THE EARL'S
Betrothal

To Jenny,

OTHER BOOKS AND AUDIO BOOKS
BY KAREN TUFT

Reality Check

Unexpected

Trouble in Paradise

THE EARL'S
Betrothal

A Regency Romance by

KAREN TUFT

Covenant Communications, Inc.

Cover image © Lee Avison / Trevillion Images

Cover design copyright © 2016 by Covenant Communications, Inc.

Published by Covenant Communications, Inc.
American Fork, Utah

Copyright © 2016 by Karen Tuft
All rights reserved. No part of this book may be reproduced in any format or in any medium without the written permission of the publisher, Covenant Communications, Inc., P.O. Box 416, American Fork, UT 84003. The views expressed within this work are the sole responsibility of the author and do not necessarily reflect the position of Covenant Communications, Inc., or any other entity.

This is a work of fiction. The characters, names, incidents, places, and dialogue are either products of the author's imagination, and are not to be construed as real, or are used fictitiously.

Printed in the United States of America
First Printing: May 2016

22 21 20 19 18 17 16   10 9 8 7 6 5 4 3 2 1

ISBN 978-1-52440-011-8

To Stephen, even though the first time we watched *Pride and Prejudice* together, he kept referring to Darcy as Mr. Grumpy Pants.

Acknowledgments

Thanks to my wonderful editor, Samantha Millburn. The editing process can be a grueling endeavor, but with Sam, it's always great, and even a fun experience. That's right—fun, believe it or not. Thanks also to the entire Covenant team, especially Stephanie and Christina.

A special thank you to my terrific children, who constantly step into the breach when I'm in my office typing away and tearing out my hair. Their support and enthusiasm for my writing always touches my heart and humbles me. I love you!

And most especially, I want to thank my husband, Stephen. He went from refusing to read my novels for fear he wouldn't like them and would have to be honest about it to reading them in secret to telling me to write faster so he'd have another book to read. You just can't beat support like that. Always and forever, my love.

Chapter 1

THE ROOM WAS AS SILENT as a tomb. Amelia Clarke handed the week's menu to Lady Ashworth, who sat quietly in a chair, watching the Marquess of Ashworth sleep. "I hope this meets with your approval," Amelia whispered. "I added a few dishes my father enjoyed when he was . . . unwell himself." She'd nearly said, "When my father was dying," which would have been a terrible mistake. It wasn't good to suggest the marquess was anything more than ill. Amelia didn't want to distress Lady Ashworth, who was utterly devoted to her husband, any more than she already was.

It had been three years since Amelia's father had taken ill and just over two years since he'd passed away, leaving her alone with few options. How grateful Amelia had been that her mother's old acquaintance, Lady Walmsley, had given her a personal reference and sent her to Lady Ashworth, who had subsequently hired her as a paid companion.

The marchioness glanced distractedly at the menu and handed it back to Amelia. "I'm sure I approve, Amelia dear. Thank you."

Lady Ashworth's short reply said much about her emotional state. This latest heart seizure of Lord Ashworth's had been particularly severe and had left everyone fearful that he might succumb this time. It was more than a family should have to bear, and Amelia's heart broke for them.

Eight months ago, Ashworth's oldest son and heir, Alexander, the Earl of Halford, had fallen while jumping a gate on horseback and had died as a result. He'd been an exceptional horseman and the accident a terrible fluke, leaving his parents and sister devastated.

His death had also precipitated the marquess's first heart seizure and a lengthy recovery.

Those had been dark days, indeed.

And then a month ago, Lord Ashworth had received a letter stating his only remaining son, Captain Lord Anthony Hargreaves, was among the thousands of British military casualties in a place called Badajoz, Spain. The marquess's already weakened heart had been unable to bear up under the news that both of his sons were dead.

"I'll take the menu to Mrs. Deal, then, shall I?" Amelia said, studying the marchioness carefully as she spoke. Lady Ashworth was a beautiful woman despite her years, but today her face was lined with grief and worry, her eyes heavy from lack of sleep. There was no reply from the marchioness, which Amelia interpreted as tacit consent. Anything she could do to lessen Lady Ashworth's burdens Amelia would do, and gladly.

She hurried down the hallway of the private family quarters toward the grand staircase of Ashworth Park, on her way to the kitchen, but stopped when she heard voices at the front entrance. The family was in mourning and was not accepting visitors, which made the disruption unusual.

John, one of the newer footmen, was trying to bar someone from entering the house as Buxton, the butler, glided across the marble floor to take matters in hand. Amelia ventured down a few stairs, curious.

Whoever was at the door was taking issue with the footman, and then a deep male voice said, "Buxton! Good to see you, old man. Explain to this young fellow who I am, and let me and my friend here come inside."

The voice sent an odd tingle down Amelia's spine, and she watched in amazement as the ever-dignified Buxton faltered.

What was going on here? And more to the point, who could this stranger possibly be?

Buxton ran a shaky hand over his perfectly groomed hair. "It can't be!" he declared in an equally shaky voice. "Lord Anthony, raised from the dead. Begging your pardon, you're Halford now. Make way, John. This is my lord's son come back to us from the grave, praise be to God!"

This was Captain Lord Anthony Hargreaves, who had been reported dead and buried in Spain?

"Buxton, you've known me since I was in leading strings; Anthony will do. And the gentleman beside me is my good friend, Lucas Jennings. Will you kindly have him shown to a guest room so he can refresh himself? The carriage with our belongings should be arriving shortly."

"Yes, my lord, and with pleasure," Buxton said. He signaled to John, and the gentleman who was Mr. Jennings followed him, passing Amelia as they went. Mr. Jennings, a great, strapping fellow, nodded a greeting at her as he went up the stairs.

Lady Ashworth must be told, Amelia thought, but before she could act, she heard a gasp behind her.

"Anthony!" Lady Ashworth cried.

The man stood with his arms spread wide as his mother raced down the stairs past Amelia. He wrapped his arms around her, and she clung to him, sobbing. He rested his head atop hers and murmured endearments to her. Amelia had rarely seen anything so beautiful. Oh, that she could embrace her own mother just once more or tell her father she loved him.

Buxton vanished discreetly. He was no doubt announcing the return of the lost heir to the rest of the staff and setting them into action.

Aware that she was intruding on what was clearly a private moment between mother and son, Amelia continued the rest of the way down the stairs as quietly as she could, intending to slip out of the entrance hall to go to the kitchen as she had originally planned to do before the new Lord Halford had returned from the grave.

As she reached the bottom of the stairs, Lord Halford's eyes shot open, spearing her with his gaze and stopping her in her tracks. They were a bright blue, the color of the seas in the West Indies, Amelia imagined, or the sky on a bright summer day. Mesmerizing eyes. But there was more to them than their arresting color. Amelia saw pain and fatigue and a world-weariness that stunned her—and a slight puzzlement too as he tried to figure out who she was.

She curtsied slightly, heart racing, and turned toward the hallway.

Lady Ashworth must have heard her movement. "Amelia, dear," she said, smiling through her tears, "wait a moment. I want to introduce you to my son."

Amelia stopped.

Lady Ashworth pulled a handkerchief from her pocket and dabbed at her eyes. Her son's free arm moved to encircle her shoulders as if he needed to maintain physical contact with his mother. "Anthony, this is my companion, Miss Amelia Clarke. Amelia, my son, Lord Anthony Hargreaves, the Earl of Halford." Lady Ashworth stumbled a little over the title, which was understandable since it had been the title Alexander had held until his death only eight months before.

Lord Halford made a short bow. "Enchanted, Miss Clarke."

"Lord Halford," Amelia said, curtsying in reply. She turned to the marchioness. "I was on my way to consult Mrs. Deal. If you'll excuse me, I'll leave you two alone and continue on with my task." Was there anything more inane she could have chosen to say? Amelia highly doubted it. But between the man's dark good looks, blue eyes, and deep voice, her brain had thoroughly ceased to function.

"Of course, my dear, and thank you," Lady Ashworth said. "She has been such a godsend to me, Anthony. I don't know what I would have done without her these past months."

"Then I am in your debt, Miss Clarke," he said with such earnestness one would have thought Amelia had single-handedly taken on Napoleon.

She made her curtsies once more and walked away as serenely as she could. When she knew she was out of sight, she ducked into the library and collapsed into a chair. Her hands were damp, and the menu she held, the one she had so carefully penned for Lady Ashworth that morning, was a crumpled mess. Amelia set it on her lap and did her best to smooth out the creases.

She had heard tales of the younger son, of course, especially when she'd first arrived at Ashworth Park. His letters from the Peninsula had been scarce, but, then, Amelia imagined writing correspondence while on march through a foreign land would be a challenge. She had seen his portrait hanging in the gallery, painted just before he'd left. Amelia had found the young man in the scarlet uniform intriguing and had occasionally pondered the youthful antics she had heard about the dignified and confident young man in the portrait.

Seeing a man who was supposed to be dead was startling enough. But to stand next to the intriguing young man from the portrait and take in the full measure of his masculinity was a bit of a shock, to say the least.

She could almost hear her father chuckle at her overblown reaction to the situation. "Gracious, Amelia," he would say to her if he were here. "I had best run after the smelling salts before you faint straightaway. After all these years, a young gentleman has finally elicited more than an eye roll from you. Perhaps I will use the smelling salts myself, come to think of it." He would chuckle again and pat her hand and think himself the cleverest of papas.

Oh, how she had adored her father, and, oh, how she missed him! And her mama too. But her mother had been gone since Amelia was twelve, while her father's passing was more recent and the pain, therefore, still acute.

She patted the small volume of poetry tucked safely in her gown pocket. Her parents had purchased a few such books, and Amelia frequently kept one with her during the day for those occasions when she had time to herself.

Today, of all days, when the Ashworth heir had returned to the family from the dead, Amelia would find an opportunity to be alone with her poetry and the memory of her parents and privately rejoice that her kind employer had been blessed in a way Amelia had not.

***

Lord Anthony Hargreaves led his mother to the sitting room off the entrance hall. It had been two years since he'd been home, and in that time this room hadn't changed at all: rose damask sofas with floral-upholstered side chairs, a portrait of his parents as newlyweds over the marble fireplace. It was his mother's favorite room, and she frequently entertained guests here. It was why he had brought her here rather than the parlor, which was much more formal.

The marchioness sank into a sofa and drew him down to sit next to her. She had aged in the time Anthony had been gone. Silver shimmered generously through her dark hair now, and she'd lost weight, although she was still extraordinarily beautiful. She always had been.

"I cannot stop looking at you," she exclaimed. "I never thought to see your face again. Oh, Anthony, it is truly you. I am so happy!"

He took both of her hands in his own, kissing first one and then the other. "Yes, Mother, I am home, and all in one piece, thank the Lord and Lucas Jennings. I am so sorry you and Father were told otherwise and suffered unnecessarily as a result." Anthony himself was struggling to accept that his older brother, Alex, was eight months dead, and his strong, vital father was mortally ill. He dropped his voice. "How is Father, truly?"

"Quite frankly, he's unwell," she said. "Doctor Samuels isn't optimistic, although I have forbidden him to say such a thing to Ashworth. I'm afraid I will lose him yet, and then where will I be?" She blinked back more tears, and Anthony released one of her hands so she could dab at her eyes again. "Having you back again will be medicine to him; I know it. But I must warn him before I take you up to him. Seeing his deceased son in the flesh might be too much of a shock otherwise."

"He may believe he's gone to his Maker, in truth." Morbid humor was better than no humor at all sometimes. "I'm eager to assess Father's condition for myself, but it can wait until you've had a chance to prepare him. In the meantime, I'll go refresh myself and see if poor Lucas has found his way through the ancestral pile to his room successfully."

His jokes brought a slight smile to her lips and eased Anthony's heart. "I'll have a tray sent up, then. I'm sure you and Mr. Jennings are famished."

"Thank you, Mother. But be prepared: we will undoubtedly devour everything in sight, except army rations and bad ale, that is."

She actually chuckled this time, and Anthony rose and assisted her up from her seat. "Oh, Anthony," she exclaimed, "Welcome home! Everything is going to be better now that you have come back to us alive and safe."

He smiled faintly and kissed her cheek. "I'm sure you're right. Let me know when you have spoken to Father, then."

"I will."

Anthony kept his smile in place until she left the room, then walked over to the windows, clasping his hands behind his back. The rose garden beyond was in full, riotous bloom, but he barely saw it. Instead, images of blood and violence made an unwelcome appearance, scenes that had haunted him since Badajoz, and a wave of nausea rolled through him.

He inhaled deeply, fighting for control over his mind and bodily functions. He was not nearly as confident as his mother that everything was going to be better now that he was home again.

He needed to get out of the confinement of the house and clear his head. Hang it all, Lucas had found his way across the length and breadth of Spain and hadn't gotten lost once; he could certainly follow a footman successfully to his guest room. And if that meant Lucas ate every last morsel on the tray his mother ordered, so be it. Anthony would survive until dinner. He had survived on less before.

* * *

Nearly the entire household staff was in the kitchen by the time Amelia arrived there. The large room was abuzz with the news of the young lord's return, except for Buxton, who, now that his announcement had been made, was sipping tea at the large kitchen table and reading the daily sheets, minding his own dignified business.

"But did he look like a ghost, Miss Clarke?" the young maid named Mary asked.

"Don't be silly, child," Mrs. Deal said, adding the finishing touches to a tray laden with sliced meats and cheeses, bread, and an assortment of fruit. "He couldn't have been dead and showed up here, now could he? Take this tray upstairs, and be quick about it."

Mary picked up the tray and then hesitated, obviously reluctant to leave when very important questions were going to be asked during her absence.

"He looked alive to me, Mary," Amelia said. Very much alive, in fact, if her wildly beating heart was any indication.

"But what did he look *like*, Miss Clarke?" another of the maids, Jane, asked.

"Tall. Quite tall, actually," Amelia said. "With dark hair and blue eyes." Eyes that had stopped her with their intensity. "He has a serious countenance and a commanding manner, as one would expect from an officer in the military, although I only saw him briefly. I left immediately after our introduction, so the marchioness and he—"

"You *met* him?" Jane sighed. "How dashing and romantic he must have seemed."

"I can show you dashing and romantic if you like," offered a footman, causing giggles among the girls.

"Enough of this," Mrs. Deal said, snapping a dish towel at the footman, who leaped nimbly away. "Mary, you're still here? Begone before I take a switch to you. Jane, you'll be keeping your girlish thoughts and eyes to yourself, now, especially around the young lord."

"Yes, ma'am," Jane said meekly.

"And I'd say it was time for the lot of you to get back to work," Buxton added, folding the dailies and standing.

They all scurried off to resume their chores. "I made only minor adjustments to the menu," Amelia told Mrs. Deal when they were finally alone but for the scullery maid cleaning pots. "However, with Lord Halford's arrival, perhaps we should go over it again."

Mrs. Deal wiped her hands on her apron and sat at the large table where Buxton had been and studied the menu while Amelia slid onto the bench opposite. "Let me see . . ." Mrs. Deal said. "The little lordlings was constantly underfoot in my kitchen as boys, the both of them, snatching treats before I'd barely got them out of the oven." She smiled fondly at the memory. "Young rascals, they were. I'll include a few of Master Anthony's favorites in tonight's meal and make it a fine welcome home for our hero."

"That sounds perfect. I'm sure Lady Ashworth will be grateful, and Lord Halford as well." She stood and brushed out her skirt. "The weather this morning is being cooperative for once, and the marchioness is undoubtedly occupied with the marquess and her son. I think I will go walking in the gardens, if she happens to ask for me."

"Take a scone with you, then," Mrs. Deal replied.

Amelia helped herself to a buttery scone and thanked Mrs. Deal before heading out the kitchen door and through the herb garden beyond. It was a beautiful day, with only the occasional cloud floating through a vivid blue sky—a sky the exact color of Lord Halford's eyes.

She mentally scolded herself. Such thoughts simply wouldn't do. Lord Halford's reappearance on the scene was a blessing, to be sure, and she was exceedingly glad for Lord and Lady Ashworth. And, yes, Amelia had found herself struck by his gaze—what young lady would not have been?—but any attraction she might feel toward him would only serve to complicate her life. She was not for him. Her status, however gently bred she had been, was far beneath his own as heir to a marquess.

She walked briskly through the formal gardens toward a wooded area at the north end of the estate. There was a path nearby that ended by a small lake. Life at Ashworth Park wasn't as vigorous as her life had been as the daughter of a parish vicar, so Amelia frequently walked in the park in order to stretch her legs and use excess energy.

Her life really had been active in Little Brenchley, especially after the death of her mother when Amelia was twelve. She and her father had mourned deeply, but the needs of the parish had never stopped, and continuing to serve the good people of Little Brenchley during that time had been a godsend for both of them. Amelia had filled her days assisting her father as he'd taught the village children or checked in on the widows and the sick, and she'd read the books in her father's modest library. The one she had with her now was a small volume of poems by Robert Burns her father had often read aloud using a Scottish accent, which had made Amelia and her mother laugh.

She missed them both and lived daily with the sweet ache for a childhood long past. The loss of her father, however, had changed Amelia's life from one of love and security to one of fear and uncertainty. She had no more family that she knew of and had been left entirely on her own. Money was nonexistent, having been shared over the years with the parishioners.

Bad planning on both her father's and her part, in hindsight.

Undoubtedly her father had expected her to marry, but Little Brenchley had not been flush with eligible men. Amelia had emphatically refused the widowed farmer who'd been looking for a mother for his seven children, as well as the local shopkeeper, a bachelor who was older than her own father. The fact that she had never married hadn't been an issue until her father had become mortally ill.

Life took unexpected twists and turns, and considering the prospects Amelia had faced with her father's untimely death, things had turned out remarkably well. He had urged her in strong terms to contact a Lady Walmsley on his passing, the dowager countess having some sort of connection to her mother, and Lady Walmsley had referred Amelia to Lady Ashworth.

And Lady Ashworth treated Amelia almost like a daughter. Amelia had clothes and food and a warm bed to sleep in, and there was enough to do to keep her occupied, even if she wasn't as busy as she had been in Little Brenchley.

She wouldn't go all the way to the lake today, she decided, as Lady Ashworth might need her, what with all the goings-on. There was a bench approximately halfway to the lake on a slight rise that afforded a nice view of the village of Ashworthy. She would walk that far and enjoy some of her favorite verses from her father's book, with his voice lilting through the words in her mind.

Chapter 2

The formal gardens looked the same as they had two years ago, the last time Anthony had taken leave and come home. He should go to the stables and check on the horses after their long ride this morning, but that could mean enduring a welcome home from the stable hands, and right now Anthony wanted to be alone.

He strode across the gardens to the wooded area beyond. A swim in the lake sounded appealing: the solitude of the place, the cool resistance of the water against muscles that ached from days on horseback. Away from Lucas's constant nagging over a wound that was almost healed.

He was nearly halfway to his goal when he spied his mother's companion sitting on a bench a few dozen feet away, reading a book. He was about to retreat when she raised her head and spotted him.

There was nothing for it now but to be sociable. "Miss Clarke," he called out to her. "Forgive me for intruding upon your privacy."

"Not at all, Lord Halford." She returned her gaze to the book.

He doubted she wanted him there any more than he desired her company, but he had been trained all his life to be a gentleman, and to simply pass by would be ill-mannered. He walked the remaining distance, cursing his luck and silently bidding a fond farewell to his dip in the lake.

"May I sit?" he asked, hoping she'd say no.

Instead, she scooted over on the bench, giving him ample room to be seated by her without actually having to touch, which was as insulting to Anthony as it was a relief. Their eyes had met briefly when he had first arrived, and he had found himself drawn to her completely against his will.

He was broken in too many ways to count, and his duties to his family would require all he had left to give. Dead brother, ill father, worried mother, the estate with all its incumbent responsibilities. He wasn't sure he was up to the task.

And then there were the men he'd left behind in Spain when he'd sold his commission and returned home. Napoleon's grandiose schemes had not yet been contained, and Britain needed all her men to achieve victory.

How did one do one's duty to one's family *and* one's country? It wasn't possible in all cases, and it exacerbated the guilt Anthony felt and that occasionally overwhelmed him.

He realized suddenly Miss Clarke was looking strangely at him. Dash it all, his mind had gone wandering for too long, apparently. He did his best to offer a reassuring smile. "I beg your pardon; I was woolgathering. May I sit?" Had he asked her that already? Of course he had. Where were his mental faculties these days?

"Of course. I presumed you would understand that when I moved over to make space for you on the bench," she said matter-of-factly.

Well, the lady had a bit of a backbone, then. He sat next to her, a little closer than she—or he—had intended. She had made it abundantly clear she wanted distance between them; however, he didn't feel inclined to give her the upper hand in this initial encounter. Better to let her know he was in charge now that he was home and that his authority extended even to his mother's personal employee. "You are given to frank speaking, Miss Clarke. I'm sure my mother appreciates such a quality in a companion."

Her eyes fluttered down to take in his close proximity, and a slight blush rose on her cheeks. She closed her book and set it on her lap, placing her hands primly on top. "I have been told so, my lord, and have striven to control my speech for years . . . but with little success, I'm afraid. You do not approve of frank speaking?" She looked directly at him now.

Her eyes were a deep shade of green, a twinkle lurking in them at the moment. Not in a flirtatious manner—it would be unseemly for a paid companion to be so bold with the son of the house—but with humor and a friendliness Anthony found appealing.

Perhaps too appealing.

He cleared his throat. "One becomes accustomed to frankness in the military, Miss Clarke. In the course of battle, there is little time to phrase things prettily." His blunt response was intended to put her on her guard, for both their sakes.

She clearly missed his intent. "I imagine there is very little about war itself that could be phrased prettily," she replied. "Although I imagine the people and the countryside were pleasant enough at times."

Images flashed through Anthony's mind: eyes filled with terror and agony, swaths of land scorched and vacated to keep the French from obtaining provisions on the way west to Portugal. "As you say," he said. He would not contradict her. "It is my fervent hope that you never experience the harshness men can inflict on others, Miss Clarke."

"I have experienced harshness in my life, Lord Halford, though nothing to compare to that of war," she said to him. "None of us are immune to such things. Even the bountiful lives of your parents have had their share of hardships. Especially lately."

"You mean to speak for my parents, Miss Clarke?" he asked.

"I would never presume, my lord. I speak for myself and from my own observations. Your father's grief over your brother's death robbed him of his health, as you know. And your mother's love for them and for you has taken a great toll on her, although not in as obvious a way as your father. It is a great blessing that you have returned to them healthy and whole."

"Healthy, perhaps, but war rarely leaves a man whole," Anthony said. He was straying too close to topics he didn't want to discuss. "But this is not a subject for a beautiful morning. England has produced a day without rain, and we should not cast a shadow over it by speaking of somber things."

He studied the young woman seated next to him. She looked to be petite, not quite as tall as his mother, though it was difficult to tell since she was seated. Her hair was dark and had a tendency to curl, with deep red highlights that were illuminated in the moments when they encountered sunlight amidst the shade of the trees. Anthony's military experience had trained him to evaluate his opponents, to assess their strengths and weaknesses. Miss Amelia Clarke wasn't precisely an opponent, but Anthony intended to be on his guard. A pretty, petite woman with chestnut-colored hair and deep-green eyes could be formidable to a man who was drawn to her, even if it was against his will.

He had too many responsibilities, too many ghosts to be having thoughts about the likes of Miss Amelia Clarke.

*　*　*

Amelia couldn't help but notice that the man who had approached her and was now seated beside her, in addition to being extraordinarily tall, was broad at the shoulders, though of a more refined build than his traveling companion. There was no padding added to his lordship's coat to give him a more masculine presence, as some gentlemen were inclined to do, and it said much about the man. He must have been the type of officer who had worked alongside his men. Amelia approved of this. Her limited exposure to men of the upper classes did not impress her much when compared to their working-class counterparts, at least when it came to physical strength.

"What are you reading, Miss Clarke?" Lord Halford asked. "I noticed you were engrossed in your book when I came upon you."

"Poetry, my lord. The works of Robert Burns."

"Ah. 'The best-laid schemes of mice and men / Go oft awry / And leave us nought but grief and pain / For promised joy!'"

Amelia smiled. "You're familiar with Mr. Burns's work. He's a favorite of mine, I must admit." She handed his lordship the book when he held out his hand for it. "My father used to read these poems to me when I was a girl. He'd exaggerate the Scottish dialect. They were happy times." She needed to be careful, or she'd break down and weep at the memory. "The poem you quoted is a lovely apology to a mere field mouse. It's a particular favorite."

"No lofty verse for you? No sonnets? No romantic idylls?"

Amelia wasn't sure if he was teasing since his manner suggested otherwise. "They have their place as well, my lord. I enjoy reading many works, poetical or otherwise."

"You are well read, then?"

"I wouldn't venture to call myself that. My father was a gentleman and well educated. He shared his knowledge freely with me, although I admit I didn't enjoy the Greek and Latin he was keen to share."

"What? You disliked Cicero or Ovid? And Marcus Aurelius, no less?" His lips tipped up slightly on one side.

Ah, he *was* teasing her.

"I confess they were less to my liking than Mr. Burns here. My mother also did her best to instill ladylike manners in me. I was something of a tomboy."

"I see no fault in your manners, Miss Clarke. Your parents must be proud of you." He caught himself, and his countenance became more serious. "Pardon me, you said your father *was* a gentleman . . ."

Amelia inferred the question he was too polite to ask. "My father died two years ago, my lord. My mother eight years before that."

"My deepest condolences, Miss Clarke. It seems we both have reasons to mourn."

"Indeed," she said kindly. Realizing she had spent more time outside than she'd intended, she rose, causing him to follow suit. "I think it is time for me to return."

"May I escort you?" he asked, clearly the gentleman in every way.

"Yes, thank you," Amelia replied.

He extended an elbow to her, which she took. As they began to stroll back toward the house, her fingertips fairly tingled from the flex of his muscles.

This was not good.

They walked in silence for several minutes, and then Lord Halford repeated the final verse of the poem, softly, almost to himself, and in English rather than a Scottish lilt. "'Still thou are blest, compared with me! / The present only toucheth thee: / But, oh! I backward cast my eye / On prospects drear! / And forward, though I cannot see / I guess and fear!'" He paused a beat before continuing. "May I be so bold as to ask how you came to be my mother's companion?"

"My mother was a schoolfriend of Lady Walmsley's niece when they were girls," she said. "After my father's death, Lady Walmsley was kind enough to give me a reference and introduce me to Lady Ashworth."

"My mother is a relatively young woman with a husband," he mused out loud, "not a dowager in need of idle conversation."

Amelia bristled. How was he to know what his mother needed? "I should hope I have provided more than idle conversation, my lord," Amelia said. "If you have concerns about my employment, you are welcome to bring them up with her, of course. Good day." She dropped his arm and hurried her steps, intent on making her way back alone, but the dratted man had a long stride and caught up to her easily.

"My apologies, Miss Clarke. I did not mean to offend."

She continued on at her brisk pace.

It didn't deter him. "I expected changes to my home, Miss Clarke, but I failed to anticipate an addition among the intimate circle of my family. A lovely addition, I might add."

She only glared at him and kept walking.

"Miss Clarke, my mother will rake me over the coals if I do not make proper amends to you. I have insulted you, and for that I am truly sorry." He kept apace of her and lowered his voice. "I am also mortally afraid of my mother, so I beg you to take pity on me."

Amelia let out an unladylike gust of air and slowed her steps. He was attempting humor to win her over, although he himself hadn't smiled at all. Well, neither would she, then, nor was she entirely convinced of his sincerity. She would take the high road and at least be civil. "You are forgiven," she said coolly and continued on toward the house at a more normal speed.

He must have had good survival instincts—he didn't offer his arm again, as she might have been inclined to smack it with her book of poetry. Instead, he clasped his hands behind his back and adjusted his stride to hers.

"Miss Clarke, may I ask—how is my father faring exactly? My mother's letters ranged from despairing to hopeful, and unfortunately, due to my varied assignments in Spain, all reached me at the same time. It was difficult to make heads or tails of them, I'm afraid. And then I arrived here this morning only to discover that my family had been informed I had died in battle at Badajoz and that my father had taken a turn for the worse at the news. You would be doing me a kindness to share your observations so I am as prepared as possible before I see him for myself."

"I am surely not the appropriate person to do that, my lord," Amelia said. "Your mother—"

"My mother felt it best to warn my father of my return, Miss Clarke, afraid my sudden appearance in his bedchamber would do him more ill than good. Is he that frail, then?"

Amelia stopped walking. Some things deserved the courtesy of being said face-to-face. "Lord Halford," she said, "your father is indeed quite ill. Your mother rarely leaves his side, and the entire household has been worried. We have all done our best to take care of him and also to support Lady Ashworth in any way possible. If we overstepped our bounds in doing so, it was only with the best intentions."

"Now you are putting words in my mouth, Miss Clarke. I do not recall saying you overstepped in any way. And I do thank you for your service to both my mother and my father."

"You may not have said I overstepped, my lord, but I saw it in your eyes, in the hall, earlier."

"Very well, I concede that perhaps I was somewhat suspicious when I spied you in the front hall this morning, but in my own defense, you had the most peculiar expression on your face at the time."

"What you observed was shock at seeing a supposedly dead man look so remarkably *un*dead. We shall have to remove your headstone from the Ashworth graveyard with alacrity. Perhaps it can be used as a table for playing chess."

A burst of air escaped his lungs, sounding suspiciously like a laugh. "Touché, Miss Clarke," he said. "My years dealing with rough enlisted men have made me cynical, I'm afraid."

Since Amelia couldn't begin to imagine the day-to-day struggles that accompanied war, she decided it was time for a truce. "I have only the highest regard for your parents, who have been all that is good to me," she said. "And I believe your return will do your father much good. Anything else, I will leave you to discern on your own."

They began walking again. Amelia prayed she had reassured the earl sufficiently, and she hoped with all her heart her words would be prophetic.

* * *

The first thing Anthony noticed when he arrived at his room to make himself presentable to see his father was the empty serving tray. While he'd fully expected Lucas to devour everything, his encounter with Miss Amelia Clarke had been oddly invigorating, and his appetite had returned.

"The maids have gotten your bath ready, although it won't be nice and hot by now," Lucas said, entering the bedchamber from the adjoining dressing room. "I also requested more food. You can't face your father on an empty stomach."

"Couldn't find the willpower to leave any for me?" Anthony asked.

"Too many months of infantry rations have left me a broken man," Lucas replied, a ridiculous hangdog expression on his face. "I have no resistance to good food anymore and find I cannot stop myself until there isn't a crumb remaining."

Anthony understood that sentiment.

He removed his jacket and waistcoat, tossing them onto the bed, then tugged off his neckcloth and shirt on his way into his dressing room. "I doubt I'll find anything that will even fit me in that wardrobe," he called back to Lucas. "I've lost at least two stone."

"I took the liberty of rummaging through it while you were gone. Luckily for you, I already found a few items in that extensive wardrobe of yours that might work," Lucas said, bringing Anthony's old dressing gown with him. "I want to check that wound of yours before you immerse yourself."

"It's fine."

"I want to see it, Captain."

"That's Captain Lord to you," Anthony joked, but he stood still so Lucas could examine the bullet wound he'd taken in his side. "As you can see, it has healed, thanks to a merciful God and you and Señora Bartolo." Anthony didn't know how Lucas had managed it, especially during the horrific aftermath of the battle, but he'd found a local woman willing to take them in and see to Anthony. Bribery, most likely. The number of killed and wounded had been staggering, and the locals hadn't been inclined to help after the brutalities the British soldiers had committed following the battle, from what Anthony had been able to gather since.

Lucas probed at the wound, making Anthony hiss. "Not quite healed but better."

"Then, with your permission, I will bathe." He removed his breeches and eased himself into the tub. The water was warm enough, especially when compared with the streams of Spain, which had been all that was available for months. He settled deeper into the water, allowing it to soothe the tension in his mind and body.

"You do realize you are no longer my personal servant now that we are out of the army," he said to Lucas before shutting his eyes and submerging himself without waiting for a reply. Lucas had enlisted rather than purchase an officer's commission, so he had been assigned to Anthony in that capacity.

Lucas was still there when Anthony reemerged and slicked the water from his face and hair. "I expect I will eventually accustom myself to the change, Captain—wait, is that Captain Lord or Lord Captain?—I get so confused at times."

"I'm thinking that the honorable fourth son of a viscount would have had any confusion regarding titles beaten out of him in school. But if you are indeed unsure, you may refer to me as Your Highness."

"Thank you, Your Highness,'" Lucas said and then grew serious. "And while I may not be your valet and personal servant anymore, I intend to remain with you for a while longer. Dash it, Tony, you saved my life on more than one occasion."

"As you saved mine," Anthony said. "I should have been buried with others in a hastily dug grave if not for your quick actions."

"Then, in gratitude let me decide my own future and allow me to remain here for the time being. I intend to see you healed before I leave."

"Fine. Now begone so I may scrub my feet and other necessary parts. And see what is keeping that tray. I'm famished."

Lucas winked and gave him an exaggerated bow. "As you wish, Your Highness."

***

"There you are," Lady Ashworth said as she hurried down the hallway toward Amelia. The marchioness looked years younger, her smile full of sunshine and hope. "Oh, my dear, you should have *seen* Ashworth's face when I gave him the good news!"

If the marquess's face looked anything like hers, it would have been a beautiful sight to behold indeed. Amelia had spent many silent hours the past few weeks at Lady Ashworth's side, watching his lordship waste away—and her ladyship as well, sick with worry for him.

"I have dashed off a note to Louisa and Farleigh," Lady Ashworth continued. "They will want to be here as soon as possible, I'm sure. Louisa will be ecstatic to see her brother alive and whole. And Anthony will be in raptures when he sees how his sweet nephew, William, has grown and little Penelope too—they've never even met, and Penny is walking and talking.

"There is much to do, Amelia, and I am going to need your good help, as always." She took both Amelia's hands in her own. It was impossible not to respond to Lady Ashworth's joy and enthusiasm. "And, my dear, how *glad* I am that we will be doing happy things for once after so much sadness. Come!" She led Amelia into her sitting room, and they each took a seat on the sofa. "Ashworth will need to rest after he is reunited with Anthony. While he does, we shall make arrangements. We must have a celebration and include everyone: the neighbors, the tenants, the village. Everyone!"

"But the family is still in mourning," Amelia said.

"It is true that my poor, dear Alexander has not been gone for a full year. But, Amelia, Ashworth and I lost *both* our sons, and we have been given one of them back again. He is *alive*. It is a time of rejoicing for the family and for everyone else here as well. The continuation of Ashworth affects all the people of the estate and village. We are their home and their livelihood. To have Anthony back means the family line will continue. He will eventually become Ashworth and hopefully have a son who will follow him as marquess someday." She patted Amelia's hand before standing again, bubbling with enthusiasm and energy. "Now, I must get back to Ashworth. We will meet for tea later this afternoon to make plans." Lady Ashworth dashed off with a lightness of step Amelia hadn't seen in months.

Well, there was nothing for it. Things were going to get busy around here—and quickly. Amelia rose. Mrs. Shaw and Mrs. Deal needed to know about the celebration Lady Ashworth had in mind, and Amelia may as well inform them now. She could pass on the necessary details later.

* * *

The door to his father's bedchamber was closed when Anthony arrived bathed and shaved, and he could hear his parents' murmuring voices on the other side of it. He paced away and then back again, tugging at the waistcoat Lucas had spotted in the back of Anthony's wardrobe. His clothes were out of fashion, being a handful of years out of date, but as they had been tailored to fit a younger, more youthful version of himself, they fortuitously hid the weight he'd recently lost.

The clothing also spared him from donning his dress uniform, the only other thing he had at hand. Since he was no longer an officer, he was disinclined to wear it now.

He was anxious but reluctant to see his father. He wanted to reassure himself of the marquess's health but knew seeing him would make the situation undeniably real. Speculation, such as it was, could be exaggerated horribly or minimized optimistically, but fact was fact.

He took a deep breath, set his jaw, and knocked softly.

His father's valet opened the door, bowing as Anthony entered the room.

"Thank you, Harrison," Anthony murmured.

"It is very good to see you, my lord," Harrison replied with touching earnestness.

The Marquess of Ashworth was sitting up in bed, supported by a regiment of pillows, wearing an elegant burgundy dressing gown. His dark hair was much more heavily threaded with silver now but was neatly groomed, and he was freshly shaven. He was still very much the marquess Anthony recognized from his boyhood and youth, but Anthony did not miss the pallor of his father's cheeks and the boniness of the wrists and hands resting on top of the counterpane.

His father's frail state was shocking, but it was the expression on his face that gave Anthony pause. It was a complexity of emotions: suspicion, pain . . . and hope, all restrained by aristocratic decorum.

"Father," Anthony said. "It is good to see you."

The marquess closed his eyes and let out a shuddering sigh before opening them again. "It truly is you, then," he said. "My son. I scarcely dared believe what your mother told me."

The marquess raised his hand, and Anthony walked forward and took it in his own. It felt familiar and reassuring, although the grip was weak. "Yes, Father," Anthony said. "I have come home."

"Praise God." His eyes roamed hungrily over Anthony's person as his hand returned to rest on the counterpane, taking Anthony's with it. "You have lost weight, boy."

"As have you, sir."

"True enough."

"And I will happily see to fattening you both up," Anthony's mother interjected, leaning over to pat her husband affectionately on the shoulder.

"Eleanor," the marquess said. "If you would be so kind, I would like a few words alone with my son."

"Do not be too hard on him, Ashworth," she replied. She stood and kissed him affectionately on the cheek. "He has only just arrived, and I have not got my fill of him yet, so I won't have you scaring him back to Spain."

"Nonsense, woman. Anthony's not going anywhere." His lips had curved up ever so slightly when she'd kissed his cheek, and if Anthony hadn't seen it for himself, he wouldn't have believed it. The Marquess of Ashworth was a proud man. To allow such a show of affection, even before his own son, was simply not done in fashionable society and was not something he would have tolerated before. "She takes advantage of my powerlessness to shower me with feminine emotions. It becomes more than a man can bear at times."

"Silly man," his equally aristocratic mother said as she flounced out the door. Yes, that was it. She had flounced.

The silly man in question, the esteemed Marquess of Ashworth, only sighed. "Sit down, Anthony. I have much to say and not much time to say it before your mother will return and tuck me in like I am but a babe in the nursery."

Anthony took the chair his mother had occupied. He could feel his jaw tensing. "Yes, Father?"

"First of all, I would know the circumstances surrounding your so-called death."

Anthony immediately rose again to gaze out the bedchamber window, but what he saw instead were the ghastly images of the war: *The weeks of miserable torrential rain and the continuous gunfire from the French. The most gruesome of deaths as men were stabbed, shot, trampled, and blown to bits; the wounded suffering and suffocating in the hellish, ever-present mud. A woman's sob, a shot ringing out, and a searing pain in his side crippling him instantly. Falling, seeing red, and then seeing nothing at all . . .*

Anthony returned his gaze to his father. "I was badly wounded in a remote part of the city," he said simply.

"I suspect there is more to it than that," his father replied, arching an eyebrow.

"True," Anthony replied. "But it is a conversation for a later time. Suffice it to say the casualties were in the thousands, and those assigned to deal with the matter were put to better use seeing to the wounded."

"Of which you were one," his father pointed out.

"As I said, I was in a remote part of the city. Fortunately Lucas found me before I met my Maker and arranged for a local woman to care for my wounds. As the two of them stayed at my side for the next several days, my whereabouts went unreported."

His father only shook his head. But since there was no way Anthony could sufficiently describe the ordeal—nor had he any wish to—he left the details unsaid.

"Perhaps one day you will feel able to tell me what you endured. I hope so. But we must deal in the here and now, I suppose. And to that end, we must face the obvious: you are Halford now," his father said.

Anthony shuddered. The simple statement spoke volumes. Alexander had been Anthony's best friend, he being only a couple years Anthony's senior. And since they had studied with the same tutor and Anthony had followed Alex to school and university, he'd also witnessed the additional training—and pressures—Alex had undergone as Earl of Halford, heir to the Marquess of Ashworth.

"I know that, Father." Assuming the title felt uncomfortable, as it had always been his brother's and Anthony had never aspired to it.

"You have responsibilities that require urgent attention as a result."

"I intend to do all I can to assume the role in Alexander's place, Father. With your permission, I will set up a meeting with your land steward today—"

"Hang the land steward!" his father exclaimed, slapping his hand on the counterpane and then stopping to catch his breath. "And hang this foolish illness of mine," he added when he'd adequately recovered. "I'm not talking about the estate, boy. I'm talking *heirs*."

Anthony clenched his teeth until he thought they might crack. "Heirs?" he managed to say, embarrassed to hear his voice squeak out the word.

"Yes, of course, heirs. I lost both of my heirs this year, and it very nearly killed me. Now that we have been given a second chance, I refuse to hand Ashworth and its people over to some mealy-mouthed second cousin from the Cotswolds. *Heirs*, boy. By some miracle, by the grace of God, I got one of my sons back," he continued, his hands now two tight fists atop the counterpane. A coiling tension spread through Anthony's body. "I've had a glimpse of my own mortality, and it isn't pretty, I can assure you."

He stopped speaking to take several more breaths, and then he sat up straight, and his countenance changed, becoming the Marquess of Ashworth in all his authority and not merely Anthony's father. "I want your word, *Halford*, that you will do everything in your power to present me with your legitimate heir within the year."

"A *year*, sir?" Images of terrified Spanish eyes and screaming mouths flashed through his mind again, vivid and horrible. He swallowed hard. "To present you with my legitimate heir? That means—"

"Marriage. Yes, yes, I know. You will have to get on with the business quickly."

Striving to sound calm and reasonable when what he felt was panic, Anthony said, "Even so, Father, there is the chance that the child in question will be female."

"It won't be." The Marquess of Ashworth delivered the statement with alarming force and absolute confidence. "It *must* be a boy. And it *will*."

While the gentlemen of the aristocracy were definitely the lords of their manors, Anthony doubted his father had quite as much say when it came to such godly matters as the procreative process, although Anthony wasn't inclined to point that out at the moment. Besides, he knew what his duty as heir required. "I will do everything in my power," he told his father, "to do as you ask."

"I'll have your word on it."

"You have it," Anthony snapped. It rankled him that his father would demand it again of him. He had just said he would, had he not? Anthony had always kept his word as a gentleman and as an officer, and that his father needed to hear the words repeated was, under normal circumstances, an affront to Anthony's honor.

His father nodded and shut his eyes, his head sinking back into the pillows. "Good," he said. "That is very good."

It spoke to the helplessness and desperation his father must feel that he would push Anthony in this way, in their first conversation, no less. His father might live to see the completion of a twelvemonth—or live for years. Or he could die tomorrow, especially if he remained as agitated as he had gotten during their conversation.

How Anthony was going to keep the promise he'd just made, he had no idea. He could barely entertain the thought of binding a woman to his side and subjecting her to the darkness and horror that haunted him day and night. And yet obtaining a wife was what he must do if he was to keep his promise and fulfill his duty as heir.

"I'll leave you to rest now, Father," Anthony said.

He needed a drink.

Chapter 3

THERE WAS TO BE A grand fete held Friday week in celebration of the return of Lord Anthony Hargreaves, the new Earl of Halford, formerly Captain Lord Hargreaves of His Majesty's Army, from his perilous adventures on the Peninsula, where he had been reported a casualty of war. So Lady Ashworth had announced to Amelia when she'd located her after leaving her son with her husband to get reacquainted.

It sounded exciting—and a good lot of fun too, Amelia thought. Buxton, Mrs. Shaw, and Mrs. Deal would take organizing Ashworth Park in hand, particularly for the ball that would be held the evening of the fete, so Amelia had volunteered to organize the tenants and villagers in their contributions for the day's activities. As the daughter of a vicar, she was accustomed to this type of thing, and in fact, it was something she enjoyed.

She tied her bonnet on her head and grabbed her shawl in preparation for the walk into the village. The weather had been cooperative lately, and Amelia wanted to take advantage of it while she could.

The village of Ashworthy was about a mile from Ashworth Park. Since no one was around, Amelia quickened her pace. It felt good to stretch her legs and to be out of the house for the afternoon.

Lord Halford disquieted her. In their first conversation, he had been blunt, almost insulting at times, although Amelia could be quite frank herself on occasion, so she allowed that her observation was just that: an observation.

It was the close scrutiny he had given her that had unnerved her. It had been startlingly thorough and had made her tingle all over while at the same time arousing her caution.

She needed to be cautious, she told herself as she headed to the village pub. Handsome as Lord Halford was, Amelia had spent her life dealing in practicalities, not fantasies.

"Ho, Miss Clarke! Good day." Thomas Braddock, owner of The Green Man, the local pub, called to her as she neared, wiping his hands on his apron. "Good news at the manor house, eh?"

"Hello, Mr. Braddock. Yes, good news indeed." Village news always traveled with extraordinary speed, and today's news, as miraculous and welcome as it was for the villagers, would fly like the wind.

"For the life of me, I'm not sure I'll believe it until I see him with my own eyes," Mr. Braddock said. "Those young lads were a fine pair, always full of mischief, they were. Nearly gave them the back of my hand a few times, despite their lofty station." He chuckled at the memory. "Aye, fine lads, and fine lords. It's been sad times these many months, what with them both dying and then his lordship's poor health and all. And now Lord Anthony has returned to us, after all that he was dead, and a service for him at the church and everything. Well," he nodded, "the family deserves today's good fortune, and that's that."

"Yes," Amelia said. "And the village as well. There's to be a fete in honor of Lord Halford's return. Can I count on your assistance with it, Mr. Braddock?"

"Oh, aye, Miss Clarke, that you can. Ashworthy has held many a grand fete, and assemblies and dances as well before you joined us here."

"Miss Clarke! Miss Clarke!"

They both turned to see who had called Amelia's name. "'Tis that old hen, Lady Putnam, if you'll be excusing me for saying so, Miss Clarke," Mr. Braddock grumbled, "and her daughters too, no less. I'll be heading back to work now, then. You can count on me the day of the fete."

"Thank you, Mr. Braddock." She wasn't sure he had even heard her reply, so quickly did he disappear back inside The Green Man.

"Miss Clarke, I would speak to you." Lady Putnam, wife of Sir Frederick Putnam, baronet, announced in a shrill tone that brooked no argument.

"Good day, Lady Putnam, Miss Putnam, Miss Charlotte." Amelia made her curtsies, and the girls replied in kind.

"Miss Clarke, I must know if it is true. I daresay one cannot rely on servants to get the facts straight, but I believe I heard Lord Ashworth's son has actually returned alive and whole from Spain. Can this be so?"

"It is, Lady Putnam." Amelia was quite sure the woman had heard the news from more than one reliable source. In fact, she could probably give Amelia details of Lord Halford's return Amelia did not know herself.

"Well," Lady Putnam replied. "Well, well, well." Her eyes narrowed in thought. "That changes things around here, doesn't it, girls?"

Amelia was tempted to say something that went beyond the realm of ladylike behavior. The woman was already plotting to snare the earl for one of her daughters, and the poor man had not been home for even half a day!

"But, Miss Clarke, what is he like?" the eldest Miss Putnam ventured. Amelia had hoped to become friends with Harriet Putnam when she'd first arrived at Ashworth Park but had been soundly put in her place when Harriet had realized Amelia was the lowly daughter of a vicar. Being a paid companion, even to a marchioness, had not elevated her status enough for Harriet Putnam.

There was nothing for it. Amelia must answer, though she loathed sharing any details with the likes of Lady and Harriet Putnam. Charlotte was a nice enough girl though, especially considering she'd been raised in the same household as the other two. "He is tall and dark like his father. Very serious."

"And he is the heir now," Harriet added, a feral glint in her eye.

"That it true," Amelia said.

"Is the family receiving?" Lady Putnam asked. "I feel it is only natural that Sir Frederick and I welcome the young man home after such a long absence."

The last thing Lady Ashworth needed was the likes of Lady Putnam showing up at the front door. "They are not receiving yet, my lady," Amelia replied. "You will understand, of course, that, while wonderful, this has been a shocking turn of events. The marquess and his wife need time alone to be with their son."

"Of course," Lady Putnam demurred, although it was apparent she wasn't happy with Amelia's answer. "Well, perhaps later, then. Come along, girls. There is shopping to be done." She sailed off, her daughters trailing behind, Charlotte shrugging her shoulders in silent apology and waving at Amelia as they went.

Amelia shook her head and made her way to the church to speak to the vicar and his wife about the fete. Poor Lord Halford if Lady Putnam's and Miss Putnam's reactions to the news of his return was any indication. Amelia suspected there would be many eager young ladies lining up to attract the earl's attention as well. He would be facing a new battle now that he was home, and it was going to be a full-scale attack on his status as an eligible young gentleman. She hoped he was skilled in defense tactics. He was going to need them if he intended to end up with a lady of his own choosing.

***

"Saddle Bucephalus for me, will you, Tom?" Anthony said.

"Right you are, my lord."

By the time Anthony had left his father's room, he was in need of air. Again. For the second time in one day. And, more importantly, distance from Ashworth Park and his father and the demands that had already been thrust upon him. He had been home less than a day, welcomed joyfully by all and sundry, and yet felt as Atlas did, with the weight of the world on his shoulders.

Bucephalus was a great black beast of a stallion Anthony had spotted in London before leaving for the Peninsula. He and Alex had wandered Tattersalls together one morning to appraise the horseflesh on sale there before going to White's.

"I am buying that horse," Anthony had said at the time. "And I am naming him Bucephalus." Bucephalus had been the name of Alexander the Great's horse, and it had seemed fitting for such a marvelous creature.

"As I recall, Bucephalus had a rather fiery temper in addition to his black color and great size," Alex had replied. He'd then moved closer to inspect the horse's flanks and been snapped at by some impressively large teeth. Alex had landed on his backside in an attempt to avoid the assault.

They'd both laughed uproariously over it at the time. "I like his temper so far," Anthony had joked. "Besides, I am better at dealing with unruly cattle than you."

"That may be so, but I am *much* better with the fairer sex than you are, little brother." Alex had crossed his arms and studied the horse from a safe distance. "By all means, buy your horse. I shall lay down a hundred quid at White's that you cannot bring him up to snuff before you leave to join your company." He'd smiled wickedly.

"Done."

Anthony had, of course, bought the horse and had succeeded with its training as well. And because he had bet against his brother—and several others who had placed bets against his success in the betting book—he'd ended up several hundred pounds the richer. The money had come in handy on the Peninsula, buying supplies and, on occasion, information from some of the greedier French deserters he'd encountered. Bucephalus had spent the time Anthony had been gone in Ashworth Park's stables under Tom's expert care.

"Here you are, Lord Anthony. Beggin' your pardon, that is, Lord Halford." Tom pulled on his forelock in deference.

In Anthony's mind, Alex would always be Halford. "Tom," he said, clapping the man who'd helped teach him to ride on the shoulder before taking the reins from him. "I have been Anthony to you for the past two decades at least. I do not see a need to change that now." He pulled a carrot from his pocket for Bucephalus, who whickered at him in recognition. "How are you, old boy? Fattened the family purse for us with your offspring yet?" He then asked the question he dreaded. "Tom, it wasn't Bucephalus who—"

"No, my lord. 'Tweren't Bucephalus. That were a different horse what was involved in Lord Alex's . . ." He coughed to avoid saying the word *death*. "Leastways, that horse is gone now. I seen to it myself."

Anthony nodded. It would have been like Alex to take Anthony's horse out for exercise while he was gone. It was a relief to know Bucephalus hadn't been the cause of Alex's death.

He mounted the horse and set out for the least populated areas of the estate, away from tenant farmers and anyone else who might be inclined to wave him down and bid him welcome. Then he allowed the horse to run.

Bucephalus's hooves churned up the ground beneath him, and Anthony allowed himself this momentary exhilaration, this feeling of pure freedom as they flew across the pasture land. Bucephalus sailed easily over fences, needing little encouragement from Anthony to do so. He would not think about Alex or the jump on horseback that had ended his life. Not now.

When Bucephalus tired, Anthony led him to a stream and dismounted. Bucephalus drank greedily. They had skirted the village completely and avoided seeing anyone so far. When the horse's thirst was sated, Anthony patted his neck fondly and scratched his withers. "Well, old boy, I'm afraid it's time to return to Ashworth Park and the duties that await," Anthony said. Bucephalus nickered in reply. "I promise we'll do this again soon. Hopefully tomorrow. I'm sure we'll both need it."

He remounted, then turned Bucephalus onto the road that led from Ashworthy back to the manor. It was only then he heard the first rumble and took in his surroundings. Devil take it; when had all those clouds gathered? He had been so caught up in his thoughts and his ride that he'd not noticed them. He must be losing his wits not to have remembered how unruly English rain could be.

A few fat drops fell, and then it began to rain in earnest. Anthony turned up the collar of his coat. He'd neglected to bring a hat, knowing full well he would be racing Bucephalus at top speed and hadn't wanted to deal with the blasted thing.

Bucephalus was winded now, so Anthony kept him at a walk and allowed himself to get reacquainted with the weather of his boyhood and youth. He lifted his face to the sky and let the rain wash over him. He had bathed once today, and he might need another to warm himself when he arrived home, but the rain felt cleansing and was oddly a source of happiness. A baptism.

He was already soaked to the skin.

He decided he'd better pay attention to the conditions of the road, which were getting slicker by the minute. It would not do to have Bucephalus hurt himself.

It was then he noticed a small figure hurrying toward the estate. A woman hunched in defense against the storm and carefully picking her steps around the puddles. Her shawl did nothing to protect her from the rain, her bonnet was a soggy, dripping mess, and her plain gray dress clung to her form.

Her rather shapely form.

She looked up as Anthony drew alongside her, and Anthony realized it was his mother's paid companion. "Miss Clarke," he said, "what the devil are you doing traipsing about in this deluge? You'll catch your death."

"I couldn't agree more, my lord, but I have only my two feet at present, and they are taking me home as quickly as they are able."

Well, that was a saucy reply! Although he supposed he deserved it.

"Miss Clarke, my apologies. I accused you of something that I myself am guilty of—that is, getting caught in a rainstorm. It goes against my honor to leave you to your own two-footed resources. I have six feet between me and my good friend, Bucephalus, here. Allow me to take you up on the horse in front of me. It will get us both home more efficiently, you must agree."

Her eyes widened at his offer, which surprised him. He briefly wondered if she was afraid of Bucephalus or himself.

"My lord, I do not think—"

"Then don't. Think, that is." The rain was coming down with a vengeance, and if Anthony was already uncomfortably drenched, Miss Clarke, in her light shawl, must be even more so. "Give me your hand, Miss Clarke, and step on my boot. I insist."

"Oh, all right," she said with more bravado than he suspected she actually had. She did as he had instructed, setting one hand in his and one on Bucephalus. It was an effort for her to reach his boot in the stirrup; she truly was a petite thing.

Concentrate on the rain, Anthony, not on Miss Clarke's lovely dimensions, he mentally chided himself as she boosted herself up onto his foot. He placed his free hand under her arm and hoisted her the rest of the way onto the saddle.

She was now seated sideways in front of him and was struggling to find her balance. "Place your arm around my waist, Miss Clarke, and you will feel more secure," he said.

Her wet, cold arm crept around him beneath his coat and clutched the back of his waistcoat tightly, and he slipped his free hand around her waist as well. "That's better," he said. "I must allow Bucephalus to find his own footing as we go, but he's a smart fellow and a gentleman, so you are in good hands."

"Are you saying you are not a gentleman, my lord?" she asked. The little minx. He was glad to see she had some spirit left, considering the fear he'd thought he'd seen in her eyes at the idea of joining him on his horse, let alone under such slippery and potentially dangerous conditions.

Dangerous in more than one way, he thought as his eyes wandered to the corkscrews of dark hair that had escaped her sodden bonnet and now clung wetly to the nape of her neck.

"It goes without saying that I am a gentleman," he said, pulling his gaze away. "But I wasn't entirely sure you had been introduced to my friend Bucephalus, and I wanted to assure you of his character."

"It's true I have not met Bucephalus *formally* before, although we have eyed each other from a distance on occasion."

"Warily, no doubt."

"True, at least from my point of view. He is quite intimidating, you must admit."

As Miss Clarke seemed to be feeling more settled atop the horse, Anthony gave Bucephalus a nudge to continue. Miss Clarke kept a firm grip on his waistcoat from behind, though. Occasionally, when she turned her head enough for him to see past the brim of her bonnet, he caught a glimpse of long lashes, spiky from the rain, and those vivid green eyes. At the moment, her skin was damp and pale from the cold, but his masculine mind told him it would be creamy and soft in more agreeable circumstances.

Hmm, not good. He shouldn't be observing his mother's companion this closely or allowing his mind to wander in the direction it was currently taking—although, to be honest, it was difficult to ignore someone who was, for all intents and purposes, sitting on his lap. He shook his head to clear it, sending a spray of rainwater shooting out in all directions, and nudged Bucephalus to a slightly faster gait.

"Miss Clarke," he said, searching for a topic of conversation. "Thank you again for the service you have provided my mother the past several months. Despite my gratitude, I cannot help but wonder at the circumstances that took you from your own family and brought you to mine."

He felt her body tense and wondered why his words affected her so. Perhaps his approach had been too blunt. He was out of practice dealing with gently bred young ladies. He would have to remedy that—and the sooner the better. He would do well to practice his skills now, since the opportunity had presented itself.

"My mother died when I was quite young, and my father was a vicar," she said. "After my father's death two years ago, a new vicar replaced him, and with his own rather large family, there wasn't room for me to remain."

"You have no family with whom you could have lived?"

"No, my lord. No one of whom I am aware."

How odd. "None at all, Miss Clarke?"

"None, my lord."

The tension in her back and the tone of her voice signaled that Anthony might have ventured into bluntness again. "My apologies for the direction of my inquiries, Miss Clarke. I am only trying to understand, and the idea of having no known relatives is baffling to me. One would expect you to be acquainted with grandparents, aunts and uncles, and the like. On either side of your family tree."

"My parents rarely raised the subject. I confess I was a curious child, but they only told me they had married for love and had no family to speak of. Eventually I replaced curiosity with resolve not to know, for if these other relations existed, they never wrote, did they? They never came to visit."

"Your curiosity was replaced with a sense of loyalty to your parents."

"Precisely."

It made sense, in a way, and yet Anthony's own curiosity was piqued now, if hers was not.

A hare chose that instant to hop out of the trees, and Bucephalus, startled, danced away from it. Anthony pulled Miss Clarke tightly against him, making sure she was secure as he brought the horse under control. He felt the woman suck in her breath and found himself hoping her reaction might at least in part be because of him. It was deuced difficult to have her so close, with those spiky lashes and green eyes peering up at him and her full, rosy lips close enough to reach with his own, and not be affected by it. He may feel broken and haunted, but he wasn't dead. Lucas had made sure of that.

And Miss Clarke, sitting before him on his horse, had proven it.

If Anthony were to guess, he would estimate her to be a half-dozen years younger than his own thirty. She would be considered well and truly on the shelf compared to the scores of debutantes gracing the ballrooms of the London Season.

He would be traveling to London soon if he was to fulfill his promise to his father. And yet the idea of courting one of those very young, very innocent young ladies he had become used to seeing during the Season before buying his commission made him shudder. How could any one of them ever cope with the man he was now?

It would have to happen somehow, heaven help him. But thankfully not today.

"Bucephalus and I apologize for the scare, Miss Clarke," he said. "We prefer to be on our best behavior when accompanying a lady home."

She peered over her shoulder at him and smiled, even though she was gripping his waistcoat as tightly as ever, and for that brief moment, Anthony's heart felt a shade lighter.

"I have full confidence in both of you, my lord. I cannot blame either of you for the unruly actions of the wildlife in the neighborhood."

"I hope we acquit ourselves better for the remainder of the ride. Are you enjoying your time at Ashworth Park?"

"Oh yes," she replied. "Ashworth Park is beautiful, and your mother is all that is kind and agreeable. She has made me feel incredibly welcome despite the circumstances of the past year."

"You refer to my brother and my father."

"And to you, my lord."

"Ah, yes, of course. Since I myself was unaware of my demise, I keep forgetting what others had been told. I'm grateful my mother had someone with her who could help ease her burdens, especially when my father took ill a second time. Ah, and here we are."

They rode up to the main entrance, and he dismounted from behind as a stable lad scurried over. He then placed his hands on Miss Clarke's waist to help her dismount.

She set her hands on Anthony's shoulders for support, and as he lifted her from Bucephalus's back and down to the ground, he suddenly found her face mere inches from his own, and he was riveted. Her eyes were the deep, lush green of home, the green of the meadows and farmlands and hedgerows of his beloved England. He had missed home.

And then his eyes wandered lower, back to those lips he'd noticed before, rosy and tempting, and he realized he wanted to kiss her. He'd only met her today, and it was highly improper for him to be entertaining such a thought. What would she say to him if she knew what he was thinking? Would she be appalled? Would she be pleased?

Would her lips be as soft and welcoming as they looked?

Her rain-dampened cheeks were now as rosy in appearance as her lips. "My lord?" she asked hesitantly.

They weren't quite the words he might have hoped for in that mesmerizing moment, but they succeeded in reminding him where they were: in the front courtyard of Ashworth Park, where anyone could see them. He needed to search for a wife. He was a gentleman who did not dally with the affections of those in his family's employment and, therefore, under its—and his—protection. What had he been thinking? Well, the answer was that he *hadn't* been thinking, not at all, not logically at any rate, and if he wasn't careful, he could ruin Miss Clarke's reputation.

He would not allow that on his conscience. Not after what he had experienced at Badajoz.

He finished lowering her carefully to her feet, then stepped away from her and clasped his hands behind his back. "I hope you don't catch your death from the chill you received," he said.

"Thank you, my lord," she said breathlessly. Despite his guilt over the situation, some masculine part of him was pleased he'd had an effect on her since she'd had an effect on him too. "I'm sure I will be well," she continued. "Thank you for seeing me safely back to the house."

"It was my pleasure, Miss Clarke," Anthony replied, and it had been a pleasure. And an aching sort of torture as well.

He bowed to her and set off for his rooms in search of dry clothing. Perhaps he would suggest a bout of boxing to Lucas. For if anyone could knock some sense into Anthony, it would be Lucas.

* * *

Amelia was unsure how she was to face Lord Halford at dinner. She had very nearly requested a tray be sent to her room instead until she remembered the words of her parents: "Amelia," her mother had often said to her when she was a young girl, "when you face challenges you think you cannot overcome, you find strength you did not know you had." Her father had put it more simply: "The hotter the flame, the stronger the steel." Their own words had prepared her to cope with their deaths.

If she could face those hardships, a simple dinner with Lord Halford in attendance should be easy by comparison.

The ride home in the rain had been a wonderful, terrible experience. She had rarely been on horseback before—the horses her father had kept at the vicarage had been beasts intended to draw his small cart to visit parishioners. They'd been hacks, not the large, exquisite beast that was Bucephalus.

But even Bucephalus had paled when compared to his master. Lord Anthony Hargreaves, Earl of Halford, was an impressive specimen of a man, and his years of military service had honed every muscle Amelia had placed her hands on. She'd been pressed against his chest with her arm encircling his waist—his waist!—and she'd been able to feel every flex and twist of his powerful body as he'd managed his temperamental horse.

Amelia's personal experience with men was limited. She had taken care of her father in his weakened state, but a male retainer had seen to bathing him and helping with his private needs. Her only other experiences had been at the village assemblies, but there, any men who had asked her to dance had treated her with deference. She was the daughter of the vicar, after all.

Perhaps they'd shown her too much deference. Or perhaps she was simply unattractive. She hadn't actually been interested in any of the men of Little Brenchley, but maybe they hadn't been interested in her either.

What a demoralizing thought.

Either way, her lack of experience had left her wholly unprepared for her encounter with Lord Halford.

She patted an unruly curl back into place and winced at her best gray dress, worn to respect the house's state of mourning, though it did nothing for her complexion. Then she made herself walk into the sitting room.

"There you are, Amelia!" Lady Ashworth said. "I was about to send Anthony in search of you. Shall we dine?"

At the marchioness's mention of Lord Halford, Amelia turned instinctively in his direction, which was a mistake. Her eyes locked with his again—and she was immediately transported back to their initial encounter and then to this afternoon when he'd helped her dismount. Rather than the impersonal assistance she'd expected, he'd held her above the ground, his brilliant blue eyes catching her own, and she'd been breathless from the flood of emotions that had surged through her.

Her lips began to tingle, remembering how his eyes had lingered on them earlier. This evening, however, in company, his eyes did not stray. "Miss Clarke," he said, "may I introduce my friend, Mr. Lucas Jennings. Lucas and I spent a great deal of time together on the Peninsula."

"A pleasure, Miss Clarke," Mr. Jennings said, bowing over her hand. "I was an enlisted man, and Halford asked to have me assigned to him as his valet, luckily for me. So whether I am Halford's friend serving as his valet or his valet serving as a friend is a mystery to us all."

"It is no mystery whatsoever," Lord Halford said. "You are my friend, Lucas. 'Tis enough."

"Then we must find you a valet as soon as possible," Mr. Jennings replied, casting his eyes up and down, scrutinizing Lord Halford's attire. "I fear you may embarrass yourself otherwise." He dramatically brushed a piece of imaginary lint from his sleeve.

The others in the room laughed. "Well said, Mr. Jennings," Lady Ashford said. "I fear he is correct, Anthony. Your clothes are in desperate need of alteration. Mr. Jennings, Miss Clarke serves as my companion, yet she couldn't be more dear were she a friend or even a daughter than she is at present, so I understand completely. And if my dear Anthony had such a friend to see him safely home from the war, then I am ever in your debt."

"As am I," Amelia heard Lord Halford murmur.

"Thank you, my lady," Mr. Jennings said, seeming not to have heard Lord Halford's comment. "As we are dining informally, may I have the unique honor of escorting you into dinner?" He winged an arm out to Lady Ashworth.

"Why, thank you, Mr. Jennings. How very kind of you to ask," she said, laying her hand on his sleeve.

"And I would be honored to escort you, Miss Clarke," Lord Halford said to Amelia. "If you would allow me."

"Thank you, my lord." Amelia set a hand lightly on his sleeve and allowed him to lead her to the dining room, surprised that she didn't go up in flames the minute she touched him.

His black evening clothes were of the highest quality, though Mr. Jennings was right—they didn't fit him quite as snugly as was the current fashion. He must have lost a bit of weight during his time on the Peninsula. That would undoubtedly change now that he was eating Mrs. Deal's creations rather than military rations. His waistcoat was silver embroidered with blue, and he had a sapphire stickpin in his neckcloth. The soft wool of his sleeve did nothing to disguise the strength of the arm under her fingertips.

"Are you well, Miss Clarke, after our adventure this afternoon?" he asked.

She dared to glance upward. The corners of his mouth were turned up in what was intended to be a smile, though it didn't quite reach his eyes. "I am well, my lord," she said. "While I thank you for your concern, I am not one to be put off by a little English rain."

"Come now, that was more than a little rain, and I would be the worst sort of gentleman and host not to ask after your health, especially under the circumstances."

"What circumstances are those, my lord? Are you saying you were responsible for the weather and my own negligence?"

"While I concede I cannot control the weather, ma'am, I also cannot help but be concerned for your welfare when I find you ill-treated by it."

There was such earnestness in these last words that Amelia looked up at him again. This was truly a man who felt his duty to others keenly, and it said much about his character.

Oh, to have such a man truly care for her, not merely because she was one of his many responsibilities but because they shared a fondness for each other, as her parents had shared for each other and for her. Amelia missed being cherished and valued in that way.

Stop this wayward thinking, Amelia admonished herself. *Lord Halford is not for you, nor you for him.* Any girlish hopes of love and marriage she'd held had long been buried under the realities of her situation. She smiled politely at him. "And how are you faring, my lord, since you were as exposed to the elements as I?"

"I have endured much worse than the rains of England, Miss Clarke. Spain has a rather extreme climate, and my men and I experienced both scorching heat and bitter cold during our time on the Peninsula. So you see, a refreshing rain while assisting a lovely lady, with the anticipation of a warm house and dry clothes, was something to be enjoyed. My happiness is complete now to know you suffered no ill effects."

He held her chair out for her and then seated himself. Amelia was relieved to be free of his close proximity. At least now the conversation would involve the four of them at the table and lessen his effect on her.

"The excitement of the day was tiring for Ashworth," Lady Ashworth said, "and yet I believe his cheeks held more color in them than they have for some time. He took a tray earlier and is resting now."

"I'm glad to hear it, my lady," Mr. Jennings said. "Anthony was worried about him during our travel here. Hopefully he will have benefitted by his son's arrival."

Mr. Jennings, Amelia noted, was in his own way as striking in appearance as Lord Halford. He was as tall as Halford, with light-brown hair and eyes that twinkled with perceptiveness and wit.

"I believe he will, Mr. Jennings," the marchioness said. "And I cannot thank you enough for seeing my dear Anthony safely home to us."

"My friend here harbors a secret, Mother, which will shock you to no end."

Startled, Amelia looked up from her soup and waited for Lord Halford to continue.

"I would have you know," he said, "that Mr. Jennings, my esteemed valet and personal servant while in the army, is none other than the Honorable Lucas Jennings, fourth son of Viscount Thurlby."

Amelia gasped, then quickly coughed to disguise the sound as the others turned at once to look at her. She unearthed a smile from the pit of her stomach and patted her mouth with her napkin.

She was the only commoner at the table.

She had become used to dining with the marchioness, though she took her meals alone when Lady Ashworth dined with the marquess in his rooms whenever his health allowed, which had become more frequent of late. But to be seated to dine and discover she was the only commoner in the group was disconcerting. As a fellow employee, she'd felt an unspoken camaraderie with Mr. Jennings that was now gone, along with most of her appetite.

"I'm not the least bit shocked to learn this, Anthony," the marchioness said, "since your friend has better manners than you and speaks very well. I'm not familiar with Viscount Thurlby, though, I must admit," the marchioness said.

"My family hails from Lincolnshire, my lady, and my father chooses to remain there rather than spend time in London. I am the fourth of five sons and have three sisters as well."

"A very prolific man," Halford mused.

"That goes without saying," Mr. Jennings said, shooting him an amused glance. "But, then, he's a farmer and is used to producing things in volume. Thus, you can see why I enlisted, Lady Ashworth, rather than put my father to the expense of buying a commission for me. It was quite an adventure for a young man."

"I keep telling Lucas," Lord Halford said, "that he has seen to his duty and brought me safely back to the bosom of my family, and yet the man stubbornly refuses to listen, remaining here and fussing over me like a mother hen."

"If what I hear is true, Mr. Jennings," Lady Ashworth said, taking a dainty sip of soup, "that you saved my son's life, then you are an honored guest and may stay as long as you wish. But isn't your family anxious to have you home with them?"

"Thank you for your hospitality, my lady. My family is aware of my whereabouts, but my intention is to remain here with the captain for the time being."

"I'm not a captain any longer," Lord Halford said.

"Hardly matters," Mr. Jennings replied. "You're still pompous and bossy, aren't you?"

Lady Ashworth chuckled, while Amelia attempted another spoonful of soup, utterly unable to contribute to the conversation.

Lady Ashworth dabbed at her mouth with her napkin. "Dreadful weather we had this afternoon after an especially promising morning. I hope the sudden rain didn't interfere with your errand in the village, Amelia."

"No, my lady," Amelia said, giving up on her soup entirely and allowing a footman to remove the dish. "And I was spared a lengthy walk in the rain by the arrival of your son on horseback."

Three pairs of eyes turned to look at her, one of which was a pair of brilliant blue eyes that sent electricity straight through her.

"It's true," Lord Halford said, still looking at her. "I took Bucephalus for a run and am very thankful I chose to do so, as it allowed me to be of service."

Mr. Jennings coughed and took a sip from his goblet.

"Well," Lady Ashworth said as her soup dish was cleared away and the next course presented to her. "I suppose that is a good thing, then. But both of you . . . on Bucephalus? In all that rain and mud? I hope you will be more careful in the future, Anthony, especially after what happened to your brother." She stopped speaking and gripped her napkin. "And you too, Amelia," she said when she had recovered her emotions. "I would hate for anything untoward to happen."

While there were many ways to interpret the word *untoward*, and Amelia was sure Lady Ashworth was referring to Alexander's untimely death, Amelia realized the word was an appropriate reminder that she and Lord Halford had been alone together, unchaperoned.

"Bucephalus was every bit the gentleman," Lord Halford assured his mother.

"I don't doubt it, Anthony," she retorted. "It is you who needs to be trained to the bit now that you are back."

He barked out a laugh, and Mr. Jennings chuckled. "Well said, Lady Ashworth," Mr. Jennings said, raising his goblet to her.

Lady Ashworth returned to her original subject. "And how are the plans for the fete, Amelia? I hope you were met with enthusiasm in the village."

"Oh, yes, my lady," Amelia said. "Word of Lord Halford's arrival had already made the rounds, and by the time I arrived, the celebration was as good as planned. I had but to inform everyone of the day."

"Wonderful! It is as I had hoped." She placed her napkin aside. "I confess to having had a joyful but tiring day. If you will excuse me, I think I will retire and see how Ashworth is faring. Good evening."

She rose, Lord Halford standing to assist her, Mr. Jennings rising from his seat as well. "Good night, Mother," Lord Halford said, kissing her on the cheek. "And sweet dreams."

"Thank you, Anthony. Oh, my dear, dear Anthony!" She laid her hand on his cheek. "How good it is to have you alive and home! I shall be thanking God on my knees for quite a while tonight."

It was as good a time as any for Amelia to make her own exit, especially since her desire for food had abandoned her. She rose, and Mr. Jennings held her chair for her. "If you gentlemen will excuse me," she said, "I believe I shall retire as well."

Mr. Jennings bowed over her hand. "Good evening, then, Miss Clarke."

She turned toward Lord Halford, who also took her hand. "Good evening. I am glad our little escapade this afternoon did not leave you the worse for wear." His lips lightly brushed her knuckles, setting them on fire.

"Thank you, my lord," she replied, grateful her voice didn't sound as shaky as she felt.

She walked sedately from the dining room and then hurried to her room, shutting the door safely behind her.

* * *

Anthony stared at himself in the mirror on his washstand, feeling weary to the bone. After dinner he'd spent several hours in his father's study, familiarizing himself with the estate accounts and his father's business correspondence. By the time he looked at the clock, it was nearly three in the morning.

He tugged off his neckcloth—a form of torture if ever there was one—and then his shirt, tossing both onto the chair where he'd previously dropped his coat and waistcoat, and splashed water on his face.

Lucas entered the room and handed him a fresh towel. "It's been a long day and an even longer night, Tony. I'll help you with your boots."

"Why aren't you asleep?" Anthony asked.

Lucas gave him a speaking glance.

"I don't need a nursemaid," Anthony grumbled. He crossed to the bed and collapsed, grateful for the assistance all the same. He really shouldn't allow it. Now that the others knew of Lucas's aristocratic background, he shouldn't be behaving like a servant. But Anthony had gotten comfortable with Lucas as his personal servant in the army, and old habits died hard, especially when one was nearly too exhausted to move. Perhaps he was tired enough to actually sleep through what remained of the night.

Boots removed, he rolled fully onto his bed and dragged the quilts over himself. He was barely aware of Lucas blowing out the candles.

Anthony was sure he'd scarcely closed his eyes when he heard a commotion. Gunfire and explosions. Scuffling. Someone screaming.

A woman.

Was it Miss Clarke? Was she in peril?

Panicked, he struggled to sit up, fought to go to her rescue. Her screams were frantic, high-pitched sounds that struck at Anthony like knife blows. Something or someone was holding him back, and he fought, flailing out furiously to free himself. It couldn't be happening again.

"Stop!" he cried at the top of his voice, fighting, fighting. "Stop! Stop!"

"Tony!" he heard in the distance. "Tony!"

Someone grabbed his shoulders and shook him. The screams turned to sobs, and Anthony raged and despaired. He was too late! He'd failed again! He pushed at the restraining arms, tried to aim a blow at the man responsible for his failure to assist.

"Tony!"

This time his name was accompanied by a slap to the face. Shaking his head to clear it, he looked, *really* looked this time, and saw Lucas.

There was no sobbing outside his door. There were no men attacking Miss Clarke or anyone else, for that matter.

"It was the dream again," he said. He was clammy, and his heart was beating out of his chest.

His friend had a look of resolve on his face and only released his grip on Anthony when it was obvious he was fully awake. "Yes," Lucas said. "And this is why I intend to remain for a while yet. You don't need a stranger wondering about your nightmares."

Meaning someone who hadn't been there. Hadn't experienced Badajoz, didn't know of its horror.

"You don't suffer from nightmares."

"I have my own demons to fight, I assure you, but I wasn't an officer like you. I wasn't responsible for the actions of others. Or, more aptly, I didn't *feel* responsible for their actions like you did. Will you be able to sleep again?"

"I doubt it. What time is it?"

"Nearly dawn. You did well tonight, considering."

He'd slept a measly two hours, but at least it was something—more sleep than either of them expected.

"Has the weather cleared? Perhaps I'll take Bucephalus for an early run."

Lucas parted the curtains and peered outside. "No rain. I believe I'll join you on that run, if you'll let me."

"Of course."

Lucas left to dress, and Anthony rose, untangling himself from the blankets that had twisted around his legs in his distress, and quickly pulled on his clothes. The scent of acrid smoke filled his nostrils, so real had been his dream. Would he ever get past the horror of Badajoz?

Shots rang out and mingled with the screams and cries of the soldiers as they pressed forward and were immediately felled and those behind struggled over the fallen to take their places. Explosions and gunfire illuminated the smoky, murky sky, revealing men subjected to the unfathomable atrocities of war.

In what had seemed an eternity to Anthony but was a mere few hours, French commander General Philippon surrendered to General Wellesley. But the surrender did not stop British soldiers fueled with bloodlust from their looting and vicious reprisals on the innocent citizens of Badajoz. Anthony fought a new battle now against his own men, but without success.

As he made his way down one putrid, narrow alley, he encountered the worst sort of brutality imaginable—a gang of men savagely attacking a woman, her eyes wild with fear and pain. Anthony had had enough and raised his pistol. "Stop!" he yelled. "I order you to stop this instant."

A filthy soldier turned to look at him with glinting, unseeing eyes. "Leave be, Captain, and let us have a little fun."

"No," Anthony said. "I command you to stop. Now!"

He charged at them, tearing a few of the men away from the woman as she struggled and screamed. He fought, taking hard punches and landing a few of his own. The woman sobbed, and he lunged, throwing himself between her and her attackers. And then he heard the shot from a pistol and felt intense fire in his side, and then nothing at all . . .

Anthony dropped into a chair and hung his head, covering his face with his hands. The images of Badajoz haunted him constantly, but none more than that of the woman. Had the men killed her? And, if so, how long had she been forced to suffer before they had?

He'd been helpless to save her. He'd failed. There was nothing he could do now but pray for her soul and hope she'd found peace, but it was not enough. It would never be enough. Not for her or for so many others.

It wasn't until he joined Lucas in the hallway that he paused to wonder why it had been Miss Clarke who had been in his dream.

Chapter 4

When Amelia had initially begun her employment as Lady Ashworth's companion, Lord Ashworth had spent a great deal of time and energy bringing his eldest son to heel. Lord Alexander had been a dashing, amiable man who had been kind to Amelia on the few occasions when they'd spoken, but he'd been inclined to reckless behavior, from what she had been able to observe.

The staff had occasionally gossiped about the antics of the young earl, although they'd stopped talking whenever Amelia had happened by. As a newcomer who spent most of her time with the marchioness, she hadn't been privy to their chatter, despite her general acceptance among the servants. Still, Amelia had caught bits of conversations: Lord Alex racing to Brighton in his curricle, the young master losing hundreds of pounds gambling, then winning it all back on a single hand of cards, the dashing young man who was such a favorite with the ladies . . .

And then Amelia had seen the young man laid out in the parlor, his neck broken when his horse had failed to clear a fence. Those had been terrible days, terrible months—the marchioness weeping, the ill marquess staring woodenly out the window. Lady Louisa inconsolable at the loss of her eldest brother, with Viscount Farleigh, Lady Louisa's husband, standing helplessly by. The news of the younger son dying in Spain.

Now the family Amelia had grown to love as dearly as if they were her own could rejoice. And she would do everything in her power to make the fete a joyous one. She thought again how she would love to see her mother or her father and discover their deaths had not occurred!

The last few days had been extraordinarily busy ones. Lady Ashworth had quickly dashed off a letter to Lady Louisa, informing her that her brother was home from Spain and very much alive. During the subsequent mornings, Lord Ashworth—invigorated by the return of his son—had his steward and Lord Halford meet with him in his bedchamber so he could oversee their estate discussions from the comfort of his bed. During that time, Amelia helped the marchioness write invitations to the local gentry and particular friends for a formal dinner to be held the evening prior to the festivities. In the early afternoons, Lady Ashworth took luncheon with the marquess before he rested.

Which was why Amelia had an hour to herself at present.

A footman bearing a silver tray approached Amelia as she came down the staircase into the great hall. "This arrived for you, Miss Clarke," he said, bowing slightly.

"Thank you, John," she said. Undoubtedly it was from the vicar's wife, who had promised to update her on the plans for the scheduled daytime activities. She tucked the letter into her pocket and headed in the direction of the music room—her favorite room in the house.

The plans for the festivities, now less than a week away, were under control. Mrs. Shaw already had the housemaids dusting every inch of the place, and the laundry maids had been tasked with ironing every piece of linen.

Feeling a trifle hungry, Amelia decided to stop by the kitchen first. Mrs. Deal had been busy making cakes and tarts and various other preparations for the fete, and the place bloomed with mouthwatering aromas.

"Miss Amelia," Mrs. Deal said, using her apron to protect her hands as she removed a large copper pot from the fire. "You're in time for a fresh scone. Lizzie, fetch some butter; that's a good girl."

"Dear Mrs. Deal, you read my mind." Amelia sat on the bench next to the kitchen table, where the scones were cooling. The young scullery maid set a crock of butter and a dish of currant jam on the table.

"Thank you kindly, Lizzie," Amelia said.

The girl dipped a polite curtsy and returned to her task of scrubbing pots.

Amelia helped herself to a warm scone, giving it a good dollop of butter and jam before taking a bite and savoring its utter deliciousness. Mrs. Deal was known throughout the area for her cooking. "Will you be baking something for the contest this Friday?" she asked nonchalantly, knowing full well what Mrs. Deal's reaction would be.

The woman huffed and ran a sleeve across her damp forehead. "As if I don't have enough to do, what with providing fancied-up meals to all them gentry folk what will be here and all. Of *course* I'm entering something. I'll not be having people thinking I'm not up to snuff, and that's that. Now take another scone and be off with you. I've work to do."

Amelia laughed and kissed Mrs. Deal on her reddened cheek before slathering butter and jam on another scone and tucking it into a napkin to eat later.

There had been an old clavichord in her home growing up, and Amelia had fond childhood memories of her mother playing it. She'd given Amelia lessons until she'd become too ill to continue.

The music room at Ashworth Park was home to a lovely, modern pianoforte and had warm, golden walls and high ceilings elaborately painted with scenes from Greek mythology. Large banks of windows overlooked the grounds and gave the room an open, airy feeling.

She wandered over to the windows to take in the scene and open the note she'd received. It was indeed from Mrs. Villiers, the vicar's wife. She had convinced some of the village men to organize a cricket match and, later, if it met with approval, a tug-of-war.

Amelia smiled. From what she had been told in the village, a tug of war between the men of Ashworthy was traditionally done over muddy ground and was particularly amusing to watch.

She read further. The ladies of the parish who were organizing the baking contest wondered if Lord Halford would be so kind as to judge their wares, and would Miss Clarke please put their request to him.

That made her heart skip a beat. It meant approaching him, and the idea was both frightening and exhilarating. Too exhilarating for Amelia's own good. Keeping her distance was in her best interest; the man had too much of an effect on Amelia's common sense.

She continued reading. Mrs. Villiers seemed to have everything well in hand, so it only remained for Amelia to plan the games and contests for the children, which she had happily volunteered to do. She adored children and had spent many wonderful hours assisting her father at the school in Little Brenchley.

Satisfied that the plans were going well, she tucked the letter back in her pocket and seated herself at the pianoforte. Amelia ran her hands lightly over its wooden cabinetry, enjoying the satiny finish. Above the keyboard was a lovely floral pattern of inlaid wood, the perfect touch for such an exquisite instrument.

She set her fingers to the keys and began to play.

* * *

Anthony had spent another long morning with his father and his father's steward, Fawcett. Honestly, the man had been old when Anthony had been a boy; he looked like Father Time now, though he was still as sharp as a tack. And while his father was looking better than he had on the first day of Anthony's arrival home, he tired easily and, therefore, relied on Fawcett's recommendations.

None of which would have been bad if the man didn't look at Anthony as though he was still an infant in leading strings.

Adding insult to injury, after Fawcett had made his obsequious bows and had finally left the room, Anthony's father said, "Your mother has assured me there will be eligible young ladies at the dinner to be held in your honor. Be sure to do your part."

"I know my duties in that regard, Father. You have made them perfectly clear."

"I hope so." His father straightened the few papers that remained on his lap desk. "You should know that we had nearly completed the settlements between your brother and Marwood's daughter before he went off and got himself killed on that wild horse of his. She'll be there, so look her over carefully. Most of the work is already done, so the marriage can be expedited if she suits."

Clearly implying his father wanted them to suit.

Anthony remembered Lady Elizabeth Spaulding, the Duke of Marwood's only daughter. She was extraordinarily beautiful, every bit the daughter of a duke and a diamond of the first water. How could Anthony, with his blemished soul, bind such an exquisite creature to him? The answer was he couldn't. Besides, she had always been intended for Alex, and Anthony regarded her as a sister. "I understand completely," Anthony said, wanting the conversation to end. "Now, if you'll excuse me, I will leave you to rest."

"Devil take it! I'm not tired, and what could be more important than the topic we're discussing? I'd like to know," his father said.

"The age of your steward, for one," Anthony replied. "The man is ancient. I must learn what I can from him as speedily as possible, for he is apt to crumble into dust at any moment."

"Bah," the marquess said. "Fawcett's too mean to die. It's what I've valued about him for all these years."

"Seriously, Father, the man has earned the right to a generous pension and some leisure time while he can still enjoy it. I will be his diligent pupil in the meantime. I know I have much to learn if I am to assume my duties effectively."

"I am not sure Fawcett would know what to do with himself if I pensioned him off, but I take your point. Go, then, off with you, and see what pearls of wisdom you can glean from him before it's too late." The marquess settled deeper into the pillows at his back and closed his eyes. "You're a good lad. Always have been." He sighed. "And there I am, calling you a lad myself."

"I take no offense, but thank you instead, Father," Anthony said as he lifted the lap desk from his father's bed. The man wasn't known for sprinkling compliments. "I will do my best."

"Just don't forget Lady Elizabeth while you are at it," he said, his eyes closed, his hands clasped on the counterpane.

Anthony shook his head and left his father's bedchamber, determined to speak to Fawcett and assert his authority over the man. The old steward was undoubtedly in the study, so Anthony went in that direction. As he made his way down the hallway, however, he heard an unfamiliar sound.

Music.

That was odd. His sister, Louisa, was the only one who played the pianoforte, and even before she married, she'd rarely spent time at the instrument.

Dealing with Fawcett could wait.

He walked to the music room and stood outside the door, listening for several minutes. He recognized the piece as a simple country tune, but the performer was embellishing it in a most delightful way.

The door to the room was closed, and Anthony didn't wish to disturb the performance, so he carefully turned the knob and opened the door only enough to slip inside. It was Miss Clarke at the keyboard, and she was engrossed enough in her music that she didn't hear Anthony enter the room.

He leaned against the wall, watching her and listening. Her fingers glided over the keys, combining the lilting melody with harmonies that filled an empty place in Anthony's heart. When she finished, he waited quietly in hopes that she would play another, certain that if she knew he was there she would stop and the pleasure of listening to her would end.

He was not disappointed. She began another piece, slower, softer this time, with a tender melody and harmonies more somber than the first had had. The music ebbed and flowed, nuanced with emotions he rarely acknowledged.

The piece finally concluded, and Anthony found himself deeply moved by the performance. He was reluctant for the soothing atmosphere she had created to end, but unfortunately, it was time to make her aware of his presence. He began to clap.

She turned abruptly at the sound, a blush rising on her cheeks. He continued clapping as he righted himself from the wall and walked toward her.

"Brava, Miss Clarke," he said. "Forgive my intrusion on your privacy, but I was drawn to the music and could not resist. You are very accomplished."

"I think not, my lord, though I thank you for the compliment," she said. She hesitated and then added, "I do have permission to be here."

"I don't doubt it," Anthony replied. "I'm certain the moment my parents heard you play they insisted on making this room available to you at any time. You have great ability."

"Any ability I have I owe to my mother. It was she who taught me."

"And a fine job she did too," he said, "but you have a natural gift as well." More and more Miss Clarke was showing herself to be a puzzle that piqued Anthony's interest. She read Robbie Burns and played the pianoforte beautifully. Her manners were impeccable.

Of course his mother wouldn't have chosen a companion who was not accomplished. That wasn't the puzzling part. As the daughter of a vicar, Miss Clarke would have received a decent enough education, but she was well read, not merely literate. And music lessons to the extent Miss Clarke had obviously received would have been a luxury of time in a vicarage.

Her father's livelihood meant he very likely could have been the younger son of a nobleman. It was a common career choice for many younger sons. It also meant her mother was probably gently born. And yet Miss Clarke claimed no other family, none beyond her now-deceased parents. But if her father had been an only child, he would have inherited his father's title. It raised questions in Anthony's mind.

"It seems your childhood was an idyllic one," he said, hoping to gather more clues from her as subtly as possible.

"It was," she said. "My parents doted on each other and on me too. I loved tagging along after my father as he saw to the needs of the parish."

"The parish of?" he casually asked, holding his breath.

"Little Brenchley," she said, and Anthony exhaled. "It's a tiny village in Kent," she continued. "And a lovely place. Mama began teaching me my letters when I was quite young, but I begged and begged to be allowed to attend school with the other children. I thought spending all day with them would be much more fun than staying home with Mama." She sighed. "If I'd known she'd be gone so soon, I would have chosen differently."

"No one can foresee something like that." He thought of Alex and all the other deaths he'd witnessed on the Peninsula. "Anyway, I'm sure she was happy to see you run off to school every day and learn along with your friends."

"Perhaps," Miss Clarke said. "And she did teach me a great deal. The piano, for starters, although my skill pales in comparison to hers. Embroidery—which I detest, quite frankly. I cannot, for the life of me, seem to make the needle and thread go where I intend them, and I am forever tangling things into the worst imaginable knots."

Anthony chuckled. "I would dearly love to see a piece of your needlework, Miss Clarke, to judge it for myself."

"I can assure you with all gravity that you would find my work dull, my lord, unless you look at the back, in which case you will not be able to find an adjective to describe what you see." Her green eyes twinkled.

On impulse, Anthony sat next to her, facing the opposite direction she was. The bench wasn't large, which meant they were pressed together, thigh to thigh. It had been a long time since he'd been in the company of a genteel young woman, and the intimacy surrounding them was both calming and exhilarating—an irresistible combination for his empty, hungry soul.

She did not shift, which meant she had a bit of steel inside her, but he'd rattled her, nonetheless, he knew, as she had become as still as a rabbit being hunted by a fox. He'd surprised himself, frankly. But he liked that she held her ground and did not let him intimidate her.

He leaned back against the piano's wooden frame, putting him nearly face-to-face with her. She hadn't been using any music—she had a true gift—but now it meant she didn't have anything to look at except him.

He smiled at her, out of practice though he was at the expression.

* * *

He was smiling at her.

Sitting so close they were literally touching, he was smiling as if it were the most normal thing in the world for him to do, when it most assuredly was not since the smile did not reach his eyes.

He was also scrutinizing her too closely.

It seemed to Amelia as if Lord Halford had made some sort of strategic move, like he might have done under General Wellesley, and that he was waiting now to see how she would counter his move.

Well, she thought, she would not retreat, despite the logic that strongly urged her to do so. Nothing would result from his flirtation, if that was what this was about.

He leaned back against the pianoforte and stretched a long, muscular arm across the top of it—right in front of Amelia's eyes. This brought him even closer to her and deepened the sense of intimacy between them.

Oh, but she needed to be careful. He was impossibly attractive.

"You do your parents credit," he said. "It's not every vicar's daughter who has impeccable manners, exquisite musicianship, and a kind, generous heart."

She wondered if he could hear the pounding of that heart. "Thank you, Lord Halford. My parents were my world; I would want them to be pleased."

"Miss Clarke," he said, "I know we have only known each other a short week, but please call me Anthony. My brother was Halford. Perhaps in time I will wear the title more comfortably, but for now it conjures only sadness."

Anthony. It was so tempting to do as he asked . . . "I cannot be so familiar, my lord," she said reluctantly. "It would be improper."

"I don't see why," he said. "The older retainers do. I'm Master Anthony to them. Sometimes I'm even referred to as 'that young rascal.'"

Ah, his smile nearly reached his eyes that time. They were so blue they deserved to sparkle like the sky on a sunny day, but Amelia could see shadows lurking in them still, despite his effort to be lighthearted. She wanted to take those shadows from him.

"Well then," she said, "I shall call you 'that young rascal,' and you may call me Miss Clarke."

He laughed outright. "I believe that perhaps *you* are the rascal, not I. Very well, *Miss Clarke*, I concede. Whatever you choose to call me, I shall answer. But you know my wishes in this matter." He took her hand in his and raised his eyes to hers, and Amelia's breath caught in her throat. His eyes were blazing now, and he held her gaze while he turned her hand over and kissed her palm and then her wrist.

The feel of his lips was so unexpected, so exquisite. "Oh," she breathed. She'd never been kissed like this before. Never been tempted to *allow* kisses like these before. This was not at all like the cautious gentlemen and unappealing suitors of Little Brenchley.

Lord Halford brought his face close to hers then, his beautiful, masculine mouth a mere inch away, and she wanted to close the distance, fought not to close the distance, afraid he was going to kiss her, panicked he would not.

"Amelia," he whispered, and then his lips found hers.

The sensation was delicious and subtle and electrifying. He cupped her cheek with his hand, and Amelia felt cherished in a way she hadn't since losing her parents and her home. His lips were soft, and they caressed and explored hers, and then inexplicably her hands were in his hair, and she drew his head closer to get more of him. She was on fire, and her heart thundered loudly in her ears.

Too soon he drew away from her. "Amelia," he said again. "Amelia." He ran his hands gently down her arms and took hold of her hands, placing them over his heart. It was a touching gesture, and he looked handsome and vulnerable, yet so very strong. His hair was mussed now, so she pulled one hand free and smoothed it down, feeling off-balance and a little shocked, frankly, that she had reacted so intensely to him.

He stood and offered her his hand. "Undoubtedly it would be wise for me to leave, but I find I am reluctant to do so just yet. Would you care to stroll in the garden with me?"

"I think I would, thank you," she said, feeling much as he did.

"Shall I call for a maid to join us?"

"That won't be necessary," Amelia replied. "I am not a young debutante who must be protected from scandal. I am a spinster, on the shelf for so long I have collected a distinctive layer of dust." To illustrate her point, she brushed a hand over her sleeve.

"You are nothing of the sort, Miss Clarke," he said, chuckling. "I take great exception to your description of yourself. Shall we, then?" He extended his hand to her.

Once she rose from the piano bench, she immediately released his hand. Touching him would only reignite the flames inside her. Better to extinguish them with cool formality.

He held the door to the music room for her and walked beside her, his hands clasped behind him, until they reached the formal gardens at the back of the house.

"I am interested in your stories of Little . . . Brenchley, was it?" he said as they strolled past the marchioness's roses, which were in full bloom and particularly fragrant this afternoon. "It sounds delightful. You must miss it dreadfully."

"Yes, Little Brenchley. It was indeed a happy place to grow up, as I am sure Ashworth Park was as well."

"True enough." Lord Halford—Anthony—pointed to a cluster of oaks growing nearby. "You see those trees? In the past, they served as a pirate ship, a carriage, and a jungle of darkest Africa for two daring young boys."

She smiled. "And those two boys would have been you and your brother, of course. What of your sister? Was she allowed to join you on your daring adventures?"

"No, not at all. She was a mere infant in our eyes, not to mention a *girl*." He shuddered dramatically. "We could not have our masculine refuge overtaken by such a beastly creature, you know. Alex and I were very young ourselves, and our opinion of the fairer sex was not as appreciative as it became when we grew older."

Amelia was only too aware of how appreciative he could be.

"Eventually our lives were filled with tutors and school and university. Alex had the added responsibility of being the heir, and I realized early on that I must find a suitable living for myself for my own sake and sanity. The law held no interest for me and the church even less. That left the military, which sounded dashing—much like our escapades in the oak trees." The bleak look was back in his eyes again.

"But you did not find it so," she said.

"No, Miss Clarke, I did not. Far from it, in fact."

He said no more on the subject. They strolled quietly side by side, eventually reaching the path that led past the oak trees in question toward the lake. Here he offered his arm once again since the path was uneven. She placed her hand in the crook of his elbow and fought back the urge to draw closer to him.

"It was in the army where you met Mr. Jennings, I take it," she said, redirecting her thoughts away from his physical person.

"No, actually," he said. "Lucas was a year behind me at Cambridge, although he left after a year and enlisted. He actually has more years in the army than I do, and yet as an enlisted man, he was a mere corporal to my own rank of captain by the time I met up with him. When I recognized him, I asked to have him assigned to me as my personal servant. We were able to keep an eye on each other that way." He became silent again.

He seemed reluctant to speak much about his time in Spain, and Amelia didn't want to press him on an uncomfortable topic. "You studied at Cambridge? And yet your family seat is here in Oxfordshire."

"Oxford was not for me, my dear Miss Clarke, or for Alex. Young men in university do not wish to be too close to their parents. I was for Cambridge."

They had reached the lake, and he left her and walked to the shore.

"There used to be rowboats on the lake," he called back to her. "I will check with the head gardener to see if they've been stored somewhere on the estate. It would be good to have them out again, and they would be a nice addition to the festivities everyone is so occupied with planning."

Even from a distance, he was irresistible, and she was weaker than she realized. She rose and joined him on the shore. "That sounds fun. I have never been in a rowboat before. There was a small stream outside Little Brenchley, and my father took me fishing there a few times, but nothing as large as this."

He picked up a stone and sent it skipping across the water. "Another talent to add to your growing list: fishing. I'm impressed."

"Yes, well, it is not such a surprise when you realize I was a substitute son for my father on many occasions. We definitely fished, and the fish tasted all the better for our efforts."

"Well done, Miss Clarke. My father took Alex and me fishing on several occasions as well. I wonder which of us is the more skilled angler."

"I cannot say," she replied archly, enjoying herself, "but I am inclined to believe it would be me."

"There is a challenge if I ever heard one," he said. "In the meantime, I think we shall see who is better at skipping stones."

They spent several minutes searching for the best stones before taking turns letting them fly.

Lord Halford was the more accomplished of the two, without question.

"I hope you feel better having bested me," Amelia said. "Although, considering you grew up with a lake upon which to practice, while I did not, it comes as no great surprise. I applaud you for your masculine superiority."

"Cheeky wench," he said, holding back a laugh.

"I intend to thrash you soundly when it comes to fishing. You will see."

"Name the place and weapon," he replied, winking at her.

She smiled.

He pulled his watch from his waistcoat pocket and checked the time. "Blast, just as I thought. I must return to my duties. Shall we go back together, or would you like to remain here for a while?"

"I will return with you."

He seemed contemplative on the walk back to the house, and Amelia chose not to disturb him. It was a pleasure simply to be in his company.

When they reached the house, he bowed over her hand and kissed it. "Adieu for now, Miss Clarke," he said. "I thank you for your music and your company. You have lightened my heart this afternoon." He turned and strode down the hallway toward Lord Ashworth's study, no doubt to work with the steward.

Amelia watched him until he disappeared from sight. She would treasure their kiss in the music room and the time they'd spent together this afternoon, and she was glad she had been able to do something to ease the burdens he seemed to be carrying, but it could not be repeated. She was growing too fond of him, which, when added to her growing attraction to him, was a disaster waiting to happen. And it would be she who suffered as a result. In the meantime, she would do all she could to make the fete a wonderful occasion for him to enjoy.

She was suddenly reminded of the letter from the vicar's wife in her pocket. And the scone.

Heavens, she had forgotten to ask him about judging the baking contest!

Chapter 5

For the next few days, Anthony was extraordinarily busy, spending nearly all his time with Fawcett. His father was getting stronger with every passing day, thankfully. Strong enough to prod Anthony much too frequently about the necessity of filling his nursery quickly.

"I have seen my own mortality, and that of my sons," he'd said—*again*—to Anthony only yesterday. "There is no time to lose."

"I already gave you my word, Father," Anthony had said. As soon as this infernal celebration concluded, he was off to London on that particular errand, if Lady Elizabeth or the other young ladies who would be attending the fete did not suit.

He thought of the kiss he'd shared with Miss Clarke, and guilt twisted through him. He should not have kissed her, knowing he must most likely face this year's crop of debutantes in the Marriage Mart very shortly.

And yet he could not be altogether sorry either. For too long, the hollow-eyed look of the Spanish women and girls he'd encountered had haunted him. How he was to flirt with the innocent darlings of London society with those images in his mind, he did not know. He'd been reassured by his encounter with Miss Clarke. He didn't want to lead her on with his overtures, but he at least now knew he could probably manage to court someone when he arrived in Town since it was expected of him.

The guests would begin arriving today for the dinner this evening and the day-long festivities tomorrow. He would play host and be at his mother's side and receive them so his father could be rested enough to attend the dinner.

Anthony had just finished washing and dressing and was on his way to find his mother when he heard a commotion coming from the entry hall.

"Mother!" he heard a musical, familiar voice sing out. "How is Father? Is he much improved? And where is—Oh, Anthony! Anthony!"

He hurried down the stairs, and then Louisa was in his arms, weeping and laughing and hugging him as tightly as he was hugging her.

He realized there was a distinct roundness protruding from her middle. "My dear Lady Farleigh," he said. "You are looking well, and it seems you are to present me with another niece or nephew in a month or two or three."

"You rascal!" Louisa said. "You've never called me Lady Anything before. You always had some terrible nickname for whatever the occasion called for. But you have guessed we are again in the family way. Farleigh, look! It truly *is* my despicable brother back from the grave. When I received Mama's letter, I could not believe it. Then Farleigh said, 'But surely your mama would not tease about such a matter.' And he was right, the dear man, and here you are. Oh, my dear, you have played with our affections most cruelly." She sniffed and rummaged in her reticule for her handkerchief.

Anthony retrieved his own from his pocket and handed it to her. "Darling little sister, I would never wish to add to your suffering, and I apologize most profusely for the pain this has caused you all. William, good to see you, old man." He shook his brother-in-law's hand firmly. He and William Barlow, Viscount Farleigh, had been schoolmates at Eton.

"Welcome home, Tony," Farleigh said. "It is good to have you firmly back among the living."

"Agreed. And can these two fine individuals truly be young William and Penelope?"

His nephew and niece were standing nearby, vibrating with excitement.

"Bow to your Uncle Anthony, William. Penelope, you may curtsy now, as we practiced," Louisa said.

Young Will, whom Anthony figured to be about four years old—good heavens, could that be right?—gave him a formal bow, bending deeply at the waist and forcing Anthony to hold back a laugh as he returned the favor. The young lad was the spitting image of his father, with light-brown hair and dark-brown eyes that held a mischievous twinkle.

Anthony crouched next to tiny Penelope.

She blinked two large blue eyes at him—she had inherited the Hargreaves blue eyes—clutched her little skirt in both hands, and curtsied, nearly toppling over in the process. Anthony caught her before she hit the marble floor and presented her with a distinguished bow as well. That girl would steal hearts when she grew up. She already had his.

"Amelia! Oh, I am so glad you are here!" Louisa said, causing Anthony to look up. Indeed, Miss Clarke stood on the staircase, and it was difficult for him to look away from her. "Nurse didn't handle the coach ride very well this morning, the poor dear," his sister continued, "and the children are wild to get some exercise."

"There is nothing I would enjoy more, my lady. Come, then, Will and Penny," she said as both children ran to her side and the children's poor nurse slipped out of the hall, looking green-tinged and miserable. "I happen to know," Miss Clarke said to the children, "that Mrs. Deal has hot chocolate and biscuits waiting in the kitchen for two very special children."

"And we're those special children!" Will crowed.

"You are. Afterward we shall go to the stables, where I have it on good authority that there are kittens looking for playmates."

"Kitts!" Penelope said, skipping along, holding tightly to Miss Clarke's hand. "Kitts! Kitts!"

"No, Penny, I'm hungry. Biscuits first," Will insisted, firmly attached to Miss Clarke's other hand.

"Kitts," Penelope said, sticking out her lower lip.

Anthony braced himself for the tempest he saw looming on the horizon.

"We will take refreshment first, shall we, Penny?" Miss Clarke said softly, crouching to address the girl. "While the chocolate is nice and hot. And then perhaps Mrs. Deal will find a treat we can take to the kittens. Does that meet with your approval?"

Little Penelope nodded, and Anthony relaxed.

"I thought you might agree. Very practical of you. Let's be on our way, then," Miss Clarke said.

Anthony watched the trio disappear down the hallway leading to the kitchen until he became aware that the hall had grown quiet. Too quiet . . .

"What are you all looking at?" he asked, feeling defensive. Everyone was focused on him for some reason, his sister's eyebrows raised, his brother-in-law coughing back a laugh. He needed to defuse the situation quickly. "Chocolate and biscuits would tempt anyone."

His mother's look of contemplation was the most worrisome to Anthony and made him uneasy.

"As you say," she eventually said. "Come, Louisa. I'm sure you would like to rest for a while. What of you, Farleigh?"

"I should like to accompany Louisa to our rooms and see her settled comfortably." Anthony's brother-in-law offered his arm to Louisa. "Is that all right with you, my dear?" he asked her softly.

"Thank you, Farleigh," Louisa said, eyes glowing. "You are so good to me."

Anthony made his bows to the group and beat a hasty retreat to his father's study. His family had observed something peculiar in his behavior, though he'd changed so much in the past few years he couldn't be certain what it would have been. But he could venture a guess.

For Anthony, however, it was Louisa's and Farleigh's behavior that had been noteworthy. Theirs had been an arranged marriage, much as Anthony was fated to experience himself. But it had grown into a love match, for which Anthony was exceedingly grateful. More so now than he'd been at the time, he had to admit.

He'd known Louisa had married well enough, that Farleigh was a decent chap and would treat his sister kindly. It had seemed sufficient and was more than most married couples of the ton could claim. It was *de rigueur* to marry for advantage alone and unseemly to suggest otherwise. Love rarely had anything to do with marriage among the *beau monde*.

But since then he'd witnessed firsthand what ill treatment of the fairer sex was like, and he regretted his earlier opinions on the matter of matrimony. He would not have the opportunity to marry for love either, but he vowed that whatever wife he chose he would treat with fidelity and respect. If he was lucky, they could eventually share a type of affection.

He dared not hope for more than that.

***

Amelia sipped her tea and watched Penelope dip a biscuit daintily into her cup of hot chocolate. The girl sat perched on a box placed on a kitchen chair and was swathed in a voluminous apron. It was a grand event to take refreshment anywhere other than the nursery and was doubly fortunate today, as it allowed their nurse the chance to rest and let her stomach settle.

Travel with two young children was taxing enough, but Amelia knew from past experience that Nurse Pratt didn't fare well when traveling by coach. Amelia had gotten used to keeping company with Will and Penny when the family paid a visit. They were energetic, delightful children, and she loved spending time with them. It also prompted happy memories of helping her father at the village school.

Will, wearing a large napkin tied around his neck, slurped down the last of his chocolate and plunked his cup down. He wore a chocolate mustache now, which Amelia hated to wash off, finding it a charming addition to the little boy's face.

"Are you done, Penny?" he asked his sister. "It is time to see the kittens. May we, Miss Amelia?"

"Kitts," Penny said as she dunked her biscuit once again.

"Come on, Pen!" Will tugged at the napkin unsuccessfully. "Let's go!"

"Let me help you with that," Amelia said. She set her own cup down and proceeded to untie the knot at his neck. "Sit still, William, so I can wash the chocolate from your face."

She dipped the napkin in water, then returned to the table to dab away the chocolate. By that time, Penny had decided she was through eating, and Amelia cleaned her up as well.

"Down," Penny said as Amelia worked to untangle her from the protective apron. "Kitts."

"Yes, darling, it's time to visit the kittens."

"Hooray!" Will shouted. "Hurry, Pen!"

The three of them properly thanked Mrs. Deal, who had found a few bits of bacon for the kittens, and then set out for the stable. One of the boys had set up a nest for the mother and babies at the back of the building, past Bucephalus and the estate's other fine horses.

Amelia had no desire to supervise two rambunctious children around such large beasts. "Tom," she called to one of the stable hands from the doorway. "Would you please bring some of the kittens outside for Master Will and Miss Penny to see?"

"Yes, ma'am," he replied, tugging at his forelock.

Amelia led the children to a shady area under some nearby trees. It was a lovely grassy spot, and she settled the children and then herself on it.

"Here you are, ma'am. Mind, they're still babes yet and need to be handled gently." He directed that last bit of conversation to the children.

"Oh, we shall!" Will said.

"Kitts!" Penny cried.

Amelia only smiled and picked up the one closest to her, a fluffy ball of orange fur, and set it on her lap.

Penny poked a cautious finger in the direction of another orange ball, which nipped at her and made her squeal, while William flopped onto his back and placed the black kitten on his belly. The kitten began prowling up his chest and nuzzling his chin, sending William into peals of giggles.

"Here, Penny," Amelia said. "Come and pet this one. It won't bite you."

Penny stroked her tiny fingers down the back of the orange kitten on Amelia's lap, then looked up at Amelia, her big blue eyes glowing with delight. "Ooh! Nice kitt."

"What is this I see? My young nephew bravely wrestling a huge jungle cat. A panther, I'll wager." Lord Halford approached the trio, looking as dangerous to Amelia's state of well-being as a jungle cat. She kept her eyes focused on the children and the kittens . . . and Lord Halford's highly polished boots.

"No, it's not," the boy crowed. "It's only a mouse catcher! And a baby one, at that."

"So it is. May I sit?"

He directed that last bit to Amelia, and what could she say? In any case, the dratted man didn't wait for her reply before lounging down next to William, who now had two kittens crawling all over him.

"Of course," she murmured belatedly.

He eyed her suspiciously, so she bent her head and fed a bit of bacon to the orange kitten. "I've been instructed to ask you if you will judge the baking competition tomorrow," she said.

He sighed. "I suppose they will not take no for an answer?" he asked.

"I doubt it."

"Fine, then," he said without much enthusiasm.

He had come outside to enjoy a moment with his niece and nephew, and she'd inadvertently added to his burdens. "I can tell them you would rather not, if you like."

He chuckled without humor. "I can either judge and offend all the ladies whose baking I do not choose, or I can offend them all at once by refusing to judge at all."

"I see your point," she said. "I will tell them you are extraordinarily happy to have been asked and accept wholeheartedly."

That raised a genuine smile on his face. "Please do that for me," he said. "Penny, love, what is that I see by your feet?"

Penny, feeling much more confident, grabbed the calico sniffing at her shoes and handed it to her uncle. "Nice kitt!" she said.

"It certainly is, sweeting." He pulled the child onto his lap and held the kitten for her examination, running his finger down the kitten's neck.

Amelia's own neck began to tingle. She cleared her throat. "I am actually surprised Penny went to you so willingly. Had you even seen her since she was born?"

"No, but she obviously has great instincts when it comes to people. Don't you, Miss Penny?"

The poppet beamed up at him. He apparently had an effect on females of all ages.

William suddenly plopped the two kittens on the grass and darted off.

"Where are you going?" Amelia called after him, but he returned as quickly as he'd gone, holding a longish stick.

"Watch," he commanded and then ran the stick around in the grass for his two kittens to chase, which they did with relish.

Penny pointed. "Kitts!"

"It's obvious I am going to have to work on expanding my niece's vocabulary while I'm here," he said.

Amelia looked at him with alarm.

"I mean," he corrected, "while *she* is here, of course."

"I do not think that is what you meant at all," Amelia said.

"No, you are right. It is only that after the celebration tomorrow, I must go to Town for several days. Weeks, possibly." He dropped his gaze and stroked Penny's curls.

A knot formed in Amelia's stomach. "But your parents. They have only just gotten you back. Why weeks?"

"I have duties that must be fulfilled," he said, "and the sooner I attend to them, the better for all involved. I have been absent too long."

"You are speaking in riddles," Amelia said. "I have no right to pry, I know, but I will be heartbroken for your parents' sake and hope you will be able to return to them quickly."

"Heartbroken, the lady says . . . but for my parents' sake. It is for my parents' sake that I go, Miss Clarke. But let us say no more on the subject, for it is a fine afternoon and we have kittens that must be enjoyed."

Amelia noticed Penny had nearly dozed off from the gentle ministrations Lord Halford had given her curly head. The kitten too had curled up for nap. William's two were worn out from chasing the stick, and Will had lost interest in the game anyway and was chasing a butterfly. Staying any longer would only add to their sense of familiarity with each other, and there had been something resolute and unnerving about his plans to go into Town. Amelia rose to her feet. "I think it is time for the kittens to return to their mama," she said, then called softly to Will. "Let's go find Tom, William, and then we can go to the lake."

"Brilliant!" Will cried, then clapped a hand over his mouth when he saw Penny was asleep.

"I will see that Penny reaches the nursery," Lord Halford said.

"Thank you." She left him with Penny and the kittens and, after informing Tom, led Will to the lake, where he was content to pitch pebbles into the water and watch them splash.

Amelia was not content, however. Her thoughts were a jumble. Why was Lord Halford leaving so soon after arriving? Why did he consider it his duty to leave? It made no sense. He may have business that needed urgent attention; he'd been gone from England for the better part of five years, except for the occasional leave. And yet it seemed to be something of an abrupt decision on his part.

Was he going away because of her? Certainly she wasn't important enough to take him from his family so soon, despite their kiss in the music room. He'd been friendly and pleasant to her in the days since but had also maintained a careful distance, tacitly reminding her that the kiss had been an impetuous mistake on both their parts.

Mistakes of that nature were agonizingly sweet and tempting, which made them difficult to forget. And yet she must.

Her thoughts did not settle, not after she returned Will to the nursery or while she saw to the final details of the fete. She needed to be clearheaded that evening. The remainder of the guests were arriving during the afternoon, among them Lady Walmsley, to whom Amelia owed her position here. She would not do anything to make Lady Walmsley regret her letter of reference.

And yet the idea of Lord Halford leaving the day after the celebration cast a pall over everything for her. She expected his parents were not ready to have him gone so soon.

And she acknowledged to herself that she was not ready either.

* * *

Tonight's dinner will be endured only through what little mental discipline I developed on the Peninsula, Anthony thought as he finished dressing.

His kind mother had absolved him of greeting every guest upon their arrival that afternoon, saying he could be presented to all of them that evening at dinner. He had been immensely grateful.

She'd found him shortly after he'd ducked into his father's study and had chided him for hiding. "Go outside and get some fresh air," she'd said. "You seem restless to me. The exercise will do you good, and you need to be in good humor in time for dinner."

And so he had, immediately stumbling upon his niece and nephew in Miss Clarke's care, and it had done him a world of good to be in their company.

How wonderful it would be to have the blessed innocence of Penelope and the jolly outlook of little Will again. How weary and old Anthony felt by comparison.

After he had taken tiny Penelope up to the nursery, he'd saddled Bucephalus and gone for a ride across the estate. Blessedly alone and, for the moment, free of guilt and obligation.

Setup had already gotten underway for the fete tomorrow. The staff had set up tables for the food-tasting competitions, and there were seating arrangements in shaded locations that would allow for conversations amongst the guests. An area had been roped off for the children's games, and the head groundskeeper had located the rowboats, which were now lashed to the small dock at the north end of the lake.

Once past all that, Anthony took Bucephalus on a good run. He longed for more physical exercise, though, and was looking forward to the cricket match tomorrow, as well as the tug-of-war he'd heard rumors about.

Back in the day, when he and Alex had been boys, the men of the village had held a tug-of-war at every fete. There was a traditional spot near the green where the stream that wound near Ashworthy cut nearest to the town. The women had done everything they could to get the spot as muddy as possible, and it had made for great entertainment as the men had slipped and pulled and exerted all their strength. The losers had always bought the winners a round at the pub later.

Both boys had looked forward to the day when they could participate, but school and university had limited those opportunities. Anthony had seen instead his share of mud and grit at Badajoz. Perhaps tomorrow's tug-of-war would be a way to replace a bad memory with a good one.

He checked his neckcloth one more time in the mirror.

"You look fine," Lucas said. "It's one of my better knots."

"I should have said no when you offered to tie it; it feels like a noose," Anthony said. "I think you are trying to get back at me for your having to dress and dine with us, although you are as grand as half the people who will be in attendance."

"Fortunately, the attention of all the marrying mamas and young ladies will be directed at you, despite my superior looks," Lucas said, flicking imaginary lint from his sleeve. "I would bow out to ensure your success in that regard, but I would be throwing off the seating numbers, and we cannot do that to your mother at such late notice, now can we?"

Anthony's only response was a growl, making Lucas laugh before they both left Anthony's dressing room and joined the guests.

A footman opened the door to the sitting room in which the guests had gathered, and Anthony braced himself as he and Lucas entered. It was much more crowded than he'd anticipated, and he tugged discreetly at his neckcloth again. Lucas quickly melted into the crowd, blast the man. Anthony was on his own.

"Ah, there he is now," he heard his mother say as she made her way toward him. "We were just speaking about what a miracle it was that you returned home after the dreadful news we'd received. I've already made apologies for your father," she added in a lowered voice so that only he could hear. "He was adamant about attending but was feeling tired. I told him not to be pigheaded and foolish. Your Grace," she said, raising her voice again, "I do not believe you have met my younger son, the current Lord Halford. Anthony, may I present the Duke of Marwood, the Duchess of Marwood, and their daughter, Lady Elizabeth Spaulding."

"Your Graces, Lady Elizabeth," Anthony said, bowing to each in turn. "An honor to make your acquaintance." The Duke of Marwood was a large man with a stocky build and pale, ruthless eyes. His wife was tall and too thin. She would have been a handsome woman but for the pinched expression she wore. Lady Elizabeth, however, was as beautiful as Anthony remembered. He wondered if she and Alex had been in love.

"Halford." The duke harrumphed. "Met the other Halford. Decent chap, if a bit wild. Hope you are more settled than he was."

His mother paled, and Lady Elizabeth blushed at her father's implications, which matched what Anthony's father had suggested: that since the marriage agreement between Alex and Lady Elizabeth had been near completion, it made sense that Anthony simply step into the breach. He was not happy with the duke's assessment of his brother's character, however. "I expect the military disciplined a great deal of wildness from my character, Your Grace," Anthony replied, trying not to bristle. "If you will excuse us, my mother is anxious for me to greet our other guests. Duchess, Lady Elizabeth."

Bowing to each again, he and his mother moved away. "I cannot believe the nerve of that man sometimes," she whispered to him. "Saying such things about you and Alex that way, as if the two of you were bloodstock at Tattersalls."

They'd reached the cluster of people nearest them. Unfortunately it happened to be Sir Frederick Putnam, a local baronet, and his wife and two daughters. Anthony winced inwardly. The Duke of Marwood had been pompous and arrogant, but the Putnams were social climbers of the worst kind. Sir Frederick wasn't entirely a bad sort, but Anthony could already feel Lady Putnam's eyes boring through him, and the

Misses Putnam were eyeing him like a prize bull. Miss Harriet Putnam, the eldest, wasn't much younger than Louisa, but the years hadn't been as kind to her as they had his sister. Miss Charlotte Putnam had always been a silly girl, and it appeared maturity hadn't changed that aspect of her personality, although she was relatively harmless—he hoped.

After greeting each member of the family, Anthony opened his mouth to make polite conversation before moving on—they were neighbors, after all—but Lady Putnam beat him to the punch.

"Lord Halford," she said loudly enough for the entire room to hear. "What a joy it is to have you back among your bosom friends! I cannot tell you how it made us feel when we heard the news! We were all in raptures, were we not, girls?"

"Oh, yes, Mama," Miss Harriet exclaimed, clasping her hands dramatically against her overly exposed bosom. Anthony suspected it was a tactical maneuver, however badly it failed. "Absolute raptures!"

Miss Charlotte giggled behind her gloved hand.

"Yes, well, I was quite in raptures myself to return home," Anthony managed as politely as possible. "If you will excuse us—"

"And I said to Harriet," Lady Putnam continued. "'Harriet,' says I, 'we *must* have that young man over to tea soon and welcome him back properly to the village.'"

"That is very kind of you, my lady," Anthony said, glancing at his mother, but she was intentionally ignoring him and smoothing down her skirts.

It appeared he would have to rescue himself.

"Harriet has gotten very good on the pianoforte," Lady Putnam said. "Everyone compliments her. I am certain you would enjoy listening to her perform her latest Haydn sonata."

Anthony glanced frantically about the room. "I am sure I would," he said. "I shall make a note of it. I have many new responsibilities requiring my attention that take precedence over everything else, unfortunately, but I shall endeavor . . . Mother," he added, hoping he didn't sound desperate. "Who is that young lady seated in the chair by the window? I must take you to task for not introducing me to such a lovely guest."

"But she *isn't* a young lady," Charlotte Putnam piped up. "She is as old as a crone."

His mother looked up. *Finally.* "But of course, son," she replied smoothly, ignoring Charlotte's remark. Even Lady Putnam managed to look embarrassed. "Please forgive us, Lady Putnam. I have neglected my duties as hostess and must introduce Halford to Lady Walmsley."

Anthony made a point of bowing over each of the Putnam ladies' hands and left with great relief. Lady Putnam had hardly spoken to him in his youth, and the girls had been indifferent. Alex had been the heir, not he, so Alex had been the object of their fawning attention. Anthony suspected Harriet was holding out for no less than an earl. She would probably be married with children of her own, like Louisa, if she and her marriage-mad mama hadn't cared more about the title than the man. Harriet was not for him.

And Charlotte Putnam would drive him mad in a week with her silly comments and incessant giggling.

When they reached the silver-haired lady in the chair, Anthony realized Miss Clarke was seated next to her, looking especially lovely in a pale-green muslin gown.

"Lady Walmsley," his mother said, "may I present my son, the Earl of Halford."

Anthony took Lady Walmsley's hand in his and bowed low over it. "An honor, my lady," he said, remembering that it was she who had given Miss Clarke her reference.

"Welcome back from the grave, young man," she said. "You have returned from a place I may soon make my residence. Perhaps you can share your knowledge with me so I will get along better once I arrive there."

"Oh, but you must not speak so!" Miss Clarke exclaimed, taking the hand Anthony had relinquished and kissing it fondly.

He had felt those lips on his own and knew they were full and soft and—devil take it! His thoughts seemed to travel in that direction no matter what he did. And to complicate matters further, he was finding it a great pleasure to feast his eyes upon her now. Her simple green evening dress was modest and not quite in the latest fashion but still very pretty, and the color of it matched her eyes and set off her auburn hair nicely. It was the first time he had seen her in anything but gray.

His father had called an end to the year of mourning beginning this evening, what with Anthony's arrival home and the celebrations and all, and Anthony could not be sorry. If Alex could see Miss Clarke right now, may he rest in peace, he would not be sorry either.

"Halford," Lady Walmsley said forcefully, bringing him out of his thoughts. "I have decided I shall be staying here as your guest for the next fortnight at least. Perhaps longer. My own companion was in need of a vacation, but instead she chose to visit her relations in Yorkshire, foolish woman. She's due back any day now, but she will be that much the worse for wear, so I am writing to say I am staying here and ordering her to Bath for a long rest when she returns from the north. Ashworth Park appears to have plenty of diversions to keep people from being bored silly"—she paused and gave a speaking glance at Charlotte Putnam—"well, some people at least."

Anthony bit the inside of his cheek in order to maintain his composure. "You are welcome to stay as long as you wish, my lady," he replied in a solemn voice. Lady Walmsley seemed the sort to keep an entire household merrily on its toes. "We will enjoy getting to know you better, and I am sure Miss Clarke is looking forward to spending more time with you."

"Oh yes," Miss Clarke said. "Did you know, Lord Halford, that Lady Walmsley was a friend of your grandmother's? And her niece and my mother were at school together. That is an amazing coincidence, do you not agree?"

"Amazing indeed," Anthony said. In fact, it was another piece of the puzzle, he thought. He seemed to recall that Lady Walmsley was the daughter of an earl, and her niece, therefore, the granddaughter of an earl. And Miss Clarke's mother had been at finishing school with her . . . It must have been a fairly elite school, then, and helped explain how Miss Clarke had arrived at her own impeccable manners and speech.

"That is all fine and good," Lady Walmsley said, waving her hand about. "But it is a conversation for a different time, when we may sit comfortably away from all and sundry and talk freely about such things. I do not share my history with the undeserving public." Anthony coughed, and Lady Walmsley narrowed her eyes at him. "Do *you*, young man?" she asked pointedly.

"Do I what?" Anthony had lost the thread of the conversation somehow.

"Share your personal history with all and sundry," she replied impatiently. "Lady Ashworth, you did not tell me your son returned home from the war without his wits."

Lady Ashworth looked at her son.

"I retained my wits, I assure you," Anthony replied. "I am merely dazzled by your beauty and find myself tongue-tied as a result."

"Ha!" Lady Walmsley cackled. "I daresay you *do* have your wits after all."

"But promise that you will share your stories with us—I mean, me," Miss Clarke said, casting a furtive glance in Anthony's direction. "I should dearly love to hear anything you can tell me about my mother, even if it is not much."

"I have stories, my dear," Lady Walmsley said, patting Miss Clarke's hand. "But I see that dinner is to be served. Not a moment too soon either. Help me to my feet, Halford."

"Of course," Anthony replied, noting that his mother and Miss Clarke were both fighting not to smile at Lady Walmsley's command.

Buxton had indeed entered the room to announce dinner. Anthony assisted Lady Walmsley to her feet, though she wasn't as frail as he'd originally thought. "You, my lady, are a force to be reckoned with."

"Flatterer," she said, cackling and smacking him with her fan. "If I were a decade or two younger, I would be hot on your trail."

Terrifying thought, that.

He wished he could escort Miss Clarke, but it would be bad form. As host, he was required to escort the lady of highest rank, which happened to be the Duchess of Marwood. His brother-in-law, Farleigh, arrived to escort Lady Walmsley. Anthony glanced around for an escort for Miss Clarke, reluctant to leave her on her own, and was relieved when his father's physician, Dr. Samuels, stepped forward.

Samuels was older, probably in his fifties, but Anthony recalled that the man was a widower and had spent a great deal of time at Ashworth Park attending to his father and, therefore, would be well acquainted with Miss Clarke.

Suddenly the idea of Samuels escorting her didn't seem like such a good idea.

Anthony could not help his impulse to protect Miss Clarke. And yet any attention he paid to her would be perceived as the lord of the manor dallying with a subordinate, taking advantage of his position. It simply was not done.

"Farleigh, I need your help for a moment," his sister Louisa said from across the room, drawing Anthony's brother-in-law away from Lady Walmsley momentarily. Anthony opted to stay with the elderly woman. The Duchess of Marwood would simply have to wait a moment for his escort, if she wished it.

"You are woolgathering again, boy," Lady Walmsley murmured to him. Only someone like Lady Walmsley could get away with calling him 'boy.' "Pay attention," she said.

"Forgive me. I shall try to be more attentive."

"Apology accepted," she said. "Now, if I were a young man, I would be keeping an eye on her too." She gestured with her fan in the direction of Miss Clarke and Dr. Samuels. "Lovely girl, unlike most of them here. Levelheaded, with a kind heart to boot."

"What are you suggesting, my lady?"

"You could do worse. The evidence of that will be sitting around the dinner table with us. Oh, the Marwood chit is well enough, if only her father would loosen his grip on her. She has almost lost what spirit she has. But the Putnam girls"—she snorted in disgust—"there is only one brain between the two of them, and unfortunately most of it belongs to the eldest, who only uses it for her self-serving ends. And that mother of theirs . . . Well, I have said enough for now. Ah, there you are, Lord Farleigh."

Anthony left Lady Walmsley in his brother-in-law's capable hands and went to offer his escort to the duchess and then led the way to the dining room.

He seated himself at the head of the table, his mother seated opposite. The other guests for the evening, in addition to Lucas, included the Reverend Villiers and his wife, Alice; old Fawcett; and Christopher and Phillip Osbourne, neighbors and particular friends of both Anthony and Alex. He had not been able to greet them earlier, having been commandeered by Lady Walmsley, but he would be sure to speak with them at length later.

If he remembered correctly, their father had died while Anthony was gone, and Christopher—Kit to his friends—was the Earl of Cantwell now.

If there were any two people alive who would understand Anthony's position at the moment, it would be the Osbourne brothers.

Miss Clarke, he noted, had been seated between Dr. Samuels and Mr. Fawcett. Anthony, on the other hand, had Lady Elizabeth seated at his left and her mother at his right.

It promised to be a dull evening.

He rose from his seat and delivered the speech he'd mentally prepared while Lucas—who'd insisted—had shaved him for the second time that day. "On my father's behalf, may I welcome you all to Ashworth Park and hope your stay with us will be an enjoyable one. I am happy to report that he is getting stronger and is determined to join us for part of the day tomorrow—"

A round of "Hear! hears!" erupted, and some of the men raised their goblets.

Anthony continued. "Additionally, I would like to say that I am gratified to be home and reunited once again with family and friends and am humbled by the celebration that has been planned for tomorrow in my honor. But I cannot allow things to proceed further until I have raised a glass to my brother, Alexander, who left us all too soon. I was spared a similar fate while in Spain, but I would not have had it thrust onto him." He raised his goblet. "To my brother, Alexander."

"To Alexander," the others at the table echoed.

* * *

Amelia found herself seated between Dr. Samuels and Mr. Fawcett, which did not bode well for an enjoyable dinner. She might have found it interminable if not for her conversation with Phillip Osbourne, who was seated across from her at the table. She had a previous acquaintance with Mr. Osbourne and his brother, Lord Cantwell; they had been frequent visitors to Ashworth Park two years ago, visiting even more so during the days immediately following Lord Alexander's death.

They had ridden over frequently during that terrible week to console the family and to be consoled. Their estate was nearby, and the four boys had been the best of friends. Amelia had been privileged to hear them tell stories of the antics they had got into. Even Lady Louisa had tearfully shared jolly anecdotes of her childhood attempts to be included in the band of four.

Amelia could not help but be distracted by the conversations at the other end of the room, however, where Lord Halford was.

"I have suggested, my dear Miss Clarke," Dr. Samuels said, "that Lord Ashworth allow me to bleed him daily, but he has refused. If he does not listen to my advice, I cannot vouchsafe his continued return to health."

"And yet, sir," she replied as patiently as she could, "if his health is improving as you say, he may not require such extreme methods." She really did not wish to discuss Lord Ashworth's blood—or anyone else's, for that matter—at a formal dinner party. Lord Ashworth himself would be appalled.

"The subtleties inherent in the practice of medicine are many, dear lady. Perhaps we may stroll on the terrace following dinner and I can instruct you further."

The type of instruction Amelia was sure Dr. Samuels intended to provide, if the way he was ogling her was any indication, had nothing whatsoever to do with the treatment of patients, and she was determined to avoid it at all cost. "Thank you for your generous offer, Dr. Samuels," she said, "but I shall be retiring shortly after dinner. Tomorrow promises to be a busy day, and as I have much responsibility for it, I must be well rested."

"My dear Miss Clarke!" he exclaimed. "Your own health will be at risk if you are not careful. I shall speak to the marchioness on your behalf and set the situation to rights. It simply cannot be borne."

Could the man not take a hint? "I beg you, do not, sir. I will be happily occupied with my tasks tomorrow. I volunteered for them." In a last-ditch attempt to extricate herself from Dr. Samuels's attentions, she looked determinedly at Mr. Osbourne. "And what of you, Mr. Osbourne? May we hope to see you participate in the cricket match tomorrow afternoon?"

"That you will, Miss Amelia," he said, his eyes twinkling. The scoundrel. He'd used her Christian name intentionally to get under Dr. Samuels's skin, as Amelia had not given the doctor permission to do so. "And I plan to be involved in the tug-of-war I've heard rumors about," he added. "I hope you will be there to see me at my impressive best."

"I wouldn't miss it," she said.

Dr. Samuels grumbled about impertinent young men as he drained his goblet and gestured at a footman to refill it.

Mr. Osbourne winked conspiratorially at Amelia.

She smiled and took a bite of pheasant, then glanced around the table while she savored it. Lady Ashworth was engaged in conversation with the Reverend Mr. and Mrs. Villiers; Mr. Fawcett was busy refilling his plate. At the other end of the table, the duke and Lord Cantwell conversed with Lord Halford. Amelia had stolen glances at him during dinner, but this time he looked up and caught her at it.

She quickly looked back at her plate and sliced away at the pheasant. Had he sensed her watching him? Oh, she hoped not! How mortifying that would be!

"Miss Clarke," he said loudly enough to be heard at her end of the table—and to silence the other conversations taking place. "The Duke of Marwood has just said something of note, and I should like another opinion on the subject. A lady's opinion."

For him to single her out and refer to her as a *lady* amongst this lofty group set Amelia's hands to shaking. She gave up on the pheasant, set her utensils down, and placed her hands in her lap.

"Well, I should be happy to respond," Sir Frederick said. "Whatever His Grace has said, I'm sure it's quite correct, and I shall go on record as saying so." He smiled ingratiatingly at the duke.

Lord Halford ignored him completely. "Miss Clarke?" he repeated, his eyes locked on her.

How could he put her on the spot like this? She was but a companion, not quite a servant, but lowly when compared to the others present. She was seated at dinner only by virtue of the marchioness's affection for her, and yet Lord Halford now wished her to offer public commentary on a duke's point of view. "I should do my best to offer an opinion, my lord," she said, "except that I did not hear what His Grace said." She was tempted to say she had been busy discussing bloodletting with Dr. Samuels, but she would do nothing that would reflect poorly on her parents or the marchioness—or Lady Walmsley, for that matter.

Mostly, though, she hoped her answer would excuse her from any further reply.

"Would you care to repeat what you said, Your Grace, or shall I paraphrase for the lady and the others?" Lord Halford asked.

Drat the man.

The Duke of Marwood flicked an elegant hand at Lord Halford. "You may speak, Halford. And she may reply, though I doubt we shall hear anything more riveting than has already been offered on the subject, which is to say, nothing at all."

The Duchess of Marwood and Lady Putnam looked decidedly put out at the duke's remark, while Lady Elizabeth stared squarely at her plate. Charlotte Putnam was busy helping herself to more food, oblivious to what was going on around her.

Harriet, however, glared hotly at Amelia. Why she did, Amelia was not entirely sure, though she could speculate. Amelia had certainly not volunteered for this attention.

"His Grace's comments came about when the subject of the education of women arose, Miss Clarke," Lord Halford said. "Kit here—excuse me; I mean Lord Cantwell. I am afraid old habits die hard—mentioned the cleverness of some of the French émigré ladies he has become acquainted with in London. He wondered if perhaps the English were doing their daughters a disservice in their formal upbringing by comparison."

"A disservice, bah," the duke said. "A man's education is unnecessary for a lady and only serves to upset delicate female sensibilities. My Elizabeth here is the very epitome of English womanhood; she is accomplished in all the gentle arts and is a diamond of the first water as a result."

The lady in question blushed beautifully—not a splotchy red, Amelia noticed, but a delicate pink that only enhanced her appearance.

"And so she is," Lord Cantwell said smoothly. "I would never wish to imply otherwise. But perhaps other young ladies may benefit from a slightly more comprehensive education."

"Radical thinking," Dr. Samuels said, dabbing at his chin with his napkin and staring at Amelia as though *she* were the tasty pheasant being served.

"It is the responsibility of highborn parents to ensure their daughters are trained in all the genteel arts, as the duke says," Sir Frederick said. "We English have excelled in this regard. One only has to visit the Continent to recognize the superiority of our womenfolk, flowers of the upmost grace and deserving of gentlemen's protection and guidance. My own daughters are fine examples and are held in the highest esteem by the best of families."

Harriet and Charlotte preened at their father's observation.

"There is no need," Sir Frederick said, "for young ladies to worry themselves over masculine subjects that will strain their tender sensibilities. It is a gentleman's duty to see to such matters."

"You see where things stand, Miss Clarke," Lord Halford said. "It seems to be the general opinion that we gentlemen are foresworn to protect our fair English ladies above all else. They are the weaker sex, you see, and in need of the strong hand and guidance of a man's greater intellect in order for civilized society to succeed."

"Anthony," the marchioness warned.

"Precisely," the Duke of Marwood said. "And so, *Miss Clarke*," he said, dripping with condescension, "what have *you* to add to the subject?"

"I would tell you what I think," Lady Walmsley muttered, "but it would leave you with indigestion for a month."

"And yet the French ladies of my acquaintance acquit themselves very well and are a source of pride for their husbands," Lord Cantwell said.

"But they're *French*," the duke said. "They count for nothing with the English. Speak, Miss Clarke. We are gasping to have you enlighten us."

Amelia took a moment to choose her words wisely. If they were going to insist she speak, she may as well share her true feelings and not pander to those with an opposing viewpoint, especially the Duke of Marwood. Later she would also share a piece of her mind with Lord Halford for subjecting her to this embarrassment. "I am no philosopher, Your Grace," she said, trying to hide the tremor in her voice. "I do not possess your worldly knowledge, nor do I claim to. I have only my own experiences, and so I can speak only to them. Women have few choices in life, and after the death of my parents, my circumstances were bleak, except for the kindness of Lady Walmsley and Lady Ashworth."

"You are well worth it, my dear," Lady Walmsley said. "As anyone can plainly see if they would only *look*."

"Thank you, my lady," Amelia said. "Despite my good fortune, I confess I have found it difficult to be dependent on others for my survival, and I suspect many women share my feelings in this regard. I can only be grateful, therefore, that my father was generous in sharing his education with me despite my being a daughter and not a son. It is my knowledge I may rely on in the future, should I need it, as any man would rely on his for securing his place in the world."

The duke only raised his eyebrows and drank from his goblet.

"You compare yourself to a man. I wonder at your lack of decorum," Lady Putnam said.

"But no gentleman would do business with you, Miss Clarke. It would be *most* inappropriate," Sir Frederick said.

"I thank you for your honesty, Miss Clarke," Lord Halford said. "While there may be those present who disagree with you, I am sure we can all appreciate the courage it took to give such an honest answer."

"Not an honest answer at all," the Duke of Marwood drawled, sitting back in his chair. "A self-serving one. It is this kind of rebellious thought that threatens the very fabric of our society, putting ideas into the minds of wives and daughters—and sons—and pushing them toward disobedience."

"Hear, hear," Sir Frederick said, lifting his glass, as did Dr. Samuels. Lady Elizabeth set her utensils down and pushed her plate away. And yet the Duke of Marwood had not been looking at his daughter as he spoke but at Amelia.

He had called her dishonest and self-serving.

Amelia should say nothing. He was a duke, she a mere paid companion. And yet her father's voice came to her unbidden in that moment: *The hotter the flame, my dear, the stronger the steel. Remember that.*

She stepped into the flame. "I would ask, Your Grace, if it is more self-serving to want to improve one's mind in order to improve one's circumstances, or to keep others from doing so in order to maintain power over them?"

The room fell silent, and all eyes turned toward Amelia. The duke glared at her. "How dare you—"

"Well," Lady Ashworth said, standing abruptly and interrupting him. "What an invigorating conversation! I am sure everyone would agree. Perhaps this is an excellent time for the ladies to remove to the sitting room and leave you gentlemen alone to your port. Ladies?"

The gentlemen rose as the ladies departed the room, despite the fact that they hadn't been served the dessert course yet. Amelia immediately sought out the marchioness. "Lady Ashworth," she said in a hushed voice. "I am truly sorry if what happened just now gave you distress."

"It was very bold of you, my dear," Lady Ashworth replied. "And yet I am not sorry, at least not entirely, and so I would not have you be sorry. I am only perplexed at Anthony's intentions." She laid her hand on Amelia's arm. "But you must beware, my dear. You have not endeared yourself to His Grace this evening; quite the contrary. Indeed, you may have made an enemy."

"I did not expect the duke to ever acknowledge my existence and would have preferred that it stay that way. I am certain I will be nonexistent to him once again."

Lady Ashworth nodded. "Hopefully you are right. In the meantime, you have my permission to take Anthony to task over his presumptuous question if you like."

"Perhaps I shall. May I be excused now, my lady?" Amelia asked. She'd had enough excitement for one evening. "I should like to be well rested for tomorrow's activities and am a bit tired."

"Of course, my dear," Lady Ashworth replied. "And good night."

Amelia hurried to her room, grateful that the marchioness was so forgiving of her reply to the duke. She knew she herself would lay awake into the wee hours of the night, despite her best efforts to sleep, thinking of little else.

***

"What were you thinking to put Miss Clarke on the spot like that?" Lucas hissed to Anthony as the gentlemen exited the dining hall and made their way to the sitting room to rejoin the ladies. "You may as well have drawn a target on her back."

"I realize that now," Anthony replied. "I acted rashly, and now I must be certain Miss Clarke does not suffer any consequences for it."

"I repeat, *what* were you *thinking*?" Lucas said, taking him by the elbow and leading him down the hallway, away from the others.

"You heard the tone of the conversation among the men—Marwood braying on in that pompous way of his, the older men slavering over his pronouncements like hungry lapdogs. I do not understand how the ladies seated around him did not stand up and whack him on the head with the nearest plate available."

"Many of the ladies agreed with his point of view, as would most of society."

"Undoubtedly true, but I cannot get the images—" He stopped and ran a hand over his face. "Forgive me, Lucas. You were there. You know better than anyone else what it was like."

Lucas clapped his hand on Anthony's shoulder. "Tony, you take on too much of the responsibility for what happened there. You were one captain amongst many, the others all officers and men of good conscience. I will wager Wellesley does not flagellate himself over it as much as you do." He slapped Anthony on the back. "Now, you must go entertain your guests. I, on the other hand, am a guest who has decided he is done for the night."

"Deserter," Anthony whispered, but Lucas only raised his hand in farewell.

The minute Anthony entered the sitting room, his mother hurried to greet him. "What were you *thinking*, Anthony?" she whispered as he leaned in to kiss her cheek.

"You are the second person to ask me that question in as many minutes," he said, nodding to the Villiers, who had acknowledged his return.

"I do not doubt it. You stirred up a veritable hornet's nest. Make amends, and quickly." She drew him over to the Duchess of Marwood's side. "Your Grace, here is our returning hero again. Perhaps he would be willing to share some of his more entertaining war stories with you. I must see to Lady Walmsley." And then she deserted him just as Lucas had done.

He deserved his fate, he supposed.

"Your Grace," he said in his most solicitous tone, "I hope you are enjoying your stay at Ashworth Park so far. Your rooms are acceptable?"

"Yes, yes, everything is fine in that regard." She waved his questions away with her hand. "We are in the rooms we always stay in when we visit. But I cannot understand why you chose to address that *servant* at dinner just now. Marwood was not happy about it at all. And I do not believe your father would be pleased either . . . were he to be informed of it."

Was the lady attempting to threaten him? The idea was ludicrous. Her emotional blackmail might work on her poor daughter, but it would not work on Anthony. He had dealt with too many hardened soldiers to be intimidated so easily—even by a duchess.

"The lady in question is a family friend," he told her as politely as he could. "I am sure you are equally as solicitous of your friends. Now, I hope you will excuse me. I am afraid I am neglecting our other guests."

The duchess seemed mollified for the moment, and since his mother had drawn Lady Elizabeth into conversation with Lady Walmsley and he intended to avoid the Putnam ladies with a vengeance, he searched until he spotted Louisa and Farleigh speaking to Kit and Phillip and joined them with a sense of relief.

"Anthony, you are too bad!" his sister said. "I nearly spat out my food when you asked Amelia to speak. And on the education of women, no less!"

"Do not get her started, Halford," Farleigh said. "Louisa has too many radical ideas of her own without your filling her pretty head."

"Farleigh exaggerates," she said, playfully swatting him with her fan. "He adores me all the more because I had two elder brothers and had to learn to hold my own with them."

"I am her besotted slave, it is true," Farleigh said.

"And yet Miss Clarke was brilliant," Louisa added in a low voice, checking to make sure the duke was out of earshot. "She landed quite a blow. I wanted to stand and cheer."

"My wife, the silent champion of women everywhere," Farleigh said wryly, taking Louisa's hand in his own and kissing it.

"I find myself quite jealous of the two of you," Kit said. "All this marital bliss makes me want to weep."

"Truly," Phillip chimed in. "I keep encouraging Kit to take a bride and fill his nursery so I may relinquish my role as heir and trip merrily off to deepest Africa—or America, if we could ever cease being at war with them."

Anthony laughed along with the others, but the word *heir* stuck in his mind. It was apparent that the Marwoods considered him Alex's replacement for Lady Elizabeth—that, at the very least, had become apparent in the dinner conversation.

But Lady Elizabeth was not for Anthony. He knew it and had known it since his introduction to her. Perhaps even before that. Out of respect for his parents, however, and for Alex, he would not be precipitous in making his wishes in this matter known.

He looked at Lady Elizabeth once more. She was smiling and nodding agreeably at Lady Walmsley, who was waving her hand dramatically in emphasis of whatever it was she was saying.

Lady Elizabeth, despite her wretched parents, was kind.

Anthony determined he would do everything he could to make his marriage preference—or lack thereof—known to her with as much care as he possibly could.

Chapter 6

Amelia awoke bright and early, though not as well rested as she would have hoped, washed and dressed, and had a breakfast tray sent to her room. Even so, by the time she went downstairs and out to the garden, the place was buzzing with activity.

The ladies of the church auxiliary already had their baked goods out for the tasting competition, so Amelia hurried over to greet them. "Ladies," she said, surveying the cakes and pies on display, "these all look splendid, and I'm sure they will taste equally so."

"Good morning, Miss Clarke," Mrs. Villiers said. The vicar's wife was always warm and friendly, but this morning her demeanor was cool. "May I presume that you asked Lord Halford to be our judge for the event?"

"I did, Mrs. Villiers. He is looking forward to it."

"Yes. Well. That's good, then. Millie, move those last few cakes closer together. I'm sure we'll have some late entries. We always do." Amelia had been dismissed.

Millie glanced apologetically at Amelia and then set about her task. Amelia realized that none of the other women had greeted her, and most were avoiding eye contact with her.

Ah.

Apparently she had been the subject of their morning gossip. Mrs. Villiers was a kind woman but staunchly traditional, and Amelia's opinion was undoubtedly an extreme one in her opinion. Amelia shouldn't be surprised, really, but she was hurt by their actions. She had been asked for her honest opinion at dinner, and she'd replied as honestly and circumspectly as she could under the circumstances. At least, until the duke had accused her of dishonesty.

The words could not be undone, and she had too much to do today to dwell on it. She set her hurt feelings aside as best she could and began greeting the tenants and villagers as they arrived.

Soon the grounds were filled with friends and neighbors enjoying a day off from their labors. They were used to rising at dawn and would be back in their fields and shops early again tomorrow, but they would spend today fully enjoying themselves.

Amelia watched men greet each other with handshakes and backslaps, women hug one another, and children laugh and dance about in anticipation of the day's planned activities. The official guests of the manor would join the festivities later in the day, as most of them weren't used to rising so early, and Amelia was glad of that. Based on her experience at dinner the night before, she feared their illustrious presence might dampen the spirits of the otherwise jovial crowd.

"Miss Amelia!" a voice called out to her as she walked up a small incline next to the lake. Several of the village's young men were taking turns rowing the boats for the girls, who were dressed in their Sunday finest and doing their best to flirt with the boys in return, and Amelia's heart ached watching the scene before her.

"Miss Amelia!" the voice called again. She turned to look this time. Young William was chugging toward her as fast as his little legs could carry him. "Papa says I am old enough to be in the three-legged race, and he is to be my partner! It will be jolly great fun, and we shall win!"

Amelia could see Farleigh heading toward her, little Penny in his arms, undoubtedly intending to bring William to heel. It was touching to see Farleigh with his children this way. She crouched down as William reached her, red-faced from his exertions and grinning. "I will be cheering loudly for you both," she said to him.

"Will you watch us, then? Oh, it will be the greatest of good times! Penny is not so big as I am, and Papa says she is too little to do it. But I am not."

"Meela!" Penny called out to her.

"Good morning, Miss Penny," Amelia said, waving at the tiny girl.

"Good morning, Miss Clarke," Farleigh said as he reached her and his errant son. "The fickle English weather has decided to cooperate with us for a change. It is a lovely day, is it not?"

"Indeed," she replied. "I understand from Master William here that you are to participate in the three-legged race."

"Well, that remains to be seen," he said, giving a pointed look to William. "Will has been given strict instructions not to wander off on his own, and yet his enthusiasm for the day has already made that a challenge."

"I shall do better, Papa, I promise! It is only that I needed to tell Miss Amelia all about it."

Amelia bit her lip to avoid smiling. It would not do to undermine Farleigh's parental warnings.

"Meela," Penny said again, holding her arms out to Amelia. "Down."

"You are obviously a favorite of my children, Miss Clarke, for which I can only be grateful. However, Penny," he said as Penny began to wriggle in earnest, "you will be staying with Papa at present. I intend to spend the morning with my children, you see, Miss Clarke. Louisa is saving her limited store of energy for the ball this evening, and I have given Nurse leave to enjoy the activities herself for part of the day."

"I am sure the children will enjoy it. May I offer to watch Penny for you while you and Will race?"

"It will not be a burden to you to do so? I understand you have responsibilities related to the day's activities."

"Not at all," Amelia assured him. "Everyone is pitching in wonderfully. It would be my pleasure."

"Then I will take you up on your kind offer, Miss Clarke. Thank you."

"The children's games are over there." Amelia pointed toward the area that had been designated. "And just beyond it, there is lawn bowling set up especially for the children."

"Thank you again, Miss Clarke," Farleigh said, offering a slight bow, elegantly done considering he was balancing a wiggling toddler in his arms. "Make your bow to Miss Clarke, Will."

The boy did, bending fully at the waist.

She answered with a curtsy.

Amelia watched Farleigh walk toward the lawn bowling area with William in tow. Penny waved back at Amelia over Farleigh's shoulder. "Bye, Meela!" she called.

What darling children they were! Amelia adored them, loved them more and more each time the family visited Ashworth Park.

It saddened her to think she might not have children of her own. Marriage was not likely in her future. The local men found her education and gently bred manners intimidating—other than Dr. Samuels, unfortunately—and she was too lowborn for the other gentlemen.

She wandered the grounds, watching families laugh and play together, feeling alone, and missing her parents. She wanted to belong somewhere, to somebody.

The kiss she'd shared with Lord Halford flashed through her mind. He had made her feel cherished in that moment, and the feeling was an irresistible one. How was she to fight it or her attraction to the man who had offered it to her? And yet she must, for both their sakes.

She was still upset that he had directed such a controversial question to her last evening, and as she had reflected back on it throughout the night, she had seen a glint of challenge in his eyes, like he had been daring her to say what she truly thought despite the lofty company. And she had responded to his challenge.

It was nearing midday, and people began spreading out blankets for their picnic luncheons. It was also time for the judging to begin. Lord Halford had said he would do it, and he seemed the type of man who kept his word. Considering his reluctance, it might prove entertaining. He had put her on the spot last night; she would enjoy seeing the tables turned today.

By the time she arrived back at the judging area, a large crowd had gathered. Lord Halford and Lord Cantwell were standing next to Mrs. Villiers, who fluttered nervously about them.

Finally Lord Halford spoke. "Good people of Ashworthy, I am happy to be home and with you all once again."

Enthusiastic cheers and applause erupted at his words. He bowed in acknowledgment before raising his hand to silence the crowd. "I have been recruited to judge the delicious items you see before us."

"Watch out for old Nelly's pie there, yer lordship," a man called from the back. "Her cat died this week."

The crowd hooted while a woman Amelia assumed was Nelly swatted the man with her bonnet. "I wouldn't do sich a thing, me lord. 'Tis me very best currants in that there, as this old humbug knows."

"I am confident in your fine baking skills, Nelly," Lord Halford said to the woman, grinning. "However," he replied to the crowd, "I have asked my good friend the Earl of Cantwell to judge in my place. I fear my palate has been tarnished by so many years of army rations. I would not do the task justice."

Lord Cantwell bowed to the group. "I am pleased to do the honors," Lord Cantwell said. "Although I am certain I have never faced such a daunting challenge in all my years."

There was some booing and clapping at that, Amelia being inclined to boo herself, and Mrs. Villiers and women from the church auxiliary set about cutting a slice from each entry so Lord Cantwell could taste them. Lord Halford picked up a fork and dug in as well. Apparently he was not opposed to eating the baked goods, only judging them.

The crowd began to disperse a bit, and it would be awhile before the judging would be completed, so Amelia decided this would be a good opportunity to see if Lady Ashworth needed her for anything since she hadn't come outside yet.

Amelia slipped through the crowd and started off in the direction of the house—and immediately ran into Harriet and Charlotte Putnam, of all the luck.

"Ah, Miss Clarke," Harriet said. "Up at the crack of dawn, were you? How I admire your work ethic."

Amelia ignored the poorly disguised jab at her status as an employee. "Good morning, Miss Putnam, Miss Charlotte," she said. "I hope you both slept well last night."

"Well enough," Harriet said.

"I am *so* looking forward to the ball this evening," Charlotte said.

"Charlotte," Harriet purred. "Everyone is looking forward to the ball. You need not state the obvious. Well, Miss Clarke, we must be off. We are breaking our fast al fresco with some of the gentlemen and must not keep them waiting. Good day." She and Charlotte trotted off in the direction of Lord Halford and Lord Cantwell.

Harriet's plans really shouldn't have come as a surprise, but Amelia felt a stab of jealousy anyway. She stood there foolishly watching them greet the two gentlemen, who were still busy tasting pies and cakes. Amelia could see that Lord Halford was smiling at whatever Harriet was saying. And then he looked in Amelia's direction and spied her watching him.

She spun on her heel and walked swiftly to the house. How mortifying to be caught staring at him that way!

She went to her room instead of looking for Lady Ashworth, tossed her bonnet on the bed, and plopped onto a chair. Lord Halford could not have any serious interest in Harriet Putnam, could he? Harriet Putnam, of all people?

And yet the Putnams had something Amelia did not, which made them more eligible prospects for him than she could ever hope to be.

They had a father who was baronet. Amelia could not say the same.

* * *

"They are all quite good, are they not?" Cantwell said to Anthony as he stabbed his fork into a slice of gooseberry tart he'd already tasted previously. "I would share with you, ladies," he apologized to the Putnams, "except that we have been forbidden from doing so until the judging is over."

Mrs. Villiers stood nearby and nodded her head with authority.

Anthony's natural reaction whenever the Putnam sisters showed up was to make his excuses and run. Miss Harriet had made it perfectly clear that she was on the hunt and he was her quarry. Miss Charlotte was less of a threat marriage-wise, except that wherever she was, her elder sister was sure to be nearby.

He had never thought himself a coward. He had faced many battles during his stint in the army and had never shirked his duty. But the last few days he had grown to understand how a fox felt when the hounds were on the scent.

To make matters worse, when he had greeted the sisters, as polite manners had required of him, he had inadvertently glanced in the direction of the house. Miss Clarke had stood not far away, still as a statue, her eyes large as saucers. He had wanted to go to her, but she had turned and hurried away.

"Ooh," Miss Putnam said silkily, sliding her hand through his elbow. "How delicious everything looks! I am positively *ravenous*, are not you, Lord Halford?" She smiled demurely at him. "Charlotte and I had your cook prepare a special little picnic for us. I do hope you still have your appetite. Would you care to join us? And Lord Cantwell too, of course."

"A picnic, Miss Putnam. How thoughtful of you." Anthony ignored the double meaning attached to her comments, impressed that he had managed his reply without outwardly grimacing.

Kit caught a whiff of his unenthusiastic tone, however, and his eyes wrinkled with humor. "You are too kind, Miss Putnam, to have thought of us in such a generous way. Unfortunately we have been informed that the cricket match will begin shortly, and we should not be able to do our best if our stomachs are too full. The baked goods will have to suffice for the time being. May we hope that you ladies will be present to cheer us on?"

Smooth work indeed, for which Anthony was grateful. He sighed in relief. He was beginning to find the crowds and the noise grating, and Miss Harriet and her silly sister even more so.

"Are you all right, old man?" Kit asked him once the Putnam sisters had reluctantly wandered off. "You look as though you have been face-to-face with Old Boney himself."

"I would almost certainly rather face Bonaparte than Miss Putnam," Anthony said. "The lady is on the prowl. And yet I have promised my father I will marry as soon as possible and produce an heir."

"Fortunately for me, I have Phillip as an heir, so I am under no such rush to be leg-shackled and fill my nursery." He clapped his hand on Anthony's shoulder and lowered his voice. "I am sorry about Alex, by the way. I have not had a chance to tell you that."

"Thank you, Kit. Ironic, is it not, that the soldier faced his mortality several times but returned, while the heir, living in the security of his home, died?"

"Alex made his choices and experienced the consequences of them, the same as all of us. I was there. I know."

"Did he truly make his own choices? Do you have choices, *Cantwell?*" He used Kit's title intentionally to make a point.

"We are all born to a certain station in life, *Halford*, whether it is as an earl or as the son of a stable hand. It is what we do with that station that defines us. God does grant us choices, regardless of our lot in life."

"I am not convinced of your philosophy, Kit. We may make choices for ourselves, but they are small ones. Can the stable hand's son become an earl? Does he have the means to educate himself and move out of the stable? And what of Miss Clarke's answer at dinner last night? Do you think her opinions on education for women made her any friends at the table?"

"So that is what this is about," Kit said.

"What do you mean?"

"I mean," Kit said, "you have developed tender feelings for Miss Clarke. I am not surprised, old man. She is a joy to look upon, and her conversation is refreshing, much like the French ladies to whom I referred."

"You should not mention them again if you wish to remain in good graces with the other guests. I can only imagine what kind of ladies they were."

"Very respectable, I assure you," Kit said, laughing.

"It is true I find myself drawn to Miss Clarke," Anthony said, going back to the original topic, "but I meant my comments generally."

"I do take your point," Kit said. "Bonaparte would choose to be emperor, and see where that choice has got us all." He set his fork and plate down and patted his stomach. "I think it is time for us to name a winner of the contest. Although it will not be Nelly."

"Poor Nelly. Not that her pie tasted like cat, thank goodness. In fact, it was a rather decent currant pie, overall," Anthony said.

"I think I shall help myself to another slice of this apple cake, though, before we make the announcement." Kit looked around to make sure Mrs. Villiers wasn't watching, then dished another slice onto his plate. "It is really quite tasty."

"Is that your choice as winner, then?" Anthony pinched a piece of it off Kit's plate and put it in his mouth. "It is good, I agree."

"It is the winner, then. You don't happen to know who made it, do you?"

"No idea," Anthony said. "And you are not to say that I had any part in your decision. I have to live with these people and wouldn't want anyone's feelings hurt for the world."

"You have my word on it, Anthony." Looking serious, he added, "As your friend, I would urge you to take care. I know Ashworth is in a rush to have you wed, but you have already seen more battles than any man should. I would like to see you choose a wife who will provide you with a peaceful life."

"Back to discussing choices again, eh? I hardly have the time to be so choosy, do I, if I am to keep my promise to my father?"

"You would do your father more of a service if you were to find a lady wife who can help you lay your ghosts to rest. You brought several home with you from Spain."

"Lucas has been telling tales, the traitor."

"He said nothing I had not observed for myself," Kit replied. "And now I have said my piece. At the very least, avoid the Putnam chits. Married life to either of them would only add to your nightmares."

"Who said anything about nightmares?" Anthony asked with alarm. Lucas wouldn't have dared share that secret with anyone.

"No one, Tony." Kit looked at him strangely. "Figure of speech, is all."

"Right. Of course." Now he felt a fool for having said anything.

"But if you *were* having nightmares," Kit said somberly, "it would hardly be a surprise. Come. Let us join that cricket match, shall we? We will wait until people start to leave for dinner before announcing the winner here, and give your mother and the other ladies a chance to be in attendance. What do you say?"

"Sounds good. And thank you, Kit. You are a good friend and always have been."

"You can return the favor someday. I am sure I shall need one."

*　*　*

Amelia chased a giggling Penny near the roped-off area where the three-legged race was being held. There were multiple heats running, based on age group. Parents' legs were tied to children's legs, especially in the youngest group, aged six and under. Lord Farleigh, good sport that he was, had shed his coat and rolled up his sleeves before tying his son's ankle to his own, and then he and William had practiced their strategy for staying together. Will was a bright little boy, but whether he even knew his right foot from his left, let alone would be able to keep that information straight while running, remained to be seen.

Penny, on the other hand, cared little that her brother and father were racing. She was busy picking daisies and handing them to Amelia. Rather than see the happy blossoms go to waste, Amelia began turning them into a daisy chain. It would make a lovely springtime crown for the little girl.

"Are we in time for the race?" Lady Louisa asked as she and Lady Ashworth walked up to Amelia. "William was insistent that I be here for his moment of glory."

"They are about to begin," Amelia said.

"Thank you, darling," Lady Ashworth said as Penny handed daisies to her grandmama.

"What lovely daisies, sweeting," Lady Louisa said to Penny, bending down to give her a kiss. "What would Mama do without her precious little girl?"

"Here, Penny, I've made a crown for you," Amelia said as she fastened the final daisy into place. "We shall make you queen of the festival."

"Ohhh," Penny said, her eyes growing wide.

"Let me show you how it will look," Amelia said, crouching next to her. She placed the daisies on her own head. "It is lovely, is it not, with all the pretty flowers chained together like this? You will look like a fairy queen and shall reign over all of our fun today. Won't that be jolly?"

"Me, Meela! Me now!" Penny said, her tiny fingers wiggling to get hold of the crown.

"A fairy queen, indeed," a deep male voice said. "Good afternoon, Mother, Louisa. Miss Clarke."

Amelia felt her cheeks heat up as she removed the flowers and set them on Penny's head. The dratted man was always making her blush. One would think she was a schoolgirl, the way she reacted to him. She straightened and brushed off her skirt before offering a polite curtsy.

"Kit and I were on our way to the cricket match when we realized the races were happening first. Has Will dragged Farleigh to victory yet?"

"It will most likely be the other way around," Lady Louisa said. "William has lofty ambitions but very short legs."

"Up!" Penny commanded, so Lord Halford dutifully picked up his tiny niece and settled her on his hip. She patted her crown. "Pretty!"

"Pretty, indeed. You are the very image of springtime," Lord Halford said, kissing her cheek and then acknowledging an exuberant Will, who was waving at him from the starting line. "Hm, perhaps we should test our own racing abilities, Kit," he said.

"I would hate for you to lose your dignity in front of your family when I beat you, Tony."

Lady Louisa and Lady Ashworth laughed. "There is a challenge if I ever heard one, Anthony," his mother said.

"I feel a wager coming on," Lady Louisa said.

Lord Halford set a wiggly Penny back on the ground. She was ready to be free now that she had gotten her kiss. Amelia told herself it was foolish to feel envious of the child.

"It is a three-legged race, Kit, if you had not noticed," Lord Halford said. "We will each need a racing partner if this challenge is to occur." He turned to Amelia. "Miss Clarke, how about you? Will you be my partner in the three-legged race? I need someone young and capable, you see, and so I must ask you quickly before Kit here beats me to it."

Amelia looked at Lord Halford in alarm.

"Quite so," Lady Louisa chimed in. "Mama would never do it, and I would not be an asset to anyone in my condition."

"Not to mention, Farleigh would lock you in your room for the rest of your confinement," Lord Halford pointed out.

"True enough." Lady Louisa sighed.

"I will search for a worthy partner, then," Lord Cantwell said. "I think I see Lady Elizabeth. Perhaps she will do me the honors." He walked briskly toward her.

Lady Elizabeth participating in a three-legged race seemed ludicrous, but Amelia was too intent with getting over her shock to pay any heed to it.

"What do you say, Miss Clarke? Are you up to the challenge?" Lord Halford said.

"What fun! Oh, I do envy you, Amelia," Lady Louisa said.

Amelia turned to Lord Halford, determined to refuse. Oh, but it was tempting to say yes, to participate fully in the activities of the day and not feel as though she existed only on the fringes. To actually belong.

His bright blue eyes shone with merriment . . . and something else, something that dared her to take up the gauntlet he had thrown down at her, the same look he had given her when he had asked her opinion during dinner the night before.

"Very well. I accept," she said.

The corners of Lord Halford's mouth curved up slightly.

"Oh, well done!" Lady Louisa clapped enthusiastically.

Amelia wasn't so sure.

The call for the beginning of the first race, the one for the youngest children, was made, returning their attention to Lord Farleigh and young William. And then the starting gun fired, and mayhem ensued. The crowd laughed and cheered as fathers and mothers and children tumbled and twisted forward toward the finish line. Several pairs of runners collapsed to the ground, legs hopelessly tangled, while the more successful ones lurched onward, including Lord Farleigh and Will.

Amelia hoped no one broke a limb this afternoon.

As they neared the finish line, Will tripped and fell flat on his face, with Lord Farleigh cartwheeling awkwardly over him to avoid landing on top of him. Lady Louisa gasped, and Lady Ashworth threw her hands over her mouth.

Lord Halford and Lord Cantwell laughed and yelled encouragement.

When Lord Farleigh found his balance, he yanked Will up, anchored him next to his thigh, little Will's feet dangling a few inches above the ground, and hobbled to the finish line, taking a respectable third. It would ensure that they received a ribbon, and Amelia imagined any ribbon would be enough for Will.

The next two races, one for the older children and one for youth in their teens, followed as the family congratulated Lord Farleigh and Will on their accomplishment. Will had the ribbon pinned proudly on his chest.

"It's nearly time for our race, Miss Clarke," Lord Halford said over the hubbub. "Let us get ourselves leg-shackled, shall we?"

Lady Ashworth looked at him suspiciously.

"That is not amusing!" Amelia whispered as he took her by the arm and guided her over to the starting line. "You know very well what your words imply, and it will not do for anyone to hear you say such a thing."

"Come, my dear Miss Clarke, it was merely a jest. A simple play on words. And yet, truth be told, I fear that our brief time as partners in this three-legged race may be the only time I will ever enjoy being leg-shackled."

"Surely not," she said. He could not have such a negative view of marriage. His parents and sister enjoyed happy marriages, from what she had observed.

"I am pressed for time, you see," he said, "due to a promise I gave my father upon my return from Spain. So I am bound to marry in haste, as the old saying goes, and, therefore, will most likely be repenting at leisure for a lifetime. Allow me."

He knelt beside her, his foot parallel to hers. She carefully raised her skirt just enough for him to secure the rope around both their ankles before tying the knot. It felt an oddly intimate thing for him to be doing, at least to Amelia—even though everyone around them was doing the same thing.

"We must work out our strategy of movement, Miss Clarke. Place your arm around me, and I shall do the same to you. Then, on the count of one, we will move our tied legs forward and on two our other legs. Shall we try it for a bit before the race begins?"

He wrapped his arm around her shoulders, and she slid her arm about his waist, precisely where it had been when they had been on horseback in the rain. It was exhilarating to hold him thus, having his arm around her as well. Except the words he had just spoken served to remind her that there was a gulf between them despite their physical proximity at the moment, and she realized she was frustrated by it all. "I am still angry at you, you know," she blurted out.

"One," he said, but she wasn't ready for it, so she stumbled as his foot moved without hers. "Sorry, I should have warned you," he said, ignoring her comment. "Two."

She moved her opposing foot, and he repeated the numbers until they got into a rhythm of walking without them.

"Excellent," he said, giving her shoulders a slight squeeze. "We have got it now."

"You are trying to distract me," she said. "But I will not be put off."

Anthony sighed. "I am sorry you are angry with me. I was not at my best last evening. I am afraid I became impatient with the Putnam girls' rapt attention and Marwood's puffing his opinions about. He expects me to make an announcement between Lady Elizabeth and myself any day now, and yet the Putnams were just as busy with their own strategizing. I felt like a prize goose. And they completely ignored Kit, who's an earl in his own right, not to mention Phillip and Lucas. I merely hold a courtesy title."

"A courtesy title as heir to a marquess," she pointed out. "A prize that would be a victory for any lady."

"Would it be a victory for you?" he asked. Amelia stopped walking abruptly, and it was Lord Halford who lost his footing this time. "Forgive me," he said softly. "I have stumbled in more ways than one, I am afraid. It was wrong of me to put you on the spot like that. It was precisely what I did last night. I keep finding myself doing and saying things when you are about that I would never . . . And yet—"

The call came for their race to begin.

"We will speak of this later," he said. "I owe you a full apology when there are not so many listening ears around."

She did not know how to respond.

"Come, they are about to begin," he said, urging her forward.

They lined up with the other participants and awaited the firing of the starting pistol. Amelia spotted Lord Cantwell and Lady Elizabeth not far from them. Lady Elizabeth had actually agreed to participate, and Amelia couldn't help but like her better for it. She was sure the duke and duchess wouldn't approve if they were to see her.

The pistol sounded then, and Lord Halford tightened his arm around her shoulders. "One," he said, and they stepped rightly together. "Two."

They proceeded smoothly while others got off to a rocky start. A few couples fell, petticoat ruffles blossoming like the daisies growing throughout the park, before they righted themselves and continued onward.

Amelia became consumed with listening to Lord Halford's number cadence and words of encouragement. Before she knew it, the finish line was in sight, their only remaining competition the blacksmith and his wife right behind them and Lord Cantwell and Lady Elizabeth, who were slightly in the lead.

And then, as they neared the finish line, the crowd cheering their support from the sidelines, Lord Halford managed to stumble into Lord

Cantwell and send him and Lady Elizabeth careening to the ground, putting Amelia and Lord Halford in front.

The finish line was only a few feet away now. They had managed to regain their rhythm after crashing into Lord Cantwell, and they were assured the victory until Lord Halford tripped over his own feet and he and Amelia tumbled head over heels, Lord Halford gracefully twisting so he landed beneath her and cushioned her fall.

Too gracefully, Amelia realized.

The blacksmith and his wife staggered over the finish line to the wild cries of the crowd. The blacksmith, a burly man with a bright red beard, tugged their rope off and picked up his small, round wife and kissed her soundly as he twirled her about.

Lord Cantwell and Lady Elizabeth finished in second place, with Amelia and Lord Halford coming in close behind them for third.

"Dash it all, Tony!" Lord Cantwell said, laughing as they untied their ankles. "What was that all about?"

Lady Elizabeth, standing next to him, was flushed, and her hair was coming out of its pins. Amelia thought she looked disheveled . . . and happy.

Lord Halford didn't respond to Lord Cantwell's question. Instead, he hauled Amelia with him to congratulate the blacksmith.

"Well done, Perkins," he said, shaking the man's hand vigorously. "Mrs. Perkins." He made a polite bow to the blacksmith's wife. "An excellent win today."

"We cannot believe our good fortune, my lord," Perkins said, grinning widely. "The missus will know what to do with them coins, you can be sure."

"I imagine she will." Lord Halford gave Mrs. Perkins a wink. "She is a clever one, to be sure."

"Aye, that she is."

"Thank ye, me lord," Mrs. Perkins said, red-faced and beaming, before she and Perkins were overtaken by their children and several of the villagers who rushed over to celebrate with them.

Lord Halford only chuckled.

"You bounder. I see what you are about," Lord Cantwell said, grinning. "Well played, Tony. You put the winner's purse into the hands of someone who could use it."

They received their prize ribbons to much applause, and Lord Cantwell and Lord Halford left to join the cricket match. Amelia lightly traced the third-place ribbon now pinned to her bodice with her fingers. She had a small box in her room for her treasures—her father's pocket watch, her mother's brooch—and she would put the ribbon with them later for safekeeping, a frivolous keepsake from a special day.

She turned to excuse herself from Lady Elizabeth, who was standing beside her, since Amelia was scheduled to play games with the tinier children for a while. Although, come to think of it, Lord Cantwell had gotten her to participate in a rather rambunctious three-legged race. Perhaps Lady Elizabeth liked to do such things when her father didn't have his watchful eye on her. "Lady Elizabeth," Amelia said. "I wondered . . ."

"Yes?" Lady Elizabeth asked. She'd repinned her hair, and her polished demeanor was back in place. She might have seemed intimidating but for an errant curl she kept pushing behind her ear and the smudge of dirt on her chin.

"I have volunteered to play games with the children next, and I thought perhaps you would care to join me."

Lady Elizabeth's face brightened. "I can think of nothing I would enjoy more. Thank you, Miss Clarke."

Amelia smiled and linked her arm with Lady Elizabeth's. "Call me Amelia," she said. "And let us go, then."

Chapter 7

Anthony had expected a day being welcomed by the entire village to be taxing, but with all the hearty greetings and hand kissing and baby jostling, he was feeling even more drained than he'd thought and was verging on irritability now that it was midafternoon. The wound in his side, though healed, was aching and only added to the pressure he felt.

It also didn't help that he had not slept much the night before. It had felt like a night on the eve of battle.

He was glad to see everyone, friends and neighbors alike, but he was not in a frame of mind to do the job required of the heir to the manor. And the Putnam sisters had especially taxed him, showing up wherever he had gone, doing everything in their power to insinuate themselves into his activities and conversations. Kit had been his saving grace, being willing to judge the pies and cakes for him. What should have been a simple task had been one too many for Anthony today. He was not even sure which team had won the cricket match; he had become fully disconnected from what was going on around him by then.

His only moment of respite during the entire day had come when he had impulsively asked Miss Clarke to partner with him in the three-legged race. He had seen the Putnams advancing and had quickly employed a counteroffensive.

He enjoyed Miss Clarke's company, and as a man, he had to admit it had been extremely enjoyable having her pressed against his side again. She seemed to soothe and excite him at the same time.

She was attracted to him too; he could tell.

He needed to find an opportunity to offer her a full apology for his careless, impulsive behavior at dinner the night before. He had made her uncomfortable, and for that he must make amends, especially since the duke had reacted so strongly to her comments. After he apologized, he would find a way to keep distance between them, especially as he must soon leave for London to fulfill his promise to his father.

The thought dropped his mood even further.

"Ho, Lord Halford, sir, I have been sent to summon you to the men's tug-of-war." One of the new stable hands—Anthony didn't know his name—rushed up to him. "They are waiting on you."

"Tell them I am on my way." He needed a few minutes more to collect himself before once again facing the crowds and noise and expectations.

They were holding the tug-of-war next to the lake, on a shore not far from the pier where the rowboats were located. A small wooded area lay next to it. It was a lovely spot to visit, shady and quiet, similar to the one where Anthony had discovered Miss Clarke reading on his first day home, but this one was at the opposite end of the lake. Anthony and Alex had taught themselves to swim here.

It was the last large event before people would leave to prepare for the evening festivities. The villagers were having a feast and bonfire on the village green outside The Green Man since they had children to put to bed and work early the next day. The other guests would attend the ball and supper inside the manor later that evening. Anthony was not looking forward to it.

By the time he arrived at the lake, a large group of people had gathered, and the men had already chosen sides and were ready to begin.

"Pick a side, yer lordship," Perkins called. "I mean to outplay you twice today!"

There were guffaws and cries of indignation, and the man standing behind Perkins cuffed his head, nearly resulting in a good-natured fight.

Anthony shed his coat and waistcoat and tossed them to the ground. Lucas and Phillip were on one side, with Kit on the other. Farleigh stood next to Louisa, bouncing Penny on his hip.

"What, you are not joining in, but I must?" Anthony called to him.

"My wife informs me that such antics are for the unattached gentlemen in the group, as it gives them the opportunity to flaunt their rugged manliness for the ladies. Since I am attached and may flaunt my manliness to her at will, I have no need to get muddy this afternoon." He grinned. "I am heartbroken not to be participating."

His rationale hadn't stopped Mr. Perkins. "I can see that you are," Anthony said. He headed toward Kit and then stopped in his tracks.

Mud.

Anthony shuddered violently. Of course there was mud; he had known there would be. The ground was a wet, sloppy mess. The tug-of-war in the past had always been done this way. Anthony had hoped coming over here would relieve him of some of his ghosts, but seeing the filth...

He swallowed back the bile that rose in his throat and strode forcefully toward Kit, taking a place on the rope behind him. He barely had time to grip the rope before the starting gun fired.

It was on. Anthony dug in, slipped, and dug in again, the rope twisting and rubbing against his palms. The man behind Anthony lost his footing and knocked Anthony's feet out from under him. Anthony clung to the rope and struggled back to his feet. The pitch of the crowd rose higher and higher as Anthony's teammates lost ground and regained it. A child shrieked—and Anthony's memories came back in a rush:

The horrible, slippery madness. The rain. The trenches of mud and slime that constantly mocked their efforts. The endless gunfire and the boom of cannons. Fireworks squealing and bursting, the ghastly images they illuminated through the smoke and darkness in those moments: men shot, stabbed, trampled, blown to bits... Dying, all dying gruesome deaths.

Anthony fought to keep his wits. He gripped the rope harder, like a lifeline, and dug in. He slipped again and fell, splattering mud on his chest and face, and he prayed he could endure this silly contest without unmanning himself. His stomach roiled, but he focused on the task, desperate to ignore the escalating noise of the crowd and the torment in his mind and body.

He was back again.

The woman, a screaming child clutched at her breast, pleading with a soldier before he callously shot them—a British soldier, lost to reason and humanity from hardship and fury and a long night of hell. The soldiers breaking windows in the aftermath and stealing anything they could lay their hands on, destroying what they couldn't, battering the poor citizens who remained, ripping the jewels from women's ears if they didn't comply quickly enough. The orgy of drunkenness that went on for hours. The horror and helplessness Anthony felt.

The other team lost ground and then regained it. The wound in his side burned from his exertions now. Someone yelled "Pull," so he did with everything he had, and his team gained a few feet of ground, upending several of the other team's competitors. The crowd roared their approval, but it was a horrible noise to Anthony.

Finally, *finally*, they managed to bring the other team to defeat, everyone brown and nearly unrecognizable from the revolting stuff.

He could take no more and strode off in the direction of the woods. When he had gone far enough that he knew he could no longer be seen, he fell to his knees and vomited.

* * *

The crowd was celebrating, and the participants jumped into the lake to wash the mud from their bodies and clothes. Children scampered about excitedly. But Amelia had eyes only for Lord Halford, and she had watched him stride off into the woods as soon as the contest had ended. For being a member of the victorious team, he had seemed strangely out of sorts, so she hurried toward the woods, skirting people as much as she could as she went after him.

She was not prepared for what she saw when she found him. "Oh, Anthony," she whispered, dropping to her knees next to him. "Oh, my dear."

He turned his face away from her. "I'm fine," he muttered. "Leave me be."

She left, but only so she could hurry back to the lake and wet her handkerchief. The crowd had already begun to disperse, the men anxious to get clean and dry and the women wanting to get their families ready for the evening's festivities. Amelia was relieved. It meant Lord Halford might be able to make his way back to the house in privacy.

She returned to him, careful not to draw attention to herself and therefore inadvertently to him in his weakened state. "Here," she said, dropping next to him again and handing him the handkerchief. "Are you ill? Can I assist you back to the house?"

"No!" he said with an intensity that set her back on her heels. He dropped his head. "No, Miss Clarke, but I thank you." He wiped his mouth with the damp cloth and grimaced. "I will be fine. I only need a few minutes alone."

"I do not intend to leave you here until I have satisfied myself that you are well enough to manage on your own. Let me take that now."

He carefully folded the soiled handkerchief but didn't give it to her. "I shall have it laundered first."

"Give it over." She thrust her hand at him, palm up, in a manner that would brook no nonsense. She had taken care of her ailing father and had a good idea of the struggle the male ego underwent at such times. Her strategy worked; he scowled and handed it to her. "Thank you," she said. "Now hold still."

She proceeded to dab at the mud on his face. Despite a pale cast to his tanned skin, the muddy stubble on his jawline gave him a rough and implacable look. Amelia could picture him on the hills of Spain wearing this expression.

He pulled away from her touch. "It stinks here," he said. He rose, and she rose with him, and they walked a few feet away from where they had been. She spied a fallen log and gestured to it.

He let out a huge sigh as he sat and then remained silent for several minutes, his eyes closed. Amelia sat patiently beside him.

"Oh, Amelia, what must you think?" he said.

It was the first time he had called her Amelia since they had kissed. "I think that you might be in need, my lord," she said gently. "Are you ill?"

"Only in my soul. The tug-of-war conjured bad memories, 'tis all."

Bad memories, indeed, if this was the result. Lord Halford was a man of strong character, but he had been brought to his knees today. Amelia folded her hands in her lap, offering no words in return, only hoping her quiet presence could be a comfort to him.

They sat this way for several minutes, and then he opened his eyes and took one of her hands in his muddy one. "No more 'my lord' now, if you please. I should think that after this you should call me Anthony. You did when you first spied me here."

Had she? Goodness, in her alarm at his physical state, she had indeed. "Perhaps," she said, "but only if we are alone. It would be improper for you to be seen as too familiar with your mother's paid companion, you know." There was no reason to give him permission to use her Christian name; he had already chosen to, obviously.

"That is not what one would expect to hear from someone who spoke so eloquently about women's education last evening."

"About that—"

"It was poorly done of me," he said, interrupting her. "I know it. Anything you have to say I will hear and humbly beg your pardon. And yet"—there was a slight twinkle in his eye now, thank goodness, not the utter bleakness she had seen before—"I was proud of how you handled yourself and what you said on the matter."

"Were you?"

"You were brilliant, my dear Amelia, and certain individuals needed to be put in their place. The Duke of Marwood is a bore, and I should like to thrash him for what he said to you, let alone what he has done to his own daughter. The poor girl has no spirit left. He treats his cattle better than he does his own child."

Hearing him speak about Lady Elizabeth was difficult for Amelia, but he was hurting, so she did her best to ignore it. "Your own sister isn't lacking in education."

"Of course she isn't. Ashworth may be traditional in many ways—too many to suit me at present—but he was quite forward thinking in his views about his womenfolk. I am sure my mother had a great deal to do with that. Louisa spent part of the day with Alex and me and the tutor and part of the day with her governess. Quite unheard of at the time. She actually did better in Greek and Latin than either of us, although we surpassed her when we went off to school. She is also good with numbers."

"Did you learn to do needlework, then?" she said, daring to tease. His complexion wasn't nearly as chalky as it had been, and the shadows in his eyes had lessened somewhat.

"Ashworth was not quite that radical, thank goodness." The corner of his mouth twitched upward before settling back into its bleak line. He sighed deeply, then tipped his head back and closed his eyes again. "War is the very devil, Amelia."

She still did not know what had caused his sudden sickness, but now was not the time for questions. "I cannot imagine it, I confess."

"I would never wish you to. There are too many despicable acts in war. The very goodness of men is tried in a crucible of rage and death, and many fail terribly."

"But surely there is honor too."

"It is difficult to remember one's honor when hell is seething all around."

She pondered his remark and the remorse she could hear in his words. Had he failed in some horrible way in Spain? He was so inherently *good*, she had difficulty imagining he could have done something heinous, as he seemed to imply.

He straightened, appearing to collect himself, and brushed a bit of dried mud from the back of her hand. "I have gotten dirt on you now," he said, observing muddy patches on her skirt. "I am sorry for that."

"Do not be," she assured him. "I am not. Your well-being is worth much more to me than a pristine appearance."

"Is it?" He looked deeply into her eyes, searching.

She was afraid of what he'd see there but was unable to hide it. "Yes. I confess I care about you, Lord Halford—"

"Anthony," he softly corrected.

"Anthony." There, she had dared to say it. "But you needn't concern yourself about that. I only wanted to help."

He lifted her hand and pressed a kiss to it. "Ah, Amelia. I am disgusting at present, my dear, and I must be grateful for it. Otherwise, I am afraid I would press my advantage, and that would be unfair to us both."

"Yes," she said.

He rose to his feet. "I believe I am sufficiently recovered now." He held out his hand for her and assisted her to her feet. She was sorry this private time with him was at an end. "I am in your debt, my dear. May I escort you back to the house?"

"I think not." It would only start tongues wagging, and neither of them would benefit from that. "If you are truly well enough, I will leave now. You may wish to clean yourself in the lake before returning."

"Excellent advice," he said. "Very well. Adieu, then, Amelia."

"Good-bye, Anthony."

She let his name roll sweetly over her tongue as she said it, and as she made her way through the woods and back to the house, she wondered if it would be the last time she would say it to him.

* * *

After a dinner from which Amelia had been noticeably absent, Anthony made his way to the entrance of the ballroom in anticipation of greeting the guests as they arrived.

Much to his surprise, his father, in formal dress, was seated in a chair, a cane resting against it, his mother standing nearby.

"I fully intend to greet my own guests on this occasion," Ashworth said to Anthony, reading his expression accurately.

"I tried to talk him out of it," his mother said, scowling at her husband. "He is not having one of his better days, but he is so stubborn as to be nonsensical. He wanted to attend the dinner, and I put my foot down at that."

"The woman is a terror," Ashworth said, patting her hand.

His father's health had improved significantly in the time since Anthony had returned home, but he was in no way strong enough to exert himself in such a manner, especially if he had not been well today. "I am happy to do the honors, Father," he said.

"No such thing," Ashworth said. "I missed out on the festivities earlier, and I intend to greet our guests and introduce them to the new Earl of Halford, returned to us so recently from the dead." He coughed and cleared his throat. "Now, enough of this. I will use my cane, and should I require it, this chair will remain at the ready."

"You will be prudent though, Ashworth?" the marchioness asked. "I could not abide it were I to lose you."

"Hush, woman," he said. "I did not marry a watering pot, and for good reason. After I greet the guests, I will return to my room and rest, as instructed. You may join me there after the ball and then cry all you wish."

"Foolish man," she said. "I could throttle you at times." He chuckled as she leaned over and kissed him on the cheek, something Anthony was not sure he had ever observed either of them do before. It was startling, actually, but rather more pleasant to observe than he would have thought.

"Halford," his father said when the marchioness left to attend to some final details in the ballroom. "I would speak with you."

"Yes, Father?" Anthony said.

"Marwood wants an announcement made this evening, and you know my own wishes on the issue of matrimony. The work is already done, and Lady Elizabeth has been given certain expectations regarding marriage to Ashworth's heir, as you already know. I need to know if you have come up to scratch yet."

Anthony should have anticipated this. "I assure you I intend to do my duty as expeditiously as possible," he said, "but I have not had an opportunity to speak to Lady Elizabeth privately. She deserves better treatment than to rush things in such a manner. I am afraid Marwood must wait."

"And yet, Marwood wants the deed done even more swiftly than I and thinks the ball the perfect place to make the announcement. I confess I cannot entirely disagree with his reasoning." He sighed gustily and shifted a bit in the chair. "Although I suppose your argument makes sense too. Very well, but see to speaking with Lady Elizabeth soon, do you hear?"

"I do. Thank you for understanding, Father," Anthony said.

"Don't thank me. Just see you get the business taken care of. Marriage and producing heirs is your primary responsibility as far as I am concerned."

"In that order, I presume," Anthony said.

"Don't be impertinent," Ashworth growled, then chuckled again. "Of course in that order. I want *heirs*, not just more grandchildren, fond as I am of the first two."

"All is in order," Lady Ashworth said upon returning to their side. "Oh, it is so exciting to be hosting a ball at Ashworth Park again! What did I miss?"

"Not a thing," Anthony said.

"I doubt that, considering to whom I am speaking. Now, smile, both of you. The guests are arriving," she said. "Ah, Sir Frederick, Lady Putnam, as you can see, Lord Ashworth is here to greet you this evening. Is not that wonderful? And your lovely daughters are behind you, I see. Allow me to present them to my husband, the Marquess of Ashworth."

From the narrowed, calculating look in Lady Putnam's eyes, Anthony was almost certain she'd overheard the last bit of his exchange with his father, specifically the part about marrying and producing heirs. What could possibly be more foreboding than that?

It was time for the ball to officially begin. Heaven help him.

* * *

The ball had begun, but Amelia was not ready. Knowing she would be pressed for time, she had asked for a dinner tray to be sent up to her room.

She had arrived at Ashworth Park with two worn day dresses and an evening dress that was also suitable for church. Lady Ashworth had generously provided her with an expanded wardrobe, which included two evening gowns. They were modest, certainly not the first stare of fashion, but well suited to a lady's companion. She had worn the light green muslin at dinner last evening.

Tonight she was wearing the plum-colored gown, the more elegant of the two. It was made of silk rather than muslin and set off Amelia's auburn hair and green eyes nicely. Lady Ashworth had insisted on the fabric when she'd seen it at the modiste's, and the resulting gown was Amelia's favorite. She had worn it only once before and was excited to have another opportunity. She wanted to look her best tonight of all nights and was feeling both nervous and excited to be at her first formal ball.

Lady Elizabeth and Harriet and Charlotte Putnam, along with other young ladies from the surrounding area, would be dressed in their finest, and Amelia wanted to feel at her best around them. A small part of her also hoped Anthony would view her in a flattering light; she did have some feminine pride, after all.

On her dressing table sat her small treasure box; she'd left it out after adding her third-prize ribbon from the three-legged race to its contents. She moved to the box and opened it again. Her mother's brooch caught the light and gleamed. It was a beautiful piece of jewelry, gold with colored gemstones set in unique, ornate patterns. Tonight was a special occasion, Amelia thought, and the brooch would add a festive touch to her otherwise unadorned gown. She removed it from the box and put the box away.

Her mother's brooch. She tenderly ran her fingers over it. It was an exceptional piece—surprising considering her father had sold anything of value they'd had in order to help the poor of their parish and had done so with her mother's full consent. Amelia was grateful this piece had been spared to become a special memento.

Her father had not given it to her until the very end; he had waited intentionally, he'd told her, as he had suspected Amelia would have sold it for medicines otherwise. "A waste of resources on a dying man," he had told her at the time. Amelia had wept.

She brushed aside a tear now and tried to pin the brooch to her gown. It would not show at its best against the deep plum color of her dress, but Amelia didn't mind as long as it kept her parents' memory near her heart for the evening. When she could not pin the brooch on with ease, she examined it further and discovered the clasp needed repair.

Disappointed, she carefully returned the brooch to her box of treasures. As much as she longed to wear it on this special occasion, she did not want to chance losing it in the crowd of people at the ball. She would be devastated if that happened.

She pulled on her evening gloves, slipped the loop of her fan over her wrist, and descended the staircase.

Lady Ashworth and Anthony were near the entrance of the ballroom, greeting everyone in turn. As Amelia drew closer, she could see that Lord Ashworth was with them as well. He was seated in a chair and still looked thin and pale but better than he had when she had seen him last. Amelia had not spent much time in his room keeping company with Lady Ashworth lately since she had been busy preparing for the fete. The marquess's health was obviously improving, and Amelia's heart gladdened at the sight of him.

"Miss Clarke, how very fine you look this evening," Lord Ashworth said.

She curtsied deeply before him. "Thank you, my lord. I am pleased to see you looking so well."

Lady Ashworth took her hands and kissed her cheek. "Amelia, you do look stunning! I am *so* glad I insisted on the plum. I knew it was the right decision."

"Miss Clarke," Anthony said, his voice vibrating through her like the low tones of a cello. He bowed over her hand and kissed it, lingering slightly. "You look so exquisite tonight I fear I cannot resist you." He delivered this last bit with a flirtatiousness that was typical among the *beau monde* and, therefore, would not be taken seriously by anyone observing their interaction. "You must reserve a dance with me. I insist."

"It would be my pleasure," she said, feeling like a debutante. And then she was past them and in the ballroom.

She had been in the ballroom many times, but tonight it looked especially magical. Hothouse flowers spilled from urns everywhere, spicing the air with their fragrance, and the chandeliers blazed brightly overhead. The orchestra was tuning their instruments, the signal that the dancing was about to begin.

The room, spacious though it was, was filled to overflowing. It was a veritable crush: ladies in their finest gowns adding their own bouquet of colors to the scene, set off beautifully by the men in their black evening wear.

Lady Elizabeth was the first person to approach Amelia. "How fine you look this evening, Amelia," she said with true friendliness. "I love the color of your gown. I can never wear such a bold shade, you see, but it goes wonderfully with your hair. I am quite envious." Her eyes twinkled.

Lady Elizabeth, in contrast to Amelia, wore a gauzy dream of a gown that gave her an ethereal quality, especially when combined with her blonde hair and pale-blue eyes. "You have no reason for envy, Lady Elizabeth. You put everyone in the shade."

Lady Elizabeth was beauty personified, in fact, and she was Anthony's best choice for a bride, Amelia reminded herself. Ignoring the pit in her stomach, she took the lady's hands in hers in greeting. "I never could have imagined seeing you run a three-legged race," she said. "It is an image I shall treasure for some time."

Lady Elizabeth laughed merrily. "It is an image that would have haunted my father for decades had he seen it. And remember, I am merely Elizabeth."

"I shall endeavor to get used to it."

"You know, it has been so long since I did something as frivolous as that race," she said. "I enjoyed myself thoroughly. Lord Cantwell is a jolly sort of fellow."

"Indeed—"

"What a *lovely* gown," a strident female voice said, interrupting their conversation. "I was just saying that exact thing to you, was I not, Charlotte? That Miss Clarke's gown was especially lovely?"

Lady Elizabeth shot Amelia an understanding look before turning to face the Putnam girls. "Ladies, how breathtaking you both look. I envy your ability to wear that particular shade of yellow, Miss Putnam. Yellow does absolutely nothing for my own complexion. And Miss Charlotte, the ruffles on your gown are delightful."

Her words stopped the Putnam girls in their tracks. Elizabeth had smoothly and graciously deflected the attack. She was kind and beautiful, Amelia thought, and Anthony could do no better in finding a suitable wife. Amelia wanted Anthony to be happy above all else, and he needed someone who could provide him with comfort. Lady Elizabeth would be that kind of wife.

But the thought deflated her, even as Phillip Osbourne asked her for the first dance. Lord Cantwell then invited Lady Elizabeth to dance as Harriet Putnam looked on with simmering contempt.

Chapter 8

When Anthony finally entered the ballroom, the first thing he saw was Phillip Osbourne dancing with Amelia, and he had a sudden and compelling urge to plant the man a facer.

Amelia's deep-purple gown shimmered with her movements, and her auburn hair looked aflame under the chandeliers. He could not take his eyes off her. Phillip, confound the man, seemed taken with her. Anthony suddenly could not seem to remember why he had thought her an unsuitable choice as a wife.

He shook his head to rid it of the thought. He had matters to attend to before he could allow himself to ponder that question. He must mingle with the guests, and he must speak with Lady Elizabeth.

The first dance was just ending when he finally spotted her. She was on the floor with Kit. The Osbourne brothers certainly had not wasted any time acquiring the loveliest ladies in attendance as their dance partners.

He moved to intercept them. "May I have the honor?" he asked Lady Elizabeth when the dance finally concluded and Kit escorted her off the floor.

"I think you can do better than this lackwit," Kit said to her with a wink.

"Lord Cantwell!" she said, aghast. "Oh, you are joking. I would be delighted, Lord Halford." She placed her hand lightly on Anthony's sleeve and allowed him to lead her back onto the dance floor.

Whereas Lady Elizabeth had appeared relaxed and quite animated while dancing with Kit, she now seemed reserved and formal. Apparently she too was anxious about their betrothal status. It was time to resolve the issue once and for all.

"Lady Elizabeth," he said as the music began, "I hope you have been enjoying your stay at Ashworth Park."

She looked up at him with concern. "Of course," she said. "Have you heard something to the contrary?"

"Not at all."

The moves of the dance took them apart briefly, and when they were reunited, he said, "You are no doubt aware of our fathers' intentions for us." She swallowed, the movement of her throat as delicate as a bird's, giving her an air of vulnerability. "What is your opinion on the matter?" he asked gently.

"What do you mean?" she asked cautiously.

"Come with me." He took her by the elbow and led her from the floor toward a quiet corner where they could speak more privately. "I meant exactly what I asked. What is your opinion?"

"I . . ." She seemed at a total loss for words. "I have never presumed to have an opinion on the matter. I knew marriage to your brother was a good match, and I accepted his courtship and proposal willingly, as everyone expected me to do."

"Ah," Anthony said. This was going to be harder than he had anticipated. It all led back to duty; it always did. Even for her. As surely as Anthony knew his own duty, she knew hers, which was to marry well, an arrangement that did not necessarily include love, especially among the ton. In fact, it rarely did.

"You must know, Lord Halford, that I grieved for your brother when he died," she said.

"Thank you." Anthony paused so he could choose his next words carefully. "Lady Elizabeth, what would your opinion be if I were to suggest that we not continue down the path set out by both our fathers? Would that be your preference? Or are you set on the match?" She grew quiet, so Anthony sought to put any concerns she may have to rest. "I will, of course, honor the agreement that has been made, if that is your preference. However, I have made it clear to my father that no announcement will be made under any circumstances without your full consent."

He drew her farther aside so he could whisper this next part. He did not want anyone but her to hear what he was about to say. "I was only just informed of your father's wish for an announcement to be made this evening. Forgive me, then, for my abrupt manner in bringing up the subject. I would have preferred discussing this with you under more accommodating circumstances. I would never want to rush any lady in such a manner. But his insistence requires that I receive an answer from you."

She searched his face to see if what he was saying was in earnest. "Do you truly mean what you are saying? That if I choose not to accept your proposal at this time, you will honor it?"

"Yes. However, I must be frank, my lady. I have given my word to my father that I will wed at the earliest convenience and therefore cannot promise I will be free later should you change your mind."

"I see," she said. "I understand completely."

Anthony suddenly remembered her animation when dancing with Kit—and Kit had also run the three-legged race with her. With that knowledge shoring him up, he realized he was not doing her a disservice. Probably quite the opposite. "You are an exceptional woman, Lady Elizabeth, and I am not the only person to recognize this, am I? I am fully confident you will marry well and find great happiness in the match. I believe you know in your own heart it will not be with me though, don't you?"

"Yes, not with you." She smiled. "I hope you do not take offense at that."

"Not at all." He smiled to reassure her. "It is why I am having this conversation with you in the first place."

"Thank you for your honesty and your concern for my happiness. You are a true gentleman, Lord Halford. I hope we shall remain friends."

"I am certain of it, my lady." He took both of her hands in his and kissed each one. "And now," he said briskly, "I shall go find your father so I may tell him of our decision."

"I would never let you do that alone, Lord Halford," she said, lifting her chin and looking every inch the daughter of a duke. "My father is not the most reasonable man once his mind is made up. I will go with you, and we shall face his wrath together."

Anthony admired her all the more for it. "As a gentleman, I cannot let you," he said. "Were I to ask for your hand, I would approach your father on my own. It will be on my own that I face him now as well."

"But he must be made to understand this was a mutual decision."

"Lady Elizabeth, we are not betrothed, nor have we ever, until this moment, even discussed the matter. I will simply make it clear to him that it is not to be and that it is my decision. I would not have your relationship with him tarnished."

"What relationship?" she asked sadly. "I am merely a pawn my father moves at will to accomplish his ends."

"Nonetheless, he is your father. Now, if you will excuse me, I shall go find him. But promise me something first?"

"What?" she asked.

"Enjoy yourself tonight. You deserve to." He kissed her hand again and left her in order to find the duke, whom he suspected would be spending his time in the room set aside for cards.

Had Anthony been obliged to marry Lady Elizabeth, they would have had an amiable arrangement, which was more than most marriages of the ton could claim. Perhaps he had made a mistake in freeing them both.

And yet he did not think so. Despite the time constraints, Anthony needed to hope he would find a woman who could complete him, thin as that hope was.

But in truth, what he needed was someone who would not be frightened by his ghosts.

* * *

"Come here, you naughty child, and keep me company for a few minutes," Lady Walmsley commanded Amelia from her seat at the side of the ballroom, gesturing rather wildly for a lady of her years.

Amelia dutifully sat next to her, grateful to be able to rest her feet.

Lady Walmsley was wearing a gray satin gown and more jewels than Amelia had ever seen in her life. Necklaces and brooches filled her bosom, and each of her fingers sported a dazzling ring or two.

"Now tell me," the lady said as the ostrich feather in her hair bobbed up and down. "Are you enjoying yourself?"

"Of course. Everything is lovely." Amelia was trying to enjoy herself, that was. The orchestra was wonderful, and the ballroom was awhirl with every imaginable color. It was a feast for the senses and undeniably the most elegant event Amelia had ever attended, but she had seen Anthony and Lady Elizabeth slip off together, which had left her with a pit in her stomach. "And are you enjoying yourself, Lady Walmsley?" she asked.

"More than I expected to at my age. I saw you dancing with that young Osbourne fellow earlier. Nice enough chap but not for the likes of you."

"I am not here angling for a husband, Lady Walmsley," Amelia assured her. Unlike certain other ladies she could mention.

"Oh, pah. You should be if you are not. You want to be a companion forever? Of course you don't, clever girl like you. You want children, lots of them, and you have all the qualities it takes to keep a husband in tow." She patted Amelia's hand. "Lord Walmsley, God rest his soul, and I were not blessed with children of our own, but we rubbed along well together for all those years, nonetheless. Had a niece I was fond of; was her godmother, in fact. My sister's girl." She had a far-off look in her eye. "My sister married a younger son, and then off to India they went. There was money to be had there, you know, and younger sons need money."

"Yes," Amelia said.

"Did very well for themselves too, especially in the early years. Cotton primarily but other textiles as well. People want more than wool for their clothes, now don't they? So there's always a demand."

"Did they eventually return to England?" Amelia wasn't certain where this conversation was going, but Lady Walmsley was such a dear. Amelia had grown extraordinarily fond of the woman. "Your sister and her husband?"

"No, they never did." She fumbled in her reticule for her handkerchief. "Sent their only child to me though, so she could get a proper English education. Name of Julia. Lovely girl. She had a terrible time leaving her parents. I felt bad about that, though I did the best I could. I doted on her, sent her to the best schools, and her friends came to visit on holidays. Wonderful times, they were. But, goodness, listen to me rattle on and you listening so kindly. Now, off with you." She wiggled her fingers at Amelia in a shooing gesture. "Dance all you can, and flirt even more. Ho, young man," Lady Walmsley called to—hm, Amelia didn't know the gentleman who had turned in response, which could prove awkward. "Yes, *you*. Come here, if you please."

The gentleman in question approached and bowed formally to them.

"I am Lady Walmsley, and you are?" she asked.

"Rupert Seymour, at your service, my lady," he said. He seemed at a loss, Amelia thought, just as she was. He was also something of a dandy. His hair was heavily pomaded, and his waistcoat was lavender silk with heavy embroidery work.

"Mr. Seymour," Lady Walmsley continued. "May I present Miss Amelia Clarke? Miss Clarke, Mr. Seymour. I am too old to care about formalities," Lady Walmsley said. "But there you are; you have been introduced. Mr. Seymour, this young lady is in need of a dance partner, and it appears you are available."

The poor man flushed bright red, which clashed terribly with his waistcoat. "Well . . . um, certainly I . . ."

"My lady," Amelia quickly interjected, hoping to spare the man more embarrassment. "I am afraid I cannot accept Mr. Seymour's generous offer as I am promised elsewhere at the moment. Please forgive me." It was a pathetic excuse, and Lady Walmsley shot her a knowing look, but desperate times called for desperate measures. She smiled politely at Mr. Seymour, who bowed once more and made his escape.

"Lady Walmsley, you are a troublemaker," Amelia whispered.

The old woman only cackled and tapped Amelia on the arm with her fan. "Off with you, then, girl, to keep this so-called 'promise' I know you do not happen to have. Go break some hearts."

Amelia leaned down and planted a kiss on Lady Walmsley's papery cheek. "I shall try, my lady. Stay out of trouble, or at the very least, do not overtire yourself."

"If only I dared. Oh, to be young again," Lady Walmsley said as Amelia took her leave.

The elderly lady really was a dear.

*　*　*

The Duke of Marwood was sitting at a table with a few of his cronies, playing cards, just as Anthony had suspected.

In what little time Anthony had been around the man, he had grown to dislike him exceedingly. He was a power-mongering windbag with a surprising number of bad habits, including gambling and drinking to excess. Anthony had met a few such individuals in the army, arrogant and full of themselves; he had learned it was better to ignore them as much as possible and face them man to man only when the situation called for it.

Marwood's rank and his status as a guest of Anthony's parents meant Anthony would need to choose his words carefully. He cleared his throat to get the gentlemen's attention, so engrossed in the game they were. "Your Grace," he said. "May I have a word?"

The Duke of Marwood looked at his cards and the size of the pot and said, "Must it be now? I am in a game here, in case you had not noticed."

The other players looked up at Anthony with interest.

"I suppose, if you insist, we can have the conversation here," Anthony said. "However, I do not believe your daughter would appreciate an audience while we discuss certain matters."

Marwood glared at him, slapped his cards on the table facedown, and stood.

"Thank you, Your Grace," Anthony said.

He led the duke to a small study down the hall from the card room and gestured for him to enter first. Once the door was closed behind them, the duke spoke. "I am assuming you are officially asking for Elizabeth's hand, although you needn't have bothered with the formality, especially when I had a winning hand. Your father and I are in agreement. The betrothal will be announced before the supper dance."

"You and my father may be in agreement, Your Grace, but Lady Elizabeth and I are not. I have informed my father thus, and now I am informing you. There will be no betrothal, not tonight or at any other time. The lady does not wish it, and neither do I."

"Her wishes are not my concern, nor are yours. Lady Elizabeth understands her duty to her family and defers to me in such instances. I find it appalling that you are less informed about your own duty."

Anthony knew his duty only too well.

"I will not marry the lady without her consent," he said.

"Then you would do well to earn it before the supper dance, or I will take matters into my own hands."

"With all due respect, Your Grace, I would suggest not doing that." Anthony was working hard to control his temper, which felt perilously close to the surface, especially after the demands of the day.

"You are an impudent boy who thinks to deter *me*, the Duke of Marwood. I wonder that you managed to come home from the war alive, as insubordinate as you are to your superiors."

Anthony's entire body vibrated from the insult, from the insinuation that his survival in Spain had resulted from less than honorable means and that he had been deficient as an officer. They were words that struck Anthony where he felt most vulnerable, for, despite his efforts, he had failed to control his men when the siege had ended; he had failed to protect the innocent citizens who had remained in Badajoz from their so-called saviors. Sometimes, especially at night after yet another nightmare, he thought that perhaps he should have died in Spain after all.

Leave be, Captain, and let us have a little fun.

"I have spoken my piece, Your Grace," he said. "The decision is final." He made an elegant bow that bordered on mockery. "Now, if you will excuse me, I shall leave and allow you to return to your very important game of cards."

He did not bother to look back as he left the room.

Chapter 9

Anthony would have preferred to avoid the crowded ballroom and go out onto the terrace for a few minutes so he could get himself under control before facing his guests. Unfortunately Lady Putnam nabbed him before he could, her daughters trailing in her wake.

"Lord Halford," she purred. "We had quite despaired of seeing you dance at the ball this evening. A few brief steps with Lady Elizabeth hardly count, now do they?" She tapped him playfully with her fan. "I myself do not feel the slight, but I am sure the young ladies here this evening do. Am I right in saying so, Harriet?"

"Yes, Mama," Miss Putnam cooed. "And a young lady gets *so* few opportunities to dance with eligible young men of quality in the country." She fluttered her eyelashes at Anthony.

He was trapped, devil take it.

"Miss Putnam," Anthony said through gritted teeth. "Would you do me the honor?"

"Why, thank you," she said, casting a triumphant look at her sister, who stuck her tongue out at her in retaliation.

Paragons, both.

Hiding his annoyance, he reluctantly offered Miss Putnam his arm and escorted her out onto the floor.

Thankfully, the orchestra began a lively tune for a dance that did not require much actual contact with his partner. It was the first bit of luck he'd had all evening. He danced and willed the music to end, all while reminding himself he had endured worse things—until he noticed Amelia dancing with Phillip for a *second time*. Anthony's simmering temper heated up several more degrees.

The music came to an end not a minute too soon, from Anthony's point of view. Rather than return Harriet to her mama, however, he escorted her to some of her friends near the french doors leading out to the terrace.

"Thank you, Miss Putnam," he said with an abrupt bow and was off before anyone could utter a word to him.

Feeling irritated and exhausted, he stole through the french doors and walked along the terrace until he found a dark and secluded corner. Luckily the terrace wasn't overly occupied at present.

He held on to the balustrade with both hands and fought to regain his composure. He had only a few minutes to collect himself before he would feel pressed by duty to return to the ballroom.

There was that word again—*duty*.

He studied the scene before him, the formal garden and the ordered symmetry of the flowerbeds located there. A shy quarter moon peeked out from behind the clouds, and a sprinkle of stars shone nearby. Through the french doors, Anthony could hear the sedate beginning notes of a minuet.

He must find a way to face his guests and play the host and guest of honor. He must think of a strategy for countering Marwood should the man decide to act on his threat and make a betrothal announcement on his own.

But right now Anthony could do neither. He could not think at all. His mind was a churning, boiling mass of images and emotions: his father's lined face, his mother's worried yet hopeful one, the slaps on his back, the expectations, the cheers. Dull eyes staring blankly from both the dead and the living, the looks of betrayal from the citizens of Badajoz, the mud, the blood, broken glass, broken limbs . . .

He gripped the balustrade harder, eyes squeezed shut, trying to block the images assaulting him. He feared he had nothing left inside to get him through the demands of the evening, simple though they ought to have been.

So absorbed was he that when someone laid a hand on his arm, he jumped and swung around to defend himself.

"Oh!" a female voice cried.

Anthony's senses slammed back to the present. It was Amelia. She had taken a step back from him and was looking at him with alarm, not that he blamed her.

"I am sorry to have startled you," he said. He rubbed his hands vigorously over his face. *Startled* was an understatement. He really needed to get a hold of himself.

"I think," she said, "it was *I* who startled *you*." She drew near to him again, reassured, no doubt, when he was not raving at her like a lunatic. "I saw you leave and sensed something was wrong."

As though she needed to justify herself. She had seen him this very afternoon casting up his accounts like a sickly little boy, all because he had lost his nerve over some mud. *Of course* she suspected something was wrong. "What you must think of me," he muttered, turning to gaze once again at the parterres. Anything to avoid looking directly into her eyes.

"I do not know what to think," she said, turning to gaze out to the garden herself. She rested her forearms on top of the balustrade, and Anthony dared to glance at her. The waning moon offered little light but still managed to cast her profile in a lustrous silhouette, her hair a banked fire of curls. "I only know you are troubled, and I wish to help."

"You wish to help," he echoed. "If only you could. Lucas wishes to help, my mother wishes to help; I imagine if my father were in better health, he would wish to help too—most probably in ways I would not like, and he's done enough of that already since my return."

"I do not understand," she said. "You speak as though that is a bad thing, and yet I cannot believe it is. In our own ways, we all wish you to be happy."

"Oh, now, there I believe you are wrong, Miss Clarke. Must I call you Miss Clarke since we are in a public setting, although speaking privately at the moment? How confusing that is! How we must be careful for propriety's sake." His temper was rising again, so he paused to gain control. "Pardon me. That was uncalled for. I apologize."

He stared at the gardens. "But since you have asked the question, my dear Miss Clarke, I shall answer. Lucas saved my life in Spain. Oh, I saved his a time or two; we watched each other's backs quite diligently. But during my last battle, at a town called Badajoz, he saved my life. I was surely dead, with a gunshot wound to the side. Had he not found me and also found a woman willing to take me in, I would definitely be dead, and the letter informing my parents of this would have been quite accurate.

"As it was, it was a near thing. I was fevered and unconscious for days, and I have Lucas and Señora Bartolo to thank for my recovery. Lucas did not dare leave my side, and so I was reported missing and presumed dead. As Lucas was an enlisted man, the reports back home about him were less complete, and his family was spared any misinformation. My friend, the fourth son of the Viscount Thurlby, has fulfilled any obligation he may have had to me in full, and yet he refuses to leave until he is certain I am 'healed.' You saw me at the tug-of-war; is it not obvious that I am unwell? In body and in spirit?"

"Anyone who has experienced what you have would need time—"

"Ah, but Lucas experienced those things with me, and he does not need time. My mother is doing her best, but she is not quite sure how to help her undead son take the place of his dead brother. My father, on the other hand, knows precisely how to *help* me: he has outlined his priorities for me and has issued a command that I be about those priorities posthaste. He is concerned, and rightly so, for the marquessate and my role in its continuance.

"And you, Miss Clarke? You would help me too. How do you propose to do that when I am not sure *what* will help?"

She rested her hand on his forearm and answered softly, "I can listen. And I can pray."

"Ah, yes. The vicar's daughter to the rescue. Will you read sermons to me too?"

"That is an unkind thing to say when all I want is your happiness," she said, removing her hand from his arm and leaving him feeling bereft.

"Happiness is beyond me," he said. "I would be satisfied with a little peace. Every soldier during the siege at Badajoz was praying. Those prayers did little to save many of them."

"I do not claim to know God's will, but like you, I have faced death," Amelia said. "I prayed as a child for my mother to get well, but she was taken nonetheless. And I prayed desperately for months that my father would be spared, and again God did not answer the way I had hoped. But He gave me the strength to see to my father's needs and be thankful for each day I had with him."

"I hear your words," Anthony said hollowly. "But they do little for me at present. I returned home a broken man, and yet I have a father who has been near death and may yet die, and my duties in that regard overwhelm me. I was never meant to be Halford. My brother was." He gestured toward the estate and the village of Ashworthy beyond. "These are my people, or they will be when I am Ashworth. They depend on my father and, therefore, on me—for their livelihoods, for their very lives. I lead them. I must care for them—as I did as an officer for my men."

"I understand that," she said. "What I do not understand is this despair you are feeling."

"Despair," he said. His heart felt rent in two. The anguish was such that he feared he would collapse. "Despair barely covers it. I am responsible for them. I feel acutely the need to be someone they can look up to and trust."

She drew closer and laid her hand once again on his arm. He shuddered, aching with need from her nearness. "You are that person and more. I have watched you this past fortnight. You are the most honorable—"

"Honor!" Anthony spat the word from his mouth, the taste of it bitter and vile. He turned and grabbed her by the shoulders, intent on making her understand, fearful that she would and would cringe from him afterward. "War does its worst to men, Amelia. The devil rattles his saber and screams for blood during battle, then whispers the worst sort of fears and evils in the aftermath. Hell opens its mouth, and men, women, and children are all caught in a maelstrom of fire and agony."

"Stop, my dear," she said. "Oh, Anthony, please stop."

Sometime during his rant she had placed her hands on his chest, over his heart. She must have bruises on her shoulders, so hard was his grip on her. "Forgive me," he said, his voice breaking. "Forgive me." He did not know if he was asking it of her or his Maker.

"Anthony," she repeated, and the sound of his name on her lips was balm to his soul. He was not a captain or Halford here with her now, on the terrace and away from the din. He was merely a man. He was his true self, as he had been from birth.

She cupped his jaw then with a tenderness that undid him.

Broken by her innocence and by a touch that both soothed and ravaged him, he shared his darkest secret. "I was caught in that maelstrom, Amelia. I was in those trenches and fought with the same fury as any of my men. I watched them fall, wounded and dead. I saw the blood. And when it was over and Badajoz was ours, I felt the rage along with the others. I wanted to partake in the horrific things I saw my men—*my own men*—doing. I did not want to call them to order. I wanted—"

"Hush," she said, softly stroking his jaw. "Hush."

But there was only one way Anthony could stop the flow of words now that they had begun. He brought her to himself and took her lips, plundered them, taking and taking. He was so empty, and she was so full of goodness and light . . .

And then suddenly, miraculously, she was giving, giving to him, who was so undeserving, her lips generous and sweet, and he rejoiced and was humbled that this woman—this *good* woman—did not despise him for the confession he had made.

Her arms came around him and held him close, and he encircled her waist with one arm while his free hand moved to cup her head. He cherished her. He kissed her cheeks and throat and then pressed his lips once again to hers. He felt her clutch at his back as she had done when they had been on Bucephalus in the rain—it seemed ages ago now—only this time she was keeping *him* secure, assuring him of the safety he needed. She was a strong woman, although her slight appearance made her seem otherwise. There was such a grace to be found in her strength.

"Anthony," she said again, an edge in her voice that only intensified his ardor. He would never tire of hearing his name on her lips.

"Amelia," he said in reply, lost in her femininity, kissing her again.

"Lord Halford," he heard, only it was not her voice this time. Whose was it? Familiar, grating . . . Instinctively he adjusted slightly to put Amelia behind him and hide her from whoever it was while he struggled to regain his bearings.

"Oh, merciful heavens! Turn your head, Harriet, this minute!"

He looked over his shoulder. Devil take him for a fool! It was Lady Putnam, with eyes the size of saucers, and Harriet, her mouth gaping like a halibut straining for air. Behind them were Sir Frederick and Charlotte, a handful of guests Anthony was in no mood to identify, and his mother, whose expression he was unable to decipher.

He must act quickly to remedy this farce and salvage what he could of Amelia's reputation, for it was she who would suffer the consequences of his actions. She would be ruined in the eyes of the ton as surely as any of the women of Badajoz had been in truth.

Anthony could not, would not allow that to happen.

"Mother, Lady Putnam, Sir Frederick," he began, keeping a secure arm around Amelia, who stood frozen in place next to him. "You catch us at an inopportune moment, for which I beg your pardon. I am confident, however, that you will forgive us both when you learn that Miss Clarke has made me the happiest of men, having just accepted my proposal of marriage." He used his most authoritative voice, the one that had normally sent the men under his command running. He would not have anyone question the intent of his words. It was the only way to protect Amelia.

He felt her tremble and had a moment of guilt that he had compromised her, and yet he could not entirely regret it either. She was not, perhaps, the sort of woman others would expect an earl to marry and who would become a marchioness in due time, but it settled a responsibility Anthony had dreaded facing. If he was to marry and produce heirs quickly, tonight's indiscretion had saved him the time and trouble of wife hunting. Besides, he and Amelia got on very well together, and he was obviously attracted to her, an added bonus.

His mother approached them, a practiced smile on her face, and took Amelia's hands in hers. "My dear Amelia," she said, kissing her cheek. "What wonderful news! I am to have a daughter-in-law." She turned to face the onlookers. "We must share this with our other guests. Anthony, I leave it up to you to make the full announcement. Come with me." With the dignified bearing of the marchioness she was, she cut her way through the gathering crowd, leading him and his new fiancée into the ballroom.

God bless his mother for taking matters in hand and publicly stating her approval. Whether she meant her words or not, Anthony did not know, but it allowed them all to save face.

That was all he dared hope for at the moment.

* * *

Amelia was still reeling with shock from Anthony's words as he held her hand firmly in his and strode into the ballroom behind Lady Ashworth. He had told the people on the terrace—and his mother had been one of them—that they were betrothed, and now he intended to announce it to the entire room.

He gripped her hand like a vise, and Amelia winced from pain. The music dwindled and came to an end, and she could hear murmurs rolling over the dancers as word that something gossip worthy was about to occur.

As the three of them approached the dais on which the orchestra was seated, a hush descended over the room. A group of gentlemen entered from the back. Lady Louisa, looking confused, stood next to Lord Farleigh. Lucas Jennings and Lord Cantwell were with them, grim and resolute.

"My good friends," Anthony said in a booming voice. "I am pleased to announce that this lovely lady, Miss Amelia Clarke, has just now consented to be my bride."

The murmuring started up again.

Anthony held up his hand for silence. "I am grateful to have returned to my home and family and to your good fellowship, and it is with great pleasure I look forward to the future with my soon-to-be wife."

Considering the bleakness she had heard in his voice out on the terrace only moments before, Amelia did not believe a word he was saying.

"What's this?" a man hissed loudly from the back of the ballroom.

The Duke of Marwood pushed his way through the crowd, stopping directly in front of Anthony. Anthony's eyes locked with Marwood's, his jaw set, his mouth in a firm line. "You are *betrothed*, Lord Halford?" the duke said sarcastically. "May I be the first to congratulate you, although it was but *minutes* ago you jilted my daughter. Now I see why: you have been caught dallying with a servant who is no better than she ought to be."

Gasps and more murmurs flew around the room, and Amelia felt dizzy at the duke's insinuation.

"Watch yourself, Marwood," Anthony replied in a low voice. "You are speaking of my future wife."

"And such a wife as you deserve, no doubt. It must come from years of mucking about with commoners and light-skirts across the Iberian Peninsula."

Anthony fairly vibrated with rage, and Amelia was afraid he might do something drastic, so strained were his emotions already. It was within his rights to challenge the Duke of Marwood to a duel over the duke's comments about her. She prayed it would not come to that.

Oh, this was dreadful, and it was all her fault—her fault! If only she had not gone looking for him this evening, concerned though she had been. She should have sent Mr. Jennings to him instead or even Lord Cantwell, but no, she had gone herself.

And now this.

She must make things right. How, she didn't know, but she must for Anthony's sake. She turned to Lady Ashworth, a woman who, up until a few moments ago, Amelia had considered a friend as well as employer. "Lady Ashworth, your son honors me with his words, and I am truly humbled." Amelia made a deep curtsy to her, hoping her deference would go over well with the onlookers.

"Pathetic," Marwood sneered. "Only last night the chit was expounding her radical views and spewing defiance toward those of the highest rank. I was appalled."

"Marwood," Anthony said. "You have already been warned. Pray, do not force me in this matter."

"Anthony," his mother murmured. "Have a care. You are addressing the Duke of Marwood."

"If your father were standing here, he would disown you," Marwood spat. "I am sure I would rather have *no* heir than one who flaunts propriety as easily as you do."

Lady Ashworth's hand flew to her mouth at the remark, and Anthony took a step forward. Amelia's heart leapt to her throat.

"Enough. I am leaving," Marwood said with a slash of his arm. "I will not stay another minute in this house. You will excuse us, Lady Ashworth," he said, giving her a curt bow. "Come, Lady Marwood, Elizabeth." He pivoted and exited the room, the duchess and Lady Elizabeth trailing after him. Lady Ashworth followed, her head held high.

The whispering began again, so Anthony held up his hand again. "My dear guests," he said in a clear, loud voice. "I regret you were forced to witness that exchange, for this is meant to be a festive occasion, now even more so as we celebrate my betrothal."

He raised Amelia's hand, there in front of everyone, and kissed it. "Miss Clarke, may I lead you out for the next dance?" He smiled, but his eyes were blue ice.

"Thank you, my lord," she answered, surprised her voice worked at all. "It would be my honor to dance with you."

He led her to the center of the floor, although no other couples followed. Determined, he gestured to the maestro for the orchestra to begin, then turned to face Amelia.

The first notes began, and Amelia tensed. It was a waltz. She had never had reason or opportunity to perform the dance before. He held out his left hand for her to take and snaked his right hand around her waist.

"My lord, I cannot—"

"You can, and you shall. Begin as you mean to go," he said curtly.

"I mean, I have never waltzed before," she said, looking about her. "I shall humiliate myself and embarrass you and your family even further."

"Nonsense. I'll help you. Place your hand on my shoulder." He drew her closer than was proper, but it gave her some security and allowed her to stare at his neckcloth rather than at all the gawking people in the ballroom. "Are you familiar with the steps?" he asked.

"Theoretically, yes, but—"

"Then you will be fine. Ready: one, two, three, one, two, three . . ."

He kept up the counting, holding her steady while Amelia figured out her footwork. Thankfully it was a slow waltz. Amelia hated to think what would have happened had the music been up-tempo.

Gradually, other couples began to join them on the dance floor, and Amelia felt like less of a spectacle. It was time for her to make amends. "This is entirely my fault," she said. "Had I sent Mr. Jennings to you rather than look for you myself, you would not have felt compelled to claim we were betrothed as you did."

"Were you actually there, Amelia? On the terrace with me? Because I seem to recall it was not your concern for me that resulted in our betrothal but my impetuous behavior. I believe it was I who kissed you. Now hush. Everyone is watching us."

He put her in a gentle spin, and she ended up closer to him still, which would only add to the gossip, she supposed, but for the moment, there was nothing she could do to make things right. She closed her eyes and let herself imagine what it would be like to be truly betrothed to him, to marry him and give him children.

"What are we to do?" she whispered.

"We will discuss it tomorrow," he said, his breath tickling her ear. "One thing at a time."

Tomorrow. Tomorrow would be daunting. They could not simply turn from such a public betrothal announcement and say it was all in jest, especially not after Anthony's encounter with the Duke of Marwood. The betrothal would have to continue for a time. Even then Anthony would never cry off, Amelia was certain. He was too much of a gentleman, with too strong a sense of honor and duty. It would be up to her to end the betrothal.

She hoped she would be strong enough to do it when the time came.

Chapter 10

ANTHONY'S FATHER SUMMONED HIM TO his room much too early the following morning. He'd had precious little sleep the night before. The ball, as balls were inclined to do, went on into the wee hours of the morning, and Anthony had proceeded to toss and turn the remainder of the night.

How the devil had he allowed himself to get into such a mess? And not only himself, oh no; he'd had to drag Amelia into it with him. If she had any brains in her head, she would pack her things and run as far away from him as she possibly could.

"Hold still," Lucas grumbled as he shaved Anthony's face. "Or I shall cut you, and it won't be on accident."

Anthony had awakened him despite knowing that Lucas would be lacking sleep as well. But if Anthony was to face his father and declare that, one: he was not betrothed to Lady Elizabeth, two: he had managed to make an enemy of Marwood in the process, and three: he'd gotten himself betrothed to his mother's companion, to boot, he intended to look every bit the Earl of Halford, and that would require his friend's assistance, as his own hands were feeling exceptionally unsteady.

"Your words strike no fear in me whatsoever," Anthony said as he stared at their bleary-eyed reflections in the mirror. "You have had too many opportunities to let me expire to imagine you would let your previous good efforts on my behalf go to waste."

"Don't be so sure," Lucas said. "I never took you for a fool before last night. What got into you, Tony, that you would take on the Duke of Marwood like that?"

"What got into me," Anthony said, "was the fact that he made derogatory remarks about the lady to whom I am betrothed. I had no choice but to return fire."

"Yes, and about that betrothal." Lucas handed Anthony a towel. "What do you intend to do?"

"Honor it, of course." He wiped the remaining soap from his face and tossed the towel onto the dressing table and then allowed Lucas to help him into his waistcoat. "I compromised Miss Clarke, and it is my duty to make it right."

"You think the entire world is your duty, Tony," Lucas said. "Now hold still again. I am only willing to tie one neckcloth this morning, so it had better be right the first time. After that, I am returning to my bed and dreaming of dancing with lovely young ladies."

"My father asked me to marry quickly. He is getting his wish."

Lucas only looked at him as though he had lost his mind. Perhaps he had. "Marwood is a powerful man," Lucas said, "and you have gotten out of step with him. Your father will not be pleased. He seemed intent on having you wed Lady Elizabeth in your brother's place."

"Only because it was convenient." He ran a hand over his eyes. "I wish I had seen Alex and Lady Elizabeth together to determine if it was a love match or not. She isn't like his usual type of woman."

"She seems very nice to me. Do you mean she is too quiet? Too bland, perhaps?"

"I would never call Lady Elizabeth bland, although Alex did seem to prefer a livelier sort of lady. Perhaps he fell in love with her and was setting aside his wild ways."

"Perhaps." Lucas finished the knot and assisted Anthony into his coat.

"Why should Marwood care so much about an alliance with Ashworth that he would turn hostile over a broken betrothal? And not even a betrothal, at that," Anthony continued. "It seems all out of proportion to me. Louisa had several beaus ask for her hand, and my father even began negotiating settlements with one young man's family until Louisa changed her mind."

"It is indeed a mystery." Lucas studied Anthony's appearance. "You look as good as you are going to this early in the morning," he said.

They were interrupted by a soft knock at the door, and a footman stepped inside. "Your father is ready for you, my lord."

"Tell him I will be there shortly," Anthony replied.

"I think the sapphire stickpin," Lucas said. He selected the stickpin from Anthony's jewel case and deftly slipped it into the folds of his neckcloth. "There. I have done all that I can for you. The rest is up to you. Good luck." He yawned and returned to his own room.

Anthony shot his cuffs, tugged at his waistcoat, and went to face his father.

He discovered upon his arrival at his father's suite of rooms that both his parents were there to meet with him. His father, fully dressed and looking serious, sat in an overstuffed chair near the fireplace. His mother stood next to him, her hand resting on his shoulder. It was a daunting family portrait, to say the least.

Anthony bowed formally. There would be no cutting corners on propriety this morning. "Father, Mother. Good morning. I hope you both slept well."

"Rather not, I am afraid," his father said. "I was awakened late last night with the news that some of our more esteemed guests left abruptly. Care to explain?"

"The Duke of Marwood insulted Miss Clarke," Anthony said. "And I would not stand for it."

"There is more to the story than that, or so I have been told."

Anthony looked at his mother.

"I do not keep secrets from your father, Anthony, and he needed to know as soon as possible," she said.

"I am assuming Mother told you I am now betrothed, then, an arrangement that should make you happy."

His father closed his eyes. He looked tired, the deep brackets around his mouth making him look older than he was. "Perhaps I should speak to Halford alone, my dear," he said. "Man to man."

"Not on your life, Ashworth," his mother retorted. She left his side and sank onto the sofa that faced his chair. "Have a seat, Anthony, for pity's sake."

He did, sitting next to his mother on the sofa.

"I spoke to Lady Elizabeth," Anthony said. "As I told you I would. I do not know what sort of understanding she and Alex had before his death, only that she was not inclined to accept a proposal from me. I told her I would speak to Marwood, and I did. He was not pleased."

"But what of the betrothal to Amelia, Anthony?" his mother asked.

What to say? How to protect Amelia, even from the judgment of his parents? "I have gotten to know Miss Clarke over the past few weeks, and I have an affection for her. Proposing to her saves a great deal of time and allows me to focus on my new responsibilities."

"I should have held firm on the matter with Lady Elizabeth," his father said. "In your rashness, you have exchanged the daughter of a duke for the daughter of a mere vicar. As much as I admire Miss Clarke, it is nonsensical."

"It may seem so to you, Father. But what makes no sense to me is the Duke of Marwood's reaction to the entire business. He was incensed that I would not hold to the marriage contracts between Alex and Lady Elizabeth, all out of proportion to the situation, if you were to ask me."

"Yes, well," his father said, looking grumpily at his wife and clearing his throat. "We were quite determined to have your brother marry and settle down. I wanted Halford to have a bride of the finest quality, and I was willing to be generous to secure Lady Elizabeth. We worked out a very detailed arrangement. Marwood and I both got what we wanted from it."

"Apparently the Duke of Marwood cared more about the union than his daughter did," Anthony observed wryly.

"Your brother courted the girl properly, and she agreed to the match, whatever you may think," his father snapped.

"He really was fond of her, Anthony, and she of him," his mother added. "We would never have wanted their marriage to be an indifferent one."

"Enough of that now. I want to know more about this business with Miss Clarke," his father said impatiently. "I truly cannot fathom it."

"I do not see why not, Father. Miss Clarke is clever, and her manners are without exception."

"That may be true, and we are certainly indebted to her," the marquess said. "She was a great support to your mother during Halford's death and with my own indisposition. But I needn't remind you that she is a hired companion, with no family to speak of. She will be looked down upon, viewed as your inferior. Tongues will wag, and people will assume the worst. From what your mother has told me, they already are. What do you intend to do about it?"

"I have already begun making plans," Anthony said. "I spent part of the night drafting a letter to our solicitor in London, outlining amendments to my will reflecting my change in marital status." He did not add that he had also asked the solicitor to look into Miss Clarke's family background. He found it odd that she had never been told anything about her grandparents or aunts and uncles, for that matter, and he wanted to find family members who could be with her at the wedding.

"Additionally," he said, "in three days' time, I will take Miss Clarke to London. She needs a wardrobe fit for a countess—"

"Oh, yes, Anthony, of course," his mother interrupted. "But who will take her to see the modiste? Who will be her chaperone? You must behave with the utmost propriety in Town, especially after the scene last night. But

I cannot leave your father, and I am sure Farleigh will not allow Louisa to gallivant all over Town, tiring herself in her condition. Perhaps I can write to one of my friends."

"We will sort it out, Mother," Anthony said. "Also, while I am there, I plan to arrange for a special license."

"That is wise," his father said. "The sooner the deed is done, the better, and the tongues will eventually begin to wag over something else. But now I am for my bed." He reached for his cane, and Anthony stood. "Send that letter, and start making the arrangements."

"I shall. But before I go," Anthony said, "I want you both to know I will do everything in my power to make things right and minimize any scandal that may occur from this."

"Do not make promises you cannot keep, Halford," his father said.

"I never do," Anthony assured him.

He hoped he wasn't this time.

***

Amelia slept until noon, so exhausted she was from the events of the day and night before. How she had managed to keep her head up and a smile on her face while ladies whispered behind their fans and gentlemen looked at her with raised eyebrows, she didn't know.

Anthony had led her out for the supper dance and had gotten her a plate of delicacies. Mrs. Deal had exceeded herself with her cooking, by all accounts. But Amelia had barely tasted anything she had put in her mouth.

Eventually the ball had concluded, and Anthony had escorted her to her room.

"I cannot be sorry for what happened," he had whispered in her ear. "Even though I should be. Good night, my dear."

He had kissed her then, a chaste kiss on the cheek, and had vanished down the hallway. Considering what had resulted from their previous kiss, Amelia had not been surprised. What had surprised her was how much she had wanted a repeat of the passion they had shared on the terrace.

Perhaps she had wished for reassurance that he had real feelings for her, that the kiss had not been merely the result of the emotional tumult he had been in. Perhaps then she would feel less guilty that he had leg-shackled himself to a woman so clearly beneath him in status.

They had joked about being leg-shackled earlier in the day. He had thought it amusing at the time. It definitely was not amusing now.

She washed and chose her most somber day dress to wear, then rang for toast and tea to be sent to her room. She was not ready to face anyone quite yet.

What could they possibly be thinking?

There was a quiet knock at her door, and then Jane entered bearing Amelia's morning tray. "Oh, there you are, miss," she said, standing awkwardly inside the door. "Where would you like your tray, miss?"

Amelia sighed. "On the same table where you have put my morning tray every time I have requested one since I arrived here at Ashworth Park."

"Of course, miss. Is there anything else you need?" She set the tray down and returned to the door, looking as if she needed to escape.

"Yes, Jane, there is." Last evening, Anthony had said she must begin as she meant to go, and so she would. Whether a countess or companion, she was the same person today as she had been yesterday. "My betrothal is going to be an adjustment for everyone, including me. What I need most, therefore, is help I am unaccustomed to receiving."

She crossed to her dressing table and sat down. "I have been having trouble with my hair this morning." On the occasions when she wasn't wearing her mobcap, Jane's hair always looked lovely, and Amelia had long been impressed with the girl's skill. "Today is going to be a challenging one, I am afraid, and I would feel more confident if I thought my hair looked just right. Perhaps you would be willing to help me."

"Oh, miss! Yes, miss!" Jane exclaimed. "I have younger sisters, you see, and Ma was always asking me to do their hair and such, considering she was busy with the cooking or with a baby. You have such pretty hair too, miss. I would love nothing more."

Amelia picked up her brush and handed it to her. "Have at it, then. Make me look a proper fiancée to the Earl of Halford." It would not only delay her presence a few minutes more, but if Jane worked magic, it would indeed help Amelia face the scrutiny that awaited her.

What Amelia was not sure she could face after that was her own guilt. She would make it up to Anthony somehow. She would play her part in the charade, and then she would end the betrothal—for there would surely need to be an ending.

And she would do everything in her power while she was betrothed to him to help him heal from the wounds he had suffered both physically and emotionally during his time in Spain.

* * *

"There you are. *Finally*." Lady Ashworth looked up from her needlework as Amelia entered the marchioness's sitting room. "Something is different about you. Let me see." She gestured to a chair near where she was seated, so Amelia crossed the room and sat. "It is your hair, is it not?"

"Yes. I asked Jane to try something different from what I usually do myself."

"It suits you nicely. I had no idea Jane was so talented." She set her sewing aside. "I hope you are rested this morning because we have much to do. Last night was quite eventful."

"Lady Ashworth," Amelia said, "I am sorry. I had no intention—"

"I am certain that is true, my dear, but what happened, happened. May I speak frankly?"

"Of course."

"I am terribly fond of you, as you know," the marchioness said. "However, I cannot say in good conscience I would have chosen you as a wife for my son."

"I understand that, of course." The words were difficult to hear, nevertheless, especially from Lady Ashworth.

"Marquesses and their heirs are amongst the highest of the peerage, and it is no easy thing to marry one of them. I know this from personal experience." She smiled briefly. "However, I also know you are clever and learn quickly. You will have to learn quickly, for the society you will be joining through your marriage to my son will be watching you closely and hoping you fail. Now, ring for some tea, will you?"

Amelia obliged and returned to her seat.

"Ashworth and Anthony and I discussed things earlier and put together a plan," Lady Ashworth said. "You and Anthony are to leave for Town in three days. You need to be fitted for a new wardrobe, and you also need to be seen on Anthony's arm out in public and at a few of the smaller parties. If people get used to seeing you behaving with decorum, you will cease to be a topic of gossip, and idle tongues will find something new to amuse them. Tea please, Mary," she told the maid who had arrived.

"Yes, my lady." Mary bobbed a curtsy and left.

Amelia had not considered needing a wardrobe. How would she ever repay such a thing? "I cannot feel good about a wardrobe, Lady Ashworth. The betrothal was merely Anthony's way of protecting me. I should never hold him to it in the end."

"Would you not?" Lady Ashworth studied Amelia closely. "You know how honorable he is. His duty will not allow him to cry off."

"I shall play the part of fiancée the best I am able, my lady, but my intention is to free him when the time is right. If I must dress the part, then I would prefer the fewest garments possible. And I will repay you for them."

"With what money? What income do you have, Amelia, other than the one you receive from me? They will be your clothes, and there's an end to it. Besides, we have more important things to discuss." Lady Ashworth folded her hands in her lap. "His father wishes him to marry speedily and fill his nursery, and yet this betrothal will need to last a few months at least to allay any scandal. That means valuable time will be lost in fulfilling Ashworth's expectations."

The idea of bearing a child—Anthony's child—struck a longing in Amelia's breast so strong she ached from the pain of it.

Mary returned then with the tea tray, which was a relief. After she left, while the marchioness poured, Amelia worked to regain her composure.

"Frankly," Lady Ashworth said after taking a sip of her tea, "I thought the vicar's daughter I had brought into my home as my companion was not the type of single young lady who would allow such intimacies with a gentleman."

Amelia choked on her tea.

"Are you all right?" Lady Ashworth asked.

Amelia nodded, coughing, and set her cup and saucer down until she could recover.

"I think I would have spotted such a character flaw in you," Lady Ashworth continued without missing a beat. "And yet I did not. Which is why I was surprised to discover it was *you* out on the terrace with Anthony."

"I meant only to comfort him, Lady Ashworth," Amelia said in a small voice, still recovering from the tea, not to mention her shame. "He seemed distressed, and I was concerned."

"More than concerned, I think," the marchioness replied archly. "Do you have an affection for him, then? An attachment of which I am unaware? Ah, but I saw you together at the three-legged race and suspected something, did I not?"

Amelia could say nothing, hoping her eyes didn't betray her feelings completely.

"Ah," the marchioness murmured again. "I see."

"I am truly sorry, my lady," Amelia said. "It was not my intention—"

Lady Ashworth held up her hand. "Intentions matter little at this point. What is done is done. You must begin this very instant to act as the fiancée of an earl would act. Your education will begin this very morning. There is much to do before you leave with Anthony three days hence. We must also arrange for you to have a lady's maid. It would seem Jane is an obvious choice."

"Yes, Lady Ashworth. With your permission, I shall ask her straightaway."

"She will be ecstatic, I think. Very well."

The marchioness set her empty cup and saucer back on the tray and stood. Amelia rose as well. "We will meet in my sitting room after luncheon while Lord Ashworth is resting, and I shall begin instructing you on the responsibilities of a nobleman's wife."

"Is there anything you wish for me to do in the meantime?" Amelia asked.

"Pray," Lady Ashworth said. "Pray and prepare yourself for the challenges ahead."

Which did not sound at all encouraging.

* * *

"Where has everyone *been* all day," Lady Walmsley complained at dinner that evening, an event which Anthony's father felt well enough to attend. "The house has been a veritable tomb. Marwood up and left, taking his women with him. That was exciting to watch, I confess, all that huffing and puffing. I do not miss him or his wife much, but his daughter was a sweet thing. She at least spoke to me as though I still had some wits rattling around in my head."

Anthony's only real regret about the night before was that poor Lady Elizabeth would be on her own dealing with the repercussions of their decision not to marry. He hoped Marwood did not place the blame on her.

"I am not sorry those Putnams left this morning either," Lady Walmsley continued. "I'd had my fill of them, to be sure. But I have not had a decent chat with anyone all day—not that I would have had one with any of them. My wineglass, boy." She tapped the rim of it with her finger in an authoritative manner. The footman hurried over and topped it off. "That is better. As I was saying: it went from talk, talk, talk to silence and whispers in the space of an evening. I was there. I know what happened. But I've half a mind to return to London if it's going to be so dull around here."

"I'm sorry you felt neglected today, Lady Walmsley," Amelia said earnestly.

"Excellent duck this evening, Lady Ashworth," Anthony's father said, unwilling as he'd always been to be pulled into gossip.

"Thank you, my dear," Anthony's mother replied. "I shall inform Mrs. Deal. She will be pleased."

Anthony, however, had caught something different in Lady Walmsley's comments and looked up from his plate. "You are planning to return to London after your visit with us, Lady Walmsley?" His brain was making swift calculations.

"Yes," she said. "Although I had intended to enjoy myself here for another week or so."

"Would you care to walk with me in the gardens after dinner, Lady Walmsley?" his mother asked. "I am afraid I was rather preoccupied with instructing Miss Clarke this afternoon."

"No surprise there," the lady answered. "The life of an aristocratic wife is a demanding one. I should know. You are a fortunate man, Halford, to have secured such a jewel, and there is no mistaking it. She will be up to snuff in no time. I accept your offer, Lady Ashworth, and thank you. Besides, these two young lovebirds will be wanting some time alone, I suspect."

"Not too much time alone," Anthony's father grumbled. "That is what started this whole business."

Amelia blushed beet red. Anthony bit the inside of his cheek to keep from laughing.

"Perhaps I shall join you," Louisa said. "After resting most of the day, I think I would enjoy stretching my legs a bit."

Anthony was feeling lighter today, truth be told. Amelia was clever and sensible, and she already knew something of his experiences in Spain. She knew some of it and had not rejected him for it. And he was attracted to her. He had dreaded finding himself in a marriage of convenience, one in which he and his wife would go their own way once the requirement of an heir and a spare had been dutifully met. His honor would not allow him to break his marriage vows by taking a mistress, although the practice was common enough among the ton. He had always intended to be faithful to his wife.

He had hope now for a marriage of affection at least, and possibly more. He must find a way to convince Amelia that while the betrothal may have begun as a means of protecting her reputation, it held potential for more. He thought he would like it to become a betrothal in truth.

"Lady Walmsley," he said, "Amelia and I are leaving in a few days for London ourselves. She is in need of a wardrobe, amongst other things. Would you care to act as chaperone for her?"

Everyone at the table turned and looked at him and then at Lady Walmsley.

"Hm. Chaperone, you say." Lady Walmsley drummed her fingers against the table in thought.

"I should love nothing more than to act as chaperone," Louisa said. "What fun to help Amelia shop for new gowns and bonnets! But Farleigh says I am not to exert myself during my delicate condition except for what is absolutely necessary. He is firm on that point, sadly."

"Quite true, my love," Farleigh said while dishing her another slice of beef.

"You are so good to me," Louisa said.

"And I must remain with Ashworth while he gains his strength," Anthony's mother said.

"I will not be staying at your place in London if I agree to this arrangement, Halford," Lady Walmsley said. "Amelia will have to stay with me. And I am not as young as I used to be, mind, as much as it pains me to say it."

"Amelia will be taking Jane with her as her personal maid," Lady Ashworth said. "Perhaps she can act as chaperone on those occasions when you cannot."

"It would be nice to have a young girl in the house again after so many years. Very well, I shall do it." She nodded decisively.

"Thank you, Lady Walmsley," Anthony said. The first step of many had fallen into place nicely, he thought.

"Oh, thank you, Lady Walmsley," Amelia said. "It is such a relief that if I am to do this, I will be with someone I already know. I look forward to sharing your company and getting even better acquainted."

"And I will enjoy your company as well. Although I am not so old as to forget that it is you and young Halford who will be getting to know each other the most."

"You are my favorite kind of chaperone," Anthony said. "For I intend to get to know my betrothed much better during that time. It is gratifying to know I will be aided in that endeavor."

"Not *too* well, I hope," his mother warned.

Lady Walmsley cackled, and Farleigh chuckled.

"Really, Anthony," Louisa said. "Do not let him rattle you, Amelia."

"Have you ever noticed, Farleigh, how delightful young ladies look with a blush on their cheeks?" Anthony asked.

"It was one of Louisa's most charming attributes," Farleigh concurred. "Was what brought me up to scratch, in fact."

"You foolish man," Louisa said, shooting him a melting look.

"This frivolity is all very well and good," Lord Ashworth said, "but do not lose sight of what is at stake here. Amelia's entrance and acceptance into Society is critical."

"Oh, Ashworth, I wish you were well enough to travel. I will be on tenterhooks the entire time," Lady Ashworth said.

"I will write to you," Amelia assured her. "And we will be back before you know it."

"In the meantime, Mother," Anthony said, "you can begin planning the wedding. I meant to discuss this with you earlier, Amelia. I had presumed we would be married here at the family chapel, if that is agreeable to you. But I forgot to consider that you have friends in Little Brenchley or may wish to be married in the church where your father was vicar. We can change the arrangements, if you would like."

"There is no reason to return to Little Brenchley," she said. "I would rather have the Reverend Villiers officiate, in any case."

Anthony had never asked her about the man who had replaced her father at the vicarage. There was much he didn't know about her, in fact. He was going to make it a priority to learn everything he could about her, and he planned to enjoy himself in the process.

Enjoy himself. Now, there was a thought. Perhaps he was actually putting some of his ghosts to rest. It was a relief to have something to look forward to after so long. He was beginning to feel alive, in truth. His parents had thought him dead—and perhaps in some respects he had been. Now that could finally be changing.

Chapter 11

The first thing Anthony did once they arrived in London and he had seen the ladies safely to Lady Walmsley's house was visit his solicitor.

Mr. George Swindlehurst had a sterling reputation—despite his unfortunate surname—and, like his father before him, served as the solicitor for Ashworth and the holdings of the marquessate. Anthony had had Swindlehurst draw up a will for him prior to his leaving for the Peninsula. When Anthony had written to him from Ashworth Park, he had informed the solicitor that he wanted to amend the will now to make Amelia his beneficiary.

He had also asked Swindlehurst's investigator to learn what he could regarding Amelia's family of origin. Anthony himself was curious, but he also hoped Amelia would be surprised and pleased to discover he had done this for her. She had resolved not to have any contact with them, but surely she would be willing to listen to their side of things and possibly forgive and accept them and allow them to rejoice with her at her wedding.

He had seen strong men brought to tears by a letter from home and too many widows made with each battle for him not to at least try to mend the breach between her family and her. He was done with breaches of any kind.

"Halford. Good to see you. Come in and be seated," Swindlehurst said, shaking Anthony's hand. "May I offer you some tea? Brandy?"

"No, thank you," Anthony replied. He removed his hat and took the offered chair.

Swindlehurst was a middle-aged man, well turned out for a solicitor, which illustrated how successful he was at his business. He returned to his desk and sat, then picked up a sheaf of papers. "Here are the amended documents you requested. I believe you will find them to your satisfaction.

If you would like to peruse them here, we can have Marlowe come in and serve as an additional witness while you sign them."

Anthony's personal property was modest. There was a small house and some land that were his outright, having inherited them from a great uncle on his mother's side, and he had been frugal with his officer's pay, investing the savings for a modest rate of return. He was also now able to draw income from properties belonging to the courtesy title of Earl of Halford.

It was not much, but it would keep Amelia secure if something were to happen to him. He knew firsthand how quickly life could end, and he would take no chances, especially after trapping her into marriage with him.

He quickly read through the will, Swindlehurst called for his assistant, and Anthony signed the documents.

"Now," he said after Marlowe excused himself and left the room. "I am curious to learn what you have discovered regarding my other questions."

"Ah," Swindlehurst said, drumming his fingers on his desk and looking diabolically pleased. "That has been a delightful mystery. My man Abbott has found a few answers and is still following up on other leads. This is what he has learned to date: it would seem your betrothed is none other than the granddaughter of John Clarke-Hammond, Viscount Winfield."

"Interesting." Anthony had heard of Winfield. The man had a reputation for being an overbearing tyrant, but that alone did not explain the rift. "I presume her father shortened his name to distinguish himself from the rest of the family."

"Yes," Swindlehurst said. "The Reverend Mr. Edmund Clarke-Hammond was well respected as vicar and was a beloved member of the Little Brenchley community. Apparently he was not cut from the same cloth as his father. Defied the man, in fact, in order to marry the lady of his choice."

"And Amelia's mother?"

"Now, *there* Viscount Winfield had a right to question the union. The young lady, a Miss Sarah Rigby by name, was a scholarship student at a girl's finishing school in Somerset, which is apparently where Edmund met her, as that is where the Clarke-Hammonds hail from. Local lads mingling with the schoolgirls at a village fete or some such, I would imagine, although Abbott's letter from Kent did not address their meeting. Apparently the girl was well known for her exceptional singing voice and was recommended to the school as a scholarship student, which allowed her to advance her musical training."

Amelia had mentioned that her mother had taught her piano. Considering how accomplished Amelia was, what Swindlehurst said made sense.

"The marriage caused quite a row, from what Abbott was told. Winfield was furious with Edmund and disowned him, while the young man in turn calmly renounced his family in favor of his chosen bride and changed his name, to boot—all while the poor girl and her family stood by watching."

"That does not explain why her family, at least, did not stay in touch with Amelia's parents through the years. It is surprising enough Winfield did not eventually reconcile with his son."

"We have not uncovered a reason for that last bit. As to Sarah's family, the locals say it was not so different from what happened to Edmund. They were never entirely comfortable with their daughter going off to school, 'developing airs,' as it were. The distance between her and her family grew wider each year, and when the son of a viscount offered for her, they told her she was too important for the likes of them and cut themselves off. Bacon-brained, the lot of them." He shook his head in disgust.

"All those years wasted," Anthony said. "I do not want your investigator to get in touch with any of her family personally, at least not yet. I want to ponder this news for a day or two."

"I shall inform him, my lord."

"Thank you for your time, Swindlehurst." Anthony rose to leave and then paused. "Do you mind my asking—what would your opinion be on this matter? Are you a family man yourself?" Strange, he had never thought to ask the solicitor that question before.

"Why, yes, sir, that I am. Married to Mrs. Swindlehurst for nearly twenty years now, with four daughters and a son. Delightful, each and every one of them."

"I am happy for you all. And so, then, if you were in my shoes? What advice would you give me?"

"Well, my lord," Swindlehurst said. "I have always thought that blood was thicker than water, and quarrels should be got over. But I have also learned as a solicitor that people don't always act as they ought."

"Wise words, though they have not exactly cleared things up in my mind."

"It's a sticky business, to be sure, my lord."

"You will let me know if your investigator learns anything helpful, then," Anthony said, taking up his hat.

"Certainly."

"Good. I will be at Ashworth House while I am in town." He had given up his bachelor quarters when he had bought his commission and would need to stay in the family townhouse for the time being.

"I will be in touch, my lord."

Anthony left the premises and tapped his hat into place, hoping he was giving Amelia a true gift by locating her family, and not doing her a huge disservice.

Only time would tell.

* * *

Amelia was at once excited and apprehensive about being in London. Having never been to Town before, she was eager to see the sights she'd read about, and what few landmarks they'd passed on their way to Lady Walmsley's house had only served to pique her interest even further.

Anthony had bid Amelia and Lady Walmsley good-bye on the steps of Lady Walmsley's London residence, saying he would escort both ladies to the theater that evening, which offer both ladies happily accepted.

However, the realities of London society were foremost in Amelia's mind. She knew gossip spread like wildfire here; word of Anthony's betrothal to a paid companion would certainly have reached Town already. During the trip, Anthony had outlined his strategy for dealing with the scandal, and he had sounded every bit the former army captain while doing so.

They would make an appearance at a few public locations first: the theater, Hyde Park, and the like. Then they would attend a few minor social gatherings. He was sure he would receive invitations, he had told them, probably more than usual, considering the circumstances. And he assured them he would not subject Amelia to anyone he suspected to be less than accepting of her.

That last bit had not reassured Amelia much.

"Would you like a tour of the house so you will feel more comfortable knocking about while you are here?" Lady Walmsley asked Amelia after luncheon.

"I would like nothing better," Amelia said. A tour would be just the thing to keep her mind occupied with something other than her appearance at the theater tonight.

After guiding Amelia through the various parlors and sitting rooms and studies, Lady Walmsley led her to the portrait gallery.

"Most of the family portraits of any significance are with the current Lord Walmsley," Lady Walmsley said. "But there were a few I was particularly attached to, and so I brought them with me before he took residence in the family seat." She pointed to one portrait in particular. "That is my dear husband. How I enjoy seeing his gruff old face." She gestured to the painting next to it. "There he is again, painted twenty years earlier. Why would I let the new earl keep them? He barely knew the man. He is more than welcome to them when I die, but not before." She ran her fingers fondly down the cheek of the younger man. "He was such a lovely rascal. I fell for him the moment I laid eyes on him, although it would never do to tell him that. He had to work to get me, I will have you know."

Amelia studied the painting in which the Lord Walmsley was standing next to his horse. "I imagine you had plenty of beaus to choose from."

The old woman gave Amelia a saucy look. "I had my share. I was quite popular."

"I do not doubt it." Amelia chuckled and strolled to look at a portrait of a young couple wearing the fashion of a generation past, the man in silk breeches and ruffles and wearing a wig, the lady seated before him in a resplendent gown of lavender satin. "Who are they?" she asked.

"That is my sister, Frances, and her husband, Joseph Carhart. I told you about her before, if you will recall. They married and went off to India, and that was the last I saw of them. This was their wedding portrait."

"They were a beautiful couple," Amelia said. And indeed they were—dressed in their finest. There was a twinkle in Frances's eye and a slightly raised eyebrow the painter had caught that Amelia had seen on Lady Walmsley's face a time or two.

"And here," Lady Walmsley said warmly, "is a small portrait of their daughter, Julia. I had it done soon after she arrived from India."

The girl in the painting had a strong resemblance to her mother, although her overall coloring was fairer. There was a sadness to her countenance despite the smile on her face that Amelia could understand. Julia had left her home and parents and traveled to an unfamiliar land. She must have felt alone and missed them terribly.

"And here I am with Walmsley shortly after our marriage."

Amelia turned to view the painting in question. "You were a beautiful bride, my lady."

"It seems like only yesterday. Life is to be seized, my dear—a much more difficult endeavor for us ladies than it is for the gentlemen, unfortunately."

She pointed at Amelia. "Do *not* be put off by the opinions of others, Amelia. If Halford is the man you want, then marry him, and the sooner, the better. If he is not, cry off and be done with it. Either way, you must retain what little power you have as a woman, or you are lost."

It was quite a declaration but was much easier said than done, in Amelia's opinion.

"Halford seems the sort of gentleman who would not be intimidated by a clever wife," Lady Walmsley added. "That is a rare quality in a man."

"My father was such a man."

"Of course he was. Otherwise you would not be *you*, would you? Now Marwood, on the other hand . . ." She left the remainder of her comment unsaid, which was just as well.

Amelia was not keen to reflect on the disparaging remarks the duke had made about her. "Do you have a garden here, Lady Walmsley?" she asked, determined to change the subject.

"A small one, not too impressive, I am afraid, but a pleasant little spot. Come, I will take you."

They went through the house to the back and to a garden boasting golden yews and hardy blooms that would require only minimal upkeep. "It is lovely," Amelia said.

"Enjoy it all you like," Lady Walmsley said. She let out an inelegant yawn. "Goodness me! I had better lie down for a spell before we head out to the theater tonight, especially if I am to keep up with you young people. Can you find your way around without me?"

"I am certain I can, although I only intend to remain for a few minutes." Amelia also needed rest herself in order to prepare for the evening ahead.

She enjoyed some quiet time in the garden and then returned to her room. She even slept for about an hour before it was time to dress for their evening at the theater.

Because Amelia had only the two evening gowns, Louisa had generously given Amelia some from her own wardrobe.

"Nonsense," Louisa had replied when Amelia had attempted to refuse. "I have more gowns than I can ever hope to wear, and at any rate, I cannot wear any of these now." She had laid a hand over her rounded belly. "Someone may as well get some use out of them."

Amelia had eventually accepted, and she and Jane had spent the day before they had left for London altering them to fit Amelia's shorter height and smaller frame.

The gown she had chosen for tonight was ivory lace. It was simple and elegant, and Louisa had assured her that it would serve as a demure contrast to the daring gowns that were the current fashion.

Amelia washed and dressed, making sure to give Jane plenty of time to style her hair.

"That gown looks ever so nice on you, miss," Jane said as she pinned up Amelia's thick tresses. "Especially with this hair of yours. I wish my hair took the curl the way yours does."

Amelia had fretted over her hair for years, which curled naturally and fought staying in the practical chignon she usually wore. Now, as she studied herself in the mirror, she tried to see herself through Jane's eyes.

Jane had piled Amelia's hair into a tumble of curls at the top of her head, allowing a few loose strands to coil gently at her neck. It was a soft style that appealed to Amelia and matched the artistic simplicity of her gown perfectly.

"Jane," Amelia said. "You are a genius."

"Oh, no, miss," she answered, blushing furiously, obviously pleased at the compliment. "It is because your hair is such a wonder, 'tis all."

"And yet I can never recall my hair looking as fine as it does right now," Amelia said. "That is your doing."

"Thank you, miss."

The only thing Amelia lacked was jewels, though she cared little about that. It would be nice to be able to wear her mother's brooch at some point, and that was something she intended to remedy while in Town. She would locate a jeweler near the shops she and Lady Walmsley would be visiting and have him repair the brooch. Perhaps she would also look for a small, suitable gift for Anthony.

As it was, she would face the world unadorned. But thanks to Jane's work and Louisa's generosity, Amelia felt she could stand next to the members of the ton and not be looked upon poorly.

She rose from her seat in front of her dressing table and smoothed her skirt. It was time to join Lady Walmsley for dinner before Anthony arrived to take them to the theater.

* * *

Anthony ate dinner with Lucas at his club and then returned home to shave and dress. Once again he would be wearing clothes he'd purchased before he had bought his commission.

"You should have tried them on before you left for the solicitor's," Lucas lectured him. "You could have gotten one of the maids to alter them, you know."

"The waistband on the breeches is only a bit loose, is all. No one will be looking at me that closely," Anthony replied as he studied himself in the mirror. He had been physically fit before heading off to Spain and had gained muscle through his arms and shoulders while there but had lost weight in his midsection following his wound at Badajoz. "The curious onlookers will be more interested in Amelia."

"They will be interested in both of you," Lucas said. "The army captain who returned from the dead to become an earl and his middle-class fiancée."

"Once they get a glimpse of my 'middle-class fiancée,' as you so charmingly phrased it, they will be in awe and will forget all about me and whether my clothing fits properly."

Lucas picked up Anthony's tailcoat and helped him into it.

"It has been a long time since I was in Town, Lucas, and I dread the Marwoods of the world coming out in force, ready to cut Amelia down for a match she had no say in agreeing to. I would not have her suffer for my faults." He passed his hand over his eyes, tired suddenly.

"How are you sleeping these days?" Lucas asked, scrutinizing him closely. "Nightmares happening less? I have not heard you cry out lately."

"I am fine," Anthony replied. He still had nightmares, but lately he had only awakened with a start, not screaming his fool head off and causing Lucas to run to his assistance like an old nursemaid. "You do not need to sleep on the cot in my dressing room, you know, when you have got a perfectly good guest room to use."

"But the cot is such luxury when compared to Spanish soil."

"That is certainly true. But I am doing much better, Lucas, my friend, so you may worry less." He tugged his waistcoat down and shot his cuffs. "Now, I must be off. I have two lovely ladies to escort to the theater."

"Enjoy yourself, my lord," Lucas said, making a theatrical bow.

"Or," Anthony said, "I could wait for you to change and join us. I am sure Lady Walmsley would enjoy having a handsome escort."

"No," Lucas said emphatically. "Besides, I have an engagement of my own."

"Cards and brandy, is it?"

"Yes, actually, with some of our former army colleagues."

"Not nearly as exhilarating as the evening I am offering."

Lucas made a rude noise, and Anthony cracked a smile and headed to the door of his bedchamber.

"Wait," Lucas said. "You are forgetting the most important thing."

"Right." On his dressing table was a small box, a gift he had purchased for Amelia on his way home from the solicitors. He took the box from Lucas and put it in his pocket, then hurried outside, where the coach he had ordered ready awaited him.

Lady Walmsley's residence was one of the older, more distinguished ones in the city, not many blocks from Ashworth House. When the coachman pulled to a halt in front of it, Anthony took a deep breath before exiting and making his way to the door.

It was all very well and good to convince oneself events would go according to plan—and something altogether different for it to actually happen. He had selected the theater as Amelia's introduction to society because people would only be able to *look*, and conversations would be limited to intermission.

And, of course, they could leave at any time if things went awry.

There was always the chance something could go wrong, he thought as he approached the front door. He must be prepared for it and keep Amelia from harm as diligently as he could.

The butler opened the door and bowed, inviting him inside. "I shall inform the ladies you have arrived," he said, leaving Anthony in the entrance hall.

Anthony removed his hat and waited, tapping his fingers against his thigh. He stalked over to a painting that hung on the wall and studied it. He brushed invisible lint from the sleeve of his coat. The butler should have shown him to a parlor if the ladies were going to be so late—

"Lord Halford, how dashing you look!" Lady Walmsley's voice echoed through the chamber. She descended the stairs slowly, holding carefully to the banister.

Anthony hurried to her and assisted her down the remaining stairs, relieved to have something to do.

"Thank you, young man," she said, beaming up at him when they reached the bottom. "I have it on good authority that Amelia will be down shortly. Ah, there she is now."

Anthony looked up—and his heart stopped.

Amelia was wearing a creamy confection of lace that flattered her figure in ways her normal day dresses most emphatically did not. Her hair was piled in loose curls on her head, and Anthony wanted to take her hairpins out one by one and run each curl through his fingers and across his lips.

"Miss Clarke, you are a vision this evening," he said huskily. He took the stairs two at a time to offer her his assistance, his eyes never leaving her. "Allow me," he murmured, offering her his arm.

Amelia smiled radiantly up at him as she laid her gloved hand on his sleeve. She truly was a vision, with glowing skin and sparkling green eyes and full, soft lips that looked rosy and inviting. Anthony fought not to claim them there and then.

She wore no jewelry, and Anthony was glad he'd had the foresight to remedy the situation. The members of the ton would notice such things.

"I brought you a betrothal gift," he said.

Those huge green eyes of hers looked up at him in surprise.

"You did? Well, my opinion of you has risen once again," Lady Walmsley remarked.

He shot the elderly woman a quelling look, but she only cackled and moved to the far end of the hall, where she pretended to study the painting hanging there, the one he had been pretending to study earlier.

He removed the box from his pocket. "Would you care to open it now?" he asked, suddenly concerned the gift was not as impressive as it should have been.

"Yes, please." She took the box from his hands and opened it. "Oh," she breathed. "How beautiful! Thank you."

Lady Walmsley trotted back over to see what he had given Amelia. "Pearls!" she said, sounding put out. "You got her *pearls? They* will not impress anybody. Diamonds. Now, that would make a statement. Rubies, even, or emeralds. Honestly—"

"They are perfect," Amelia interjected. "I love them. Will you help me put them on?"

"It would be my pleasure," Anthony said.

Amelia turned to face the hallway mirror and took the necklace from the box. Anthony removed his gloves and turned to stand behind her. The necklace he had purchased was a single strand of pearls with a teardrop pendant and had matching ear bobs. He had wanted to give her something simple and exquisite, and when he had seen the pearls, he had thought them ideally suited for her. He slipped the necklace around her throat and fastened the clasp, his hands itching to stroke the tender skin at her nape.

She fastened the ear bobs in place and then turned to face him, her eyes luminous now. "I have never had such a lovely gift," she murmured.

"I will be the most envied man at the theater this evening," Anthony replied truthfully.

"But only if we actually *arrive* at the theater," Lady Walmsley said. "Our wraps, young man, if you please."

"Yes, my lady," Anthony said. Amelia bit her lip, trying not to laugh, and Anthony's gazed lingered there.

"Ahem!" Lady Walmsley said, tapping her foot impatiently.

"I am busy at the moment, madam," he said, keeping his eyes on Amelia and making her cheeks bloom a rosy pink.

The delicious moment passed, however, so Anthony helped each lady with her shawl and then assisted them into the carriage, taking the seat opposite.

It was time to escort his beautiful fiancée to her debut into London Society. And not for the first time, he found himself hoping they had done enough preparation to make a good showing this evening. He wanted Amelia to enjoy herself tonight.

But even if the evening went according to plan, he understood there were more battles to face before he could claim victory.

* * *

When the trio arrived at the Theatre Royal in Covent Garden, they did not encounter any crowds arriving or milling about.

"Where is everyone?" Amelia asked.

"They are inside the theater already, enjoying the performance. We have arrived late," Anthony said.

"But why are we late?" she asked him. "We are missing part of the play. I should think that would make it difficult to understand the plot."

"Because, my dear," Lady Walmsley replied before Anthony could respond, "the point tonight is for people to see *you*, not for you to see the play."

"Precisely," Anthony said. "I am afraid we are the actors most of the theatergoers will recall from tonight. And I would rather they see you from a distance first rather than have you face a crush as we make our way through the lobby. Shall we?"

He offered his arms to both ladies and led them through the elegant foyer, up the grand staircase, and down the hallway to the box held exclusively for the Marquess of Ashworth. The moment they were seated, Amelia felt hundreds of eyes turn in their direction. Across the theater, Amelia could see the Duchess of Marwood and Lady Elizabeth seated in a box, along with some others, though she could not see the duke, thank goodness.

She had difficulty concentrating on the performance, despite her best efforts. She felt too self-conscious, too aware that she was on deliberate display, to fully relax. Her eyes constantly wandered over the audience, trying to read the expressions of the people she saw who continually glanced in their direction.

Before she realized it, the first act had ended, and it was intermission. Anthony rose. "Would you ladies care to walk?" he asked.

"Not me," Lady Walmsley said. "My legs have decided they are content where they are. If any of my friends wish to greet me, they may do so here."

"Amelia?" he asked.

She must face the *beau monde* sooner or later, so she stood. "I suppose my reputation will not be helped if I cower here."

He smiled at her, obviously pleased by her answer. "We shall face the dragons together, then."

They had no sooner left the box when Lord Cantwell and some of his friends greeted them. "Tony!" the earl said, shaking Anthony's hand vigorously. "I have already told these gentleman you are betrothed to the lovely lady they spotted in your box with you. Miss Clarke, how exquisite you look this evening." He bowed over her hand before introducing his friends to her.

"Unfair, Halford, for you to snatch up such a charming creature before she could be presented to any of us," one of the gentlemen, who gazed at Amelia through his quizzing glass, drawled.

"My thoughts exactly," another gentleman said. "Charming, indeed."

Amelia had never flirted before; it would have been unseemly as a vicar's daughter *and* as a companion, but she had learned to deal diplomatically with a few of the more ardent men of Little Brenchley. "Such flattery, gentlemen, and in front of Lord Halford, no less," she said. "I wonder that you esteem your lives so lightly."

The men laughed in response and then began asking Anthony about his return from Spain, so Amelia allowed herself to relax. It seemed Anthony's friends were here in support and not in judgment.

As they bid farewell to the gentlemen and began to return to their box, however, the Duchess of Marwood walked down the hallway toward them with several other ladies. Amelia braced herself for a confrontation, but instead, the Duchess paused briefly, looked directly into Amelia's eyes, and then turned away from her, the other ladies following suit.

She had been given the cut direct, and because it had been by a duchess, it was damage that would be difficult to overcome.

She felt Anthony's arm tense beneath her hand. "Come," he whispered. "Do not trouble yourself over the Duchess of Marwood, my dear, or her friends. They are only a few of many, and our efforts are only beginning."

She returned with him to their box, where they found Lady Walmsley chatting with Lady Elizabeth, who stood as soon as they arrived.

"I heard," Lady Walmsley said in an ominous tone. "Lady Elizabeth has told me what happened."

"I am sorry, Amelia," Lady Elizabeth said, looking breathtakingly lovely in pale-blue satin. "I cannot seem to make my parents see reason."

"It was not your doing," Amelia said.

"They hold much influence," Lady Walmsley said, "but are not invincible."

"I must go now," Lady Elizabeth said. "Mama will be looking for me. I only wanted to offer what little support I can."

Amelia took her hands in her own. "I do not blame you. I consider us friends."

Lady Elizabeth smiled at her and then was gone.

Amelia sat through the second act, wondering if all their efforts would be worth it. Lord and Lady Ashworth—oh, and Anthony too—had been adamant that they must remain betrothed long enough to protect Amelia from harm and, she was certain, ensure that Anthony was regarded as a nobleman of the highest character.

And at the end of their betrothal? What then? What would she do? The truth was she did not know. She would not be able to return to Lady Ashworth's employ. She could not bear to see Anthony with a wife and children while she herself sat silently in the corner, longing for what might have been.

And yet for at least two months she must be betrothed to him. Two precious months. She would simply cherish every moment they shared and store the memories against a lifetime of loneliness.

Chapter 12

The following morning, Amelia and Lady Walmsley, with Jane and a footman in tow, proceeded to Oxford Street. Amelia had reservations about the money being spent on a wardrobe for her when she would inevitably be a paid companion once again, but Lady Walmsley hadn't tolerated her protests.

"Foolishness," the lady had said. "Trust me when I tell you the money that will be spent is a mere pittance when compared to the income of the Ashworths. Do not let Halford's time in the army lead you to conclude he is not wealthy in his own right."

And so here they were at Madame Veronique's, the madame herself clucking and fretting over Amelia, who stood on a small platform in one of the dressing rooms, wearing only her chemise as one of the seamstresses measured her, while Jane looked on in wonder.

Lady Walmsley had settled herself into a comfortable-looking chair in the front of the shop, and when Amelia had left her, the lady had been sipping contentedly from a cup of tea and reviewing fashion plates.

When Madame was *certainement* that the seamstress had every measurement correct, Amelia was allowed to dress and return to Lady Walmsley. Anthony had arrived while she was being measured and was studying the plates along with Lady Walmsley. Amelia hadn't expected him this morning, and seeing him here set her heart racing nervously.

He rose when he saw her and crossed the room to kiss her hand.

"What are you doing here?" she asked.

"If I have an opportunity to help choose the wardrobe for my future wife, do you think I would forgo such a pleasure?" he said.

"Yes, quite frankly, I do," she replied.

His mouth twitched upward.

"Ah, mademoiselle, but no," Madame Veronique said. "Many a gentlemen, they wish to see their—how you say?—sweetheart looking so beautiful for their eyes. Ees true."

"Ees true," Anthony echoed, subtly using Madame's accent.

Amelia rolled her eyes. Madame was about as French as Amelia was.

Madame Veronique did not seem to notice Anthony's comment. Of course, considering the amount of money he would be spending here today, Amelia was not at all surprised.

They spent the next hour deciding on dress styles and fabrics—Anthony insisting on a deep green velvet for one of her ball gowns—before deciding they were through and it was time to visit the next shop.

"Madame," Anthony said. "You have been all that is helpful today. I would ask one more favor of you, however."

"But of course," the modiste replied, her eyelids fluttering like twin butterflies. "Anything you say, monsieur. I am only so happy to do it."

"My fiancée is in need of some gowns rather quickly. Is there anything you can do—"

Madame Veronique held up her hand. "Say no more, monsieur. Claire, Marie!" she called, and two seamstresses came running from the back room. "Mrs. Hardwicke's new gown, the blue one. And the peach-colored muslin as well."

"Yes, Madame," the girls said, scurrying off again.

"It will be no problem," Madame said, waving off Amelia's attempt to protest. "The blue looks terrible on her, but I could not convince her otherwise. I will find something she will love, and she will not remember the blue. The peach will be ready later this afternoon, the gold tomorrow. The rest of mademoiselle's clothes will be ready next week. Will that do?"

"Yes, thank you, it will."

"Anything for you, monsieur, the great hero who defied death."

A muscle twitched in Anthony's cheek at the modiste's words.

"Quite," he said. He turned to Amelia. "Are you ready, my dear? Lady Walmsley?"

Both ladies recognized their cue. Anthony offered Madame Veronique a proper bow, and they left the premises.

Despite his efforts to appear otherwise, Amelia knew Anthony still suffered from his experiences in Spain. If she could do nothing else, she would help him heal before she released him from their betrothal.

* * *

Anthony excused himself from the ladies once they left Madame Veronique's shop. "I have business to attend to that requires I leave you both briefly," he said, "but I shall join you at Gunter's later for tea—and for ices, if you are inclined to try one, Amelia."

"Oh, yes!" she exclaimed. She had heard of Gunter's famous ices, and so she was more than inclined—she was thrilled.

Lady Walmsley, despite her years, was a lively companion who seemed to take delight in showing Amelia all the finery available for purchase in London. She also seemed to think that Amelia needed it all. Amelia quickly found herself the owner of new bonnets, a variety of gloves, and stockings—both silk and practical cotton ones—as well as undergarments made of the most delicate lawn Amelia had ever touched.

They had only to shop for slippers and halfboots, and Lady Walmsley hadn't so much as yawned. Amelia, on the other hand, was beginning to wilt. "Perhaps," she ventured, "we can shop for slippers tomorrow."

"No such thing," Lady Walmsley said. "I am home for visitors tomorrow. You must be there too since you will be the main attraction."

Amelia sighed. Gunter's ices could not come too soon for her.

After purchasing the footwear Lady Walmsley insisted Amelia have, they sent poor Jane and the footman home in the carriage, with Amelia's many parcels stowed within.

When they were nearly to Gunter's, Amelia noticed a jeweler's shop. "Lady Walmsley," she said. "I have one more stop I would like to make. Perhaps I can meet you at Gunter's afterward, if you do not mind." She wanted to buy a gift for Anthony and preferred that it be kept between her and Anthony only.

"I believe my feet could use a rest," she said, her eyes twinkling. She had noticed the jeweler's as well and had undoubtedly figured out Amelia's intentions. "I shall wait at Gunter's for you, then."

Relieved to get her way with Lady Walmsley so easily for once, Amelia hurried to the shop, a place called Phillips.

"Good day," the jeweler said, looking up from the piece he was working on. "How may I assist you?"

"I would like to buy a gift for a gentleman," she said. "My fiancé, to be precise," she added when the man, whom she presumed was Mr. Phillips, looked askance at her.

"Ah," he said, seemingly unconvinced.

Begin as you mean to go. She stood straight and raised her chin slightly, in order to look as dignified as possible. "The gentleman in question deserves something very fine, and yet I have limited funds and must rely upon you for guidance."

He studied her carefully over his spectacles and must have finally approved of what he saw, for he nodded and gestured to a glass case at the end of the counter. "Perhaps a watch fob would suit his tastes."

"Thank you." Amelia moved to the end of the counter and studied the items in the case. There was one fob in particular she was drawn to, made of carved gold and inset with a smooth, oval stone of rich blue. "How much is that one?" she asked, pointing to it.

"Ah, the lapis. A very nice choice." He told her the price, and she blanched. She had obviously entered a world in which she had no concept of expense, especially since Anthony had insisted that the bills for her wardrobe be sent directly to him. Lady Walmsley had simply waved her hand as if shooing the idea of cost away when Amelia had questioned her about it.

"Perhaps not," she said, suddenly feeling discouraged. "In the meantime, I wonder if you can help me with another matter. I have a brooch with a broken clasp and would dearly love to have it fixed." She opened her reticule and drew the brooch out, setting it carefully on the counter.

The man gasped. "Where did you get this?" he demanded.

His reaction was strange, Amelia thought. "It belonged to my mother," she said.

"And who was she?" he asked. "This work is highly unusual." He picked up the magnifying glass from his worktable behind him and studied the brooch intently.

"She was the wife of a vicar," Amelia replied. The words sounded demeaning to her mother, who was much more than that in Amelia's eyes. "I imagine it was a gift from my father."

"From a vicar?" The jeweler shook his head. "Not likely. And, yes, I can fix the clasp." He picked up the brooch as though it were a religious relic. "It would be my honor to do so."

He obviously saw something unusual about the piece, but Amelia could not imagine what, even with all the sentiment she attached to it.

"I think we can come to an arrangement regarding the fob too, Miss . . ."

"Clarke," she replied, thoroughly confused now. "And thank you." She handed over the banknotes she had brought with her, barely half the amount the man had quoted to her for the fob.

"Paid in full," he said as he put the money in his cashbox and then removed the watch fob from the case. "The brooch will be ready for you tomorrow afternoon," he said. "May I have it delivered to your place of residence?"

"I am a guest of Lady Walmsley," she said.

"Very good. I shall have both items delivered tomorrow, if that pleases you. Would you care to have the fob engraved with a monogram?"

"Oh, I couldn't, surely," she said, surprised by his offer. She was already paying half the price for it.

"It would be my pleasure," the jeweler said. "A single initial, perhaps?"

He seemed earnest, so Amelia thought through the options. She could have an *H* engraved, for Hargreaves or Halford, but Anthony was to be Ashworth one day, and it was the initial for his Christian name as well. "Perhaps an *A*, then. And thank you again."

"It has been my pleasure, ma'am," he said.

Amelia exited the shop and walked toward Gunter's, surprised by her good fortune and hopeful that Anthony would be pleased by her gift.

* * *

By the end of the week, Anthony was ready to quit London and return to Ashworth Park. Not that every minute in Town had been unpleasant. He had relished seeing Amelia in her new gowns and showing her the sights. But his regular bachelor haunts were just that: haunts.

Everywhere he went, whether he was visiting his boot maker or inspecting the latest crop of thoroughbreds at Tattersalls, he was invariably met by old friends and acquaintances, all of whom had heard he had died and were bluntly curious to learn of his miraculous return. And this invariably led to questions about his experiences on the Peninsula.

Dealing with the barrage of questions and the backslaps and jovial comments left Anthony frustrated and angry. Was he the only person in all of England who had survived battle? Of course not. Yet everyone treated him like some sort of paragon, like a hero.

He did not feel like a hero.

His only respite this week had been in Amelia's company. Before leaving for London, Anthony had met with his mother and sister and set out the plan for introducing Amelia to society, the general consensus being that he carefully select when and where to take her. Eventually the gossips would see what a lovely, serene young lady she was and the scandal surrounding the betrothal would fade, with other on dits taking its place.

As a result, Anthony had escorted Amelia to the theater, Gunter's, Hyde Park, and a few small dinner parties. These had given her the visibility she needed at present.

He intended to go to Doctors Commons today to obtain a special marriage license. Tonight he was escorting Amelia and Lady Walmsley to Vauxhall Gardens, and the day after tomorrow he and Amelia would return to Ashworth Park. Lady Walmsley intended to remain in London until the wedding took place, at which time she would arrive at Ashworth Park with all the other guests.

He tipped his chin up so he could spread lather more easily on his neck. "I have decided we are returning home day after tomorrow," he said.

Lucas rested a hip on the edge of the washstand. "You are always the most chatty when you have a deadly instrument in your hands," he observed.

"I wonder," Anthony said, deftly finishing his task and rubbing a towel over his face, "why you persist in hovering when I am clearly no longer an invalid. You ought to be relieved, you know, since you must be anxious to return to your own family."

Lucas studied his own image in the looking glass. "I will return home soon, but not quite yet."

"As you wish. What do you suppose we will learn from Swindlehurst's man when he returns from Kent?" Anthony asked. "I find it extremely odd that Amelia has no family to speak of on either her mother's or her father's side. There must be someone. Speak up, man," he said when Lucas still did not reply.

"My family do not need me at present," Lucas said, ignoring Anthony's question about Swindlehurst. "And I am content to remain here for the time being—unless you would care to explain to a valet you have yet to hire about your nightmares and bouts of nausea. You would do well to warn Miss Clarke too before the nuptials take place."

"I do not foresee that as a problem," Anthony said. "The lady has already seen me indisposed."

Lucas's eyebrows rose in question. "Indisposed, eh? And she did not run screaming for the hills? Very brave of her."

"Indeed."

Lucas grew serious. "If you are to rid yourself of your ghosts, Tony, you must first come to terms with certain truths. Truths I have told you before."

"Please share."

"Certainly." Lucas ignored Anthony's tone. "As the fourth son of a viscount, I was clearly made to understand I must be responsible for myself—

finding a suitable career and income. I was not to depend on my father for anything beyond the barest of essentials, except in extreme circumstances. Owing to the fact that my father had five sons and three daughters, I understood what he was saying.

"You, on the other hand, were the spare to your brother, the heir. You would have understood that you had to be ready to act," Lucas said, "despite your loathing to do so. You were reared with the understanding that you were responsible for the welfare of others. It is what made you a good captain, Tony, and why your men respected you as they did."

"Not all of my men." Anthony had a scar to prove that. "Your attempt to explain your theory is failing miserably, and I grow tired of trying to make sense of it."

"I mean only this: that I was responsible for myself and my own actions. There were no expectations of anything beyond that, and that is what I did—other than save your pathetic hide once you were wounded.

"But you felt responsible for everyone's personal actions besides your own. I daresay you felt responsible for more than that, considering your upbringing. So when things went horribly wrong and you saw those under your command dying or, worse, doing egregious, dishonorable things, you naturally thought *you* had allowed them to occur and felt powerless as a result. Your own near death did not serve to help any of this either. You were in a bad way for a while, you know."

"Pray, tell me, Dr. Jennings," Anthony said, irritated. "How am I to overcome these things? Have you a remedy? An elixir, perhaps?"

"Of course I don't," Lucas said softly. "I only wish to heaven I did."

His reply took the wind out of Anthony's sails, and he sank deeper into his chair, running his hand behind his neck to rub the tight muscles there.

"But if I could offer anything along those lines," Lucas said, "it would be that you begin by finding a way to forgive yourself."

"For what?" Anthony asked.

Lucas smiled wistfully. "You are the one who must figure that out."

Chapter 13

THE FOLLOWING MORNING, A BOY arrived at Ashworth House with a letter from Swindlehurst, which Anthony read immediately. It stated that Swindlehurst's investigator had returned from Kent and asked Lord Halford to suggest a time when they could call on him.

Anthony wrote a quick response, saying he would meet Swindlehurst at his office at eleven o'clock, and sent it back with the boy, tossing him a half crown for his efforts. Anthony had a piece of business he wanted to attend to first thing, and it would be more convenient if he spoke to Swindlehurst and his man there.

His first item of business was to place the announcement of his betrothal to Amelia in the newspaper. It was not necessarily a commonplace thing to do, although the society writers for the paper frequently included such information in their columns. For Anthony to place his own announcement, however, was a way to ensure the correct information was disseminated amongst the ton and would also serve to reinforce the Hargreaves family's acceptance of Amelia into their midst.

Anthony arrived at Swindlehurst's office promptly at eleven. Marlowe, Swindlehurst's assistant, showed Anthony straight into the solicitor's private office.

"Come in, my lord," Swindlehurst said. Another man, whom Anthony presumed to be the investigator, rose from his chair when Anthony came into the room and shook his hand. "John Abbott at your service, my lord," the man said.

"Mr. Abbott," Anthony replied. "Your reputation precedes you."

"Thank you, my lord."

When both men were seated, formalities out of the way, Anthony asked bluntly, "What have you to tell me, Mr. Abbott? Good news from Little Brenchley, I hope."

"Interesting news to be sure, my lord." Abbott was a lean and wiry man, roughly forty years of age, with a neat mustache and dark, intelligent eyes. "As you have already been informed, Miss Clarke's surname is not Clarke, but Clarke-Hammond."

"Edmund Clarke-Hammond being her father," Anthony said.

"Correct. The vicar of Little Brenchley and son of John Clarke-Hammond, Viscount Winfield of Somerset," Abbott said. "I have the documents in hand from Kent to confirm this."

Excellent, Anthony thought. "And what of his wife?"

"Maiden name of Sarah Rigby, as Swindlehurst will have told you," Abbott said. "The older residents of Little Brenchley recall her beautiful singing voice. She performed frequently at church—until her illness and death, that is. Took quite a toll on the vicar and their daughter, from what I understand."

"And her family?" Anthony asked.

"Well," Abbott said. "I happened on one woman who was a particular friend of the former Sarah Rigby. She told me Miss Rigby's mother was a seamstress and her father a coal miner until the black lung made him too ill to work; they are both now deceased. It makes one wonder," Abbott mused, "how the daughter of a coal miner and the son of a viscount could have met, let alone married."

"Similar occurrences have been known to happen," Anthony said wryly. "My own situation, for example. I presume you plan to uncover the details of their marriage with some alacrity," Anthony said.

"Quite so," Abbott replied. "In fact, as soon as we are finished here, I am bound for Somerset."

"Learn what you can there," Anthony said, "but do not speak directly to the Clarke-Hammonds. I would prefer to handle that myself, if and when the time is right."

"Understood, my lord." Abbott rose from his chair. "Discretion is always uppermost in my mind." He tipped his hat and was gone.

Based on what Abbott had said, Anthony doubted there was much of any family on the Rigby side, not if her grandparents were already dead. And on her father's side? That connection would need more finessing than Anthony had time to provide at present.

When Abbot was gone, Swindlehurst sat back in his chair. "Brandy, Halford?" he asked.

"No, thank you."

"Are you sure?" He rose and took up the decanter on a tray behind him, splashing a modest amount of amber liquid into a glass for himself. "You just learned that the woman you are to wed is the granddaughter of a coal miner and a seamstress."

"And a viscount," Anthony added.

"Do you think it will be enough to appease the critics?" Swindlehurst asked, taking a sip of his drink.

"It will have to be," Anthony said. "I cannot and will not jilt Miss Clarke, or Clarke-Hammond, as the case may be. It will be up to her to cry off, if it is to happen at all."

If she knew her nights would be disturbed by his thrashing and bellowing and her days spent dealing with his somber moods and self-recriminations, would she cry off? Anthony realized more and more that he did not want her to end the betrothal once the scandal had passed, even for all that he thought it would be in her best interest.

Lucas had suggested that Anthony would benefit by forgiving himself.

How could he possibly do this when he had no idea how to begin or if he deserved forgiveness at all? How did one rid oneself of the ghostly faces, the gunfire, and the screams of agony and despair that were always there in his mind?

He stood. "I will be leaving for Ashworth Park soon. I presume you will keep me informed of any updates in the investigation."

"Certainly," Swindlehurst said. "Good-bye, my lord, and many felicitations on your upcoming marriage."

Anthony nodded and left, striding past Marlowe in the outer office. He leaped into his curricle and grabbed the reins from his surprised groom. He flicked his whip, and the horses sprang into action. How, he thought, pain cutting through his chest, every bit as raw as the wound he had taken at Badajoz, could he bind Amelia to him in his broken state? He craved her practicality and kindness, longed for her softness and the sensation of her in his arms, but what did he have to offer her? Not much, if he was honest. The security of his home and income. Affection. Children.

She deserved someone who could give her his whole heart, something Anthony was unsure he could ever do, as hollow as he often felt inside. Could he be so selfish as to wed her anyway?

He was afraid he could. And the thought grieved him at the same time it offered him a perverse kind of solace.

***

Anthony arrived home from Swindlehurst's office, handing his curricle over to his groom and instructing him to get Bucephalus and another mount ready. Then he strode into the house, barely giving the butler, Gibbs, time to move out of the way after opening the door.

He tossed his hat and gloves onto the table in the front hall and took the stairs two at a time, not stopping until he located Lucas reading in one of the sitting rooms. "Change your clothes," Anthony said. "We are going riding in Hyde Park. And I refuse to hear that you do not have suitable riding clothes you can be seen wearing in public. I happen to know you have organized a decent wardrobe for yourself, despite the limited amount of time we have been in London."

"Of course I have," Lucas said, setting his book aside, not perturbed in the least by Anthony's tone. "I have always known that sooner or later I needed to resume my role as a viscount's son. May I ask why we are suddenly to be trotting about the park?"

"Because I need to ride, devil take it, and there is nowhere else to do it but there, despite the people who will be thronging the place at this hour to see and be seen. I need you along to smile at all and sundry and deflect any attempts at conversation away from me."

"I see," Lucas said.

Pronouncement made, Anthony stalked off to his bedchamber, where he jerked his coat off and began unbuttoning his waistcoat. He paced to his wardrobe and yanked it open. "Riding breeches. Where are they?"

Lucas leaned against the doorjamb and watched. "Most likely where they always are when they are not on your body."

Anthony ignored Lucas and sat on the bed to tug off his boots. Lucas walked over and grabbed a heel and pulled.

"Maybe you'd like to explain what has happened?" he asked.

"Nothing has happened. Nothing bad anyway," Anthony said, tugging his shirt off from over his head.

"Because you *always* act like this when something good happens," Lucas said wryly. "Unlike most people, who tend to smile in those instances."

Anthony glared at him. "You are neither my doctor nor my confessor."

"True," Lucas replied. "I am merely your friend."

"Then, as my friend, come riding with me, and let the rest of it go for now."

By the time they dressed and went downstairs, both horses were waiting for them. They mounted and turned in the direction of Hyde Park.

Anthony could sense Bucephalus's energy beneath him, and he patted the horse's neck. "Just a few more minutes, old fellow, and we'll be there." He longed for a gallop so the wind in his face would set his memories free and clear away his guilt. Hyde Park was large and was maintained with a rural aspect, including dense woods in areas, and was sufficient for a good run in the early hours of the morning. Unfortunately this afternoon he would be limited to riding Bucephalus at a sedate pace, but it was better than nothing.

It was the height of the social hour by the time he and Lucas arrived, and Hyde Park was teeming with people. Anthony put a hand to his eyes to shield them from the afternoon sun and gazed out over the swirling mass of humanity before him. Ladies strolled together, followed discreetly by their maids; matrons rolled along in their open landaus; gentlemen rode by on horseback or in their curricles.

Anthony was not in the mood for any of it. "This way," he said to Lucas, veering off in a less-populated direction. "Unless you'd rather remain here and chat."

"I may do just that," Lucas said, bringing his mount abreast with Bucephalus. "I might find more congenial company if I did, considering the mood you are in. But I am nothing if not loyal." He urged his mount ahead of Bucephalus.

Rotten Row had few people on it, so against the rules for the time of day, Anthony allowed Bucephalus to move into a canter, leaving Lucas behind. The steady rhythm of the horse beneath him took the edge off the guilt and helplessness he felt.

Eventually he brought Bucephalus to a walk, then he and Lucas proceeded toward the gate they had originally entered. He managed to tip his hat to a few ladies without having to engage in conversation, and Lucas deftly interceded with those who did not take the hint from Anthony's polite but distant responses.

They were nearing the gate when a couple of Anthony's friends from university hailed him. He and Lucas rode toward them, both men dismounting when they reached the group. Anthony shook hands with each of them and introduced Lucas, referring to him as his nursemaid, making them all laugh.

"I am not at all surprised," Hugh Wallingham said, "considering the fact that at last report you were dead."

"I am entirely responsible for the life and health of the current Earl of Halford," Lucas said with a wink. "As I remind him daily."

The men laughed again. "But seriously, Tony," Sir Richard Egan said, "what happened to you over there?"

Anthony glanced at Lucas and then said, "It is as Lucas told you. I was wounded, and he managed to find a willing Spanish lady to assist in my recovery. He saved my life."

Anthony's words elicited an array of congratulatory backslaps, particularly addressed to Lucas's person, which Anthony personally enjoyed watching—until one member of the group asked Anthony in a hushed tone, "Just how willing was she?" The guilt and frustration Anthony had worked to alleviate this afternoon flooded back at the insensitive question.

"Bad form, Freddie," one of the men murmured.

Lucas shot Anthony a speaking glance, but Anthony had had enough. These young men were noblemen who had chosen not to fight—and had had every right not to, considering their responsibilities to their families—but for one of them to make light of the people suffering at the hands of Napoleon or the armies that laid waste to their homelands, whether in conquest or defense, was intolerable.

"Señora Bartolo," he said in a low voice that carried weight nonetheless, "watched in horror as her city underwent a lengthy siege and the bloodiest battle imaginable, followed by a thorough pillaging at the hands of the so-called rescuers. That she was 'willing' to assist at all is a blessing for which I am daily thankful." He looked at Lucas. "Would you care to add anything?"

"Yes, Captain," he said, using Anthony's former rank to make a point. "I was grateful to find somewhere in the city where you could be treated for your wounds, considering the number of casualties there were. Resources were greatly strained at the time. And I doubt you would have survived had I been obliged to remove you from the city."

"And thus you see," Anthony said, "I have returned from near death, owing to the grace of the Almighty, and am able to converse with you gentlemen on this lovely afternoon in Hyde Park." He nodded to the group and turned to mount Bucephalus.

"Tony," Hugh said, stopping Anthony and causing him to turn. "Well done, the both of you. I hope we can meet up one day soon."

"Thank you, Hugh. Likewise." He appreciated his friend attempting to make amends for what had been said, although Anthony was still seething.

He moved to Bucephalus's side and was preparing to mount when he noticed a familiar person walking alone a short distance off, a maid and a footman trailing behind.

"Watch my horse," he said to Lucas and hurried off toward the person in question.

"What are you doing here in the park by yourself?" he said to Amelia when he reached her side, his heart pounding in his throat.

She had been caught off-guard by his abrupt appearance and cast startled green eyes at him. "What do you mean by myself? Jane and Harold are with me." She turned her head to look at them, and Anthony saw Jane give a small wave.

"I mean," Anthony said, striving to control himself when he thought he might be violently sick at the moment, "without Lady Walmsley or me accompanying you. We are trying to introduce you to society gradually, and when you go off on your own like this, there is no way for us to prepare for the unexpected. This is London, not the country."

"I do not believe I did anything wrong," Amelia said. "I have a maid and a footman with me, as you can clearly see."

He glanced at Jane and the burly youth dressed in livery who was presently scuffing his feet in the dirt and looking self-consciously about.

Anthony knew he was behaving irrationally, but at present all he could think about were cutthroats lurking on London side streets, unsavory characters easily spotting an innocent from the country, new to Town and its dangers. He refused to consider the fact that having Lady Walmsley with her would have done nothing to protect her from those unsavory types. "You are new to Town," Anthony said, realizing his tone was a little too much like the one he had used on new enlistees, "and would be better served to have a more experienced escort with you until you have been here awhile."

"I am a person who has reached her full majority," Amelia said, matching his tone, "and I have been used to walking around Little Brenchley and Ashworthy unattended. Lady Walmsley wished to rest, and I needed fresh air. It is as simple as that, my lord."

Ah. The fact that she had referred to him as "my lord" showed exactly how perturbed she was with him. Well, he was irritated with her and her . . . independence, especially considering she was in a large and strange city, where anything could happen.

"Walk with me, if you please," he said.

He offered his arm to Amelia, which she reluctantly took, and then he escorted her toward a wooded area of the park not too far off at a pace a little too fast for fashion. Jane, he saw, was wringing her hands.

Amelia noticed too. "Jane," she called, pointing. "There is a bench where you may rest yourself. Lord Halford wishes to show me something." She turned back to Anthony. "The poor girl has no experience whatsoever on her own in Town either, and yet you are not overly concerned about her."

"I am not betrothed to her!" Anthony exclaimed, then rubbed the back of his neck with his hand and lowered his voice. "You are quite correct. But the footman will watch over her, and Lucas is nearby. That is not the point, however."

They entered the wooded area and were soon hidden from view.

"What is the point, then?" she cried. "I am able to care for myself, you know. I took care of my mother and then my father when they became ill, and I had no one to help me. And yet I survived and have even thrived."

Her face was flushed, and her chest was heaving from her passionate response, and Anthony reached his limit. "*This* is the point." He pulled her to him, encircling her waist with one hand, clutching the fabric at her back in a firm grip, and with his free hand, he yanked at the ribbon of her new frilly bonnet and tore it from her head. Then he crushed his mouth to hers.

She gasped, seeking air, but as soon as she filled her lungs, his mouth returned to hers, softening his kiss now, seeking to learn the contour of her lips. He threaded his fingers into her rich, auburn hair and held the back of her head so he could keep her close and direct the movement of his lips over hers.

Her hands sought his chest, a weak attempt to control the fire that had erupted between them. Her touch only made Anthony's heart beat faster, however, and he fought his own battle to control the flames. Somewhere in the back of his mind he was aware that the rest of the world was not far away, that he had already compromised Amelia once, forcing a betrothal, but it was a struggle, especially when her hands crept to his shoulders and Anthony felt her fingers in the hair at the nape of his neck.

Drawing upon all the strength of character he could find, he took a deep breath and moved his hands to her shoulders, taking a step back before resting his forehead against hers and working to regain his composure. "That is the point, Amelia," he whispered. "I desire you, and I am not the only man who would if given half a chance."

He shook his head, realizing he was making a hash out of what he was trying to say, struggling to get his thundering heart under control. "You are wonderfully capable and independent, and you are right; you have flourished despite the circumstances life has given you. In that regard, you are different from every debutante who will grace the ballrooms of the ton this Season. It is what will draw people, men in particular, to you." He retrieved her bonnet, which had fallen to the ground, and ran the ribbons through his fingers. "I am afraid I am not altogether rational at present when it comes to men's attentions to the gentler sex."

She cupped his face in her hands. "I am not quite the sheltered miss you think I am," she said. "Little Brenchley may not be London, but the daughter of a vicar is privy to more of the struggles of life than you might think. You needn't worry so."

"And yet I do worry. I feel responsible."

She dropped her hands and moved back, and Anthony wanted to draw her into his arms again. It was too late, though, if the resigned, determined look he saw on her face was any indication.

"It seems to me," she said, "that perhaps too many responsibilities were thrust on you too quickly since you arrived home. I can help you with that."

Anthony's stomach knotted, knowing what her next words would be. She clasped her hands firmly together in front of her. "I am a nobody from nowhere—"

"Not true," he interrupted. "Your father was the son of a viscount. Winfield, to be precise."

Her face blanched at his announcement, and he regretted his impulsive words. This was not the time or place to tell her he had looked into her family connections, but it was too late now. He was seven times a fool.

"I am nobody from nowhere," she repeated firmly. "No one will notice me, nor will I be missed when I am gone. And *you*," her voice cracked on the word, "do not need to feel responsible, at least in regard to me. I would not do that to you. Therefore, I absolve you of your responsibility and of the betrothal you offered when circumstances seemed to require it. Thank you for your concern over my welfare. And now please excuse me; it is time for me to return to Lady Walmsley, lest she worry as well. Good day."

She turned on her heel and strode, back straight, toward Jane, who quickly gathered her things and trotted after her. Anthony watched until he could no longer see Amelia in the crowd of people before returning to claim Bucephalus from the footman.

"Don't ask, if you know what's good for you," he said to Lucas, who stood by with an inquiring look on his face.

She was strong and brave; she was his Amelia. But if she thought she was no longer betrothed to him, she was mistaken, and he would set her straight soon enough. The scandal was too recent for them to be out of trouble yet, and he refused to leave her on her own until he could be sure her reputation was sound.

He could still feel the warmth of her hands on his face.

***

Amelia was still upset when she reached Lady Walmsley's house. How could he kiss her like that, with so much passion, and then claim he worried about her because he felt responsible?

She hurried up to her room before she broke down in tears right there in the front hall. Responsible. That had been what hurt the most. The kisses were merely the product of a man's attraction to a woman, that was all. He had said other men would be attracted as well and he must protect her from their worldly, pleasure-seeking pursuits. Because he was *responsible*.

She had thought his kisses meant something more. She had been wrong.

She didn't even want to think about the *other* thing he had said, that her grandfather was a viscount. Winfield, Anthony had called him. Oh yes, although her heart had been breaking, she had heard the name and remembered it.

Tears threatening again, she brushed her hand across her eyes, refusing to give in to the raw emotions she was feeling, before sitting down at her dressing table.

She opened the side drawer and removed one of the two boxes there. The box that remained in the drawer held her mother's brooch, now repaired and ready to be worn, along with her father's watch and the third-place ribbon.

She opened the lid on the box she held in her hand. Inside was the watch fob she had purchased for Anthony. She had chosen it with gratitude, true, but also with affection—no, with love. She loved him.

She had known better, so the way she felt now was her own fault. She had never aspired to be anything other than who she was, but the handsome, troubled Earl of Halford had touched her heart from the very first. Despite her best efforts, she had fallen for him. And she had thought he'd at least cared for her too, which was why she still had difficulty believing the intensity of his kisses resulted from an indifferent attraction and a sense of responsibility.

She removed the fob from the box and ran a finger over the engraved initial *A* before returning it to the box and putting it back in the drawer.

Since it was engraved, she doubted the jeweler would be willing to take it back, but Amelia did not think she could bear to keep it.

Perhaps she would leave it with Lady Ashworth when she left Ashworth Park and her employment, after she returned there to retrieve her personal belongings. The marchioness could give it to her husband or her son, whomever she wished.

Amelia would not care.

At least that was what she told herself as she curled up on her bed and willed herself to sleep.

* * *

It was dusk when Amelia awoke. Her eyes felt gritty, and her heart ached. Lady Walmsley would be wondering what had happened to her.

She rose from her bed and splashed cool water on her face before inspecting her appearance in the mirror at her dressing table. Her eyes were puffy, but there was nothing she could do about that. She changed for dinner and tidied her hair. When Amelia decided she looked as good as she was going to, she descended the stairs in search of Lady Walmsley.

"There you are, dear," the lady said when Amelia entered the parlor the butler had indicated. "You must have been dreadfully tired! And that is exactly what I told Lord Halford when he showed up on my doorstep earlier. 'She is sleeping,' said I, 'and I would not awaken her if you were the Prince Regent himself.' But you do not seem well, Amelia, even after your long rest." She patted the cushion next to her on the sofa. "Are you ill? Shall I send for the doctor?"

"I am not ill," Amelia said, smiling to reassure her, although it was a meager attempt at best. "But I am afraid I do have bad news. Lord Halford and I—"

"Say no more," Lady Walmsley said. "I know all about it. Halford explained that the two of you had a disagreement and he wished to make amends to his betrothed."

"But that is exactly it. I am not—"

"Tut, tut, my dear," Lady Walmsley said, taking Amelia's hand in her two wrinkly ones and patting it gently. "Every betrothed couple has their little disagreements. It prepares them for the big ones once they marry."

"He is not my betrothed," Amelia said gently but firmly. "We disagreed, yes, but the nature of the disagreement made it clear that we cannot marry." The pain she felt saying the words aloud was a horrible, oppressive weight. She had expected to feel relief at freeing him from the betrothal.

Lady Walmsley looked at her sorrowfully. "I refuse to believe it. Anyone looking at either of you would know it to be a love match. Surely this little misunderstanding will pass and all will be well tomorrow."

Amelia shook her head. "I think not, Lady Walmsley. He would marry me out of a sense of responsibility, and he has too many of those already. I cannot hold him to the betrothal. It is his duty to find the most suitable match for the heir to the Marquess of Ashworth. The daughter of a vicar is not that person." She did not mention what Anthony had told her earlier, that her father had been the son of a viscount and that she was, therefore, a viscount's granddaughter. She had never had a relationship with the man, and she was not about to start one now, not when her father had died with Amelia as the only family at his side. "In fact, I had better write to Lady Ashworth tomorrow informing her of my resignation. It would be unfair to all of us if I were to remain." She had not entirely worked out the details of where she would go. "Perhaps you would be willing to give me another reference?"

"I will do better than that, my dear. You shall stay with me." Lady Walmsley said this with an emphatic nod of her head. "Lady Ashworth will be saddened by the news though. I know she has grown terribly fond of you."

"And I of her," Amelia said. "Perhaps she would be kind enough to have my things packed and sent to me here. Thank you, my lady. I appreciate your invitation, and I will take you up on it in the short term, but I am determined to look for permanent employment outside of London." Anthony would be obliged to spend part of each year in London establishing himself with others of the peerage for the time when Lord Ashworth died and Anthony assumed the title of marquess. For her own sake, Amelia would search for employment somewhere in the country so she could avoid all contact with him. And perhaps, in time, she would forget about him—and that she loved him.

"There is no hurry, you know," Lady Walmsley said. "I enjoy your company exceedingly. I have not felt this young in years."

"You are a dear," Amelia said, leaning over to press a kiss on the lady's cheek. "I am very fond of you too."

She went up to her bedchamber and wrote the letter, carefully choosing her words so the marchioness would know of Amelia's affection for her despite her resignation. Then she sealed it and took it downstairs so it could be posted first thing in the morning.

She would miss Lady Ashworth dreadfully.

She would miss Anthony even more.

Chapter 14

The day after Anthony's encounter with Amelia in the park, he returned to Lady Walmsley's house only to be told, "Miss Clarke is indisposed." He understood this, he supposed, all things considered.

On the second day when Anthony called at Lady Walmsley's house, the butler apologetically told him the ladies were not at home to callers.

On the third day when he was given the same information, Anthony grew suspicious.

By the fourth day, he was more than a little determined.

He rapped on Lady Walmsley's door and, when the butler opened it, pushed past him into the front hall. "Please inform the ladies," he said in his best captain's voice, "that I am not leaving until I have spoken to Miss Clarke."

Lady Walmsley opened the door to the sitting room, where she could not have missed overhearing his comments, and crossed the front hall to greet him. "Lord Halford, how lovely to see you."

He shot her an ironic look, considering it would have been she who had instructed the butler. Holding her gaze, he said, "I would appreciate it if you would inform Amelia that I am here."

"She does not wish to see you," Lady Walmsley said. "I have given her my word in that regard, unfortunate as I think the circumstances are."

"Thank you for that, at least," Anthony replied. "However, I am not leaving until she and I have discussed the matter further, even if it means camping on your doorstep. I had to endure much worse in Spain, lest either of you think it an idle threat."

He heard a gasp.

Turning in the direction of the sound, he saw her at the top of the stairs, a hand pressed to her bosom. She started down the stairs, her eyes fixed on his, and he fought to hold back a smile, keeping his expression as fiercely determined as hers was.

"Lord Halford," she said as she neared the bottom. "What a surprise to see you here. I had thought we'd discussed our current situation to its conclusion at Hyde Park the other day."

"Not a surprise at all, I should wager. And we have not discussed our situation nearly enough, my dear. Please excuse us, Lady Walmsley," he said as he guided Amelia toward the sitting room Lady Walmsley had just vacated. "Miss Clarke and I have something we need to discuss."

"And about time too," Lady Walmsley said with a cackle. "The girl has been in such a depressed state since your encounter at the park, I have practically had to stand on my head to get a smile out of her."

"Lady Walmsley!" Amelia exclaimed.

Lady Walmsley's comment gave Anthony more hope than he had had in days.

"Now," he said once he had closed the sitting room door behind them. "We are going to talk. Please have a seat." He gestured to the sofa.

"I prefer to stand," she said, crossing her arms in front of her chest.

"Very well." He turned to her, and she backed a few steps away from him, but he was undeterred. "I have come to see you every day since we were together in the park," he said in a low voice. "And every day I have been turned away."

"There was no need for you to call, Lord Halford. I am not your responsibility. I thought I made that perfectly clear to you."

"I did not call because I felt responsible for you. I called because I *care*." He locked eyes with her. "I care, Amelia. And I was not happy when you ended our betrothal so abruptly." He took another step, successfully trapping her against the back of the sofa. He placed a hand on either side of her. "Not happy at all," he whispered. "I do not intend to leave you here until we understand each other on this matter," he said.

He nuzzled the soft skin behind her ear, making her shiver, before kissing her there. "The last few days have been torture," he murmured as his lips traced her jawline. "I needed to see you, and I felt frustrated and helpless but not because I felt responsible, Amelia. Do not mistake me about that."

"Oh," she said breathlessly.

She had stopped trying to push him away and was trembling, so he told her what he had come to say. "When I saw you, I neglected to see the strong, independent woman before me and instead saw a vulnerable one who could not sense the danger that surrounded her."

"I was in no danger," she said.

"A woman is always in danger. I learned that at Badajoz," he said.

"Oh, Anthony," she said softly. "I am not a casualty of war, but I fear you are." She stroked a soft hand down his cheek before turning her mouth to his.

He gloried in the offering she was giving him, relief flooding through him. Her lips were giving and sweet, and he was desperate for them. His hands moved to her waist and then made their way up to caress her back and press her close. She was so alive, and when he was with her, he felt alive too.

Her hands went around his neck and then in his hair, and it felt like heaven, but Anthony was aware, despite the delicious distraction that Amelia was, that Lady Walmsley could interrupt them at any moment. Reluctantly he ended the kiss.

She had ended their betrothal, though Anthony had a differing opinion of the matter. His best recourse, he realized, was to court her, convince her of his intentions, and use the special license he'd procured as quickly as was prudent.

She looked at him then, her beautiful eyes like deep green velvet, her lips rosy from his amorous attention to them, and his heart somersaulted in his chest. He wanted her to be his own. He intended to make her his countess. Whether she was the granddaughter of a viscount or the daughter of a simple vicar, it mattered not to him. The scandal would pass quickly enough and all would be well. He would make certain of it.

It was time for battle once more, and former Captain Lord Anthony Hargreaves vowed to himself it would be an all-out assault. He would lay siege to Amelia's arguments against the match, convince her it was not mere attraction or a passing fancy or—heaven help him—*responsibility* he felt toward her. And she was attracted to him, he knew, or she would never have allowed herself to be caught in a situation that would compromise her in the first place. One did not spend twenty-two years as the daughter of a vicar to behave with anything but the highest propriety. That she had succumbed to him that first time as she had again today explained a great deal.

"Amelia," he said. "I do not want the betrothal to end. Give us—*me*—more time before you make a decision. Please do not end it based on our conversation in the park."

"I cannot see how it can ever work," she said, those beautiful eyes full of sadness . . . and longing.

The longing gave Anthony hope.

"One week," he said. "One week is all I ask, and I intend to court you properly for that week. At the end of that time, if you still feel we do not suit, I will walk away and never bother you again. But if at the end of the week you consent to be my wife, we will marry the week after."

"So soon?" she asked, her brows drawing together. "But—"

"Yes. I do not want to give you time to change your mind again."

He kissed her again with the intent of persuading her to his point of view.

* * *

Lady Walmsley, informed that Amelia and Anthony had come to an agreement, invited Anthony to join them for dinner that evening. After dinner they retired to the music room, where Amelia played the pianoforte while Lady Walmsley did needlework and Anthony pretended to read.

Amelia could tell he was pretending because whenever she looked at him—which was more frequently than she was willing to admit—she caught him gazing at her instead.

Knowing he was watching her so carefully, she used what little skill she had gained from her mother and played from her heart, trying to express through her music what she did not dare say to Anthony in words. She loved him, but she was afraid. Was it enough to marry the man she loved, even if he did not love her in return? Or would she come to resent the fact that he only cared for her but did not love her? There was a huge difference between the two.

Eventually Anthony gave up the pretense of reading. He shut his book and simply sat and listened, his eyes closed. It was the most serene Amelia had seen him. Playing the pianoforte had always been a blessing in her life. It had allowed her, even at an early age, to express a wide range of emotions—anger, passion, reverence—through the notes of the great composers. Her fingers would fly over the scale passages of Haydn and Mozart or plumb the hidden harmonic and emotional depths of Beethoven. But whatever the case, her playing was a source of peace.

She would share that peace with Anthony now. He needed peace.

Eventually her fingers stilled on the keys, and she folded them into her lap.

"Exquisite, my dear," Lady Walmsley said in a soft voice. "My heart is full from hearing you play." She dabbed her eyes with her handkerchief before placing a finger to her lips. "I believe you have lulled our friend to sleep."

Anthony had not budged at all.

"I hate to wake him," Lady Walmsley continued. "I fear if we do, he will be startled and embarrassed."

Amelia could only stare at his masculine beauty, watch his chest rise and fall in slumber, and fall more in love with him than she already was.

"I believe I shall retire and allow him the privacy he will prefer to discover when he awakens." Lady Walmsley set her sewing aside and rose from her chair. Then she surprised Amelia by crossing to the piano and kissing her softly on the cheek. "Good night, my dear," she said. "And do give Lord Halford my regards as well." She withdrew quietly from the room, leaving the door slightly ajar for propriety's sake.

Amelia watched her leave and then returned her gaze to Anthony. The light in the room was low, with only a candelabrum on the pianoforte and two others placed on nearby tables, their candlelight flickering softly and casting Anthony's features in shadow. The air was still, and she was reluctant to disturb the tranquility of the moment.

She allowed herself to dream, to imagine a life with this gentleman—this *man*. There was such honor in him, a goodness of character she had rarely observed in others, excepting her father, who had cared for his parishioners nearly as much as he had cared for his wife and daughter.

Anthony was such a man.

She rose and silently walked to the wing chair where he sat, his head resting against its high back, a finger tucked between the pages of his closed book, marking his place. Amelia sank to her knees and gently drew the book from his hands. "Anthony," she said softly.

He did not budge.

"Anthony," she repeated.

When he still didn't awaken, she decided to let him sleep a bit longer and take advantage of the opportunity to study him at close range. His hair had grown in the weeks since he had returned from Spain. It was thick and had a tendency to wave, and Amelia fought the urge to run her fingers through it, especially since she knew how it felt.

He sighed deeply then, startling her, and shifted his position in the chair. When she realized he hadn't awakened, she relaxed and returned to her perusal.

She took in his straight, dark brows and the fringe of black lashes that curved against his cheekbones. He had a strong jaw and a firm mouth, with sensuous lips that twitched upward when he was amused or flattened to a thin line when he was vexed. He did not smile enough, she realized. And on the occasions when he did, the smile did not always reach his eyes. She would do something to change that, she vowed.

Could she marry him? Was it possible that the heir to a marquess had chosen *her*, humble as she was, for his wife? Was he really marrying her by choice and not out of responsibility?

Oh, she wanted to believe it was true. She knew the Earl of Halford was a plum catch in the Marriage Mart because of his title and ancient aristocratic family. Any young lady would be thrilled if she was fortunate enough to catch the earl's attention. But none of that mattered to Amelia; in fact, it was the reason for her reluctance. It was Anthony Hargreaves she loved. The rest of it was a responsibility they would share together.

And she would help him bear the responsibilities that had been placed on him. She had a lot to learn, and life would be complicated on occasion, but she would do it, for him.

If she married him.

It truly was time to awaken him, she decided reluctantly. Otherwise she might crawl into his lap and sleep with her head nestled on his shoulder, so appealing did he look sitting there. "Anthony," she whispered again, and brushed his hair from his forehead.

His eyes opened partway, and he seemed surprised to see her there—as if in his slumber he had forgotten where he was. That irresistible mouth of his slowly turned upward in a relaxed, appreciative smile. "I see an angel," he said in a low, gravelly voice. He blinked a few times and looked around as he gradually awakened and remembered where he was. "Right," he said. "You were playing the pianoforte."

"You fell asleep," Amelia told him. "I was reluctant to wake you; you were sleeping so peacefully."

"Was I? That will be news to Lucas. I have not done that in longer than I can remember. Quite the contrary, in fact." He sat up straight and stretched. "It appears I also managed to bore Lady Walmsley enough that she left us to ourselves." His contented smile turned into a mischievous grin, and he reached for her and tried to tug her onto his lap.

"Oh, no, you don't," she said, resisting despite her earlier yearnings to be precisely there. "You are going home to continue that peaceful sleep of yours."

"You are right, of course, but it doesn't sound nearly as much fun." He rose to his feet, drawing her up with him and pulling her close. "Thank you for playing the pianoforte for me," he said, running his hands up and down her back. "Next time I vow to remain awake for the entire performance."

"We shall see," she said. "Good night."

"Walk me out?" he asked.

They blew out the candelabra, taking a single lit candle with them, and strolled slowly through the dark, silent house, her hand tucked in the crook of his arm.

"What did you mean about your sleeping being news to Lucas?" she asked softly.

Anthony heaved a huge sigh. "Nothing, really. Nothing for you to fret over, at least."

"Anthony," she said in a soft, chiding voice. "If we are to marry—*if*—then we must be honest with each other and share those parts of ourselves that make us feel vulnerable. It is part of the bond of marriage." She was not so naive that she couldn't understand that many couples, especially among the nobility, shared very little with each other, but she refused to have such a marriage.

"You are an expert, then?" he asked, apparently reluctant to explain his comment.

Amelia didn't want to push him overly much. She knew he had suffered while in Spain. "I rely on my parents' marriage for my example, and I witnessed a loving bond between them that shared happiness and burdens equally."

"You may think in your childlike way that your parents shared equally, but I would venture there were things they each kept hidden in order to spare the other unnecessary pain."

Amelia thought about it as they walked. What Anthony had said was most likely true. She knew her mother had tried to disguise her pain from both Amelia and her father. Undoubtedly her father had been unrealistically optimistic to her mother when the end was near, for both their sakes.

"But I agree with you in principle," Anthony continued. "I should prefer my marriage to be an open and honest one, at least as much as possible."

"That is acceptable," Amelia replied. She wanted an open and honest marriage, but she also wanted a marriage made of love, especially if Anthony was to be her husband. She did not dare say it though.

Which obviously proved the point Anthony had just made.

"Well," she said, "I won't press you about the comment you made about Lucas, then. I will only say that I am glad you were able to sleep peacefully for a while this evening, and if my music had anything to do with it, I shall play for you every evening from now on."

"I shall hold you to that."

They had reached the front hall, and Anthony took up his hat from the table. He kissed each of her hands in turn before leaving a final kiss on her lips. "Good night, angel," he said, then closed the door behind him, taking all of her heart with him as he went.

* * *

The following afternoon, after a night of restful sleep that had continued after listening to Amelia's music, two large traveling coaches pulled up in front of Ashworth House. Anthony watched in astonishment as his father emerged slowly from the first coach, carefully assisted by a sturdy footman, followed by Anthony's mother, sister, and brother-in-law.

He hurried down the front steps and took his father's arm, concerned that he had left Ashworth Park, where he should be continuing to rest and regain his strength.

"Never you mind, Halford," his father said, waving off his assistance and taking a cane from the footman. "I'll be hanged if I do not enter my home under my own power."

Anthony moved to kiss his mother on the cheek, keeping a wary eye on his father nonetheless.

"He really is much stronger, Anthony, or I should never have let him come to Town," she said, taking his outstretched arm.

"And why did you come to Town?" Anthony asked. "You knew Miss Clarke and I intended to return to Ashworth Park within a week or two."

"You *and* Miss Clarke were, were you?" she said, arching an eyebrow at him. "Then why, precisely, did I receive a letter from her informing me that her betrothal and employment were at an end and thanking me for my kindness to her?"

He was saved from answering, fortunately, when Louisa hurried over and threw her arms around his neck. "Oh, Anthony!" she cried. "I was positively devastated when Amelia wrote Mama and told her the betrothal was off, was I not, Farleigh?" she added when her husband arrived to shake Anthony's hand.

"Indeed," Farleigh said, smiling at Louisa.

Anthony had always wondered at Farleigh's devotion to his pretty but emotional sister. Now that he understood the feelings himself, he wondered no more.

"We took our time traveling so Papa could rest," Louisa said. "Farleigh insisted I rest too, the dear man." She shot Farleigh a gaze that rivaled the one he had given her. "Otherwise we should have arrived yesterday. Oh, please tell us what has happened."

"Perhaps we should wait until we are inside to have this conversation, my dear," Farleigh said.

"You're right, of course. But, Anthony, I have been beside myself with worry, and Farleigh would not have me be so, despite what he just said. Please tell us."

"I confess to being in a similar state as Louisa over this," his mother said. "I am quite impatient to learn what is going on."

"You will both have to be patient a few minutes more," Anthony said, turning to lead his mother into the house. "How is Father, truly?" he asked in a low voice as Louisa hurried over to Will and Penny's nurse to make sure all was settled with the children.

"Still weak, but doing much better than Dr. Samuels and I could have hoped. I believe knowing he has a son who lives did much to restore his own will to keep living."

Anthony rejoiced at her words. He felt as though another burden of responsibility had been lifted from his shoulders.

They arrived in the sitting room, where Lord Ashworth was already seated, his feet resting on a cushioned footstool. He was pale, but Anthony could see that even in the short amount of time since Anthony had left Ashworth Park, his father had gained weight and looked much stronger.

Lady Ashworth rang for tea and then sat on the sofa next to her husband's chair. Louisa sat by her mother while Farleigh wandered over to the crystal decanter on a side table.

"Brandy, Halford?" he asked, splashing some in a glass for himself. "Ashworth?"

"No, thank you," Anthony replied.

"None for me," the marquess said, recognizing the stern look his wife was giving him. "Doctor's orders and all that."

The marchioness nodded in approval.

Anthony hid a smile and walked to the fireplace, where he leaned his shoulder against the mantel and crossed his arms. "I cannot believe that a mere lady's companion can fire off one little missive and my entire family jumps to attention. And yet here you all are."

His mother straightened, looking every inch the marchioness. "Amelia is neither overly emotional nor reactive, Anthony. If whatever happened made her willing—or worse, made her feel forced—to forgo her employment with me, I could only assume something dreadful had occurred."

"And I saw the way you both looked at each other," Louisa said. "Despite her rank, I could not allow such a love match to founder. Not every marriage is as fortunate as Farleigh's and mine."

"This is true," Farleigh said, taking his wife's hand and kissing it while winking at Anthony.

"Louisa, you are ever the romantic," Anthony said, feeling both amused and touched by her concern. "And you, Father, what is your opinion on the subject?"

Lord Ashworth was silent for a time, staring thoughtfully at the fire. "I confess I was not happy with what happened initially between you and Miss Clarke, but I do like her. She has been devoted to your mother, especially when your mother needed someone to be there for her the most. For that I am grateful.

"Additionally, Ashworth men are gentlemen of honor. In a rash moment, you compromised Miss Clarke, and it simply would not do for this same young lady to be ill used and tossed aside. I am reconciled, therefore, to the fact that while she would not have been my first choice for you, she is nonetheless a young lady of fine character."

It was quite a speech, and Lord Ashworth was winded when he finished. Anthony was deeply moved by his father's words. He crossed to his father's chair and dropped to a crouch, taking the marquess's hand in his own. "Father," he said, "how I honor you."

Lady Ashworth blinked back tears, and Louisa reached for Farleigh's handkerchief.

"None of this now," Lord Ashworth said. "Stand up, son. Neither your mother nor your sister will be able to rest until you tell them what is happening."

Anthony nodded and stood. "Amelia did indeed release me from our betrothal," Anthony said. "However, we have since discussed the matter, and I have persuaded her to give me this week to court her respectably before she makes her final decision. And lest you think otherwise, I have every intention of wooing her successfully and marrying her."

"I am *so* relieved!" Louisa said, pressing her hands to her bosom.

"But there is work yet to be done. She is still of the opinion that she is unworthy and I am only marrying her out of responsibility."

"The girl always did have sense," the marquess said. "She is correct, after all."

"I wish to convince her otherwise," Anthony said firmly. "I find she suits me. She has experienced much of life and death and seems to understand my . . . bleak . . . moods better than anyone, excepting Lucas."

"Oh, Anthony," his mother said. "My heart breaks for you and what you suffered."

"My suffering was nothing compared to others', Mother," he said softly.

"Well, I shall do everything I can to help," Louisa declared.

"Within reason, my dear," Farleigh said. "You have our child to consider, remember."

She patted her round belly. "I will, of course. And Mama will help too, will you not, Mama?"

The marchioness glanced at Lord Ashworth, Louisa, and Farleigh and then turned to Anthony and nodded. "Tell us what you would like us to do."

* * *

Amelia received a note while she and Lady Walmsley were spending the afternoon quietly reading in the solar, inviting the two of them to join Lady Ashworth and Lady Farleigh the following afternoon for tea. They were also to be joined by Lords Ashworth, Halford, and Farleigh. Amelia handed the card to Lady Walmsley.

"It would appear that your letter to Lady Ashworth stirred the pot," Lady Walmsley said with amusement after she read it. "The marquess would not have traveled from Oxfordshire with Lady Ashworth and the others unless they all concluded it was necessary."

"Oh no," Amelia said, rising from her seat and pacing about. "What if he ends up taking a turn for the worse? It will be my fault." If anything were to happen to the marquess due to the strain of travel, Amelia would never forgive herself. Besides which, having the marquess become involved in her current arrangement with Anthony was a terrifying thought.

"And I suppose it would be your fault, too, if I suddenly were to keel over and die?" Lady Walmsley said.

"Are you feeling unwell?" Amelia asked in a panic, reaching for her hand in concern.

"Of course not," she said, waving Amelia off. "But even if I *were* feeling unwell, it would not be your fault. I do not know where you get these foolish notions—you and that boy and your overdeveloped sense of responsibility. The more important question is, what do you plan to do?"

"Anthony asked me to agree to give him a week and consider marrying him with as open a mind as possible," she said.

"I know all that. I was not far away, you will recall, when the two of you reconciled. I wholeheartedly approve, by the way," Lady Walmsley said with a nod. "You are a practical girl, Amelia, and only a foolish one would turn down the Earl of Halford, regardless of the circumstances. Perhaps this week you will finally realize this. Should you decide to refuse him, perish the thought, you may remain with me as long as you like, as I told you before. I have not enjoyed myself so much in years—ever since my niece used to bring her school friends here for holidays." She paused then, a wistful look in her eye. "They were a jolly group of girls, and it was always great fun to have them here with Walmsley and me, and in the country with us too."

"Tell me about those times," Amelia said.

Lady Walmsley directed her gaze back at Amelia. "I was delighted when Julia arrived from India. I missed my sister desperately, and there was much of her in her daughter. Julia struggled at first, being away from her parents, of course, but also adjusting to England after living her entire life in India. It was her parents' intent that she attend a girls' school in England, though, and learn how to be a proper English lady. Her great-grandfather, my grandfather, was an earl, and with her connections to my husband and me, Julia had an opportunity to make a good match.

"She eventually settled in at school and made wonderful friends, including your mother, who was a frequent guest. I imagine that was why your father suggested you contact me after his death, since I had a fondness for Julia and her friends and would do whatever I could to help one of their daughters."

"For which fact I cannot be more grateful," Amelia said earnestly.

Lady Walmsley smiled and patted her hand. "Nor I, my dear. At any rate, everything began to go much better. The girls held little dramas, they sang, they embroidered. Your mother frequently played the pianoforte, much as you did the other night."

"I should love to have heard her perform on your pianoforte; it is such a beautiful instrument," Amelia said with a sigh.

"And she would be pleased, no doubt, to know how accomplished her daughter has become," Lady Walmsley said. "There, now." She patted the armrests of her chair with finality before boosting herself from her chair. "I have reminisced long enough. It is time to look forward, not dwell on the past. Halford could be your future, if you want it."

"But is it best for him when there are so many ladies he could choose from who would be better suited?"

"What does that mean, 'better suited'?" Lady Walmsley asked. "What young lady understands the loss of death better than you? Who understands the needs of the people she is tasked to shepherd over or has the capacity to care for them better than you? Halford needs *that* person, not someone who knows what signal she is sending with the snap of her fan or what the latest fashion is. He will be a fine marquess, like his father before him, but to do it, he will need a partner, not a consort."

Amelia's heart beat faster at the words Lady Walmsley uttered. She could be that for Anthony; she knew she could. Her upbringing had taught her many practical things about life and living, but it had also taught her charity and love.

Was it actually possible for her to marry Anthony after all? She loved him, and he had told her he cared for her.

Perhaps caring could grow into love. Was she willing to take that risk? And what if it was all he could ever offer? Would it be enough?

She had a week to decide.

Chapter 15

THE WEEK PASSED IN A whirlwind. Every morning Amelia was greeted by a new bouquet of flowers from Anthony, and every afternoon he took her for a drive in his curricle through Hyde Park, where she gradually made the acquaintance of many of his friends. She had been to tea with Lady Ashworth and Louisa twice, and they had all attended the opera together, except for Lord Ashworth, who was looking much better but still chose his level of activity with an eye toward his health.

Anthony too was looking healthier. More rested. And other than the evening when they had attended the opera, Amelia had played the pianoforte for him. He seemed to find tranquility from her music, regardless of what she played. He would read or write letters or simply shut his eyes and listen. Lady Walmsley always remained with them, diligent chaperone that she was, although she always allowed them a discreet amount of time alone together too.

Amelia looked forward to those times most of all, the memory of each tucked safely in her heart.

His kisses were tender, and Amelia had never felt more cherished. Once, he had wandered to the pianoforte while she had played a song he'd requested and had stood behind her, his hands resting on her shoulders, just listening and watching her fingers glide over the keyboard as though he could become one with her and the music. When she'd finished playing, he'd lowered his head and kissed the nape of her neck, raising goose bumps. "Ah, Amelia," he had murmured to her on that occasion, his head pressed to hers. "What a gift you are to me."

It was not precisely a declaration of love, but it gave Amelia hope.

Tonight Anthony was escorting her to a ball the Duke and Duchess of Atherton, close friends of his parents, were holding. Even Lord Ashworth planned to make a brief appearance, telling his concerned wife, "If I am well enough to subject my backside to a torturous journey by coach from Oxfordshire, I am capable of sitting on a stuffed chair and playing cards for an hour or two. My health may have served as an excuse to avoid attending the opera, but it will not deter me from mingling with old friends."

Amelia had wanted to hug him after that remark, certain he was doing it as a show of force for her and Anthony's sake, although the marchioness did not look nearly so pleased by his words.

Jane was putting the finishing touches on Amelia's hair. She had truly outdone herself this time, Amelia thought as she viewed herself in the vanity mirror. Her hair was held back by a pearl bandeau, and strings of tiny pearls had been woven into the cascade of ringlets that fell softly from the crown of her head.

Her gown for the evening was exquisite. It was a deep gold velvet, with a square neckline and short puff sleeves. It was simple and elegant. Perfect.

Jane carefully assisted Amelia into her gown and matching velvet slippers.

"Oh, miss," Jane breathed, "you look like a princess! Or at least a countess, if you end up marrying Lord Halford, which I am hoping you will." She blushed. "Madame Veronique was right; it is the perfect color to go with that gorgeous hair of yours. It's a right pleasure to do your hair, miss. Lord Halford is going to be speechless with wonder when he casts his eyes on you."

"Thank you, Jane. If what you say is true, it will be due to your efforts. I have had this hair all my life, and it has never made a man speechless before."

Jane giggled, and Amelia opened the drawer of her vanity and removed her two boxes. She opened the one that held the beautiful pearl necklace and ear bobs Anthony had given her. "Help me with this, will you, Jane?" she said, reverently removing the necklace from the box and handing it to her.

Jane fastened the necklace while Amelia put on the ear bobs. "There! The perfect finishing touch," Jane said.

Amelia would give Anthony the engraved watch fob this evening as a way of letting him know she had decided to accept his proposal. She had decided to make the betrothal one in truth. Oh, but the very idea made her heart flutter, whether in joy or panic, she wasn't entirely sure.

She pulled on one glove and then the other, smoothing the soft kid leather over her arms. Then she picked up her fan and tucked the box into her reticule and turned toward the door.

"Don't forget your wrap, miss," Jane said, scurrying toward her. Madame Veronique had suggested a creamy lace shawl, and indeed, it went splendidly with her dress.

The ball gown was the crown jewel of Amelia's new wardrobe. She had never worn such elegant attire before and had to admit the combined effect of wardrobe and hair left her feeling exhilarated and more confident to face Anthony's peers than she ever had before.

Lady Walmsley was in her private sitting room when Amelia went to say good-bye to her before Anthony arrived. She had opted out of attending the ball since Amelia would have no need of a chaperone, what with Ladies Ashworth and Farleigh in attendance, preferring to allow herself a quiet evening at home. She had changed into a comfortable dressing gown and was sitting by the fire doing her needlework, her lacy cap sitting slightly askew on her silvery curls.

"Oh, my dear," Lady Walmsley said, setting her work aside and rising to her feet. "You are a vision." Her pale blue eyes sparkled. "Now, be a good girl and turn around so I may get the entire effect." She drew a circle in the air to demonstrate.

Amelia dutifully did so and then snapped her fan open in a coquettish gesture, making Lady Walmsley chuckle.

"Well done!" she said. "But I think we had better get you back to the country as soon as may be or you will have so many beaus Halford will not be able to get near you."

Amelia laughed, feeling suddenly lighthearted.

There was a soft knock at the sitting room door, and a footman poked his head into the room. "The Earl of Halford has arrived, Miss Clarke."

"Thank you." Now that he was here, Amelia's pulse began to race.

"I feel very much like the fairy godmother sending off Cinderella," Lady Walmsley said. "But I am not going to warn you to return at midnight. Midnight is when the supper dance will occur, and my wish is for you to dance and dine with your betrothed."

"Oh, Lady Walmsley, how I love you!" Amelia threw her arms around the older woman, grateful to have her in her life, grateful to have someone to bid her farewell as she went to greet Anthony.

"Tut tut, child," Lady Walmsley said. "You will wrinkle your gown if you are not careful. Now, off with you, and have a wonderful time."

Amelia nodded and left the room, stopping when she reached the landing. Down in the entry hall stood Anthony. He wore formal black, with gold cuff links winking out from his snowy white linens, his white waistcoat embroidered with gold as well. He looked every inch the nobleman, his military posture adding to his aura of authority.

And Amelia was going to agree to marry this nobleman, this noble man, tonight.

He must have heard her approach, for he turned and looked up, his piercing blue eyes taking in every inch of her before locking his gaze on her face. He strode up the stairs, stopping just a few steps short of the landing so they were eye to eye. "You are utterly breathtaking," he declared in a low, husky voice. "I shall be the envy of every man this evening." He held out his hand to her.

She offered him hers, which he tucked into the crook of his arm, and they descended the stairs slowly, their eyes never leaving each other. Instead of helping her with her shawl, however, he led her into the front parlor. He ran a gloved finger lightly over the pearl necklace around her neck, and she shivered at his touch, silently glad he had noticed she'd worn it. "I have been remiss," he said. "I hope you will forgive me."

"For what?" Amelia said, mesmerized by the expression on his beautiful face.

He reached into his pocket and then dropped to one knee. "Dearest Miss Clarke," he began, and Amelia's heart raced. "Despite the fact that our betrothal is public knowledge, it dawned on me—rather late in the process, I am afraid—that I had never formally asked for your hand, and for that I am the most abject of men." He reached for her trembling hand. "For you are more deserving than that."

He reached into his pocket and extracted a ring, then held it up as an offering to Amelia. It was gold set with a large emerald, a diamond on either side. "It was my grandmother's," Anthony said. "And I knew it was to be yours. It reminded me of your eyes, although it does not do them justice . . . May I?"

Her eyes welled with tears. "Oh, my love," she whispered. "Yes."

He gently peeled her glove down her arm and off, the sensation sending shock waves clear down to her toes, and then slipped the beautiful ring on her finger and rose to his feet. "One week from today, I intend to make you my wife. I refuse to entertain any arguments to the contrary." He smiled mischievously at the remark, and yet there was a look of determination in his eyes. "I want you for my wife, my Amelia."

He reached for her wrap, and Amelia, dazed as she was, finally remembered her gift for him. "Wait," she said, opening her reticule and removing the box inside. "This is for you."

"A gift?" he asked, turning the box over in his large hands.

"A betrothal gift, of sorts," she said. When he looked at her inquiringly, she shrugged. "All right, yes. I got a betrothal gift for you awhile back."

His mouth drew into a lazy grin. "I am delighted." He opened the box and removed the fob. "And it is inscribed, I see. With an *A*."

"For Anthony," she said. "Or for Ashworth, when the time comes, if you like, although I hope that occasion is far into the future."

The mention of his father's eventual death sobered them both.

"Instead, I will always think of it as an *A* for Amelia," he said softly. He removed his pocket watch and replaced its existing fob with hers. "I shall wear it proudly as a token from my beautiful wife-to-be."

He took her shawl now and set it gently about her shoulders, then escorted her to his waiting carriage. Once they were settled inside, Anthony sitting across from her, his back to the horses, the coachman cracked his whip, and they set off to the Duke of Atherton's large London house.

They chatted comfortably all the way to their destination, and it was only after they had arrived that it dawned on Amelia that while she had called Anthony her love, he had yet to offer the same word to her, though he had said other lovely things. But not *love*.

She tried not to let it bother her, but it stung nonetheless.

* * *

The London residence of the Duke and Duchess of Atherton was located in Grosvenor Square, and there was already a long line of carriages queued up, waiting to deliver their occupants at the red carpet leading to the door.

So far, Amelia had been seen with Anthony only in Hyde Park, the theater and opera, and at a few dinner parties that included the Ashworth's closest friends. The plan had been to create allies before fully presenting her to society. Once people had an opportunity to meet Amelia and discern her true character, any remaining gossip among the ton would die a quick death. So far, the plan had been successful.

This ball was to be her formal debut.

Anthony sat across from her in the carriage, his long legs stretched out, his fingers drumming his thigh, and studied her profile as she gazed out the window at the crowds of people in attendance. He felt a heightened sense of anticipation, like what he had felt on the eve of a battle.

Their carriage finally reached the carpet, laid to protect the ladies' expensive gowns from the dirt of the street, and a groom opened the door. Anthony exited first and handed Amelia down after, then offered her his arm.

He could feel her hand trembling, and while her expression was smooth, her face was pale. What would he have said to his men at the beginning of battle that would be appropriate here? "Take heart, Amelia," he murmured inanely as they joined the crush waiting to be welcomed by their host and hostess. It was better than nothing, he supposed. He suspected his words were directed as much at himself as at her anyway.

His blood was high, his mind alert as they finally reached the Duke and Duchess of Atherton.

"Lord Halford, well met!" the duke said, grasping his hand in a firm handshake. He was a tall, vibrant man with a wide smile and shrewd eyes, his vivid red hair nearly completely faded to silver since Anthony had seen him last. "Your parents and Lord and Lady Farleigh have already arrived. So reassuring to see Ashworth for myself and know he is on the mend."

"Indeed, Your Grace," Anthony said. "Duchess," he said and bent over her hand. The Duchess of Atherton, by contrast, was short and plump, but her twinkling hazel eyes missed nothing. The duke had frequently referred to her as the general, so clever she was in all things, whether it came to running her household or offering astute opinions on politics. "May I present my fiancée, Miss Amelia Clarke?"

"You may. How do you do, Miss Clarke?" the Duke of Atherton said. His demeanor was not quite so open with her as it had been with Anthony, but he had allowed the introduction, which was a first step toward her acceptance among the others in attendance.

Amelia curtsied. "I am well, Your Grace, thank you," Amelia said, looking every bit the aristocratic lady, Anthony observed with pride.

"Miss Clarke, so it is you who has captured our Halford's interest," the duchess said. "I must say, after seeing you, I can understand why."

Amelia's cheeks bloomed at the comment, and Anthony wondered if the duchess was offering a general compliment or alluding to the original tête-à-tête that had resulted in their forced betrothal. He shot the Duchess of Atherton a look, which she blandly ignored.

"You give me too much credit," Amelia said with complete graciousness. "But I thank you for your generous words."

The duchess's eyebrows rose in surprise, and Anthony detected reluctant admiration on her face. "I understand a bit more of what Halford saw in you. Welcome, Miss Clarke," the duchess said.

Anthony led Amelia away from the Athertons. "Well done," he whispered as they entered the ballroom. He watched Amelia swallow, and while momentarily captivated by the movement of her throat, he understood she had been more nervous than he had realized. It was time to gather the troops in support. "What do you say we go find my family now?"

"Yes," she said. "I think that is a good idea."

"And then afterward I intend to dance with my fiancée," he said, giving her an encouraging smile.

She nodded, and Anthony gazed over the crowded ballroom, searching for his parents. The Atherton ballroom was large and opulent, its chandeliers blazing from the high ceilings, their sparkling crystals shooting rainbows of color over the dancers. Huge bouquets of flowers in all hues were set near gold-leafed pillars, adding their pungent scents to the array of perfumes—and less pleasant human smells—that were to be found in any ballroom.

The bank of french doors on the far side of the room was opened to allow cool evening air to enter and give guests an alternative to the crush, if they so chose.

Anthony eventually spotted his parents near the door leading to the cardroom. His father would spend most of his time there, where he could sit and converse with his peers in a friendly game of whist or loo for an hour or so, until he was ready to return home.

"Come," he said to Amelia and, securing her hand in the crook of his arm, began to make his way through the ballroom in that direction. Reaching them took longer than Anthony anticipated, however, as he was stopped several times and welcomed home and congratulated for his war efforts.

Amelia remained quietly poised throughout, enduring a few polite jabs aimed at him and their soon-to-be marital status.

"Caught in the parson's mousetrap, eh?" one gentleman asked with a wink.

"Thought after so many years in the army, you would have learned how to defend yourself by now, Halford—though I can see how a surrender may have been the order of the day," another said with a look of appraisal at Amelia that was more appreciative than Anthony liked.

In fact, Anthony found himself feeling more and more on edge. The sheer number of people, the din of conversation, the heavy scents of perfume and perspiration were beginning to feel claustrophobic. And as they worked their way through the numerous guests, Anthony felt like he was pushing through the crowded alleys of Badajoz all over again.

He took a gulp of air, fighting back panic and nausea. He had been feeling so much better, nearly human again the past couple weeks, especially on the peaceful evenings when Amelia played the pianoforte for him, that he had not anticipated having this reaction tonight.

"Tony!"

Anthony turned his head in the direction of the voice calling his name and saw Sir Richard Egan skirting around a small group of matrons that included Lady Putnam and her two daughters. Behind him were Hugh Wallingham and Phillip Osbourne. They were all on their way to greet Amelia and him.

Anthony couldn't avoid the shudder that ran through him at the sight of Lady Putnam and Harriet and Charlotte. But of course they would come to London. Something else he should have anticipated, no doubt.

"Good to see you again, old man," Sir Richard said, shaking Anthony's outstretched hand. "I must apologize for poor Freddie and what he said the other day. He got another earful after you and Lucas left, you can be sure."

"And rightly so," Hugh chimed in. "Old Fred can be a bit bacon-brained, but he is a good sort of chap and means well."

"Hello again, Miss Clarke," Phillip Osbourne said, offering her a bow. "You look utterly magnificent this evening."

"Indeed," Sir Richard echoed. "Do introduce us to the young lady, Tony."

"Gentlemen, my fiancée, Miss Amelia Clarke," Anthony said, feeling proud and fairly possessive. "Amelia, may I present these rogues, Sir Richard Egan and Hugh Wallingham. You remember Phillip, of course."

"Enchanted, Miss Clarke, to say the least," Hugh said.

"At your service, Miss Clarke," Sir Richard said with a deep bow. "I cannot imagine what you see in old Tony here."

"Oh, he has a few qualities hidden beneath that scowling countenance of his." She glanced up at him with amusement in her eyes.

"Very few, I should think," Sir Richard teased.

Was he scowling? Anthony thought to himself. Probably. "Who would not scowl with these ne'er-do-wells hovering around my betrothed like a pack of slavering wolves?" he said.

"I say, Tony, that is harsh!" Hugh exclaimed, grinning.

Amelia bit her lip to keep from laughing, and the sight of it lightened Anthony's mood.

"I would be honored, Miss Clarke, if you would dance with me," Hugh said, eyeing Anthony carefully. "After your protective fiancé dances with you first, of course."

"I would be delighted," Amelia said.

"But not yet," Anthony interjected smoothly. "If you will excuse us, I can see my mother attempting to get our attention. Later, gentlemen."

In fact, his mother looked worried when he and Amelia reached her side. "I am not sure what to make of this," she said in a low voice so others would not hear. "Perhaps it will amount to nothing."

"What is it, Mother?" Anthony asked.

"I overheard someone say that the Duchess of Marwood and Lady Elizabeth have arrived, and the duke will be joining them here later. Anthony, I did not even know they had come to Town! Had I known they would be here at the ball tonight, I would have sent our regrets to the Athertons."

Anthony had known they were in London, of course; Lady Elizabeth had spoken to them at the theater, but they had managed to avoid the Marwoods from then on. "There is nothing to worry about, Mother. Certainly the duke will not wish to make a scene, and Lady Elizabeth and I are in complete accord over the matter."

"I do hope you are right," she said. "It would be dreadful if everything were to get stirred up again when the worst of it was just beginning to blow over. Oh, my dear," she said to Amelia. "This is supposed to be a happy night for you."

"I am certain everything will be fine," Amelia said, a reassuring smile on her face, though Anthony wasn't sure she was as confident as either of them claimed to be. "I am inclined to agree with Anthony regarding the Duke of Marwood."

"It is strange that Marwood was so determined to see Lady Elizabeth and I married," Anthony said. Perhaps it would be wise to have Abbott look into it. "But for now, Mother, we will not court disaster. I suggest you find Louisa and Farleigh and enjoy yourself. I intend to dance with Amelia."

"Very well," his mother said. "And you are right, of course, on all counts." She attempted a smile and then turned toward Amelia. "You look utterly stunning tonight, my dear. You fairly glow."

"Thank you, my lady." Amelia's lips curved into such a sweet smile at the compliment that Anthony wanted desperately to kiss them. He would find an opportunity later in the evening to accomplish that particular goal.

When his mother left, he escorted Amelia onto the floor. The next dance turned out to be a waltz. As they twirled amongst the other dancers under the bright chandeliers, Anthony was filled with a sense of well-being and happiness, Marwood forgotten for the moment. Amelia fit perfectly in his arms, her lovely face was turned up to meet his, and he allowed himself to sink contentedly into the depths of her deep-green eyes.

Too soon the waltz ended, however, and Anthony reluctantly parted from her. "If we are to be completely proper," he said. "I may only dance one more time with you this evening. I would like that to be the supper dance, if you will permit me."

"If I am allowed to dance with you only once more, then I hope you will instruct the orchestra to choose the longest piece of music they have," she said.

"Brilliant idea," he answered, full of joy and hope. He had never expected to find any peace again, but it might actually be possible; he might be able to experience a life of happiness with Amelia. For with her in his arms, the oppression he had felt from the crowds dissipated.

They strolled over to rejoin Anthony's friends, but before they reached them, Kit arrived at their side, accompanied by Lady Elizabeth.

"Miss Clarke, how splendid you look this evening," Kit said, sending a speaking glance to Anthony after smiling and bowing over Amelia's hand. "Perhaps I can persuade you to take a turn on the dance floor with me?"

Amelia politely agreed, and soon they were engaged in a country dance while Lady Elizabeth remained at Anthony's side. "May we walk, Lord Halford?" she murmured so the other gentlemen present could not hear.

"Certainly," Anthony said and extended his arm to her.

They strolled around the perimeter of the ballroom toward the french doors, at Lady Elizabeth's suggestion, nodding to acquaintances as they went. Anthony noticed several pairs of curious eyes and a few looks of disdain.

Once outside, he led Lady Elizabeth away from the others who had come outside for fresh air.

"I must warn you," she said in a hushed voice.

"What is going on?" Anthony said.

"I am dreadfully sorry, Lord Halford. I don't know what more to do. I cannot get him to see reason, and Mama refuses to listen to me as well. Something is terribly wrong. Father has not been at all the same since the dance at Ashworth Park—he is rarely at home, and when he is, he is angry and . . . pardon me, but to speak bluntly, he is usually quite foxed. He barely says two words to me, and Mama even scolded me after our stay at Ashworth Park." Her eyes were huge and glistened with tears.

Anthony hated to see her in pain like this. "What in blazes is going on?" he asked.

"I don't know," she answered, "except that our decision not to marry seems to have been the final straw."

"That makes no sense. I am beyond confident you will have no trouble attracting other suitors, scores of them. I do not understand why your parents refuse to accept our decision and are putting you through this."

"Neither do I; I wish I did. Regardless of that, there is a specific reason I am speaking to you about this tonight. You see, my father believes Amelia is the primary cause of all this."

A sense of cold foreboding congealed in Anthony's stomach at her words. He would not allow the Duke of Marwood, or anyone else, to harm Amelia.

"Do not trust in my father's ability to be rational right now, Lord Halford. He is truly not his normal self. I fear for him. I only hope that when he arrives at the ball, he will content himself with disappearing into the cardroom and into his cups. Perhaps if he does, I will be able to convince Mama to help me take him home. Stay away from him if you can, for Amelia's sake."

"Thank you for the warning, Lady Elizabeth." He checked the scene in the ballroom through the french doors. "The current dance appears to be drawing to an end, and I suspect Kit and Amelia will be looking for us. It would seem you have an eligible suitor already."

"Lord Cantwell is very charming, but I think his only intentions are to enjoy himself tonight and return Miss Clarke to you," she said. "Now, if you will excuse me, I am going in search of my mother. I suspect she may be complicit with my father in undermining Amelia. I intend to do what I can to minimize any effect her words may have on others."

Anthony took her by the hand before she could leave and raised it to his lips. "Thank you again, Lady Elizabeth. For you to take such a stand against your parents shows courage, and I shall forever be in your debt."

"I only pray all will be well, Lord Halford," she said.

*　*　*

The country dance concluded, and Amelia curtsied to her partner. "Thank you for the dance, Lord Cantwell," she said.

He bowed in reply. "The pleasure was mine, and my name is Christopher, though that is as a big a mouthful as Cantwell is. My friends call me Kit, and as I hope we may be friends, I would like you to call me Kit also."

"Kit, then," she replied. "And, please, call me Amelia."

He was a lovely dancer, but Amelia had had a difficult time concentrating on her steps, finding herself watching Anthony and Elizabeth and wondering what their serious conversation was about.

As she and Kit headed across the floor to meet them, Kit held her back briefly.

"Amelia, I must tell you something," he said, slowing their pace to a stroll. "Lady Elizabeth is informing Tony that her father blames you for the failed betrothal between them, and he is in a frame of mind to create trouble over it."

"Oh no," Amelia said, her heart sinking. "Perhaps I should leave. My presence will only make matters worse."

"I am truly sorry to be the bearer of such distressing news. When Lady Elizabeth asked for my help, we decided the best thing was to speak to you individually, which seemed the most discreet way to let you both know. To tell everyone at once might have caused too obvious a reaction."

"Thank you for that." Oh, she was a burden to Anthony! He needed to be done with conflict, but here again was more of it. Why could the Duke of Marwood not accept the decision Anthony and Lady Elizabeth had made?

Kit gently led her to a chair in a small alcove, away from the crowd. "Would you care for a drink?" he asked her, looking concerned. "Lemonade perhaps?"

"No, thank you; I shall be fine in a minute." She rested her head on the back of the chair, feeling weary suddenly. "Is it normal for the upper classes to be so contentious about these things?"

"No, and that is the puzzling part. Lady Elizabeth and Tony were agreed that there would be no marriage. Apparently her father had other expectations. He is certainly bearing a tremendous grudge." He frowned. "At any rate, the Ashworths, Lord and Lady Farleigh, Sir Richard, Hugh, Phillip, and myself are at your service this evening, and we shall endeavor to do whatever we can to end this business once and for all."

"Why did Lady Elizabeth ask you to speak with me?" Amelia asked.

"She knows I am loyal to Tony," Kit answered simply.

"I see. Thank you, Kit. I can only hope the Duke of Marwood decides to act with honor, for everyone's sake."

"I too. Are you feeling better? If you are, I will return you to Tony," Kit said.

"Thank you, but I believe I promised the next dance to your brother."

"Are you sure you're up to it?"

"I'm fine."

He smiled at her. "Well done, Amelia. In that case, I will escort you to him and commiserate with you over your bad fortune."

"Meaning Marwood?" she asked.

"Not this time," he said, the corner of his mouth tipping upward slightly. "As you dance with Phillip, I suggest you watch your toes."

Kit had made the joke to divert her, and she was grateful to him for it. She replied in kind. "I am rather attached to my toes, so I shall be very careful indeed."

But as Phillip was bowing to her and leading her out to the floor, Amelia forgot her toes and silently prayed the Duke of Marwood would have a change of heart—or character or whatever it was that needed changing.

***

Amelia danced with Phillip, who was a much better dancer than his brother gave him credit for. Then she danced with Hugh and Sir Richard. Sir Richard flirted shamelessly with her, begging her quite charmingly to forget Anthony. "Only consider those of us who will weep piteously at your wedding," he said with the right amount of theatrical nuance. "My neckcloth will wilt from the dampness of my tears when I am forced to use it after my handkerchief becomes a soggy mess."

Amelia smiled at his attempt to distract her. "That's laying it on rather thick, wouldn't you say?" She noticed he was glancing surreptitiously around the room and turned her head to look.

The Duchess of Marwood was making her way around the ballroom, and Amelia couldn't help but notice that wherever the duchess went, eyes inevitably turned toward Amelia. Lady Putnam seemed very eager to listen to what the duchess was saying, which meant it couldn't be good, whatever it was.

In addition to this discouraging turn of events, one gentleman in particular had seemed to be watching Amelia steadily throughout the evening, and he was doing so again now, in such a way that it made her skin crawl. She did not know him, although there was something familiar about him. He was an older man, old enough to be her father, certainly, quite tall, with steel-gray hair. He was a man used to overindulging himself, if Amelia were any judge of his appearance, for, despite being dressed in the latest fashion, he had a large, protruding belly and a ruddy complexion that came from too much rich food and drink.

The fact that he was watching Amelia so intently and with such a look of malice alarmed her. Was he a close friend of the Duke of Marwood? For the life of her, she could not understand the nobility at times, nor fathom what the duke was thinking—or why this total stranger should look at her with such a clear expression of loathing.

The strange man moved closer to her as she danced with Sir Richard. The normal hum of chatter increased in volume, and the eyes of many of the guests began watching her even more closely in the wake of the Duchess of Marwood's progress around the room. Amelia dreaded the moment when the music would stop and she would learn what was being said.

The dance eventually ended, and Sir Richard offered her his arm. "Courage, Miss Clarke," he whispered, all seriousness now, apparently aware of the negative attention on them. "You have been all that is gracious and ladylike this evening. Everything will be well, I am sure."

Amelia was not sure at all. But the supper dance was next and she would be with Anthony, and that alone gave her the will to move toward him, despite the murmuring and looks of disbelief and hostility from the very people she had met earlier this evening who had been quite pleasant and congenial.

Louisa was with Anthony when Sir Richard and Amelia reached their side. "They are saying," Louisa hissed indignantly, "that you stole my brother from right under Lady Elizabeth's nose and that you are no better than you ought to be!"

Amelia paled. It was the same accusation the Duke of Marwood had made at Ashworth Park, and it implied she was a woman of loose morals.

To have all these people think that about her . . .

She shut her eyes, shielding herself from everyone and everything going on around her.

"Anthony, take her home," Amelia heard Lady Ashworth say. "She does not need to be subjected to this. Her upbringing has not prepared her to deal with the ugly side of the *beau monde*."

Lady Ashworth's words struck her. Her upbringing had not prepared her, she had said. The vicar's daughter, gently bred in a small village, where life was about family and work, birth and life, and sickness and death. But Little Brenchley had not been completely idyllic either, and while Amelia had not seen its ugliness, she was not so foolish as to think it did not exist.

She was not naive. She understood that Anthony had seen even worse in Spain. He had barely shared what he had endured at Badajoz. What of the rest of it? What of the other battles he had endured? If Amelia could not endure the gossip of a bitter woman—a duchess who should hold herself to the highest standards—then she was not worthy to be Anthony's wife.

She opened her eyes and straightened, looking each of them in the eye. "Running away will not make things better; it will only accomplish the opposite and make me look guilty." She turned to Anthony. "Were you ever afraid before going into battle?"

"Yes," he said, his eyes blue and clear. "Every time."

"Did it stop you from doing what you knew you needed to do?" she asked.

"No," he answered. "But be warned, Amelia. Battles are never straightforward. A man's moral courage is tested at every turn. Not all men face the enemy with honor, nor is the enemy completely honorable. It is difficult, and I would not have you experience it in any form."

"But you have experienced it," she said softly. "Many times."

"Yes," he said. "And it is why I know what I am telling you."

"Will we have better success at overturning the damage the Marwoods have created if I stay or if I go?" she asked.

"I cannot say with any certainty," he said. His face was tense, his eyes those of the warrior she knew he had been.

"You must cease to be my fiancé for a moment," she said. When he looked at her in alarm, she added. "I mean you must cease *thinking* as my fiancé. You must be my captain instead. What, Captain, do you think will increase our odds of success?"

His eyes softened. "I hate to say it, but my gut tells me you are right, my love."

Amelia's heart swelled near to bursting at his endearment. Why must he call her his love now, of all times? She looked into his dear, strong face. He was a man of honor, a man who had faced terrible things with courage and a respect for others—

"Lord Halford." The strange man who had been eyeing Amelia all evening interrupted her thoughts.

"Do I know you, sir?" Anthony asked. The entire group seemed taken aback that a total stranger would presume to approach him without an introduction.

"I am the son and heir of Viscount Winfield," the man said.

Anthony's eyes grew huge.

"How do you do," Lady Ashworth said graciously, attempting to defuse the tension in the air that had arrived with the man. "I am the Marchioness of Ashworth."

He scarcely looked in the marchioness's direction, instead turning his attention directly to Amelia. "Perhaps I would be more easily recognized by the commoners in this group if I were to say that my name is John Clarke-Hammond Junior."

Viscount Winfield. That was supposedly the name of her grandfather, but before Amelia could even react, he pointed his finger at her and, in a loud voice, declared. "Did you hear me? I am John Clarke-Hammond, brother of Edmund Clarke-Hammond, and this woman is a deceitful fraud!"

Amelia was barely aware of all the gasps that erupted around her at those words. She had gasped herself, and then she had gone cold.

"Tony!" someone cried—possibly Kit—and suddenly Anthony's arms were around her as her knees grew weak and she fought a threatening blackness that encroached on her vision.

"No," she said weakly.

"Edmund Clarke-Hammond went against our father's wishes and denounced his family to marry the daughter of a coal miner and a seamstress. He was disowned as a result, something that grieves my father to this very day.

"We, of course, have kept ourselves informed of Edmund's whereabouts in order to assure ourselves he would do no further damage to the family name. Therefore, when it came to our attention that an Amelia Clarke, daughter of Edmund and Sarah Clarke, deceased, was to marry the Earl of Halford, heir to the Marquess of Ashworth, I made it my duty to thwart her in her attempt to do what her own mother did to my brother."

"You needn't have bothered," Anthony said in a cold voice. "The lady you sully with your words is my choice of bride. I care not a whit who her family is or whether she is the daughter of a vicar or granddaughter of a viscount."

Amelia still felt weak, but her vision had cleared enough to see the Duke and Duchess of Marwood join the crowd gathered around them. She was also vaguely aware that the orchestra had ceased playing.

"It is much worse than that," Mr. Clarke-Hammond sneered. "The chit is not even my brother's flesh and blood! He and his wife had no living children!"

"What?" Anthony turned to look at Amelia.

A series of puzzling circumstances suddenly fell into place. On one occasion her mother had let something slip, implying how grateful she was to have gotten her, or words to that effect. Amelia had thought little of it at the time. And when she had packed up her parents' things and moved to Oxfordshire, she had thumbed through the family Bible during a bout of melancholy, missing them both dreadfully, and had realized that her entry was different from the children her mother had birthed who had not survived.

Three small entries: one for Edmund Clarke Junior, born 5 May 1786–died 6 May 1786, and one for Sarah Clarke, born 22 September 1789–died 22 September 1789. And one final entry, which read: Amelia Clarke, christened 15 March 1790.

A christening. Not a birthdate.

As Amelia had always celebrated March 15 as her birthday, she had simply presumed the entry an anomaly. Considering what little she knew of childbirth, it had not occurred to her that her arrival in the Clarke household had not allowed sufficient time for her mother to recover from the previous birth before giving birth to Amelia . . .

Oh, good heavens.

"This . . . person," Mr. Clarke-Hammond waved his hand in a disgusted gesture at Amelia, "is the illegitimate child of no one in particular. She is not what she claims to be, the legal offspring of the Reverend Edmund Clarke-Hammond—"

"Clarke," Amelia said in a soft voice. "Edmund Clarke."

"Clarke-*Hammond*," the horrible man hissed at her. "And she is *definitely not* the granddaughter of Viscount Winfield. I am only glad I was able to arrive in time, before this fraudulent marriage actually occurred and you found yourself bound for life to this . . . this common piece of *nothing*."

The din, which grew in size as the news spread through the ballroom, was a throbbing ache in Amelia's ears. She had bravely told Anthony she would stay and fight when the only cause for alarm was the accusations of the Duke and Duchess of Marwood. But, then, Amelia had known she was innocent in their particular accusations.

This man's accusations, however, she could not answer, for she did not know how. Edmund and Sarah Clarke had been her parents in every way. If they had chosen not to tell her about her origins, their reason must have been that they had wanted her to believe she was theirs.

They were not her real parents. Not in the eyes of society, even if they were to Amelia.

The world as she had always known it was turning upside down.

Anthony, his arm securely around her waist, opened his mouth to reply to Mr. Clarke-Hammond, but before he could say anything, the Duke of Marwood pushed his way through the crowd to face them. He sneered. "What a delightful discovery to find the great Earl of Halford, who could have married the daughter of a duke but now finds himself shackled to a trollop of uncertain parentage—a social climber of the worst sort."

Amelia felt Anthony tense. "You will watch your language. There are ladies present—"

"*True* ladies," the duke added.

"*Ladies*," Anthony continued in a voice that should have sent a warning to the duke. "Including my affianced bride. You will act honorably, or I will not be accountable for the consequences of my actions."

"Anthony," Amelia said softly.

He ignored her and turned back to Mr. Clarke-Hammond. "And as for you—"

"Anthony," she repeated more firmly. "This is my battle too." She stood as straight as she could, though she was grateful Anthony's arm was there to lend support, since her whole body trembled. "Mr. Clarke-Hammond," she said, addressing the man whom she now recognized as having a mild resemblance to her father underneath his fleshy appearance. "How happy I would have been to meet you on more neutral terms, where you could have told me about my father's childhood and family. He did not speak of you, you must understand, and yet I know how important family was to him in the way he cared for me and my mother—yes, I can see you wish to argue their relationship with me. But in all the ways that mattered, they were my parents, and I loved them. And they loved me. They never told me I was not their own."

"Yes, Mr. Clarke-Hammond," Anthony said in a mock agreeable tone. "I too must wonder at your showing up at this ball fully prepared to make a scene—and I must commend you on your success—when I would have respected you much more if you had come to me privately, where we could have discussed these matters in a civil manner."

"I could not trust that you would see things with the proper perspective, Lord Halford."

Amelia watched the color rise in Anthony's face.

"Well, Duchess," the Duke of Marwood said to his wife, who stood behind him, looking at her toes. "It appears I needn't have made you say anything after all."

Lady Elizabeth stared in disgust at her parents. "Father, how could you? Oh, Mother, even you. I just knew it." She turned and pushed through the crowd to run away, with Kit following after her.

"Elizabeth, wait!" the duchess cried and dashed after them.

Amelia herself was feeling slightly hysterical. It was a circus, like the one that had come through Little Brenchley when she was seven, only this time she was in the center ring. Anthony's face was getting redder by the second, his mother and Louisa clutched their hands to their breasts, and Mr. Clarke-Hammond and the Duke of Marwood looked like overstuffed geese, their chests puffed out, honking belligerently at her.

It was too much.

What should she do? What could she say that would bring this to an end?

Papa, I need you.

Pray, my child, she heard.

She briefly shut her eyes. She had been doing a lot of praying tonight, and it hadn't seemed to help so far. But there wasn't a lot of time or any other options.

Help, was the only prayer she could manage.

And then she could see her father in her mind, pulling her onto his lap and opening the family Bible, the one that held confirmation to the horrible truths Mr. Clarke-Hammond had thrown derisively at her tonight. Her papa, the good man, the vicar, would thumb leisurely through the pages until he found just the right passage to answer a little girl's question. It had been a common occurrence in their home, tender, blessed memories that would give her strength now. Her father and God's grace were with her.

"I stand accused," Amelia said, feeling calmer, "by men who are my superior of rank and birth. In my defense, I can only say that I lived my entire life believing I was the daughter of Edmund and Sarah Clarke. I loved them unconditionally as any child would love her parents, nursed them both when illness struck, grieved when they died, and then found myself alone."

"Yes," the Duke of Marwood said, "and that is precisely when—"

"You will be silent!" Anthony roared at him.

"And *you* will refer to me as Your Grace!" the duke bellowed back.

Anthony strode over to the duke until he was in his face, requiring that the man look up, as Anthony was several inches taller. "Had you acted with the honor your title implies, I should have replied in kind. Now you will simply be quiet and let the future Countess of Halford speak!"

He returned to Amelia's side like a gallant knight of old—her champion, there to guard and protect her. Oh, how she adored him.

"You may continue, my love," Anthony said to her in a restrained voice.

She looked in his eyes, and although there was an icy turbulence to them, she saw a tender emotion there for her alone. "I had no one," she said, turning to face her audience once more. "And were it not for the kindness of Lady Walmsley and the Marchioness of Ashworth, I would have been in the direst of circumstances: without home, family, or security of any kind. They are my angels on earth, and I love them."

"We are your family now," Louisa said, her voice breaking. Farleigh placed a protective hand on Louisa's shoulder.

Amelia gave them a smile filled with gratitude. "I make no claims on the connection to the Clarke-Hammond family, nor expect anything from them. My father and mother were content in their humble existence and thrived ministering to the needs of the good people of Little Brenchley in Kent."

She turned to face Anthony. This would be the most difficult part. "As for the other item of which I stand accused, I will say only that I admire the Earl of Halford above all men, and it has been my greatest honor to have been—"

"No," Anthony murmured, shaking his head.

"My greatest honor," she repeated, her heart plummeting at what she must do, "to—"

"Do not say it, Amelia. I beg you," Anthony said, grabbing her hands as she began to draw off her glove so she could remove the beautiful ring he had given her only that evening. "Do *not* let them win."

She freed her hands and placed them on his cheeks, framing his handsome, intense face and memorizing every inch of it. "I fear it is no use, Anthony. The suspicion will always remain, and you do not deserve that after all you have had to endure."

He placed his hands over hers. "How am I to endure going forward if you are not at my side?" Removing her hands from his face, he kept hold of them and turned to face the Duke of Marwood and Mr. Clarke-Hammond. "If she refuses to accept my suit because of your selfish and ill-conceived attacks to her reputation, I shall merit a form of justice on you both so virulent you will beg for death to end your misery."

The entire ballroom was completely still.

"Mark my words, Halford," the Duke of Marwood said. "I haven't finished with this business yet." He turned and stormed from the ballroom.

Anthony watched him go, a profound look of satisfaction on his face. "As to any remaining questions regarding Miss Clarke's parentage," he said, staring deeply into Amelia's eyes before turning back to the crowd. "There is nothing more to say, except that you may all congratulate me on my nuptials, which I hope will be soon. You have witnessed my fiancée stand with dignity as two members of the nobility have publicly torn apart her reputation. Who would like to be the first to congratulate us?"

"I would," the Duke of Atherton said, stepping forward. He and his duchess had been standing near Lady Ashworth, but now the crowd parted so the two of them could reach Anthony and Amelia. He shook Anthony's hand heartily and kissed Amelia's cheek as two burly footmen quietly escorted Mr. Clarke-Hammond from the ballroom. "Well done, both of you," he said.

"You brought me to tears," the duchess said. "What moving declarations! Such honesty and courage are to be greatly admired."

The Marchioness of Ashworth was next. "Amelia, I could not be more proud! I shall be quite honored to have you for a daughter-in-law. You faced those gentlemen with such a noble bearing. Please say you will marry my son. We are all better for having you in our midst."

"Thank you, my lady," Amelia said, truly touched.

The marchioness waved a finger at her. "You are to call me Mama, if you feel you can. I should never presume to take your own mother's place, but I would like it very much if you would consider me as another mother to you."

"Thank you, from the bottom of my heart," Amelia said, tears now welling in her eyes.

Anthony kissed his mother's cheek. "God bless you, Mother," he whispered.

A man cleared his throat then, and they all turned.

It was the Marquess of Ashworth. He looked tired, the lines bracketing his mouth deeper than they had been earlier in the day. Farleigh left Louisa to assist him if he needed it, but he was walking under his own power, every inch the nobleman.

"Father," Anthony said.

"Halford," he said in a cool, commanding voice.

The crowd of onlookers had not dispersed, undoubtedly eager to catch every last bit of the scene unfolding before them this evening, and everyone waited with bated breath to see what the Marquess of Ashworth had to say.

Father and son only stared silently at each other, and Amelia, for the life of her, could not figure out what was taking place between them. They were like two lions, testing each other's right and ability to rule the pride.

After what felt like an eon to Amelia, her strength beginning to wane now that the conflict was largely over, the marquess turned his cool gaze in her direction. Aware that his were not the only eyes on her, she dropped into a respectful curtsy and rose, lifting her chin slightly, unwilling to be cowed after facing down the Duke of Marwood and her father's estranged brother.

The Marquess of Ashworth reached out and brought her hand to his lips. "Miss Clarke, I will be honored and proud to call you Countess of Halford," he said.

"Thank you, Lord Ashworth," she said simply, deeply moved.

He nodded, satisfied. "I believe it is time to leave," he said to his wife.

"I could not agree more," she said.

"I shall call for the carriage," Farleigh said and hurried off.

"I am quite put out at Marwood," the Duchess of Atherton said to Anthony and Amelia as the crowd began to disperse, the excitement finally over. "If he wished to create a scandal, he only needed to arrive with his mistress in tow, the old bounder. I am *so* sorry, my dear." She took Amelia's hand in both her own. "But I must say, Miss Clarke, you were a sight to behold—a veritable Athena, such courage and grace you possessed through it all. My ball will be on everyone's tongues for weeks." She patted Amelia's hand and then left to mingle with her guests.

Anthony and Amelia watched her leave.

"Did we just hear the Duchess of Atherton refer to the Duke of Marwood as an old bounder?" Anthony asked.

"I believe we did. I believe that wasn't all she said about him either."

"Hm. So I was not imagining it." He offered Amelia his arm. "Shall we go?"

"Yes, *please*," she said. "I have had my fill of balls for one evening. Perhaps for a lifetime."

They made it nearly to the door when the Duke of Atherton stopped them. "Miss Clarke, you are a wonder," he said, his eyes twinkling with humor. "While I regret the discomfort the confrontation caused you both, I must say old Marwood has been asking for it for years. I confess I enjoyed seeing him brought down a peg or two. A pleasant evening to you both."

When they were finally in Anthony's carriage and alone, he sat next to her, pulling her close to his side rather than taking the seat across from her. "I have to say, I entirely agree with Atherton," he murmured in a voice that sent chills through Amelia as he pulled off a glove and began to trace her jawline with his fingers.

"You mean, seeing the Duke of Marwood brought down a peg?" she whispered, her own hands itching to touch his handsome, beloved face.

"That too," Anthony said. He replaced his fingers on her skin with his lips, and Amelia sighed with pleasure.

Trying to maintain composure and not lose her senses, she asked, "If not that, then what?" She honestly could not remember what the duke had said, so muddled were her thoughts right now with Anthony's lips trailing down her throat.

"You truly are a wonder," he said and moved his lips to barely an inch from her own. "And you are mine."

And Amelia was lost.

Chapter 16

ANTHONY AWOKE THE FOLLOWING MORNING, intent on finding out what he could that might shed illumination on the Duke of Marwood's actions of the previous night.

"I heard about what happened," Lucas said, lounging casually in a chair, his leg swinging from the arm as Anthony picked up his razor and began to scrape whiskers from his cheek.

"Would you care to elaborate?" he asked, glancing over at his friend.

"Watch what you are doing," Lucas said. "I know from experience that blood is the very devil to get out of clothing."

Anthony only growled at him and scraped off more beard.

Lucas laughed. "As to your question, you must realize what happened to you at the Atherton ball spread through London like a fire through St. Giles. It even made its way to the poor gentlemen's club where I was playing cards. By the way, I have been looking over the London staff, and I believe there is at least one footman who might make a decent valet for you."

Anthony stopped what he was doing. "You have decided to return home finally, have you? It is about time. I'm sure they are convinced you have disowned them."

"Speaking of being disowned, how is Miss Clarke faring?"

"She had recovered quite well by the time I dropped her at Lady Walmsley's house." Quite well indeed. He smiled at the recollection. "I am eager to see her this afternoon and reassure her once again that whatever was said yesterday, it makes no difference to me."

"It is as I thought," Lucas said. "You are smitten. I can only presume you are dreaming of meadows and buttercups, which accounts for your improved sleep." He sighed dramatically. "You have become a lovesick schoolboy before my very eyes. It would be terrifying, if not for the fact that I too have benefited from your restful nights."

"Lovesick schoolboy, you say? Perhaps you are right. And perhaps you are finding yourself jealous over my happy state and, therefore, have decided to resort to ridicule."

"Ha!" Lucas replied with mock indignation. "No parson's mousetrap for me, my friend. While I am extraordinarily pleased for you, marriage is not in my plans."

"Plans have been known to change, as we both know from experience. Now, fill me in on the top prospects for valet—but be quick about it. I am starving. Will you join me?"

"I have already eaten. I was not out as late as you were last evening."

When Anthony finally entered the breakfast room, he found his parents still eating. After serving himself at the sideboard, he joined them at the table. "I appreciate you both standing with Amelia and me last night, especially in light of the revelations Mr. Clarke-Hammond shared so publicly." He helped himself to a bite of eggs.

His father gestured at the footman standing by the sideboard, who immediately left the room so they could be alone. "Miss Clarke conducted herself admirably," his father said as he sliced off a small bite of ham. "She demonstrated she is of superior character, despite the questions surrounding her birth. I also suspect those who were in attendance will be inclined to sympathize with her, which is to our benefit, since neither of you will be able to cry off after what happened."

"Oh, Ashworth," his mother said, setting her teacup down. "You talk as if you are planning a chess move rather than discussing our son's life and as if you are not fond of Amelia when I know very well you are. When are you planning to marry her, Anthony? There are arrangements to be made."

"As soon as possible; next week would be my preference. I have had a special license in my pocket for some time now."

"I had forgotten you planned to do that," his father said before taking a sip of tea.

"Next week?" his mother added in a faint voice. "So soon?"

"Yes, but I must discuss it with Amelia first. And while we are on the subject, I am curious about something. Why is it the Duke and Duchess of Marwood cannot seem to move on from Lady Elizabeth's and my decision not to wed? Their actions were appalling, the duke's especially concerning. I have seen men on the battlefield look as he did last night, as though they were driven to the edge of reason." Anthony had witnessed it more than he cared to recall. "What is going on?"

"You do not know everything about the original betrothal, Anthony," his mother said. "The marriage settlement your father and Marwood arranged between Alexander and Lady Elizabeth was a generous one, promising the duke a huge amount of capital, which your father was willing to provide at the time. Lady Elizabeth is a paragon and of the highest rank. There seemed no one better suited for the Earl of Halford."

"Lady Elizabeth had many suitors," his father added, "and Marwood hinted that only the best offer would secure her. Alex was partial enough to her, and so I made the appropriate arrangements. I cannot account for Marwood's current behavior, however."

"The whole thing is puzzling," his mother answered. "The duchess and I came out together and have been friends ever since. And yet she was the one spreading the gossip all evening. I could hardly believe it."

"Marwood put her up to it," Anthony said, rising from the table. He intended to see what more he could find out on his own this afternoon. Once he had a better idea of Marwood's state of affairs, he would know how to proceed.

"I hope you can convince my father to rest today," he said to his mother, kissing her cheek. "I would hate to see the poor old fellow relapse after last night's excitement."

"Rubbish," his father said. "I'm as fit as a fiddle now. In fact, I believe I will take in a few rounds of boxing at Gentleman Jackson's and then spend the rest of the day at White's." He winked slyly at Anthony.

Lady Ashworth missed the wink, however, and stared at him, appalled. "Oh, no, you will not, you foolish man," she said. "I will not have spent the last several months wringing my hands at your bedside only to have you kill yourself at the first available opportunity."

Anthony bit his lip in order not to smile. His father was definitely on the mend. Anthony finished his breakfast and bid his parents good-bye, then rang for his horse to be saddled.

He had told Amelia he would join her for tea later in the afternoon. He wondered if he should send her a note urging her to stay home with Lady Walmsley but then decided against it. She would probably want to stay away from the public today anyway and let things settle a bit. Besides, she would most likely sleep late since the ball had gone into the wee hours of the morning.

He could imagine her waking, her rich, auburn hair a halo around her head, her green eyes fringed with dark lashes as they opened sleepily, her luscious lips turning upward to smile a welcome to him . . .

He wanted to wake up to that image every day of his life.

Bucephalus was saddled and waiting for him when he got outside, stamping and eager to be off. Anthony mounted him and set off for Swindlehurst's office.

"Good afternoon, Lord Halford," Marlowe said, looking up from the work on his desk. "Mr. Swindlehurst is with someone, but I shall tell him you are here." He exited, leaving Anthony to pace. Putting Marwood in his place last night had been cathartic; for once Anthony had felt like he could *do* something about the wrongs inflicted on others—in this case, someone he loved. The ability to act had been freeing.

Eventually Swindlehurst's visitor bowed his way out of the office, and Anthony was escorted inside.

"Please, be seated," the solicitor said. "I heard about what happened last night. Astonishing, if you don't mind my saying so."

"Not at all. I quite agree."

"I do hope Miss Clarke suffered no ill effects as a result."

"She was the very epitome of strength and grace. And speaking of Miss Clarke, has Abbott any new information for me?"

"Not much," Swindlehurst replied. "He had heard rumblings about her actual parentage, but he chose not to mention it until he had suitable evidence in hand to prove it. No need to raise such a delicate matter if it turned out to be untrue, he thought. He is on his way to Kent now. I hope to hear from him in a day or two."

"It would seem Edmund Clarke-Hammond and his wife went to great lengths to hide the information."

"True, my lord, but there will be those in the village who, if pressed, will remember the circumstances surrounding Miss Clarke's birth. They may feel loyal to the vicar and not wish to share, or they may feel that since he is gone, it is all for the best. It remains to be seen."

Anthony nodded his agreement. "I will be interested to hear what he discovers, although it will make no difference in the long run. As far as I am concerned, Amelia is the beloved daughter of Edmund and Sarah Clarke. Anything else is merely a curiosity." He hesitated, then decided to ask one more question. "I wonder if, perhaps, you might know anything of Marwood's situation. His behavior last night was extreme and leads one to speculate."

Swindlehurst sat back in his chair and steepled his fingers. "As a matter of fact, Abbott did mention something this morning on that very subject. He was already looking into Marwood on another matter, financial I think he said, though he did not elaborate. I can find out more when he returns from Kent, if you like."

"Thank you. The sooner I can get to the bottom of it and determine for myself that Amelia will not be subjected to more gossip, the better I will feel. Good day to you."

"At your service, as always, my lord."

Anthony rose and shook Swindlehurst's hand and then proceeded on his way. He had other things he needed to do this afternoon before he met Amelia for tea.

* * *

Amelia slept until nearly noon, surprised when she awoke to discover just how late it was. She wondered at her ability to sleep at all. It was true she had returned home exhausted from the ordeal at the ball, but she also suspected her body had longed for sleep as a way of avoiding the realities of what she had learned.

Her parents were not her real parents. She had momentarily wondered at the way her name had compared to the others in the family Bible, but growing up? She had felt confident and secure as the beloved daughter of Edmund and Sarah Clarke.

Clarke-Hammond, she corrected herself with a shudder. Although she would never refer to her parents by that name, nor herself.

She rang for hot chocolate and toast, then hurried and washed herself.

"Are you ready for me style your hair, miss?" Jane asked.

"Yes, please, Jane." She inspected herself in the mirror. She did not look any different. It was still Amelia Clarke who looked back at her with shadowed eyes. "Something simple, I think."

"Yes, miss."

And yet, Amelia mused as Jane began combing out her hair, she was no longer the person she had always known herself to be. She was Amelia Somebody, daughter of Nobody Knew Whom and fostered by a compassionate vicar and his wife. That she was not related by blood to the ghastly man she had met last night was the only redeeming fact he had hurled at her during his awful tirade.

Her toast and chocolate arrived, but Amelia discovered she was not hungry after all and managed only a few bites. "Jane," she said, pushing the tray away, "has Lady Walmsley mentioned what her plans are today?" Lady Walmsley, with her experience and humor, would be able to advise Amelia and would tell her truthfully if it was still fair to marry Anthony after this latest round of information. Amelia was most likely illegitimate. How could a future marquess attach himself to someone like that?

And yet the Marquess and Marchioness of Ashworthy had heard all and had supported and welcomed her nonetheless.

"Oh, I forgot," Jane said. "Lady Walmsley left word for you that she went to call on a friend this afternoon and won't be back till teatime. I meant to tell you that earlier. There! All done. Simple, like you asked." She had pulled Amelia's hair into a chignon at the nape of her neck, a few tendrils escaping to frame her face.

What to do now? She was dressed, she wasn't hungry, and Lady Walmsley wasn't here to advise her. She felt restless. "Jane," she said. "Grab your bonnet and cloak. I need fresh air, and you are the only person here who can go out with me."

"But, miss," Jane said, her eyes wide, undoubtedly remembering the misunderstanding Amelia and Anthony had had the last time she had ventured out to the park unchaperoned. "I don't think—"

"Jane," Amelia entreated, "I will go mad if I cannot walk. I need fresh air. No one is here but you, and I am perfectly capable of walking without a male escort in Hyde Park. Dozens of ladies do it every day." She wished she was in the country right now, where she would be free to walk and no one would be at all alarmed.

A knock sounded at her dressing room door, and when Jane opened it, a footman stood outside holding a silver tray with a note on it. "This just arrived for Miss Clarke," the footman said.

Amelia thanked him, took the note, and broke the seal. *I need to see you alone after last night*, the letter said. *Meet me in the woods by the Serpentine as soon as you can.*

It was signed *A*.

The note was from Anthony. He must be feeling as anxious as she after what had happened at the ball and was not willing to wait until tea to discuss it with her.

"There you go, Jane," she said, waving the note in front of her nose. "This is from Lord Halford, and he wishes me to meet him near the Serpentine. We are going to Hyde Park after all, and you have no need to question it now."

"If you say so," Jane replied grumpily. "But it seems more like he would be stopping by to get you if he had a mind to walk in the park."

"I am sure it is only that he had business to attend to this morning," Amelia said, donning her straw bonnet and pelisse. It was a warm, sunny day, and Jane had chosen a light muslin for Amelia to wear. Amelia was certain Anthony would have spent the morning trying to learn what he could about her parentage, and it would help her settle her mind and heart to see him again; waiting until teatime would have been nearly unbearable.

The early afternoon was not the fashionable time of day in Hyde Park when the *beau monde* went there to see and be seen, so there wasn't the normal crush of people around to notice if Amelia walked a little faster than was ladylike. She needed to rid herself of her pent-up anxieties and reach the Serpentine as quickly as she could.

It was ironic, then, to immediately run into Kit and his brother Phillip, who were on horseback greeting the few acquaintances they happened upon. When they noticed Amelia, they dismounted and walked over to speak with her.

"Amelia, how are you this afternoon?" Kit said. "I hope you are well despite the insufferable behavior you were forced to endure last evening."

"I am, thank you," she said, impatient to be on her way to the Serpentine.

"It was badly done, and him a duke, no less," Phillip said. "I would not have believed it if I had not witnessed it with my own eyes. And that other gentleman—to air one's family business like that in public. Appalling."

"After his loud declarations, it was a relief to know that he is not a blood relation at all." She smiled brightly. "There is a silver lining, you see."

"Touché, Amelia," Kit said. "May we walk with you for a spell since Tony is not with you?"

"Oh, but I am on my way to meet him," Amelia said. "Down by the Serpentine. It is where Jane and I are headed right now." She shot Jane a look, and the maid, who had moved several feet away when the gentlemen had arrived, now walked forward and dipped into a curtsy.

Kit's eyebrows furrowed in puzzlement. "You are meeting Tony? But Phil and I only just saw him back on Bond Street. He did not say anything about it."

"Not that he necessarily would have shared his plans with us," Phillip added.

"It was a late change of plans. He sent a note," Amelia explained.

"Well, he did seem to be in a rush; I am sure that explains it," Kit said.

Both gentlemen tipped their hats. "Good day to you, then," Phillip said and turned to mount his horse.

Kit lingered, however. "Amelia, I feel impressed to warn you. The Duke of Marwood is a powerful man with powerful allies, and he will not be satisfied with last night's confrontation. I would urge you to be careful."

"Your concern is appreciated. Thank you."

"Would you care for our escort until you meet up with Anthony?" he asked. "It would be our pleasure, would it not, Phil?"

"Truly, Miss Clarke," Phillip said. "We are only too happy to be of service."

"It is quite unnecessary, gentlemen, I assure you. But I thank you," Amelia said sincerely.

"Well, we shall leave you, then," Kit said. "But know that should Marwood choose to bother you again, you have only to ask and we will be there to assist in any way we can."

Amelia was touched by their gallantry and their loyalty to Anthony. She briefly watched them make their way down the path before turning back in the direction of the Serpentine.

The sky was a clear blue for once, with the occasional cloud puffing by. A breeze ruffled her skirts as she walked, and birds chirped and called to each other. There was a dense copse of trees near the Serpentine's banks, some distance from the usual strolling areas, and Amelia looked in that direction for him but could not see him yet.

"What if he doesn't show up?" Jane said. "What if he got busy on Bond Street, like the gentlemen said? We'll be out here for ages, then, to see if he ever shows."

"Hush, Jane. If he said he would be here, he will be." Of that Amelia had no doubt.

A cloud passed over the sun, its shadow making it even more difficult to see anything amongst the trees. Then she spotted a movement deep in the undergrowth. "There, Jane, I can see him." She pointed to a bench a ways off, near the banks of the Serpentine. "Wait for me there, all right?"

Jane reluctantly tromped off in that direction, and Amelia took a deep breath and headed toward the trees. But whatever she had seen move, she could not see it now. "Anthony," she called softly. "Are you here?"

There was a rustling sound, and Amelia could make out a rider on a black horse in the shadows in the distance. "Over here," his deep voice whispered.

Amelia picked her way toward him, holding her skirts and watching her step, careful to avoid tripping over roots and pushing away low-lying branches. "I do not understand," she said. "Why do we have to meet in such an out-of-the-way—"

She heard a crack and felt a sting across her shoulders, then a searing pain that brought her immediately to her knees. She glanced up, shaken, pushing her bonnet back from her face so she could see.

"Hello, Miss Clarke," the man atop the black horse said. Not Anthony, she realized now, but the Duke of Marwood, holding a whip instead of the customary crop most gentlemen carried when on horseback. "You have caused me a great deal of trouble." He raised the whip again and brought it down.

Amelia cried out and struggled unsuccessfully to get to her feet, sending up a desperate prayer for help. Oh, she wished she had accepted Kit's escort, but it was too late for that now. She needed to find a way to stand and run, to get away from the duke.

He brought the whip down on her again, and fire exploded across her back and licked at her arms.

"You are nothing but a nuisance," the duke said calmly. Somehow his words penetrated the blistering pain that threatened to consume her. He whipped her again. "A common trollop who used her wiles to take what was not hers to have. Illegitimate, no less." The whip assaulted her again.

Fire. Pain. Amelia screamed, hoping Jane—anyone—would hear and huddled to protect herself.

"Leave London, trollop. Save your wiles for other common animals like yourself. You are not welcome here." The whip seared her shoulders and back.

She turned her head to peer up at him. His face wasn't red with rage and hatred as it had been last night but was cold and rigid like a stone, and she knew then that he was not going to stop. She had to do something, but the raw agony pulsing through her was more than she could bear. She fought the pain and, with what little strength she had, pushed herself up onto her forearms.

He brought the whip down not once but twice in succession, punishing her actions. Fire encircled her throat and bit the edge of her cheek.

She moaned and collapsed onto the ground, mercifully succumbing to the blackness that finally enveloped her.

* * *

Anthony paused at the window of Phillips on Bond Street and surveyed the array of jewelry on display. After last night, he feared he was in for a devil of a time convincing Amelia to marry him. Her parentage, which had always been an obstacle to her, would be even more of a barrier in her mind. A small trinket was not the way to win over a clever and practical woman like her, but he rationalized that it wouldn't hurt either.

A pair of emerald earrings caught his attention. They reminded him of Amelia's clear, green eyes, which sparkled with life and occasionally took on the depth and serenity of a forest.

Humorously chiding himself for being so sentimental, he entered the shop and made the purchase. He would keep them in his pocket and present them to her if he felt it would aid his cause. And if his cause needed no aid? All the better. He would give her the earrings simply because he wanted her to have them.

He removed his pocket watch and ran his fingers over the fob Amelia had given him. It was hours until teatime when he could see her again. He had completed his errands more rapidly than he had expected. Swindlehurst had not heard from Abbott yet, so Anthony had purchased a piece of sheet music for Amelia he thought she might like. Now he had bought her earrings. He decided to drop in at his club before he ended up with an entire basketful of gifts for his lady. He had not been to White's in an age, and it would allow him to read people's reactions to the latest round of gossip.

He pocketed the watch and headed toward Bucephalus when he heard someone calling his name.

Galloping down the street, dodging traffic at breakneck speed, was Phillip Osbourne, of all people. "Tony," he cried. "Come quickly! It is Amelia."

Anthony broke into a cold sweat. "What about Amelia?"

"She is hurt. Kit is with her now. We must *hurry*."

Anthony leaped onto Bucephalus and rushed after Phillip, who circled his own mount around and sped off in the direction he had just come.

It quickly became apparent they were heading for Hyde Park.

What could have happened to Amelia at Hyde Park? his frantic mind asked. Other than on Rotten Row, where during the early morning people were allowed to gallop, the pace tended to be leisurely. Had a curricle overturned on her? Had an unruly horse kicked her?

Perhaps it was nothing so terrible as those, he told himself as he and Phillip turned onto Grosvenor Street and headed west. Surely she had only twisted an ankle. But if that was the case, Phillip would not be in such a state. He and Kit would merely have escorted Amelia back to Lady Walmsley's house and not gone for him in such a panic.

His heart in his throat, he followed Phillip through the park toward the wooded area near one end of the Serpentine. A group of onlookers had gathered, and when Phillip came to a stop nearby and pointed, Anthony leaped from Bucephalus and dashed into the trees. "Amelia!" he yelled.

"Tony, over here." Kit's voice carried, even though he had used a hushed tone. Chills ran down Anthony's spine at the sound, and he looked in the direction of the voice and saw Kit crouching low to the ground, his face grim. Amelia's maid Jane knelt nearby, sobbing, both hands clutched to her mouth.

And then Anthony made sense of the scene before him, and his heart stopped cold. In front of Jane, Amelia lay in a heap on the ground. He recognized the muslin as one of her new gowns. It lay in tatters on her back.

He strode to her and dropped to his knees. Ugly red welts crisscrossed her back, oozing blood, the fine, thin muslin of her gown and undergarments no protection against what were obviously lashes from a whip.

"Who?" he asked, but he already knew the answer.

"She is badly hurt, Tony. We must get her home and have a physician see to her at once," Kit said in a hushed voice as Anthony gently stroked Amelia's tangled hair from her face. He barely dared touch her for fear of the pain it might inflict. "Phil has gone to get my carriage. He was to bring you here first."

Anthony crouched low until his face was next to Amelia's. She was deathly pale and so still Anthony had to reassure himself she was still alive. He tenderly cupped her cheek. "Amelia," he whispered. "Amelia, my love, can you hear me?"

Her eyelids fluttered briefly, and she moaned.

Anthony squeezed his eyes shut, fighting the hot tears that threatened and forcing down the bile in his throat. He must be strong. He must get Amelia safely home and attended to. Her life was in danger from possible infection, and he would *not* lose this woman now that he had her in his life.

She had given him a reason to live and the hope that he could do so in peace. He would not give up easily on that hope.

But she was so pale and still.

"Everything is going to be fine," he whispered to her silent form, stroking her hair. He could see the blue veins at her temple; for some reason they made her seem even more vulnerable. "I promise you, love, I will see to it that everything is fine."

"I told her," Jane sobbed. "But she wouldn't listen, now would she? And look at what's happened."

Anthony ignored Jane, so intent he was on willing his strength into Amelia. There was a wound on her throat, and he followed the line tenderly with his forefinger. It circled around her neck and angled up, leaving a hot curl of red next to her ear.

"It was that note," Jane blubbered. "I told her to stay home, but that note convinced her to come here, and now she's as good as dead." She burst into a keening wail.

"She is *not* dead," Anthony snapped at the maid and then chided himself for doing so. He needed to be kind to the poor girl. She had been subjected to a horrible scene, and he knew only too well the effect something like that could have on a person. "She is not dead, Jane," he said again in a calmer tone. "Nor will she die. Have no fear of that."

"Amelia mentioned a note to me when Phil and I ran into her earlier," Kit said. "And here is her maid saying the same thing: she said it was you who sent her a note."

Anthony looked up from Amelia. "I never sent her a note. Had I done such a thing, I would have told her to expect me at Lady Walmsley's."

"'Tis what I told her, my lord! But she wouldn't listen. She was feeling trapped in the house, and when the note arrived—"

"Tell me about this note," Anthony said.

"Wasn't much of one, truth be told. Only said to meet you here."

"It had my name on it?" he asked her.

"Well, she only waved it at my face, but I saw a big letter *A* on it. *A* for Anthony. But it wasn't from you after all."

"No."

Jane buried her head in her apron and sobbed even more.

Anthony wanted to hold Amelia, take her in his arms, take the lashes that had been inflicted on her for himself. But anytime he attempted more than a gentle touch, she moaned, making a deep, horrible sound that scraped at his insides. It seemed an eternity before Phillip finally arrived with the coach.

"I shooed away as many of the onlookers as I could, Tony, for Amelia's sake," he said.

Phillip's words were a relief to Anthony. He loathed having Amelia's horrific wounds displayed before the curious masses. "Amelia," he said gently. "We need to move you now, and it is going to hurt terribly. I am so sorry, love."

Her eyes fluttered briefly. Anthony took it as a sign that she had understood him, and he instructed Kit to stand at her feet.

Phillip assisted Jane up, and they left to ready the coach.

"Are you ready, my love?" Anthony asked. "We will be as gentle as we can." He prayed she was able to understand his words. "Ready, Kit?"

His friend nodded grimly.

With Kit taking her legs to help bear her weight, Anthony slipped his hands beneath her arms and hoisted her onto his right shoulder. She screamed in agony, and Anthony wanted to wail at the sound. Once he had her there securely, he slowly rose to his feet.

He picked his way carefully over roots and fallen branches, doing everything he could to keep his movements from jarring Amelia. The coachman sprang into action at his arrival and quickly opened the carriage door. Inside, Phillip had set up a pallet spread with soft quilts that spanned between the carriage seats along the far side.

"Let me help you lay her down," Kit said.

"I am not letting go of her," Anthony said.

"Do you think that is best?"

"I will be better able to absorb the jarring motion of the carriage. The pallet will not. Slide it toward the center of the carriage, will you?" With the pallet moved to the center of the carriage, he wouldn't have to worry about Amelia bumping against a wall and hurting herself further.

Kit nodded and shifted the pallet forward several inches, and then he and Jane climbed in and maneuvered into their seats, leaving plenty of room for Anthony and Amelia.

"Take us to Ashworth House," Anthony instructed the coachman. He wanted Amelia under his own roof, where he and his family could see to her care. If Lady Walmsley wished to join them there, fine, but Amelia would be with him.

"I will see to your mount," Phillip said to Anthony as he jumped onto Kit's horse. He had left his own behind when he had returned with the carriage.

"Thank you, Phil. And thank you for finding me."

"Glad to be of service. Same holds, should you need us in future," he said with a look. "There are wrongs to be addressed."

"Indeed," Anthony said. He eased himself into the carriage with Amelia and stared grimly at Kit, who nodded in agreement, aware they couldn't talk with the maid present.

But they both knew the attack on Amelia had been at the hands of the Duke of Marwood. And despite being one of the highest peers of the realm, the blackguard would pay. Anthony would make certain of it.

Chapter 17

"Good heavens, what has happened?" Anthony's mother cried when they burst through the front doors of Ashworth House. "Gibbs, tell Mrs. Brewster to bring hot water and rags. Quickly!"

Anthony did not stop to answer; he climbed the staircase as swiftly and smoothly as he could, a swollen-eyed Jane trailing behind, followed by his mother, as he hurried to put Amelia in the bedchamber next to his.

"Pull down the bedcover," he barked at a wide-eyed chambermaid hovering nearby. She scrambled into action, and when she had completed the task, he carefully lifted Amelia from his shoulder and laid her facedown on the mattress. Despite his care, the slightest movement was still more than she could bear, and she cried out.

"All will be well, love," he said softly to her, stroking her forehead and placing a gentle kiss there. "I will make sure of it."

Mrs. Brewster arrived with a basin of steaming water and clean rags. She gasped when she saw Amelia's back. "Why, she has been . . ."

"Whipped. Yes," Anthony said in a clipped voice.

His mother looked at him with stricken eyes. "But who?"

He only stared at her.

"I cannot believe—"

"Believe it," he said.

"Oh, my poor girl," she said. "Jane, run and get scissors. Quickly. Mrs. Brewster, send word to Dr. Wilcox. Tell him it is urgent. Anthony, you must leave the room."

"Gibbs has already called for the doctor," Mrs. Brewster said, pulling out her own pair of scissors from the rags she had brought.

"I am *not* leaving her," Anthony declared.

"She is in capable hands now," his mother said. "You must leave her to us. It is improper for you to be here. Go!"

He stalked out of the room.

The removal of Amelia's clothing would be a delicate task, requiring them to cut away the shredded remnants of her dress and undergarments, which were stuck to her skin with dried blood. They would also need to search carefully for any bits of cloth imbedded in the open wounds from the force of the whip. That was what worried Anthony the most. He had seen arms and legs and lives lost from poorly cleaned wounds and the resulting infections. He would *not* allow that to happen to Amelia.

Dr. Wilcox arrived, bag in tow, and was barely able to utter a word before Anthony had shoved him into Amelia's bedchamber.

Anthony paced back and forth. He sat, drumming his fingers on his thigh. He rose, his stomach churning. He could barely breathe, his lungs were so constricted from fear and anxiety.

What a delightful discovery to find the great Earl of Halford shackled to a trollop of uncertain parentage.

Leave be, Captain, and let us have a little fun.

His body fairly vibrated with rage and frustration. He threw himself into the chair again.

He started when someone placed a hand on his shoulder. It was his father. "What is wrong? What's going on?" he asked as Jane dashed back with scissors and more clean hot water and rags.

"Amelia was attacked," Anthony said.

"Attacked? What do you mean?"

"Whipped like an animal in Hyde Park."

His father dropped heavily into a nearby chair, a look of incredulity on his face as the chambermaid left the bedroom with Amelia's destroyed garments.

Anthony rose and paced some more, dragging his hands through his hair until it stood on end. His eyes burned with unshed tears. "How long until that doctor is finished in there?" he growled.

"As long as is required to take care of her properly," his father replied. "Sit down, Halford. You are making me dizzy."

Anthony slammed into the chair.

"How bad is it?" the marquess asked in a quiet voice.

"At least a half dozen lashes, maybe more. This is Marwood's doing."

"Marwood?" He shook his head in disbelief. "Even after his display last night, I can scarcely believe he would do something like this. Are you sure?"

"Sure enough. He blames Amelia for the failed betrothal between Lady Elizabeth and me. I will know for certain soon."

Kit and Phillip had volunteered to go around to the gentlemen's clubs, making discreet inquiries. While Anthony was confident the Duke of Marwood was the beast who had attacked Amelia, his lofty position in society required that Anthony have evidence before acting.

"I have known the duke since we were boys at Eton," his father mused aloud. "He always had a temper as a lad, but I could never imagine him putting a whip to one of his horses, let alone a person."

"Do not doubt it, Father," Anthony said. "Amelia is suffering because of it, and he will be held accountable one way or another."

"Be careful, Halford," his father said. "You are dealing with a duke here, one who has powerful allies."

"Allies who would support a vicious attack on a woman?"

"Some would, I am sorry to say. It is the way things are in our world, unfortunately. You must think before you act."

Sitting was driving Anthony mad, so he lurched out of his chair to pace again. The more he paced, however, the more enraged he became. Kit and Phillip were taking too long getting back to him, and as for the infernal doctor . . .

"That doctor should be through by now," he said impatiently. "Unless the man is incompetent."

"Dr. Wilcox knows what he is about, lad," his father said. "He was an army doc in Canada before returning to Town. Knows his way around all sorts of wounds: gunshots, saber, probably even seen the likes of this a time or two over in the Americas. Wild place, the Americas, from all I have heard."

Anthony crossed his arms and glared at the door. "I am going in," he finally said. "Americas or not."

He reached for the doorknob only to have it open just enough for his mother to slip out and shut it again. "I need to see Amelia," he said.

"You must wait a few minutes more, dear," she said. "The doctor gave her laudanum, poor thing, so she could have some relief from the pain and he could work more easily. He is applying salve and a few light bandages now, and when she is properly covered, you may look in on her. Oh, Ashworth, her poor back!" she exclaimed to Anthony's father. "I cried at the sight of it."

"I am *not* waiting," Anthony said. "I want to see what that beast did to her. I want to be a witness of his cruelty." Before Lady Ashworth could object, Anthony yanked the bedroom door open and went inside.

Dr. Wilcox and Jane both looked up from their patient, Jane's eyes large and startled, the doctor irritated at the interruption. "What do you want?" he asked in a gruff, low voice.

Anthony didn't respond. He couldn't. He stood frozen at the door.

Amelia lay prone on the bed, the blankets drawn up to cover her legs and hips, her back bared for the doctor's ministrations. Her pale skin was crisscrossed with hot red welts, some of which still oozed blood. Jane was carefully dabbing away any blood as it pooled while the doctor gently applied the salve.

She would have scars after this.

Images stole into his mind, nightmarish images, and he squeezed his eyes shut and fought off his nausea. Fought for control. He would not allow himself any weakness now.

Amelia's entire body trembled in agony despite the laudanum, and Anthony moved to her side, bringing the chair that stood next to the wall with him. He sat and cupped the back of her head with his hand, threading his fingers lightly through her silky curls. "You are safe, my love. You are going to be fine. You are so very brave," he said to her over and over as the doctor finished applying the salve, wiped his hands, and began laying large cloth bandages on her back and shoulders. Even that slight pressure made her shudder and moan, and Anthony wanted to scream.

Finally the doctor gestured for Anthony to follow him out to the hallway, where Anthony's mother and father were waiting, leaving Jane to tend to Amelia. "I told the maid in there how to change the dressings, and there is more salve and laudanum on the table by the bed. I have done all I can for today. I will check in on her tomorrow, but call me right away if the young lady becomes fevered."

"Thank you, doctor," Anthony's mother said.

Dr. Wilcox shook his head. "I have treated a few cases like this, mostly sailors getting flogged for one reason or another. But they are men who spend their life at sea with skin tough as leather, not tender and white like the young lady in there. The salve should help reduce scarring. Terrible pity."

Anthony watched him go and then returned to Amelia's side. "I need to leave for a while, love," he whispered. "Important business to attend to with the Duke of Marwood."

Her hand fluttered at his words, though she didn't open her eyes, and he laid his own hand on top of it.

"He is going to pay for what he did to you," Anthony vowed softly. "I swear it. I will not be stopped like I was at Badajoz."

He kissed her forehead, and then he made his way silently past his concerned parents, grabbed his hat, and stalked out of the house.

* * *

Anthony was still saddling Bucephalus when Lucas entered the stable. "Wherever you think you are going, I am going with you," Lucas said and hauled his own saddle from its rack.

Anthony didn't respond; he was too focused on what he planned to say when he encountered the Duke of Marwood.

"I have a vested interest in keeping you alive, considering all the work I did the first time. It was quite a challenge too—finding a woman willing to take you in after what had just happened to her city, stitching you up, nursing you through deliriums when you were fevered, bathing you, helping you with the chamber pot—"

"I get your point."

"What do you intend to do?"

"What do you think? Amelia was whipped—*whipped*—in Hyde Park, no less. I intend to find the blackguard who did this to her and hold him accountable; that is what I intend to do." He grabbed the reins and led Bucephalus out into the mews.

Lucas followed with his own horse. "This is not Badajoz, Tony," he said. "And you are not merely disciplining one of your men."

"You are correct. This is not Badajoz," Anthony said. "That was war, and despite my best efforts, my men acted with depravity. I was unable to protect"—he choked on the word—"protect the woman they attacked, and I was not able to foresee Marwood's actions and protect Amelia either. But I can get justice for her. And I will do just that."

"Be sure it is justice you are seeking, Tony," Lucas said as they mounted their horses. "You are dealing with a duke here."

"You sound like my father, Lucas. But what of Amelia, pray tell? She is innocent of any wrongdoing, and yet she is suffering horribly. I am determined, Lucas. Marwood will pay for what he has done."

"If that is the case, then I am your man in this endeavor," Lucas replied.

When they exited the mews, they saw Kit and Phillip approaching. "It took some doing, but we found him," Kit said when he and his brother came abreast. "He is not at White's, as we had presumed. He is at a gaming establishment where the stakes are much higher, although the quality of the patrons is decidedly lower."

The establishment in question was located in a house on Pall Mall, and they went directly there. "I shall stay with the horses," Phillip said. "Prime horseflesh is too much of a temptation for the people who patronize this type of gaming den."

It was not difficult for them to gain entrance, considering who they were. They proceeded down a hallway and entered a large room, its many tables filled with gentlemen and even a few women who had the desire to wager heavily. The room was smoky, the atmosphere intense.

"There he is," Kit whispered, pointing with a jerk of his head.

The Duke of Marwood sat at a table near the back of the room.

Anthony strolled in that direction. "Your Grace," he said in a mocking tone when he arrived at the table where the duke was playing. The pot in the center of the table was a large one, and the duke tore his eyes away from the cards in his hand to glare at Anthony.

"I am busy," he said, returning his attention to his cards and indicating to the dealer to give him another.

"You only have to answer one question," Anthony said smoothly. Kit and Lucas stood on either side of him. "Did you yourself set the whip to my fiancée this afternoon, or did you order some lackey to do it for you?"

A hush went around the room. No one moved, although several eyes turned to look at the duke, awaiting his response. The smoke was acrid and burned Anthony's eyes and brought images of cannon and musket smoke to mind.

"I believe it is your turn, Lawton," the duke said.

Baron Lawton, a portly man of dubious character who was seated to the duke's right, jumped in his seat before hastily playing a card.

The duke then proceeded to take his time before selecting a card to play from his own hand.

Anthony gritted his teeth against the urge to beat the man here and now. The room was deathly silent now, as everyone had stopped to watch the scene before them. "I would have you answer my question, Marwood."

The duke casually reached into his pocket, retrieving his snuffbox, then deliberately took his time taking a pinch of snuff in each nostril. "Have you nothing better to do than spend your time annoying those of higher rank?" he said blandly, snapping the snuffbox closed and putting it back in his pocket.

"Leave be, Halford," someone said. "There's money to be made here tonight, and you're getting in the way of it."

"I would be only too happy to oblige," Anthony replied, "if the esteemed duke here would act like a man and *answer the question*."

"Enough of this," the Duke of Marwood said, rolling his eyes in affected boredom. "I wanted the pleasure for myself and the assurance of a job thoroughly done."

"It is as I thought," Anthony said. "And thank you for your candor at last." He stepped closer to the duke. "Name your second," he said.

The so-called ladies in the room gasped.

The duke rose to his feet. "Don't be a fool, you insolent cub. I will not be taken to task over the likes of an illegitimate nobody simply because she has caught your fancy."

"The *young lady* of whom you speak," Anthony said in a low, menacing voice, "is my fiancée and of finer quality and character than you will ever be. I shall meet you tomorrow at dawn, and your friends here"—he gestured around the room—"will witness your lack of honor should you decide not to show. Name your second."

The Duke of Marwood glanced around the table. When no one spoke up, Lawton grumbled, "I'll be your second, I s'pose."

"I will be speaking to you later," Kit told the baron, "as I shall be acting as the Earl of Halford's second."

"Until dawn tomorrow, then," Anthony said to the duke. He turned on his heel and left as the silence turned to murmurs. When they were finally outside, Anthony placed his hands on the side of the building and took a deep gulp of air.

"Unless you would rather act as Anthony's second," Kit said to Lucas behind Anthony.

"Heaven forbid," Lucas replied. "I will not make the arrangements for Tony to put his life in jeopardy. My job is to pick up the pieces after the fact."

"Understood," Kit said. "Marwood is a decent shot, Tony. I've a few acquaintances who have gone on the hunt with him. You need to know what you are up against. I doubt the duke will accept fault and delope."

Anthony pushed himself away from the wall and turned. "I am not expecting him to delope. And I am a capable shot myself." Anthony had made sure of it while on the Peninsula. A man could rely on others to stay alive only so much in a war.

"You are a crack shot," Lucas said. "But *challenging* the duke to a duel, Tony? What were you thinking?"

"What was I thinking?" Anthony shot back at Lucas. "You knew I was confronting the man. Did you expect we would have a little chat and he would meekly apologize and all would be well?" He closed his eyes at the image of the welts on Amelia's back. "Her back is raw, Lucas; the welts were deep and bloody ones. She will have scars from this. And *why*? Because the duke could not accept that Lady Elizabeth and I decided not to marry and chose to blame Amelia instead. What he did is beyond the pale."

"And what happens if he does not delope?" Lucas asked. "Do you intend to kill the man?"

"I do not know," Anthony replied truthfully. "I have killed before, in battle, as have you. And I am sorely tempted. *Sorely* tempted." He was through talking. He mounted Bucephalus and turned in the direction of home. It was time to be with Amelia for as long as he could and await the dawn.

Chapter 18

It was dusk, and the house was quiet when Anthony and Lucas returned, having parted from Kit and Phillip. Lucas took both horses to the stable while Anthony went inside, anxious to see Amelia now that his meeting with the Duke of Marwood was set. He hurried up to her bedchamber.

His mother sat quietly in a chair next to Amelia's bed, reading. The fireplace crackled, providing a soothing heat while Amelia slept on, a sheet lightly draped over her back. "I could not leave her," the marchioness whispered to him, setting her book aside. "She was my support when Alex died and again when we thought you were gone too. She sat with me as I stayed at your father's bedside. How could I not do the same for her?"

Anthony took his mother's hand in his and kissed it. "How has she been?"

"Asleep mostly, which is a blessing," she said. "The laudanum will begin to wear off soon though, and she will need more." She yawned as she gestured toward the bottle that stood on the bedside table.

"Go rest, Mother," Anthony said. "I will stay with her."

"Very well." She stood and placed a gentle hand on Amelia's head. "Sleep, dear girl. I am so sorry you are having to endure this." She turned away and wrapped her arms tightly around Anthony's waist. "Watch her well," she said.

He embraced her, his arms around her shoulders. "I intend to," he said, dropping a kiss on the top of her head. It was a rare, intimate moment with his mother, and he held her close, relishing the love and warmth when he still felt such rage inside.

Perhaps he had taken his family's love for granted when he had gone off to war, but no longer. He was facing a new battle at dawn, and there was no guarantee how things would turn out, despite his intention to live through it.

Eventually she drew back and left him to his lonely vigil. Dawn would come soon enough with its unsure outcome. In the meantime, Anthony would sit with the woman he loved.

* * *

Anthony felt something crawling through his hair. He jerked his head away, his hand reaching for the culprit.

There was a hissing sound followed by a deep moan.

His eyes immediately flew open. Fingers. Amelia's fingers. He had apparently fallen asleep in the chair, his head resting on the bed next to Amelia's own. Now her eyes, bleary and tight with pain, looked back at him.

Quickly loosening his grasp on her fingers, he brought them to his mouth and kissed them. In turn, she ran her forefinger slowly over his lips, her touch a benediction to his soul. "My love," he whispered, his voice gravelly from sleep.

"On fire, Anthony," she managed to say, wincing. "My back."

"I understand," he said. He kissed and relinquished her hand, and, shaking the fogginess of sleep from his mind, poured water into a glass, then added the laudanum. He held the glass to her lips. "Drink this, love. All of it."

It was difficult for her to drink, for any movement sent her into spasms of pain. Anthony tried to hold her head as she drank, and some of the liquid spilled, but he eventually got most of it into her.

"Thank you," she whispered as he dabbed at her chin and mopped up the spills as best he could from the bedding. She closed her eyes.

"Marwood will not go unpunished for this," Anthony told her. "I will see to it." He nearly told her he had challenged the duke to a duel and was meeting him in a few short hours, but it would only agitate her, so he stopped himself.

"Closer," she whispered.

He moved the chair out of the way and knelt by the bed, resting his head on the pillow next to hers. He traced her face with his fingers: her brow and delicate cheekbones, down her nose, along her jaw . . .

"Promise," she said.

"Anything," he vowed.

"Promise . . . no vengeance."

The image of the woman from Badajoz flashed through his mind again. "I could not save you from this. I must do something."

She shook her head and winced at the effort. "All my life"—she stopped speaking as she dealt with a wave of pain—"my father taught me."

"Hush, love," Anthony said to her, brushing her hair from her face. "Rest now; don't speak. Just rest." Anthony prayed the laudanum would begin to work soon.

She forced her eyes open. "God said . . . vengeance is His," she whispered.

"My brave girl," he said softly as he continued to stroke her face. "Not vengeance, then, my love. Justice. That you cannot stop me from."

"Oh, Anthony," she breathed, her eyes drifting shut, the laudanum finally, thankfully, showing its effects. "How you have suffered."

Anthony knelt there and watched as her breathing deepened and her body, freed temporarily from pain by the medicine, gradually relaxed.

She had spoken to him of his suffering when she was the one suffering now. How incredibly special she was. How he loved her.

He stood and placed a final kiss on her brow. It was nearly dawn, and he had preparations to make in order to be ready to meet the Duke of Marwood. Amelia would sleep restfully, and God willing, he would be back at her side before anyone realized he'd been gone.

He needed time to consider his promise to Amelia and how he could keep it when his blood pulsed hotly through him, urging him to take the duke's life.

Anthony had experienced it before—the blood pumping through his veins, the hellish desire to do the unimaginable. Storming the breaches at Badajoz had been a scene straight out of Dante's *Inferno*, as brave men had attacked the wall, thousands of them dying horrible deaths, others being driven to inhuman brutality.

Anthony knew well what it meant to be driven to the very edge of his humanity, and it had happened to the Duke of Marwood as well. But the duke had made the dire mistake of directing that brutality at Amelia, and for that he would pay.

One way or another, justice would be served.

* * *

The stars were fading, the sky turning from black to gray as Anthony and Lucas quietly walked their horses down the alley leading from the mews, anxious not to stir anyone from their slumber. Soon enough the houses on the square would be filled with servants lighting morning fires and hauling water, but not yet.

The men were silent, the clop-clop of the horses' hooves on the cobblestones the only sound. Mist swirled about, adding to the grimness Anthony felt.

Kit was waiting for them when they reached the corner of the square. "Phillip has gone for the surgeon," he said in a low voice. That was all that needed to be said. They mounted their horses and proceeded forward at a walk.

The meeting place that had been selected was a remote area of Hyde Park known for its duels and, appropriately enough, was not far from the spot where the duke had attacked Amelia. When the trio arrived, they could see that Phillip and the surgeon, a man Anthony recognized as an old army sawbones, as well as the duke and Baron Lawton, were already there. In the distance were the duke's and baron's carriages as well as the hackney coach Phillip must have used to bring the surgeon, their coachmen standing huddled together.

Anthony dismounted and left Bucephalus in Lucas's care. Kit walked forward to consult with the baron, each of them examining the chosen pistols, making sure the weapons were equal and in working order and measuring out the distance between the duelists. The signal to shoot, it had been decided, would be the drop of a handkerchief.

The Duke of Marwood stood off by himself while the seconds conferred. Anthony watched him closely, trying to read his behavior in order to assess his state of mind. The duke was a gambler, so he was used to steeling his nerves under pressure. But would the same hold true in a duel? Anthony, on the other hand, knew intimately what it was like to face the killing end of a weapon.

Kit returned to his side and handed the pistol to him. Anthony took a moment to check over the weapon himself. "The points are set," Kit said. "All is ready if you still wish to pursue this, Tony. But I would ask you to think of Amelia."

"She is precisely who I am thinking of," he answered, and yet he understood it was Kit's job as his second to attempt reconciliation.

Kit's words and Amelia's promise forefront in his mind, he approached the duke. "I see you are ready, Your Grace," he said.

The duke only cast a disparaging look at him.

"Do you wish to make amends?"

"Do not insult me," the duke replied icily. "The settlements were made, and you let that cheap bit of muslin distract you. She is nothing, nothing compared to my Elizabeth, who is worth her weight in gold. She ruined everything."

"I agree that your daughter is exceptional, but she is not a commodity, as you seem to forget. The lady and I both agreed we did not suit. You would do well to accept this, Your Grace. Miss Clarke is her equal in my eyes, and I will have your apology."

"Let's get on with this. You are wasting my time."

Anthony looked into the duke's eyes and saw no remorse there, only greed and dissipation. "As you wish," he replied. He turned to Kit and gestured for him to proceed.

Kit and Baron Lawton exchanged resigned expressions. "Gentlemen, take your places," Kit said in a voice just loud enough to carry over the green.

Anthony and the Duke of Marwood each walked to their designated points and saluted each other. Then they waited, pistols at their sides, their eyes on Baron Lawton, whose duty it was to drop the handkerchief.

Lawton rubbed his hands together nervously and pulled his handkerchief from his pocket. "Ready, present," the baron called, raising his arm and holding the white linen high. It caught the breeze briefly, fluttering, reminding Anthony of a flag of surrender. But it was not.

The baron dropped the handkerchief, but just before he did, he turned his head slightly, glancing toward the duke.

The duke raised his weapon and fired. Anthony, his reflexes honed from his years of military service, saw the handkerchief drop and fired his own weapon at the exact moment the duke's bullet whizzed past his ear.

The Duke of Marwood crumpled to his knees. Lawton and the surgeon hurried over to him. Anthony stalked over to him as well.

The surgeon was hunched over the duke, moving his clothing away from the wound in his shoulder so he could inspect it while Lawton flailed his hands about fretfully. "Be of some use, man, and stanch this blood," the surgeon snapped at Lawton.

Lawton's face was as gray as the duke's, and he looked as though he would keel over at any moment, but he dutifully squatted to hold a wad of rags at the ready for the surgeon and dabbed gingerly at the blood in question.

"You shot a *duke*," Lawton choked out when he noticed Anthony.

The duke in question hissed in pain as the surgeon examined the wound.

"No one would ever fault you for your powers of observation," Anthony said, earning a glare from the surgeon. Anthony did not care. He knew well enough that His Grace had not been mortally wounded by his shot, not that he wouldn't suffer for a while as Amelia now suffered. Anthony knew his own abilities well enough to know where it would hit, and despite his own inclinations, he had made a promise to Amelia.

Kit and Phillip hurried over as the surgeon assisted the duke to his feet. He was staggering and sweating profusely from the pain. "Help me get His Grace to the carriage," the surgeon barked. "He needs to be lying down if I am to get this bleeding under control. Quickly."

The men moved to carry the duke and secure him in his carriage, the surgeon climbing in afterward. Anthony had followed behind, and now he leaned in through the carriage door.

"What do you want?" the duke hissed, clenching his teeth as the surgeon applied more pressure on the bandages. "Haven't you gotten your satisfaction yet?"

"You aimed to kill," Anthony said.

"So did you. Now get out so I can leave."

"I did not. I promised Amelia I would not."

"Please, my lord," the surgeon said. "I really must get His Grace home—"

"You also fired before the signal," Anthony said. And then something dawned on him, something his reflexes had responded to that his conscious mind had not picked up on until now. "In fact, you signaled him," Anthony said, turning from the carriage door and pointing to the baron. "I saw you look at him before you dropped the handkerchief."

"No, I swear!" the baron cried, flushing beet red. "Just never been a second before. And the first time would be for a duke, no less. Nerves got the best of me."

"I do not believe you," Anthony said.

"'Tis true," the baron insisted. "I never—"

"The fool has a tell," the duke snapped. "When he has a bad hand or is into the pot too deep, he gives himself away. I was counting on it." He snapped his eyes shut and gritted his teeth.

"Blast you, Marwood," the baron said, dropping his head. He turned on his heel and stamped off to his carriage.

"I doubt those two will be playing cards together anytime soon," Kit said wryly.

"My lord," the surgeon said. "I would like to take the duke to his residence now, if you please, before he loses any more blood."

Anthony gripped both sides of the carriage door and leaned in to confront the duke face-to-face. "You owe your life to my promise to Amelia. Do not *ever* forget that or that it was *she* who exacted the promise from me."

Anthony moved and shut the door with an emphatic bang, then watched the carriage drive away before turning to join his friends, who were walking away from the carriage toward their horses and the hackney coach. The sun's rays lined the sky, softening the gray dawn and hinting of the light to come.

It was a new day. One Anthony hoped would herald the beginning of his life with Amelia at his side and his ghosts fading away with the mist.

Chapter 19

Jane had pulled the curtains partway open, so fresh morning sunlight brightened Amelia's bedchamber. Anthony quietly shut the door behind him and stood there, his hands clasped behind his back, taking in the scene before him.

Amelia was sleeping soundly, thankfully; the laudanum would be a necessity for a few more days until she healed enough that her movements would not cause her too much pain. The sheet across her back had slipped, baring one vulnerable-looking shoulder and part of her bandage. Her hair was an endearing tangle of curls that cascaded over her pillow and was shot with golden highlights from the sun's rays.

Amelia stretched in her sleep and winced, and Anthony started forward, concerned that she might be in need of more medicine, but she settled and breathed deeply and calmly again.

He took the seat he had spent most of the night in, exhausted from the duel, and laid his head on the pillow next to hers. "Amelia, my dearest love," he whispered, gently plucking an errant curl and winding it around his finger. "Sleep and get well. You are safe now. He will not bother you again."

Anthony had seen things brought to their conclusion this time, unlike his experience in Badajoz. There was such a sense of satisfaction in it—to act for himself and to achieve victory for one of the defenseless.

More than that this time though. The victory was for his woman, his love.

"Amelia," he said again. And then he closed his eyes and slept.

***

Later that afternoon, after Anthony had rested, washed, shaved, and dressed—with the assistance of his new valet, Charlie Bates by name, and under the careful supervision of Lucas—he went to his mother's favorite sitting room and found her seated on the floral damask sofa there, doing needlework with Lady Walmsley. His father was there also, seated in a chair near his marchioness, reading.

This particular sitting room was a wash of creams, yellows, and pale pinks—a decidedly feminine, sunny room. His father had always tended to prefer his more masculine study, with its dark woods and filled bookshelves.

"Ah, Anthony," Lady Ashworth said, setting her sewing aside and taking his hands in hers for a quick squeeze. "Amelia is still sleeping soundly, thank goodness. Jane has been instructed to inform us the minute she awakes." She looked carefully at him. "I must say, you look much better than you did now that you are rested. Indeed, I believe you look better than you have since your return to us." She patted the cushion next to her.

Lady Walmsley peered at him through her lorgnette after he sat. "Your mother is quite right," she said. "You are a handsome young man, tall and fit and with those dazzling blue eyes of yours, but you looked weary to the bone before. I am glad to see you looking so well, as if a weight has been lifted from your shoulders."

A tap at the door interrupted Lady Walmsley's embarrassing soliloquy about his looks, for which Anthony was grateful. Gibbs entered. "Please excuse the interruption," he said. "There are two gentlemen here to call on Lord Halford. A Mr. Swindlehurst and a Mr. Abbott." He walked forward and handed a calling card to Anthony. "I have put the gentlemen in the front parlor, my lord."

"Thank you, Gibbs." He rose from the sofa.

His father closed his book and set it on the table next to his chair. "I believe I shall join you, Halford. Gibbs, tell the gentlemen the two of us will be with them shortly."

Gibbs bowed and left the room.

"Who are these gentlemen?" Lady Ashworth asked Anthony.

Before he could reply, Lord Ashworth did. "Mr. Swindlehurst is our solicitor, my dear, as may you recall, and his companion, Mr. John Abbott, is an investigator with an extensive reputation." He rose from his chair. "Which is why I wish to speak to my son in private before he meets with them. I am afraid I have been ill and in the dark for too long." He gestured toward the door with his hand. "After you, Halford."

When they were in the hallway with the sitting room door closed, Anthony said, "There is not much to tell that you do not already know, Father. Abbott looked into Amelia's family background for me, and I subsequently asked him for information on the Duke of Marwood, which I am hopeful will further explain his attack on Amelia."

The marquess nodded. "It did strike me as odd, the way Marwood placed such a monetary value on his daughter when we went through the settlements, although such practicalities are not unheard of in marriage settlements. I am curious to discover what Abbott can tell us."

They proceeded down the hallway to the parlor where Gibbs had deposited the gentlemen. Swindlehurst was standing by the fireplace and staring at the fire, while Mr. Abbott stood looking out the window, his hands clasped behind him.

Abbott turned and walked forward when Anthony and his father entered the room.

Anthony introduced him to his father.

"Your reputation precedes you, Mr. Abbott," the marquess said. "My responsibilities in the House of Lords have made me aware of work you have done for the Crown in the past."

"I am honored, my lord," Abbott said.

"Please be seated," Anthony said, pulling on the bell cord. When Gibbs arrived, Anthony said, "Tea, Gibbs. Or would you all prefer something a little stronger?"

The gentlemen declined refreshments of any kind, so Gibbs left, and they settled in to discuss business.

"What have you to tell us?" Anthony asked.

"First," Abbott said, "may I offer my condolences on Miss Clarke's injuries? I was appalled at the news and would wish her a speedy recovery."

"Thank you, sir," Anthony said. "I shall pass your sentiments along to her." He did not wish to discuss Amelia's injuries with these men; he was more interested in learning about the perpetrator of them. "What light can you shed on Marwood's actions and motives?"

"As to that," Abbott said, "there has been gossip for some time that the duke's finances are in a shambles, near the point of ruin, in fact."

For the Duke of Marwood to be in financial peril explained much. It also meant the duke had been grossly negligent, considering the number of properties he owned. "How could this happen?" he asked. "Gaming?" Some men were known to wager an entire estate on a hand of cards.

"Partly," Abbott said. "But not entirely. The duke had several large investments fall through, leaving him with a massive amount of debt. Even with the income from his estates, word has it that it will take years for him to find his way clear."

"What kinds of investments?" Anthony asked.

"Shipping, mostly. Merchandise from the Far East and the West Indies. Problems with the French and Americans caused some of his losses, pirates and bad seas the rest. Bad luck all around. He has been doing everything he can to raise capital, not all of it aboveboard, if you catch my drift. Nothing proven as of yet, but there are those who have their suspicions."

Anthony's father remained silent, frowning at the news.

"His investments were excessive and in risky ventures, offering unrealistic rates of return," Mr. Swindlehurst said. "A few of my clients invested in those same ventures, but because they were more cautious, they suffered fewer ill effects. Unfortunately the Duke of Marwood risked more than he could afford to lose."

"He bankrupted himself," the Marquess of Ashworth said, his fist clenched on the arm of his chair. "Then he attempted to sell his daughter, his own flesh and blood, to the highest bidder. The very idea is appalling."

"And when that did not work, he took out his frustration on an innocent young woman," Abbott said.

"Precisely," the marquess said. "He is a profligate gambler on all levels and a bully of the worst sort. He should be held accountable, although I doubt the lords will do anything to one of their highest and most esteemed peers."

Swindlehurst shared a look with Abbott, and Anthony knew that word of this morning's duel had already spread through Town. "What you say is true, my lord," Swindlehurst said. "But it would seem the Duke of Marwood has already been held accountable."

"I imagine it is true that the loss of his fortune is a significant consequence to his rash actions." The marquess's brows knit together. "But I do not believe that is what you were referring to. What did you mean, then? Miss Clarke only experienced this yesterday—" His head jerked to Anthony. "What have you done?"

"I have done what any gentleman would do to protect the honor of his beloved," Anthony replied smoothly. "I challenged him. And I won."

His father's face went ghostly white. "You *dueled*? This morning?" He ran a shaky hand through his hair. "Good heavens. And you are well? Of course you are well; I can see that you are. But the duke. He is not?"

"He is alive, Father," Anthony said. "Rest easy. The constables will not be arriving on our doorsteps to take me away in chains. And I would do exactly as I did all over again, whether the constables were planning to show up afterward or not."

"Duels are risky business, Halford," his father said. "Promise me no more duels."

"I doubt I will find myself in another situation like this one," Anthony said. "And so you have my promise." He paused, watching as his father fought to maintain his composure, knowing he had wounded him with his actions. He was the man's only surviving son and heir. His parents had been through too much already.

But he had to say what needed to be said. "With one caveat, however, Father. I will not be constrained from defending those who are dearest to me. I hope that is satisfactory to you."

He placed his hand over his father's, which was clutching the arm of the chair. It was the hand Anthony had grasped as a toddler learning to walk, the strong, muscular one that had taught him to shoot and ride a horse. Now that hand was heavily veined. In a softer voice, he continued. "I have experienced enough bloodshed for one lifetime. It is not my desire to see any more—only as a very last resort."

The Marquess of Ashworth nodded his agreement, and Anthony sensed that he had proved himself to his father in some vital way. "I understand, son. And well done."

"Ahem," Swindlehurst said, interrupting them. "I believe Mr. Abbott has further information that may be of some interest to you, Lord Halford. Regarding the circumstances of Miss Clarke's birth."

Anthony kept his hand on his father's, suddenly needing his support instead, and both men turned to listen.

Abbott steepled his fingers. "The parishioners of Little Brenchley were very keen to learn their beloved Miss Clarke was betrothed to an earl, the heir of a marquess." His eyes twinkled. "Once they knew I was working to assist her devoted fiancé, they were more willing to open up and share what they knew.

"The Reverend Clarke and his wife, it turns out, tried unsuccessfully to have a child of their own but, despite this, were always among the first to welcome each new baby into the parish. They were generous, bringing baskets of food and good cheer, and never let their own lack of good fortune dampen the joy of the occasion. I was quite moved, I tell you, listening to the people speak, and everyone had a story to tell of the vicar and his good wife." He stopped speaking for a moment, seeming to collect his thoughts.

"About Sarah Clarke," he finally continued. "It seems the villagers knew she was from a poor family and had been a scholarship girl at school. So while she had the manners of a lady born, she understood the people of the parish in a way her husband did not, kind as he was. They loved her for that and were grieved when she passed away."

"Amelia will appreciate knowing these things about her parents," Anthony said, though he was trying not to be impatient while Abbott got around to the salient points.

"One day," Abbott said, "Sarah left the village and was gone for several weeks. A few villagers swore they had seen a stranger, an older woman, arrive at the vicarage beforehand, but no one thought much of it at the time. The Reverend Clarke only said she had gone to visit friends, and there was no reason not to believe him.

"Nearly two months passed before Sarah returned home, however, and when she arrived, she had a newborn with her: Amelia. It is not an uncommon thing, you know, to raise the child of a family member or friend as one's own, so no one thought anything more about it. They were happy for the Clarkes, and the little girl was the apple of their eye."

"Were you able to learn anything at all about Amelia's natural mother?" Anthony asked.

Abbott shook his head. "No. It was never spoken of, you see, and soon enough people forgot Amelia was not even the Clarkes' own flesh and blood. If you will pardon my bluntness, your lordship, perhaps it is best to leave the final mystery alone. Amelia Clarke was well loved by the vicar and his wife. That is more than many folks can say."

"It seems that may be our only option anyway, after so much time. Thank you, Mr. Abbott, Mr. Swindlehurst," Anthony said, feeling disappointed, nonetheless.

The two gentlemen took their leave.

Once they were gone, Anthony's father turned to him again. "A duel, Halford?" he said, back to the topic he obviously considered most important.

"Father—"

"I know, I know." The marquess waved a weary hand at Anthony. "I heard your promise. Allow that I am still recovering from my initial shock. I was only beginning to think I might actually live for a while longer yet, and then I learn of this duel."

"I am truly sorry about that part of it," Anthony said. "Although not the actions I took for Amelia's sake."

The marquess rested his head against the back of the chair and closed his eyes. "Had I not capitulated to Marwood's demands for a large marriage settlement—"

"Father," Anthony interrupted. "The duke's problems were of his own making. Any settlement he made in Lady Elizabeth's behalf would not have been sufficient to salvage the financial ruin he created for himself."

"I suppose you are right."

"Now, with your permission, I would like to see Amelia."

"Of course you would. Be gone with you, then."

Anthony rose, setting a hand on his father's shoulder and squeezing it briefly. "Thank you, Father." He crossed to the door and opened it, eager to assure himself that Amelia was on the mend.

"Anthony?"

"Yes?" The marquess had used his name, not his title, and Anthony's heart quickened at its sound.

"You are a man of strength and character, and I could not be more proud."

Anthony closed the door behind him and stood there in the grand hall, his hand still on the doorknob, fighting back tears.

* * *

Somewhere in the back of Amelia's mind, swimming along with the dream she was having, was the cheerful sound of humming.

She cautiously opened one eye and squinted. Between the strands of hair that fell across her face, Amelia could see Jane opening the curtains of her bedchamber, the resulting sunlight painful. She snapped her eye shut so she could adjust to the brightness of the room. Her brain was foggy, and her limbs felt heavy. "Jane," she croaked.

"Oh, miss, you're awake!"

Amelia could sense Jane moving toward the bed, so she tried again to open her eyes. They felt unnaturally heavy, but at least the sunlight was not as bad this time around. "How long have I been asleep?" she asked.

"Nearly three days, miss. The doctor said if you are not in too much pain when you wake up, you can bathe, so long as you are careful. Would you like a nice warm bath, miss?"

Amelia cleared her throat and brushed the hair away from her face with her hand. Her skin felt tight and sore across her shoulders . . .

Her sense of awareness began to return, pushing her dream further from her consciousness and restoring some hazy memories—the Duke of Marwood on horseback, a whip, terrible pain. Anthony's reassuring voice. "A bath would be nice," she said finally. "May I have a glass of water first?"

Jane hurried over to pour her a glass and helped her sit up enough so as not to spill. Amelia gulped thirstily.

"Would you like more?" Jane asked as Amelia handed her the empty glass.

"No, thank you." Suddenly, Jane's words connected. "I have been asleep for three *days*?" she asked incredulously.

"Yes, miss," Jane said. "The London doctor here said you would be better off with taking the laudanum for a few days. The salve has been doing its job, thank goodness, and we have been taking right good care of you, miss. Even the doctor was surprised at how fast your back is healing." She gave Amelia a cheerful smile. "So today you are to have laudanum only if you think you need it."

Amelia carefully maneuvered herself around until she was sitting upright and gingerly raised her arms and twisted her back. She could feel some soreness, but it wasn't too painful.

Jane helped her shift to the edge of the bed and then to her feet. When she could see that Amelia was steady, she said, "I'll go set up your bath, then. And don't be taking off any clothing until I am here to assist you. Doctor's orders."

"Thank you, Jane." Once her maid left the bedchamber, Amelia carefully eased off the bed and made use of the chamber pot and then slowly walked to her dressing table. What she saw in the mirror made her gasp and then giggle. She couldn't help it.

She looked like a mummy from her neck to her hips. Great, long bandages had been wrapped around her, over her shoulders, under her arms, and covering the tops of her drawers. She angled herself to catch a glimpse of her back. Winding bandages held a large, thick linen pad in place over her wounds.

"I want to see what they look like," she said to Jane about her wounds when the maid returned, stacks of towels in her arms.

"Your wounds? Is that wise, miss?" the girl asked, chewing on her lip with worry. "Perhaps I should see what Lady Ashworth thinks."

"Never mind," Amelia said. She was still too fuzzy-headed to make a fuss over it, and there would be other opportunities.

A tub had been set up in Amelia's dressing room and was now filled with warm water smelling of lavender. There was a small bench next to it, and Amelia sat there so Jane could remove her bandages before she slipped gradually into the soothing water.

She soaked for a few heavenly minutes and then washed herself, leaning forward at one point so Jane could gently wash her back and her hair. When they finished, Jane rinsed Amelia's hair with a pitcher of clean water and then brought a large towel that had been hung near the fire to wrap around Amelia, along with a smaller towel for her hair.

When Amelia was dry, Jane brought her dressing robe and laid it over the back of a chair. "Wait just a moment, miss, and I'll get the salve," she said and walked back into her bedchamber to the dressing table.

Now Amelia would look.

Holding the towel closed in front of her, Amelia eased it down in back so she could see most of her wounds, welts that crisscrossed her back from her neck to her hips. Some were beginning to fade slightly while a few were still red and raw looking.

"They look much better than they did, miss. I was ever so sad when I saw them. I should not have left you to go into those woods. They say it was a duke who did it to you. In all my life, a duke! But Lord Halford, he vowed to make things right, and from what I heard tell, he's done just that. If you'll sit down, miss, I'll apply the salve to them," Jane said.

Amelia nodded and sat as Jane opened a medicinal-looking jar. Working around the towel, she delicately applied the salve to Amelia's entire back, being particularly careful on a few tender spots that made Amelia grit her teeth.

"Sorry about that, if it hurt, but they really are getting better. No infection, and that's a blessing. The doctor doesn't think you'll have much scarring—maybe a small bit, is all. Hopefully they won't show too much when you're wearing your nice evening gowns and such."

"I'm sure he's right, Jane," Amelia said, hoping to reassure her. "When you have finished with that, I think I would like you to use as thin a bandage as possible, if you can manage it."

Eventually, after much coddling and care from Jane, Amelia was dressed and feeling almost normal, if a bit worn out. She longed to see Anthony. She seemed to recall his presence in some of her laudanum-filled dreams. She had heard his voice speaking to her, telling her she was safe, urging her to get well.

She wasn't sure what to do with herself now. She felt rather like a carnival attraction, that all eyes would be on her when she emerged from her bedchamber, eager to see the woman who had been whipped.

Better sooner than later though, she decided resolutely.

She took a deep breath, grimacing as her filled lungs made her clothing press a little too snugly against her back, and then she opened the door.

Anthony was waiting for her just beyond, his arm raised as though he was preparing to knock on the door. He smiled at her, looking more handsome than ever. She went to him gladly, throwing her arms about him and hugging him tightly to her, and he kissed her, his hands framing her face.

"You were with me," she said when their lips eventually parted. "I saw you, I think. I know I heard you."

"As much as I could, I stayed by your side." He held out his arm for her. "The family is waiting for you to join us for luncheon. Shall we?"

"Yes, please. I am starving!"

Anthony laughed. "That is the best thing I have heard in days."

Amelia slipped her hand into the crook of his elbow, relishing his steadiness and support since she was a bit shaky on her legs. When they reached the dining room, the entire family was there. Lord Farleigh and Lucas rose from their seats, and Lady Ashworth and Louisa beamed at her. Lady Walmsley was there as well, seated near Lord Ashworth, who was at the head of the table.

Lord Ashworth rose and came forward to greet her. "My dear Miss Clarke, how pleased we are to see you looking so well." He raised her hand to his lips. "Or may I call you Amelia since you are to be my daughter soon?"

"I should like that very much," she said, touched by his words. "Thank you."

Anthony shot a grateful look to his father and led Amelia to an empty seat next to Farleigh, who reseated himself, and then Anthony took the vacant seat on the other side of her.

"Did Anthony tell you?" Louisa asked. "About the duel?"

Amelia turned to look at Anthony in alarm.

"Louisa, please," Lady Ashworth said. "Such topics should not be discussed at table. A person would think I did not teach you better manners!"

"But, Mama, what Anthony did was ever so dashing and romantic!"

"Young women's fancies were ever thus," Lady Walmsley said, a faraway look in her eye. "I remember a few times when men came to blows over me."

"Did you marry one of them?" Louisa asked.

"Heavens, no, child!" Lady Walmsley exclaimed. "It is one thing to have young men fall at one's feet with ardor, but one simply does not marry them."

Amelia heard a choked sound from Farleigh, which he nearly successfully hid behind his napkin.

"Although," the old lady added wistfully, "Walmsley *was* a passionate man—quite exciting, really . . . and we grew very fond of each other in time."

"Duel?" Amelia asked a bit more shrilly. She had a fuzzy memory of Anthony talking about justice, but nothing more, and the idea of Anthony fighting a duel was terrifying. Besides, she already knew more than she truly needed to know about Lord and Lady Walmsley's marriage.

"Oh dear," Lady Ashworth said. "Poor Amelia will not be able to eat in peace now, thanks to you, Louisa. You may as well tell her, Anthony."

He reached for her hand under the table. "There is nothing to say," he said, looking deeply into her eyes. "The duke has been dealt with adequately to meet the demands of honor and justice, my dear. If you wish to know more, I will tell you when we have a little more privacy."

"I do not wish to wait, Anthony," Amelia said, raising her chin indignantly. "Apparently I slept through some fairly important events. I believe I have the right to know what everyone else at the table knows. Especially when the word *duel* is used in context with your name."

"I do believe our Miss Clarke is going to make a fine countess, Lady Ashworth," Lord Ashworth observed to his wife. "See how she is already taking our son in hand."

"I believe you are right, husband," Lady Ashworth said.

"As she should." Lady Walmsley nodded. "I shudder to think what Walmsley would have got up to had I not put the fear of God into him."

"The lady is a terror," Lucas said.

"I know when I am beaten," Anthony said, a twinkle in his eye. "Very well, Amelia. Yes, I challenged the duke to a duel. I had to do *something*, you see. I was not given the chance to prevail in Spain. But you, even in your drugged and wounded state, would not let me seek vengeance and made me promise I would not. The duke, therefore, is only wounded, not dead. And you are magnificent, my dear, down to your very core.

"But that will have to suffice as an explanation, for right now I would have you eat and build up your strength. My priority is to see you returned to full health so I may use the special license that has been burning a hole in my pocket for the last few weeks. What do you say, my love?" He gazed into her eyes, and Amelia saw the same expression there that she was certain was on her own face.

"I say yes," she replied, her heart full.

"I say hear, hear!" Farleigh cried, raising his glass. "Here's to Tony and his lovely bride-to-be!"

They all happily joined in the toast.

Chapter 20

It was Amelia's wedding day. She still had trouble believing Anthony Hargreaves, Earl of Halford, had chosen her as his bride. He was everything she could have hoped for in a husband: a man of strength and character, like her father had been.

Anthony had cared about the citizens of Badajoz, caught between two armies, and had done what he could to protect them—with much personal cost to himself. And he had defended Amelia against one of the highest peers of the land.

He had chosen her.

And she had chosen him, she told herself as she dressed, and she would spend the rest of her life as his companion, striving to be his support and doing what she could to make him happy. She would gladly give him heirs—and daughters too—and together make life better for those around them.

As her parents had done before her.

"Oh, miss," Jane said. "You look pretty as a picture. Lord Halford won't be able to take his eyes off you, and that's a fact."

"Thank you, Jane. Once again, you have outdone yourself." Jane had styled her hair into a work of art, as far as Amelia was concerned, viewing it with the help of a second mirror.

She removed the beautiful emerald earrings Anthony had given her the day before from her treasure box and put them on.

Her eyes lingered on the watch and brooch. Oh, but she wished her parents could be here on her special day! Oh, how she missed them!

She took out the pocket watch. Her wedding gown, a delicate muslin with a floral pattern embroidered along the hem and across the bodice, was too delicate to hide a man's watch in a pocket beneath it. She replaced it in the box. She would wear the brooch though. Her father would understand.

Removing the brooch from the box, she pinned it in the center of her bodice, where the fabric gathered under her breasts and attached to the skirt. The ornate jewels sparkled brightly and matched her new earrings surprisingly well.

It was the perfect finishing touch.

Lady Ashworth and Louisa bustled into the room, Louisa's expectant belly protruding more each day.

Perhaps someday soon Amelia would look like that, she thought. The idea of carrying Anthony's child gave her great pleasure.

"We had to see you before we left for the church," Lady Ashworth said. She reached out and took both of Amelia's hands in her own, inspecting her from head to foot. "You look gorgeous, my dear. Oh, Amelia!" The marchioness kissed first one cheek and then the other. "You are to be my daughter! I am thrilled. You have been like a daughter since the first day you arrived at Ashworth Park."

"Indeed I cannot think of anyone I would rather have as a sister," Louisa said. "You look stunning. I am quite jealous, you know, considering my waistline has abandoned me completely these days."

"You look beautiful," Amelia said. "Radiant in anticipation of a blessed event."

"And it cannot come soon enough for me," Louisa said.

"But not today!" her mother exclaimed.

They all laughed, and the two ladies left for the church, as did Jane. The Ashworths had given the staff time to attend the wedding, although they would be bustling back afterward to finish preparations for the wedding feast that was to follow. Amelia had wanted them at the ceremony.

She wished the servants at Ashworth Park, whom she had worked alongside for so long, could be here today as well. But she would see them soon enough. After their honeymoon, Anthony and she would return to Ashworth Park and hold a celebration there. A celebration that would be for the returning heir, healthy and whole of heart this time, and his new wife.

She took a last glance in the mirror, patted a stray hair into place, and went to meet the Marquess of Ashworth, whom she had asked to give her away.

He stood at the bottom of the stairway now, looking every bit the aristocrat, tall and elegant in his formal wear. He, like his son, was much healthier now. Amelia was glad. She hoped her new father-in-law would be around for years to come, bouncing grandchildren on his knee, enjoying them and the prospect of his posterity and family name continuing.

He watched her descend the staircase, smiling at her like a proud father, and made her want to weep.

"Are you ready?" he asked when she reached him.

"I am," she said.

* * *

Anthony sat on the front pew of the church, anxiously awaiting the arrival of his father and his bride. Lucas, serving as best man, sat next to him. His mother, along with Farleigh and Louisa and little Will and Penny, sat together in the pew across the aisle, Lady Walmsley with them.

The church was filled to capacity. Friends of the family had come out in great numbers to support them. Kit and Phillip were there, as were Hugh and Sir Richard. So were the curious onlookers, of course, those who wanted to see the man who had challenged a duke to a duel, the news of which was still making the rounds in the gossip sheets and being whispered about at ladies' teas and in the gentlemen's clubs.

No one had seen the Duke of Marwood since the duel, and it had been reported that he had fled the country to avoid his many creditors. The Duchess of Marwood and Lady Elizabeth had quit London for their country estate as a result. Anthony truly felt sorry for Lady Elizabeth, who had done nothing except be true to herself. He was less sympathetic toward the duchess, considering the slanders she had spread at the ball about Amelia. As for the duke himself, Anthony prayed the man would never show his face in England again.

He would not dwell on the matter any further, however, for today was his wedding day, a day that allowed for only the best of thoughts and hope for a bright future. A day that during his darkest hours in Spain he could never have imagined would occur.

A murmur began to make its way forward from the back of the church, and Anthony turned to look.

What he saw took his breath away.

The most beautiful woman he had ever seen stood at the back, dressed from head to toe in an exquisite pale gown and accompanied by his father.

Anthony could not look away. He stood and moved into place by the altar, Lucas at his side.

The organ music began, and Amelia began her walk up the aisle, her eyes only for Anthony. But when she was nearly to him, he heard a gasp and broke his gaze long enough to see that Lady Walmsley was in some sort of distress, her face pale, looking as though she had seen a ghost.

Amelia stopped. Anthony waited, his heart in his throat. *Please do not let something happen to stop the marriage from occurring*, he prayed. *Not now. Not after all that has happened.*

Louisa turned to attend to Lady Walmsley, who then seemed to assure Louisa that she was fine. Amelia's gaze returned to Anthony's.

Anthony smiled and nodded slightly, encouraging her in the only way he could to continue toward him. She took a deep breath—so did Anthony, in relief—and made her way up the rest of the aisle with Lord Ashworth, who kissed her hand and left to sit beside his wife.

Anthony took Amelia's hands in his, and the vicar began.

* * *

They had spoken the words, made the vows, and dutifully signed the register, and now Amelia, the new Mrs. Anthony Hargreaves, was in a gaily decorated open carriage, waving farewell to the wedding guests who had poured out of the church doors. Anthony was tossing coins to the laughing children racing along beside them.

She was Mrs. Anthony Hargreaves. She was also the Countess of Halford. Both new titles were full of challenges and responsibilities, and she found herself looking forward to it all.

"I wonder what was wrong with Lady Walmsley?" Anthony said when the last coins had been tossed and they were finally out of sight of the well-wishers.

"I do not know," Amelia said. "I smiled at her when I reached her pew—then it happened. I am anxious to speak to her when we get back to the house."

"In the meantime," Anthony said, shifting closer to her. "I believe I would like to kiss my wife."

Amelia looked around her. They were in an open carriage, and while they had left everyone behind, they were still out in public.

"You look terrified," he said, chuckling and sliding his arm around her to bring her closer to him. "But you see, I ended up leg-shackled due to a public display of affection. I think it only appropriate that the behavior that brought me such good fortune be allowed to continue."

He removed his hat with one hand and used it to block the view from behind while he placed his other hand under Amelia's chin, bringing her face forward to receive his kiss.

She closed her eyes, and soon she was lost in the feel of his lips, his smooth, warm skin, and the blended scents of shaving soap and cologne.

Much too soon, in Amelia's opinion, they arrived at Ashworth House.

"Welcome home, my lord, my lady," Gibbs said when they descended from the carriage. How odd it was to Amelia to be referred to that way.

"After you, my lady," Anthony said, winking roguishly at her as he handed Gibbs his hat.

"That sounds so strange," she said. "I think I prefer Amelia to such nonsense."

"And that is precisely why I love you," Anthony said. "Although you will have to grow used to the title, as it has its place in Society and our lives."

"I understand that, and I shall endeavor to do so," she said.

He wrapped her in his arms. "Know this too," he whispered, his warm breath teasing her ear. "You will always be my lady. My heart." He pressed his lips to her throat. "My wife. Would that I could make you entirely mine right now, but there is a wedding feast to be had first. I desire you intensely, Lady Halford."

"And I you," she told him. "My heart. My husband."

The rest of the family arrived in short order, along with all those who had been invited to celebrate the day with them.

"Oh, my dears," Lady Ashworth said, kissing them both on the cheeks. "It is done! And how happy I am for you both!"

"Welcome to the family, Lady Halford," Farleigh said, jostling a wriggly Penny on his hip while Will danced merrily at his side.

"You are my Aunt Amelia now," Will said emphatically. "It is what my papa said, so it must be true."

"Meela!" Penny shouted gleefully. "Meela! Meela!"

"I simply must work to expand her vocabulary," Anthony said with a grin. "I have yet to hear her say Uncle Tony."

"It is because I am her favorite," Amelia replied archly.

"Undoubtedly that is true," Anthony said. "I know for a fact you are mine."

"I am so happy for you both, I shall cry!" Louisa said, throwing herself into Anthony's arms and then hugging Amelia. "Where is my handkerchief when I need it?"

Farleigh managed to extricate his own handkerchief and hand it to her while still keeping control of little Penny.

Perhaps one day Anthony would cultivate such a useful skill, Amelia thought wistfully.

The banquet had been set up in the music room, a fairly large space intended to accommodate recitals or amateur theatrical productions; it was the perfect size to hold everyone who would be in attendance. As the guests arrived, they were directed there, where she and Anthony waited together to greet them.

Amelia could not get the picture of Lady Walmsley's stricken face out of her mind, and it troubled her. She knew she would not be able to fully enjoy herself until she was certain her friend was all right. When Lady Walmsley arrived, Amelia separated herself from Anthony and went directly over to her.

"I must speak to you," Lady Walmsley said, staring at the brooch on Amelia's bodice. "Somewhere private, please."

"Of course." Amelia shot a worried glance at Anthony, and he hurried over.

"We need a private place to talk," Amelia said.

"Certainly, my dear," he said. He left briefly to whisper their whereabouts in his mother's ear and then returned to them. "Follow me."

He led them down the hall to a small room and assisted Lady Walmsley to a chair there. When she was settled, Amelia and Anthony sat across from her and waited until she was ready to speak.

"I must know," Lady Walmsley said, her voice quivering, "where you got that brooch."

Amelia's hand immediately rose to cover it protectively. "It was my mother's. It is the only thing I have left of hers of any value. Why?"

"May I see it? Hold it?"

Amelia clutched the brooch, for some reason reluctant to let it leave her possession. Lady Walmsley's face was so contorted with pain, however, that Amelia unpinned it and handed it to her.

The woman studied it closely, bringing it near her face and looking at it through her quizzing glass. She traced the colorful design created artfully by the gems with her finger.

"It is rare, you know," Lady Walmsley said. "And I never thought to see it again."

Amelia began to tremble.

"What are you talking about, Lady Walmsley?" Anthony asked. "Where could you have seen this before? It was Amelia's mother's, as she said, undoubtedly given to her by her father and most likely one of the Clarke-Hammond jewels. You could not possibly have encountered it anywhere."

Amelia's heart began to thump in her chest. It could not be . . .

But Lady Walmsley's eyes had a faraway look in them, as if she were seeing people and scenes long past. "Not Clarke-Hammond, young man. Carhart."

She continued to caress the brooch as gently as she would a child. Neither Amelia nor Anthony spoke, the silence in the room thick with what remained unspoken.

Finally Lady Walmsley raised her eyes to Amelia. "I know this brooch well. It is the one Joseph Carhart gave my sister at the time of their betrothal."

Amelia groped for Anthony's hand and held it tightly. "What exactly are you saying?" she whispered.

"Amelia, my dear, dear child," Lady Walmsley said, tears streaming down her face. "You have my niece's brooch, and yet your father told you it was from your mother. But as sure as I live, it is the same brooch."

Amelia was stunned and unable to speak.

"Are you truly sure, Lady Walmsley?" Anthony said. "There could be many such brooches. What makes you so certain this is the brooch of which you speak?"

"The jeweler was impressed by it," Amelia said quietly. "He made quite a fuss over it."

"Look here," Lady Walmsley said, holding the brooch out so Anthony could examine it more closely. "This is an Indian design. Joseph intended to prove he had made his fortune and brought it back to England with him, along with a few other pieces." Then she turned the brooch over and pointed to one of its corners. "Do you see that?"

"Yes," Anthony said. "There is a small engraving. A *J* and an—"

Amelia squeezed her eyes shut.

"*F*, for Frances. My sister," Lady Walmsley said.

Amelia bounded from her chair and walked to the window, staring out, seeing nothing. Her mother's brooch wasn't her mother's brooch anymore. Anthony followed her there.

"Are you all right, my love?" he asked gently.

She shook her head and leaned back against him, relieved to have his strength and support. She had never even noticed the small engravings before, so focused she had been on the brooch's colorful face. Her mind was buzzing with the questions and coincidences Lady Walmsley's pronouncement raised.

But Amelia could barely think on those right now, for of all the things Amelia had endured—public humiliation and a physical attack—this seemed to tear at her heart the most. It took her mother from her again.

Anthony left her briefly and returned with a small amount of amber liquid in a glass. "Drink this."

Numbly she took it from him and swallowed, the liquor burning a trail down her throat. She coughed, and her eyes burned, and he took the glass from her. "If you can," he said, "I think we need to hear what Lady Walmsley has to say."

She nodded, so he led her back to her chair. She already knew some of the story though, having already heard part of it from Lady Walmsley herself when they had first arrived in London.

"Joseph Carhart was a fine young man," Lady Walmsley said. "Very much in love with my sister, Frances, and unusually ambitious. He went to India to seek his fortune, promising Frances he would return for her. He kept his promise to return and gave her this brooch, in addition to a betrothal ring, as a sign of his love for her and to demonstrate that he had made his fortune after all. After they were married, he took her back to India . . . and I never saw them again. I did, however, see the brooch again—when my niece, Julia, returned to England for school. Her mother had given her the brooch."

"What happened to Julia?" Anthony asked.

"Ah, my poor, poor Julia," Lady Walmsley said, her eyes bright with tears. "I did my best, but she never quite got over the separation from her parents. When she decided to return to India after her second unsuccessful Season, I put her on the ship myself. But before she could have arrived there, I received word that her parents had died. It was all a terrible mess."

"You looked for her, surely," Anthony said.

"Of course I looked for her!" Lady Walmsley cried. "She was my whole life and my only family by then. I even went to East India House in Town to ask for help in person. Unfortunately I was told there was not much they could do, although they assured me they would forward my inquiry to Calcutta. Lot of good that did," she said bitterly. "After several years of hearing nothing, I had to conclude Julia had died there, except that here is her brooch with Amelia." She held it out in her palm.

At the sound of her name, Amelia looked up. "It was my mother's brooch, and yet I never saw her wear it. My father only gave it to me before he passed away. He is the one who told me it was my mother's. He was the one who told me to go to you for help when he died. It did not dawn on me—"

"That the mother he was referring to . . . was your natural mother," Anthony finished her sentence softly.

"Oh," Lady Walmsley breathed. "And if that is true, then you are truly my niece's child. Why did she not write to me? Why did she not come to me if she needed help? I loved her so very, very much!"

"We may never know the answer to that," Anthony said. "Perhaps by the time it was too late and she suspected she would not survive childbirth, she knew Edmund and Sarah Clarke would lovingly raise her child as theirs."

"There may be truth in what you are saying," Lady Walmsley said. She turned the brooch in her hands, moving it this way and that to catch the light. "I would have been too old to care for a newborn by then." She sniffed and dabbed her handkerchief at her nose. "Julia missed her parents dreadfully. I am sure she would have wanted her child to have a mother and father who would be able to see to her care personally." She smiled sadly. "And she was right, of course. Look how well you turned out."

She started to give the brooch back to Amelia, but Amelia could bear no more. She dropped to her knees and pulled Lady Walmsley into a tight embrace. "You are my own family, my lady, my flesh and blood. Oh, I am not surprised that it is so, for I have grown to love you dearly. This is the best of wedding presents!"

"Who would have expected such a miracle at my age? Please, my dear child, you must call me Aunt Margaret," Lady Walmsley said. "And you too, young man." She smiled, her red-rimmed eyes beginning to show signs of a twinkle. "I hardly remember the last time anyone used my Christian name. I think it must be decades. What a delight!"

"Well, then, Auntie Margaret," Anthony said, "I believe we should return to the wedding celebration before everyone thinks Amelia and I abandoned them all to begin our honeymoon."

"You make a valid point," Amelia's new Aunt Margaret said.

Both of them took a moment to straighten their gowns and check their faces for any telltale signs of splotches that tended to occur after tears were shed. Amelia also repinned the brooch on her bodice. "When I thought the brooch was not my mother's after all, I was devastated," Amelia said. "But now I know it is a memento from both of my mothers. It will be twice as special to me now."

"And how grateful I am that it has brought my family back to me," Aunt Margaret said.

Aunt Margaret! Amelia thought. It was going to take her longer to get used to that than to her own new title of countess!

When they were satisfied that all was in order, they proceeded back to the music room and the joyous celebration with family and friends that awaited them.

Epilogue

Anthony was reading while Amelia sat at the pianoforte playing one of her favorite pieces by Mozart. They spent many evenings like this, content to be at home with each other.

Peaceful.

His parents would be arriving tomorrow and staying until after Amelia's confinement. They were bringing Aunt Margaret with them, who insisted on being present for the arrival of her great-great niece or nephew. Farleigh and Louisa would be arriving a few days later with their young brood: William, Penny, and baby Clara.

Anthony turned another page, then gave up the pretense. He closed the book and placed it on the table beside his chair so he could watch his beautiful wife as she created melodies that lifted his soul.

He still had bad times, nights when the dreams returned or situations that triggered memories, but they were occurring less frequently now and with less intensity. He had Amelia for support when they happened—the comfort of her warmth when nightmares awakened him, her calmness and practical cheer to remind him each day of what he had been blessed with in his life.

He watched her fingers move gracefully over the keyboard, forming tapestries of melody and harmony, richly endowed with expression and emotion that was purely Amelia. How fortunate he had been when he had impetuously kissed her and been caught at it, for neither he nor Amelia would have felt worthy to marry the other had they not felt compelled to make the situation right.

He wanted to kiss Amelia now.

He rose and walked over to stand behind her, placing his hands on her shoulders as she played her final notes and removed her hands from the keyboard. He kneaded her shoulders, and she sighed.

"That feels wonderful," she said, dropping her head down to receive his ministrations. He placed a lingering kiss on her nape.

"You must be careful not to tire yourself," he murmured as his hands moved up and down her arms, caressing her.

"The music does not tire me," she said.

"It is everything else you insist on doing, despite the fact that our child is to arrive in but a few weeks' time. You need to rest more."

"Ah, you are using your commanding voice, the one you cultivated so well as an army captain. You tend to use it when you are overly worried, like the time you saw me walking unescorted in Hyde Park."

"I was right to worry too, considering what happened the second time you went."

"I was expecting to find *you*," she said.

"I know," he said. He traced the thin white line along her neck, barely visible now, a remnant of her encounter with the Duke of Marwood. Thankfully it was all in the past.

He sat next to her on the bench. There was not as much room for him there these days; her rounding belly tended to commandeer the space, much to his delight.

He placed his hand gently there now, hoping to feel the movement of life within. After witnessing so much death, he would never take such joy for granted again.

She rested her hand on top of his, and together they waited quietly for their baby to make its presence known. They had done this often the past few months, and Anthony never tired of the miracle of it.

Ah, there it was. A kick. And then another.

Anthony looked into Amelia's eyes, love reflected back at him in her beautiful green gaze.

The future had never been brighter.

About the Author

KAREN TUFT WAS BORN WITH a healthy dose of curiosity about pretty much everything, so as a child she taught herself to read and explored the piano. She studied composition at BYU, graduating from the University of Utah in music theory, and was a member of Phi Kappa Phi and Pi Kappa Lambda honor societies. In addition to being an author, Karen is a wife, mom, pianist, composer, and arranger. She likes to figure out what makes people tick, wander through museums, and travel, whether it's by car, plane, or paperback.